LIBERTY

Also by Rebecca Belliston

Life

Sadie

Augustina

LIBERTY

CITIZENS of LOGAN POND

BOOK 2

REBECCA BELLISTON

GATED PUBLISHING

PRINT ISBN 13: 978-0-6924561-6-3
PRINT ISBN 10: 0-692-45616-3

For Dad

Who taught me the power of words

Reason, which is that Law,
teaches all Mankind
that being all equal and independent,
no one ought to harm another in his
Life, Health, Liberty, or Possessions.

John Locke

one

Greg Pierce bolted up in bed, listening. He could have sworn he heard a motor, but that was impossible. The only motor they heard in the Logan Pond subdivision was Oliver Simmon's patrol car, and the motor he'd heard hadn't sounded like a car.

He listened a moment. Nothing. Another dream.

They were getting worse. Usually he dreamt about swimming with his sister at Salvo Beach, North Carolina. Kendra's head would slip beneath the surface, and Greg would struggle to reach her. He was always too late. Why drowning, he wasn't sure. She'd died of pneumonia a year ago in a government hospital—a drowning of the lungs, he supposed. This was the first time a beach jeep patrol tried to help save her. The motor he'd heard.

With a groan, he threw an arm over his head to block out the early sun. He knew better than to fight his way back to sleep. Cursed morning person. Strangely, the thought made him smile. He wasn't the only morning person in the clan. Standing, he peeked out his window to see if Carrie Ashworth was—

He heard it again. A motor thrumming in the distance, low and rhythmic. Not a dream. Not a car.

His heart kicked into gear.

It sounded like a helicopter, only he hadn't seen any aircraft in the six years since the global financial collapse wiped out everybody's transportation, including the government's. Frantic, he searched every inch of morning sky as the rhythmic sound grew louder.

Greg slipped out of his bedroom and through his grandparents' front door for a better look. On the porch, he spotted a black dot in the sky headed toward him.

He slammed his back against the brick. His pulse matched the beat of the rotors. This better not be some new government tactic, air sweeps instead of ground raids.

How would their illegal clan guard themselves?

Even though the helicopter was miles off and Greg technically had a citizenship card, he stayed pressed against the house, scanning every inch of every yard. His grandparents were sound asleep, and this early in the morning the rest of the neighborhood looked dead, but what about the yards he couldn't see? He wouldn't have time to warn his illegal neighbors, those squatting on government property. Hopefully they were smart enough to stay inside until the helicopter passed.

Assuming it would pass.

Just as it seemed the helicopter would fly over their neighborhood, it turned sharply east and disappeared behind his grandparents' house. Greg crept along the brick, through the side gate, and past the milk goat in the backyard. Once there, he saw the helicopter's true destination.

A huge, black cloud hung in the distant eastern sky, turning the morning sun blood-orange. It wasn't a storm cloud since the rest of the sky was a promising blue. This cloud looked too dark, too...dispersed. Smoke. And lots of it. If he lived in California, he'd think there was a forest fire to the east, but he lived in a small suburb in northern Illinois. There weren't any forests east of them, only city, which meant one thing:

Chicago was on fire. Or at least a big chunk of it.

Seemed like something the new regime would do.

The helicopter headed right into the thick of the haze. When no others followed, Greg went back around to the front yard. He surveyed the neighborhood. Not a soul had come out to check on the noise. He doubted anybody even heard. He shook his head. This clan felt too safe under Oliver's care. Greg did, too. Out of the last six years, he'd only spent a few months with actual citizenship: the last two, plus a few weeks in Raleigh when he and his mom tried to save Kendra. The rest of the time he'd slept with one eye open and both ears pricked for the slightest sound.

How had he almost slept through the helicopter?

Heading back inside, he decided it was time to move out of his grandparents' house. Finally. His mom moved into Richard O'Brien's on their wedding day, and Greg planned to move then, too, but then everything fell apart. Jeff Kovach went ballistic after his wife died and attacked several in the clan, including Greg's grandpa. Greg stuck around to help after that. But now his grandpa was walking better, and Greg was desperate for space. He hadn't lived on his own since his sophomore year at the University of North Carolina, the year of the final stock market crash.

He packed up every last thing he owned. It took all of three minutes, one of the benefits of being poor. He would have left then, but there would be dramatic consequences if he didn't say goodbye first. So he shoveled goat manure, checked on Carrie's tomato plant, watched the black haze in the distance, and even got up the nerve to feed the chickens, keeping busy until breakfast.

"I thought the army had shut down," Greg said, pushing his fried potatoes around his plate.

"You think it was a military helicopter?" his grandpa asked.

"What else could it be? President Rigsby and his cronies caused enough issues when they were as broke as the rest of us, but if they have money for helicopters now…" Greg shook his head.

"Why aren't you eating, Gregory?" his grandma said, breaking into the conversation. "Eat! The only thing you should be worrying about is that sweet girl down the street. How is Carrie anyway?"

Carrie. His grandma's favorite breakfast conversation. Breakfast, lunch, dinner, and virtually any waking time between.

"Good," Greg said, scooping up a few last bites. And before she could pester him, he stood and slung his frayed backpack over his shoulder. "Well, I'm takin' off. Thanks for breakfast—and givin' me a place to live these few months. Remember, Grandpa, no movin' stuff without me, alrighty?"

"Wait!" His grandma nearly leaped out of her seat—if leaping were possible at her age. "I thought you were moving out tomorrow."

"Nah. I wanna get settled before I head into town."

"But, but…" It started. Her bottom lip trembled and she started to cry as if Greg was eighteen and leaving to some far-off country, instead of twenty-five and moving four houses down the street. Between his mom's terminal illness and recent marriage, his grandma could hardly sweep the floor without falling apart.

She followed him to the front door. "You have to come back for lunch. Dinner, too, since your mom and Richard are coming. We're having carrot soup."

"Thanks," Greg said, "but I think I'll just bachelor it from now on."

"But do you even know how to cook over a fire?" she asked.

Next she'd tie his shoes.

"I'll have you know," he said, "Ma and I traded cooking duty comin' north. I'm a pretty dang good cook."

"I'm sure, Gregory. I'm sure. Just..." She pulled off her thick glasses and wiped her eyes. "You come back and visit us soon, okay?"

He scratched his clean-shaven cheek. "Soon? Oh, I don't know. With everything goin' on, I might not make it *all* the way back here until, say, Thanksgiving."

"Thanksgiving? That's six months away!" she cried.

"Right, right. Better say Christmas," he said, working to keep a straight face. "But I promise to write y'all real soon—assuming I can find some paper. And a pen."

Finally realizing he was teasing, she swatted him. "Oh, get out of here already."

Suppressing a grin, he headed down the street. The skies still looked clear of aircraft, and the smog in the east had dissipated. Maybe Chicago wasn't a total lost cause.

Of the twenty-eight homes in the neighborhood, only twelve were occupied. Under Greg's consolidation plan, most of the clansmen had moved into the cul-de-sac to make the sub easier to guard. That left only a few open homes for Greg to take.

He stopped in front of his new two-story home. Originally he picked this one because it sat halfway between his grandma who smothered him with affection and Jeff Kovach who wanted to smother him with a pillow. Now that Jeff and Jenna were gone, he could have taken their house, equipped with a wood-ready fireplace. But he couldn't take Kovach's house—not after everything—so he stuck with this one.

The house directly across from Carrie's.

The yard looked like a jungle, a tangled mess of overgrown grass, newly-sprouted trees, and a crumbling driveway. Of course, that described all the homes, allowing them to keep up the charade of abandoned housing. But this inside was just as bad. Cobwebs, mouse droppings, and enough dust to fill Logan Pond twice over. He was glad his mom wasn't moving in with him. The dust would aggravate her coughing spasms. Same with Kendra, whose asthma always…

He caught himself too late, and Kendra's death smacked him upside the head again. The anniversary of his sister's death was a week away. Maybe that explained the nightmares. Then again, they'd started after Jenna Kovach's death. Another death he could have prevented—*should* have prevented. Different circumstances, different fight.

Same blasted outcome.

He trotted inside and looked around twice to make sure he was in the right house. Something was different. A few interior doors were missing and holes dotted the walls where TVs and pictures had once hung. Nothing new there. Dropping his bag by the front door, he wandered into the great room where the morning sun hadn't quite reached the windows.

His nose figured it out first. No more dirty, dusty smell. Instead, a warm, tantalizing aroma greeted him. He followed the scent to the kitchen where a small bundle sat on a dark granite counter. He unwrapped a hand towel to find several corn muffins. They were still warm and smelled like heaven.

Surprised, he looked around. The muffins weren't from his grand-ma—he'd have known if she'd baked—and while his mom was an amazing cook, anytime she got her hands on corn, she made grits, not muffins.

Greg bit into one. Buttery yumminess melted in his mouth. He searched the counters for a hint, and that's when he realized the full extent of the change.

His house was spotless.

Somebody had swept the floors and carpets. No more mouse drop-pings. No more cobwebs and inches of dead bugs on the window sills. Every granite counter had been shined, all except the one next to him.

Bending down, he studied the dirt on the neglected counter. A few lines had been traced into the dust as if somebody ran their finger through it. The marks were organized into letters and words. Three words, to be precise:

WELCOME HOME NEIGHBOR

Straightening, he looked out his window to the house across the street. He broke into a wide smile. Miss Carrie Ashworth. Leave it to her to pull off something like this. She couldn't help herself, as if she had an obsessive-compulsive need to help people. She probably even talked herself out of it a dozen times:

No, I can't encourage Greg. He just wants to be friends. Cleaning is a bad idea. But he's so good-looking and I love his mouth—especially when it's shut. Plus, Greg and I are still friends, right? Best friends even. Friends do nice things for each other, even clean their house?

With Jeff and Jenna gone, their little boys living with Sasha, and Carrie's own siblings growing up, she was running out of people to pamper. Greg couldn't figure out what a sweet girl like her saw in a jerk like him, but he was more than willing to be on the receiving end of her generosity.

Smiling, he turned full circle and pictured her bright blue eyes in his kitchen, alive with the joy of serving somebody, her honey-colored hair glowing in the sun-lit windows, large smile threatening to break through as she worked. He remembered their dance, how she felt in his arms, and the moment Jeff choked her to the point Greg thought he was going to lose her, too.

His smile faded.

Living across the street from Carrie would be sheer torture.

Setting the muffin aside, he grabbed his bag and ran upstairs to unpack. It took all of two minutes.

———◆———

Carrie couldn't see Greg anymore, but she stayed by her window. Her stomach twisted at the thought of living across the street from him, a stupid thing to worry about considering their new friendship. There was no reason to stress about him living in her line of vision. Every. Single. Day.

She lucked out cleaning when she had. May said he was moving out tomorrow, but Carrie sneaked in after sunrise to finish before she had to teach home school. She'd only been home a few minutes when she saw him striding down the sidewalk with that confident walk. What would she have done if he'd walked in while she was sweeping his carpets? Then again, maybe he wouldn't notice his clean house. He was a guy after all.

No. Greg Pierce noticed everything.

Her cheeks warmed. From the beginning, he'd known how she felt about him, even before she had. Cleaning was over the top, but after all he'd done for her—all he'd done for everyone—she had to repay him somehow.

Absentmindedly, she stroked her neck where the bruises had faded. Jeff Kovach hadn't just threatened to kill her, but also her brother, Zach. If Greg hadn't intervened... A chill ran down her body. She owed Greg more than a clean house and a few stupid muffins. She owed him her life.

Still, nothing said love-sick puppy like a girl scrubbing your toilets.

With a frustrated grunt, she pushed away from her window. She was acting like Amber, her teenage, boy-crazy sister. That couldn't be good.

Throwing on her dingy yellow work shirt, Carrie rolled up her bedroll and headed to May's backyard. With the whole Jeff mess, they were weeks behind on planting. She had a little time to weed before teaching school. As she walked, she took in the colors and smells of spring. The neighborhood seemed to have blossomed overnight, splaying everything with white, pink, and lime green. If she ignored the bottom half of everyone's yards—the neglected half—she could almost pretend her neighborhood was still beautiful.

Butterscotch, their milk goat, nipped at her shirt as she opened the gate, but Carrie shooed her back to inspect the garden.

Bright green sprouts popped up along the rows of early crops. Unfortunately, many of those were weeds. Bypassing the hoe and shovel, she used the tools she knew best: her hands. She savored the feel of cold soil on her fingers while the sun warmed her hair. The garden was the one place in the world she felt most alive.

When she reached the third row, she smiled. A single tomato plant stood out in the garden, out of place in the peas. Her "little fighter" was the only plant she'd started indoors that survived the government raid in March. Technically, tomatoes weren't supposed to be in the ground until the last threat of frost was gone, but after Jenna's death, Greg convinced Carrie it was ready. Now it stood out. Her little survivor.

The gate squeaked behind her, and Sasha Green entered May's backyard with two empty water buckets.

Sasha and Dylan had moved into the cul-de-sac a month ago as part of Greg's consolidation plan. That put them closer to Carrie's new well.

Maybe if other people used her well instead of May's, she wouldn't feel so self-conscious about Greg giving her the first one.

Standing, Carrie brushed the dirt from her jeans. "Morning, Sasha."

Sasha looked up. "Oh, hi. I didn't see you." She picked up the first bucket and dropped it in the deep crevice.

"I don't know if Dylan told you," Carrie said, "but the water in my well finally settled, so you can use it now."

"No thanks," Sasha said.

"But…" Carrie watched her struggle to wind up the bucket. Water was heavy. It didn't make sense to carry it twice as far every day.

Unless…

This wasn't the first time since the Jeff blowup someone had given Carrie the cold shoulder. Sasha—and maybe others—must blame her for Jeff leaving. For the rift in the clan. For Jenna's death. Emotions rose in Carrie's throat.

"How are Little Jeffrey and Jonah adjusting?" Carrie asked softly. Boys too young to understand why their parents had disappeared.

"Fine," Sasha said. "They're going to wake up any minute, so I better go. Bye, Carrie."

She started off, buckets in hand. Carrie couldn't help but follow.

"I can watch them sometime if you need," Carrie said. She used to babysit them so Jenna could rest during her horrible morning sickness. According to May, Sasha was struggling to adjust to instant motherhood anyway. Carrie ached to see Little Jeffrey and Jonah, to hold them again. "Anytime," she added desperately.

"I know. You've already offered." Just shy of the gate, Sasha turned, eyes narrowing. "By the way, I hear you and Greg are having a tiff. Is that true?"

"A tiff?" Carrie said in surprise. "What do you mean?"

Sasha huffed. "Honestly, I'm glad you two broke up. Jeff told you it would only cause trouble. For all our sakes, I hope Oliver forgives you for cheating on him. Beg if you have to." Her expression darkened. "You owe us all that much."

Stunned, Carrie watched her storm away.

What did that mean? Carrie and Greg couldn't have "broken up" because they hadn't dated. They were just friends. Best friends now, but still. Although…she hadn't seen him much the last few weeks. But Greg was the type of guy who couldn't stand to sit around and socialize.

Between his projects, helping his injured grandpa and sick mom, Greg barely had time to sleep.

An engine purred, and she saw a flash of dark green winding down the street. Oliver's patrol car, the only car they saw anymore, pulled past May and CJ's, heading toward Carrie's house like every Thursday morning. He was early today.

Sighing, Carrie went to the well, scrubbed the dirt from her fingers, and then latched the gate and headed home.

She stopped three houses away.

Greg stood in her driveway talking to Oliver. Her nerves prickled at the sight of the two men together, men who seemed to occupy all of her thoughts lately. They were as opposite as men could be: Greg, an outspoken, confident leader in an illegal clan, and Oliver, a shy, gentle protector in a patrolman's uniform. Most clansmen refused to associate with Oliver because of his government position, but not Greg. Somehow the two men had become friends in spite of their vast differences—or their feelings about her.

Oliver spotted her and waved. Greg waved, too, but then turned and trotted across the street to his new house.

Odd.

She wouldn't have thought twice about him leaving if not for Sasha. *A tiff.* Carrie shook it off. Sasha Green was just an incurable gossip.

"Morning, Oliver," Carrie said, meeting him on her driveway. "You're early today."

"I know. Sorry. I just…" Oliver shrugged. "Sorry."

"It's fine. I'm always up with the sun," she said happily. "How's your new promotion?"

He glanced down at his arm. His green patrol uniform looked freshly pressed with beige tie and black gun belt, but instead of one gold bar on his arm, he wore two, his reward for exposing two coworkers selling on the black market.

"The promotion is fine. Mostly," he said.

Mostly? He should have been thrilled with his higher rank and pay, yet his gray eyes looked troubled, almost shaken.

"Is something wrong?" she asked.

"Yes. No. Well…kind of."

He glanced across the street, and Carrie tensed. "Did Greg say something?" she asked. Greg, who tended to boss people around—especially Oliver. A trait he inherited from his grandma.

"No. Greg just asked me about Chicago. By the way, don't worry about that helicopter or smoke. It was just a small disturbance. Hopefully."

"What helicopter? Smoke?" Carrie asked.

"Never mind. I just..." Oliver scratched his bald spot. "It's just that..."

Panic rose in her chest. Oliver couldn't even meet her gaze. Maybe Sasha was right. Oliver knew she loved Greg now. Maybe he wanted a polite way to escape his obligation to their clan. He'd hidden them for years, jeopardizing his job and life week after week. Jeff Kovach and others were convinced he was only doing it because he'd fallen for Carrie, but she didn't believe it. Oliver Simmons would help them regardless of how she might feel—or not feel—about him.

Wouldn't he?

The silence stretched between them until his gray eyes finally lifted to her. "My boss is assigning me a partner, Carrie."

She relaxed. "Oh, that's great. You work so hard. Maybe now you can..."

She trailed off as his words sunk in. He was getting a partner. Someone who would be with him for every sweep, every stop by her house. Someone who would know everything he was doing.

Including hiding thirty illegal citizens.

"Oh, no," she breathed.

two

Carrie stared up at the tall patrolman, mind racing. Oliver came alone for government sweeps, and even then he only searched the abandoned homes for stray vagrants. But if he had a partner, he'd have to search every single home, every single time. Government sweeps happened two or three times a month, which meant all thirty-four clansmen would have to pack up their belongings and crowd into May and CJ's house, the only valid homeowners in the neighborhood.

If Oliver got a partner, they were in serious trouble.

"Could your partner search our neighborhood anytime?" Carrie asked. "Even without a scheduled sweep?"

"Technically?" Oliver's shoulders fell. "Yes."

She felt ill. They'd have to post guards around the clock like they had that first year. Their entire lives could be thrown into upheaval—or destroyed—in a matter of seconds.

Carrie said the only thing she could think to say. "Oh."

They stood on her driveway, him fingering his gun belt, her ready to throw up.

"What does Greg think?" she asked. Greg would know what to do. He always did.

"He left before I could tell him."

So she'd have to break the news. One little hiccup, and things felt even more unstable in her secluded world.

"I'm sorry, Carrie," Oliver said. "With this new promotion, I have a larger territory and my boss thought I needed help. I don't, but...well...yeah."

"It's fine. We'll be fine," she said. Besides, their safety was *their* concern. Not his.

He kicked the cement softly. "I'm not sure when I'll be able to stop by and see you anymore either. It will be hard to get away."

Thursdays, too?

Oliver's visits were part of her routine. He never stayed long, just long enough to warn her about the next sweep. The two of them would make small talk and then he'd leave. Nothing special, but it had been their routine for five years.

Her stomach clenched. Jeff Kovach said this would happen.

So had Greg.

"As soon as you reject him," Greg had said, *"he'll promise to keep coming, but it'll get harder and harder to see you. His visits will spread out until he stops coming altogether. And then what?"*

Even if this had nothing to do with her choosing Greg, the timing couldn't be worse.

"Beg if you have to," Sasha whispered from her memories.

"How soon?" Carrie asked.

"I'm not sure. With Jamansky and Nielsen's arrest, we're down a couple guys," Oliver said. "Chief Dario is desperate, so when he finds someone. Maybe as soon as next week. I...I'll let you know before it happens, so don't worry yet."

"Yet?" she echoed.

His forehead wrinkled. "I'm really, really, really sorry, Carrie. Really sorry."

"Don't be." She forced herself to smile. "We'll be fine." Physically, at least. She dreaded taking the blame for another thing, but they had at least a week to plan. They could come up with something by then.

Like around-the-clock guard duty?

Desperate for a different subject, she said, "The chickens are doing well. They've already lost their yellow down."

"Oh. Good. The lady told me they would be good layers. I hope they are."

Her smile faded. Oliver bought her chickens after his coworkers wiped out their flock. She struggled to picture him asking some lady in some farm shop which chickens laid the best eggs, knowing he'd never eat a single one. Patrolmen didn't need to raise chickens. They had government grocery stores. She couldn't believe he'd go to all that trouble for her—especially after she chose the other guy.

Her eyes wandered across the street. Why had Greg left? She was sure he felt something more for her beyond friendship—he'd basically admitted as much. But he kept insisting Oliver was better for her, a ridiculous notion that she hoped he'd give up. Not yet, apparently.

Oliver leaned down to study her. Cheeks flushing, she turned and pretended to take in the colors of spring around the neighborhood.

"The trees are pretty," she said. "I miss seeing Downtown Shelton in the spring. Main Street was lined with these white flowering trees that seemed to go on forever. Every spring my mom and I made a special shopping trip to walk under their blossoms. You should see them. They're breathtaking. Unless the government ripped them out." She frowned at the possibility. "They didn't tear them down, did they?"

"No. I actually saw them on the way here. They...uh..." He played with a button on his uniform. "They made me think of you."

Why was he doing this? Didn't he know her heart was taken? She didn't want to hurt him. She never even sought his attention.

"Carrie?" He cleared his throat. "Would you ever...I mean, would you want to maybe, to go see those trees? If you have time, I mean. We could even go right now for a quick drive."

"Now?"

He shrugged. "It wouldn't take long. If you want."

"But wouldn't it be dangerous?" Ten years ago, a quick drive into her small town would mean nothing. Now the thought terrified her.

"No. The other patrolmen in Shelton were arrested. Plus, I'm a senior officer now. No one should question me. But...I could write you a travel permit if it would make you more comfortable."

Which might work if she had a citizenship card: yellow, blue, or green.

Sometimes she wondered if Oliver remembered how illegal she was. Even if he forged a citizenship card for her—any color—she'd only be allowed to travel between municipalities anyway, not take some leisurely drive. If anyone spotted her, they'd arrest her and throw her into a prison work camp until she could buy her citizenship back. A virtual life sentence. She could lose everything and everyone, but he acted like it was no big deal. Maybe it was. Maybe she understood President Rigsby's card system less than she thought. She knew little of anything happening outside of her neighborhood except that she trusted Oliver Simmons. And if he thought it was safe…

The morning breeze blew her wavy hair around her face. Go for a drive. Leave the neighborhood. She hadn't ridden in a car since the Collapse—she hadn't even seen any cars besides his—but that's not why she still hesitated.

It sounded like a date.

Oliver must have read her mind because he quickly amended, "Other people can come with us. Zach, Amber, and even"—he winced—"Greg."

Greg couldn't go because it would torture Oliver. But she didn't want to go without Greg because it would only torture her. Thankfully, Zach's best friend, Tucker, came strolling down the sidewalk with his brother, Chris. And not too far behind them was Richard O'Brien, a former accounting professor from Chicago who agreed to teach Carrie's small class of teenagers today.

"I would love to," Carrie said, "but I have to teach school."

Oliver turned and saw the group heading their way. "Right. Sorry. I forgot. Um…maybe we could go another day, like next week?"

Before she could think up another excuse, her front door burst open and Zach shot out of the house. "What? Go where? Can I come?"

Oliver smiled down at Carrie's thirteen-year-old brother. "I want to take Carrie downtown to see some trees in Shelton. If she says it's okay, you can come."

"Yes!" Zach punched the air. "I'd do anything to get out of this place. Did you hear that, Tucker? I'm leaving!"

Carrie shot him a warning look. "Zach, go back inside. I'll be there in a second."

"But Oliver said—"

"Zach," she said firmly.

He glared at her, a look he'd perfected from Amber, before turning. His friends followed him inside.

"Good morning, you two," Richard said, coming up behind them. "Nice to see you again, Officer Simmons."

Oliver shook Richard's hand. "Good to see you, too, Mr. O'Brien."

"Please, it's Richard now," Richard said warmly. Then he turned to Carrie. "Am I too early?"

"No. We just need the girls. Maddie and Lindsey should be here any minute."

Nodding, Richard joined the other teens inside. When Carrie told her class they were getting accounting lessons, Amber whined about how pointless it was to learn about money when they had none. But considering Zach didn't know the difference between a nickel and a quarter, Carrie figured the lesson was long overdue. She still had hopes these kids would get jobs—and a chance at a real life—someday.

"I'm in Joliet this weekend for training," Oliver said. "Do you want to go next week, maybe Monday?"

For whatever reason, Oliver really wanted her to see those trees.

"I can go Monday!" Zach called through the window. He and Tucker had their noses pressed to the glass.

The eagerness in their faces broke down the last of Carrie's defenses. She smiled up at Oliver. "Monday would be great. Thank you."

And if she asked May to join them—someone who would appreciate the spring colors—it wouldn't look like a date, especially if she insisted May sit in the front seat. Maybe she'd ask Greg to go anyway.

"Good. Great," Oliver said, eyes bright with pleasure. "I'll pick you up around 2:00, possibly 2:15. Is 2:15 okay?"

No one in their clan had a working clock. Carrie was lucky to know which day it was.

"Anytime is fine," she said. "How many people do you have room for?" she asked, reminding him—and herself—of the non-date-ness of this drive.

"Three besides you."

Zach high-fived Tucker who had, no doubt, already conspired for the other spot. A quick drive might do them all some good. They'd been cooped up in Logan Pond long enough.

Amber's two best friends were heading down the street, laughing and giggling. Six chatty teenagers were about to overtake Carrie's house. If she didn't nip it in the bud, she would never get them to calm down enough to listen to Richard.

"See you Monday, Oliver," she said.

Oliver smiled another rare, genuine smile. "See you Monday, Carrie."

He was still smiling as he drove away.

Carrie glanced across the street, wondering if Greg had watched the interchange. Would he be glad she agreed to go? Probably. But she couldn't help feel like she'd betrayed him somehow. The feeling intensified when she walked in and Richard, Greg's new stepfather, gave her a quizzical look.

She'd barely shut the door when Amber descended on her. "I'm going with you on Monday," Amber announced. "I don't care what you say."

That got the other teens going. The room broke into a heated discussion over who got the last seat. Carrie and Oliver were driving into their small, deserted town to see some spring trees in bloom, and yet the teens nearly started a fist fight over who got the last spot. Carrie had no chance whatsoever to get her class back on task.

Or ask Greg to go.

three

Amber knocked the clan signal on the Ziegler's door. Unfortunately, Mrs. Ziegler answered.

"Braden isn't home," Mrs. Ziegler said.

No point beating around the bush. Amber liked that. She used to visit her best friends, Maddie and Lindsey, all the time, but since their dreamy older brother started paying attention to her, she and Mrs. Ziegler no longer pretended why she visited now.

"Do you know where he is?" Amber asked.

"Straining milk," his mom said. "Or at least, he better be. He has a lot to do today."

A veiled warning. Mrs. Ziegler thought Amber 'distracted' Braden from his jobs. However, Amber just kept him entertained. Since Greg finished the well in Amber's backyard a few weeks ago, her water chores had been cut in half. Luckily Carrie hadn't replaced them. Besides, Braden was an adult now and Amber would be seventeen in the fall. It was time people stopped bossing them around.

"Thanks," Amber said with a wave.

She strode down Woodland Drive, clutching Braden's finished gift.

Come on. Be there, she begged silently. *Love it.* She grinned. Of course he would love her gift. What guy wouldn't?

Amber found him straining goat's milk behind May and CJ's. His dad was turning manure into the garden. Braden's back was to the well, and he didn't hear her enter the gate, so she took a moment to appreciate the lines in his back, the muscles working in his shoulders. His hair, a soft, sandy-blond, was on the long side, hanging down over his turquoise eyes. Now that Jenna Kovach was dead, their resident beautician, maybe Braden would let Amber cut his hair like Carrie cut Greg's.

Tiptoeing forward, she jumped out in front of him. "Boo!"

The bucket of goat's milk nearly toppled, but Braden's look of shock melted into a crooked smile, showing off the adorable chip in his tooth.

"Hey, Amber," Braden said. "What's up?"

"I have a gift for you. Here."

He turned her homemade gift every which way. "Wow. Thanks. Uh...what is it?"

"It's a bracelet!"

His turquoise eyes widened.

She giggled. "Don't worry. It's very manly. And this isn't just any bracelet. I made it from my old red t-shirt. I have a matching one, see? Only mine is smaller and more girly."

"Matching...bracelets?"

Mr. Ziegler snorted a laugh from the garden. *Jerk.* But when Amber turned back to Braden, she was all smiles.

"Want me to tie it on for you?" she asked.

"Right now?" Braden said. "Okay. Yeah. Sure."

Draping the straining cloth over the well, Braden held out his wrist. Amber tied it on, letting her fingertips brush the muscles of his tanned forearms.

"Thanks, Amber," he said, admiring it. "I actually like it."

His dad coughed back another laugh which Amber ignored. Thankfully Braden did, too. He slid his hands into hers. Taking that as an invitation, she went up on tiptoes to bring her face closer to his.

"You really like it?" she whispered outwardly, while the inside of her shouted, *Kiss me!* He still hadn't. He'd held her hand, flirted like crazy, so why wouldn't he kiss her? *Maybe my breath?* she wondered. Carrie found mint leaves in the woods only a few weeks of the year, but other couples in the clan kissed all year long.

Amber leaned closer and tipped her chin up. His light beard was shorter than others in the clan, and she was dying to know what it would feel like.

Through Braden's long bangs, she saw his gaze drop to her lips.

Yes! she cheered. *Do it!*

His dad stopped raking and cleared his throat. Loudly. Braden dropped Amber's hands and leaned back. "Uh, I should get back to work."

Amber glared at Mr. Ziegler again. Braden's parents were worse than Carrie. But she sat next to the well and chatted away as Braden worked. After a minute, she felt cold sprinkles on her shoulder.

"Rain!" she cried, jumping under the safety of May's roof. "Come on. It's raining."

"It's just sprinkling," Braden said. "Don't be such a baby."

Baby? Is that why he hadn't kissed her? Maybe he didn't consider her old enough. Pretty enough. Anything enough. Her bottom lip jutted out, which only made him laugh.

"What? You think you're safe under there, water girl?" He flicked well water on her. A lot of water.

Amber yelped and backed against May's house, but he kept flinging water at her. She was ready to dump the whole bucket on his stupid head. This time of year, it took forever to dry off. But before she could yell at him, Mr. Ziegler trotted over.

"Braden, I need to deliver the milk to Sasha and the boys before the rain really starts. Finish cleaning up here." Braden's dad eyed Amber before continuing. "Don't get distracted. It's going to downpour any minute."

"I'll help him clean up," Amber offered.

Mr. Ziegler rolled his eyes but left. Considering Amber was best friends with their three children, Braden's parents should adore her. They used to. Maybe when she and Braden were married with their own kids, they'd have a change of heart.

More sprinkles fell from the sky.

"Let's go," Amber said.

Braden set the goat stuff aside and joined her under the roof. "Wait. I have a gift for you, too."

"Really? What is it?"

He put his finger to his lips and looked around to see if anyone was watching. No one was, but that didn't stop him from being careful. He was always careful. Too careful.

Leaning down, he whispered in her ear, so close the heat of his breath sent shivers down her damp arms, "It's on the side of the house. You might get wet. Do you mind?"

All that was on the side of May and CJ's house was stacked wood and smelly buckets of chicken food scraps, but she would follow Braden Ziegler anywhere. Hurricane. Typhoon. So she lied. "No."

Squeezing her hand, he pulled her alongside the brick in the small foot of space where the roof hung over the house. Amber tried to figure out what he might have hidden over there for her. A flower? A necklace? She grinned. And Maddie thought the bracelet was a stupid idea.

Once around the corner, Braden stopped and turned, giving his other shoulder a chance to get wet.

Amber shivered. "My present is here?" He better not give her some stupid piece of wood because she spent a long time making that—

Without warning, Braden leaned down and kissed her. A jolt ran down her arms as his warm lips found hers. She was so stunned she almost fell back, but he held her tight.

When he pulled back, he smiled a crooked smile. "I know it's not really a gift, but I've wanted to give it to you for a while."

"Well, feel free to give me," she paused, feeling wonderfully breathless and giddy, "that present anytime."

"I was hoping you'd say that." Then he leaned down and kissed her again.

———— ◆ ————

Greg headed over cornfields, an old golf course, and deserted woods on the trail into Shelton. The rain fell in slow, lazy drops, chilling him in his thin t-shirt. Served him right for trusting the morning sun. Illinois weather was part woman. Unpredictable. Temperamental. Anxious to punish him.

He sped up to make it before the worst of the storm hit.

As he neared town, he hung back under a large pine to study his surroundings. Citizenship card or not, open civilization still made him nervous. Too many years hiding. Technically, if a patrolman stopped him, he could flash his new yellow card and go on his merry way. But patrolmen didn't like people wandering around in the open, not even legals. Under President Rigsby's 'emergency laws,' they could detain Greg for no other reason than he sneezed wrong, so he stayed low and out of sight.

He wondered how many legals were left in the small town of Shelton, because the downtown area looked abandoned. Shop after shop had been boarded up, and trash blew down the street with the stiff wind. The only things that looked alive were the township office, the adjoining patrol station, and dozens of flowering trees lining Main Street. The cheerful white blossoms clashed with the rest of town, unaware the world had come to a screeching halt years ago.

Carrie would love them.

Rubbing the cold rain from his goose-bumped arms, he procrastinated the reason for his trip. He scanned Main Street until he spotted it, a small flower shop on the corner. Carrie's life dream, *Buds and Roses,* sat a stone's throw away.

Greg once had the idea to fix it up and turn it into a farmers' market, his attempt to generate income for the clan. Now that he, his mom, his grandparents, and Richard were taxable, legal citizens, his grandpa's cash was flying out the window. At the current rate, they'd be broke in fourteen months, and that's if they continued to barter on the black market for supplies and didn't use an ounce of electricity. Forget taking his mom to a government doctor. Once the cash ran dry, not only would they lose their citizenship, the clan would lose their safety net. No more house to hide in during government raids. No more yard for crops or chickens. They had to generate income somehow and thus his idea.

As far as he knew, starting a business was as illegal as squatting on government property, but maybe the mayor would make an exception. Greg's idea would generate money for Shelton, too. The black market had thrived in this area, so why not make trading legal again?

The wind picked up, and his damp clothes made him crave North Carolina. He should renew his citizenship card before it was an all-out downpour, but he couldn't seem to tear his eyes from that faded flower shop.

Carrie was the only one who knew about his plan. He needed some-body like her to pull it off. Two years of business and finance classes at UNC and Greg knew enough to get things going. But Carrie understood vegetables, chickens, and more importantly, people. She could be the warm smile behind the counter, the welcoming presence to help people ease back into the idea of free commerce.

At first she thought his idea was crazy—which it was—but somehow he sold her on it. That is, until he proposed. Though it was for business purposes only, his marriage proposal went over like a lead balloon. He was a citizen now. If he married Carrie, she could be, too. She had to be legal to traipse around in the open, plus she was half in love with Greg anyway. Marriage was only logical. So her rejection came out of nowhere. When he suggested she marry Oliver instead—anything to get her legal—she about punched him.

Women, he cursed.

And yet...

Checking for any signs of life, Greg sprinted across Main Street and slid around the corner. He tried the back door to the flower shop. Locked.

Wiping the rain from his eyes, he peered in a broken window. The inside looked trashed. The counter was destroyed, the tiled ceiling hung low from leaks, and plants grew within the walls that hadn't been part of the original merchandise. He couldn't see a single redeeming thing in there, but Carrie would. She always found the good in the bad, the sunshine in the storm. After seeing the miracle she performed on his house, he knew she could work miracles here.

He pictured her behind that counter, eyes bright as she explained a certain type of tomato plant to a customer, how they should only plant it under specific conditions. The customer wouldn't understand a word she said, but they'd still smile. Not because of the tomato. Because of Carrie.

They could do it. They could pull it off.

He stopped the thought cold. It didn't matter what Carrie *could* do if she refused to get citizenship.

After everything with Jeff and Jenna, maybe it was for the best. Things were strained in the clan. A marriage to Carrie—even a fake one—would only cause a bigger rift.

Who was he kidding anyway? Even with her legal, it was a one in a million chance the mayor would agree to capitalism on any scale.

The whole idea was a joke.

Giving up, he checked down Main Street. The rows of white flowering trees caught his eye again. They were stunning. Tiny white petals broke free of the branches and blew along with the trash.

Cold, damp, and not really sure why, Greg pulled his knife from his pocket and cut off a small branch from the closest tree. The white blossoms clung together in small clusters. He lifted them to smell and lurched back, catching the scent of something vile. The beautiful blossoms stunk like rotting—

"Hey!" somebody shouted. "What are you doing?"

Greg froze. Two patrolmen in uniform ran down the street toward him, guns pointed at his chest.

"Hands in the air! Up! All the way up!"

Greg raised the knife in one hand and tree branch in the other. Neither patrolman looked older than him which meant they were new recruits. New recruits were dangerous. Jumpy. Trigger happy.

"Drop the knife!" the younger one yelled. "Drop it!"

Cursing, Greg obeyed. That was his good knife.

The older of the two, maybe early-twenties, stepped forward and frisked him, while the younger kept his gun aimed at Greg's chest. After confirming Greg wasn't armed, the older guy picked up the knife and shoved it in his own pocket. That guy was lucky Greg left his slingshot home. If they'd stolen his slingshot, there'd be war.

"Card!" the patrolman demanded.

Carefully, with cold rain sliding down his face, Greg reached into his back jean pocket and withdrew his yellow citizenship card. He had two back there, his and his mom's, but luckily he grabbed the right one.

The younger patrolman snatched it up and swiped it through a small device. He waited until a light turned green before handing it back.

"He's clear."

"What are you doing in town?" the older one barked. The guy was shorter than Greg, skinnier, and his voice came off sounding like a frightened Chihuahua. Greg might have laughed if he didn't have two semi-automatics trained on him.

"Monthly check-in," Greg said evenly.

"Then why are you snooping around, destroying government property?"

It was a small branch—a smelly one at that—but Greg dropped the blossoms and zipped his mouth shut.

The older one waved his gun toward the street. "March!"

"Come again?" Greg said.

"You heard me. We order you to go to the township office and then directly home. If we catch you anywhere else, we'll...we'll arrest you." The patrolman's eyes flickered to his younger partner who nodded in support.

Stupid new recruits. The government ought to work on the whole commanding-presence thing. Greg was ready to jump them just to get his knife back. He thought about pointing out the "FREE RANGE" notice on top of his yellow card. Of all legal citizens, yellow cardies should have the most freedom. They were the only group not receiving government handouts. But apparently "FREE RANGE" meant marching wherever the government deemed acceptable.

"Go!" the younger one shouted.

Greg crossed the street through the soft rain, taking his own sweet time. The patrolmen waited by their car until he opened the glass doors of the township office. Still, Greg dragged his feet, dreading what waited for him inside.

He was met with familiar blue standard carpet and buzzing fluorescent lights. It unnerved him to come inside a place with electricity and forced heat. If those patrolmen weren't still watching, Greg might have turned right back around because an attractive blonde stood behind the counter, picking at her fingernails. She wore heavy eyeliner and obnoxious pink blush, flaunting the fact she was rich enough to wear makeup.

Greg let the glass door swing shut.

The blonde looked up and broke into a broad smile. "Mr. Pierce! Oh my goodness, it's been so long!"

He sighed. This just wasn't his day.

"Hello, Ashlee."

four

Ashlee beamed with pleasure. "You remembered my name. May I call you Greg? I'm not supposed to, but"—her smile widened—"I'd really like to."

After picturing Carrie behind the counter of the flower shop, seeing this blonde deal behind another counter jarred his brain. Carrie was all softness and warmth. *You-can-just-call-me-Ashlee* was all noise.

"Oh, dear," she said. "You're all wet."

She was a bright one. He didn't respond. In all fairness, Ashlee was the type of girl he used to chase in his college days, but now he had no patience for her.

"May I see your card, Greg?" She held out her hand. "Sorry. It's protocol."

Of all people, she should know he was a valid citizen since she issued his card. Still, he pulled it out.

"This is a great photo of you," she said, studying his yellow card. "You have such a great face. Illinois has been good to you." Her mascara-ridden eyes grazed over him, taking in his arms, shoulders, and chest. "Really good."

It was a horrible photo when he'd been twenty pounds lighter and starved to death, Illinois was about to dump buckets on him, and he wasn't in the mood for any flirting from anybody, least of all *You-can-just-call-me-Ashlee*. He grunted something of an answer.

She swiped his card through a machine, waited for the light to turn green, and handed it back. "What can I help you with today, Greg?"

"I'm here for my monthly check-in."

"Is that all?" She ran a finger over her collar bone to draw attention to her green uniform that was missing the top two buttons.

He huffed. "I wanna beat the worst of the storm. Do I need to sign anything or is showin' my face good enough?"

"Oh, showing your face is a great place to start." Grinning, she leaned over the counter to give more view of the few curves she had.

"Am I done?" he said through gritted teeth.

Realizing he wasn't buying whatever she was selling, she sighed and stood back. "No. Give me a minute to go find your file."

As he waited, he heard soft patters behind him. The all-out downpour had begun, making his light blue UNC shirt seem pathetically thin. He'd worn it nearly every day for six years, and it was down to threads. He'd freeze on the two-mile trip home.

When Ashlee came back, her lips were bright red with lipstick that screamed, *Pay attention to me!* The chick just couldn't take a hint.

"Here's your copy of this month's *New Day Times,*" she said. "I hope you've been enjoying your subscription."

Out of obligation, he took the pamphlet. Tall and regal, President Rigsby stood in front of an American flag that looked different from the one Greg had grown up with. Instead of fifty white stars in the blue corner, there was only one. A headline perched over the president's perfectly-sculpted hair read, "United We Stand." This from the guy who singlehandedly brought the class system back to America: green, yellow, and blue. Technically, there were four types of citizens if Greg counted the millions of American-born "illegals," those who refused to bend to Rigsby's emergency laws.

Greg studied that single white star. The nerve of that guy. *The United States* could more accurately be deemed *The Divided States* now. Greg wouldn't be reading Rigsby's propaganda anytime soon.

"Where should I sign?" he asked.

"Here," Ashlee said, pointing. "When your mom comes in, let her know she won't receive another copy of *The Times*. Just one per family."

Greg paused mid-signature. "Actually, I'm here to check in for the both of us."

"Oh, you can't. Your mom has to be here to sign herself. Plus I need to swipe her card."

"Wait. Here." He whipped out his mom's card from his back pocket. "I brought her card just in case. Plus I'm real good at her signature, so I'll just sign for her."

Ashlee stared at him like he'd whipped out a dead body. "You took her card? What if she's stopped by someone?"

"She won't be 'cause she's home sick—real sick. That's why she couldn't come."

Ashlee gave a fake pouty frown that intensified the obnoxiousness of her lipstick—and personality. "Oh, I'm sorry to hear that. Wasn't she recently married to a Mr. O'Brien or something?"

He tensed, hating that she'd pieced his family together. Richard had come into town after the wedding to get his yellow card. He'd start regular check-ins soon.

"Mr. O'Brien seems like a nice man," Ashlee said, handing back his mom's card. "But don't worry. Your mom still has a week to renew her citizenship."

Greg should have known it wouldn't be that easy. In a way he did, which is why he came to town early.

The anger built inside him. His mom could hardly walk across the room, let alone make a four-mile round trip.

"I don't think she's gonna be better next week. As I said, she's real sick, so"—he scanned the paper—"where should I sign?"

Ashlee snatched the paper back. "You can't. It's not allowed."

He leaned an elbow on the counter. Though he couldn't bring himself to smile at her, he looked her directly in the eyes. "I know, but I figured *you* could overlook somethin' like that. Just this once."

He hadn't flirted with anybody in so long he wasn't sure he even remembered how. And maybe it was beneath him, but desperate men had done worse.

Her eyes widened. But not in appreciation. In fear. She glanced up to the corner of the room where a small, black camera hung suspended from the ceiling. Greg wanted to kick himself. How had he missed that? He assumed a small town like Shelton didn't have money for surveillance. A camera meant he couldn't sweet talk his way out of this.

Still, he tried.

"Please, Ashlee," he said, lowering his voice. "She's real sick." So sick she'd hardly gotten out of bed when he showed up that morning. Whatever cancer she had was eating her alive from the inside out.

"I'm sorry, Greg. Maybe she can come in with your grandparents."

"My grandparents?"

"Yes." Ashlee straightened the file. "As long as it's before your mom's check-in time, she's welcome to come with them or Mr. O'Brien."

Great. His grandparents had never been required to check in monthly before. Nobody knew why, but Greg figured it was some loophole Oliver set up long ago. Now Greg would have to drag his dying mother into town *and* his aged grandparents. Thankfully Richard could help, but still. What about winter when they had to trudge through snow?

"Well," Greg said bitterly, "I guess I can carry my mom on my back."

Ashlee laughed until she realized he wasn't joking. Her fake smile faded. "I'm sorry, Greg, but rules are rules."

"Speaking of which, I need to exchange the last of my grandpa's money for the new currency."

"Of course," she said, perking right back up. "Let me grab the register. The exchange rate is seventy cents on the dollar."

Seventy cents. *Unbelievable.*

She mirrored his frown. "Switching to a new currency has been expensive for our leaders. I'm sure you understand."

Yeah, he understood. Green cardies, like Oliver and Ashlee, were paid for their government positions, and blue cardies lived off welfare in municipalities as virtual slaves. But yellow cardies had been financially independent before the banks collapsed. They had places to live and enough money stashed away to ride the times. They didn't have to bow down and worship the President, so Rigsby devised a way to steal the rest of their saved money and force them back under his control. Seventy cents on the dollar cut Greg's timing down. Now they only had ten months before his grandpa's wallet ran dry and the bottom fell out from under them.

Ten freaking months!

Ashlee gave him crisp red bills in exchange for his worn-out green ones. President Rigsby's face looked up from the new bills, mocking him.

"Say," Greg said, "did they ever repeal that emergency law?" The one that turned Rigsby into a dictator overnight.

"I don't think they call it that anymore," Ashlee said.

I bet they don't.

"Guess my mom and I will be back next week. When do you work?"

As expected, Ashlee misunderstood and lit up with another lip-sticked smile. "I'm here every day but Tuesday."

Tuesday it is.

As he turned to leave, he saw rain falling in sheets outside. It might be sixty degrees out, but he'd have hypothermia by the time he made it home. Squinting, he spotted the abandoned flower shop across the street, and that prompted him to make the stupidest decision of the day.

"Hey," he said, "can I talk to the mayor?"

"Not without an appointment."

Greg was done with *You-can-just-call-me-Ashlee.* He started for the hallway. "His office is this way, right?"

"Wait. You can't go back there!"

Watch me.

He strode down the hallway, Ashlee hot on his heels. There were four doors, two on each side. Checking the nameplates, he found the one he needed: *Lucas Phillips, Mayor.*

"You can't go in there," Ashlee said, hands on her hips.

Greg knocked hard.

"Yes?" he heard from the other side.

That was invitation enough.

Greg entered and saw the mayor seated behind a small desk, a man pushing sixty and rounder than anybody should be given the global financial crisis. He looked up at Greg with a scowl. "What is this?"

"Sorry, Mayor Phillips," Ashlee said. "I tried to stop him."

"Excuse my interruption," Greg said, "but I'm new to Shelton, and I've just got a quick question for you."

Mayor Phillips folded up the *New Day Times* and held out his hand. Greg went to shake it before he realized that's not what the older man wanted. For the third time in ten minutes, Greg pulled out his yellow card. The mayor swiped it through his own verifying machine before handing it back.

"What do you want, Mr. Pierce?" the mayor asked.

"I've got a..." Greg turned, remembering Ashlee by the door.

The mayor waved her off. "That will be all, Miss Lyon."

Ashlee stomped off with a huff.

Greg shut the door and began again. "I've got a business proposition for you, Mayor Phillips."

With a snort, the mayor picked up his paper again. "We don't do business with citizens."

"But this business venture could benefit yourself and this town as much as it would me"—*and my clan.* "It could bring this downtown back to life and increase your revenue, possibly also the taxable citizenship."

The mayor didn't look up but neither did he tell him to leave. So Greg stood, feet apart, hands clasped behind his back, feeling suddenly nervous. He hadn't planned to speak with the mayor until he could get all his ducks in a row—especially the most important duck, Carrie. But he started anyway.

"I heard the black market is booming in this area, sir. People say it even corrupted some of your patrolmen, and two of them were arrested a while back."

That got the mayor's attention. His eyes narrowed. "Where did you hear that?"

So Jamansky and Nielsen's arrests weren't public knowledge. Too bad. Oliver could use some good public image right now. Greg kept his face impassive. "The citizens are talking, sir."

"Where? Who?" the mayor said, face reddening with rage.

Panicked, Greg charged on. "I've got a plan to make the trading business legal again. What if we start up a—"

"Get out," the mayor said, pointing to the door.

"Beg your pardon?"

"You think you're the first person to come waltzing in here, trying to take over my town? How do you even know so much about the black market? Are you working it? And who do you think you are, purporting that my patrolmen are corrupt? Get out before I have you arrested!"

"But—"

"Out!" The mayor reached for the phone to call for backup. That was all the encouragement Greg needed.

"Thank you for your time," Greg said, and then he quickly bowed out.

Ashlee met him around the corner, arms folded, smug expression. Greg stormed past her and into the rain without a backward glance. Even before he reached the end of the street, he was drenched.

Halfway around the pine tree, he stopped and doubled back to the nearest blossoming tree. He broke off a branch that was three times larger than needed and then sprinted for home.

five

Carrie dealt another round of cards to CJ, May, and Mariah. "I hate the thought of posting guards again," she said. "Oliver said not to worry yet, but I still think we should warn everyone. Maybe tonight at the adult meeting?"

CJ gave a long, tired sigh. He didn't like the idea of thirty neighbors moving back in. Since Jeff attacked him, he talked less than he used to—and he'd never been much of a talker. He stroked his thick, white beard. "Yes, I suppose you can bring it up."

Me? Carrie hoped he would break the news. She had enough enemies.

"Have you told Greg yet?" Mariah asked, picking up her cards. "He'll wanna know before the meeting tonight."

"No." Carrie would rather have all of her teeth yanked out. Greg wasn't going to be happy about it. Although in a way, he'd been preparing their clan for such a scenario. Building a barricade to block the southern entrance. Consolidating to the cul-de-sac. Really, if anyone should break the news to the clan, it should be Greg who basically ran the adult meetings anyway.

CJ heard the hesitation in her voice and smiled. "Would you like me to tell my grandson about Oliver getting a partner?"

"Yes. Please," Carrie said.

Greg's mom and grandparents chuckled. They knew him well.

Smiling, Carrie adjusted her cards. The storm dimmed the natural light in May's kitchen. Still, candles weren't permitted this time of year, so she squinted to make out her hand, hoping Mariah had better cards. Greg's mom had learned the rules to Euchre quickly, but she and Carrie still struggled as partners. After fifty-plus years of marriage, May and CJ virtually read each other's minds, making them insurmountable opponents.

"I pass," Carrie said.

May did, too, which left it up to Greg's mom. Mariah propped up her head as she surveyed her cards, looking worn down and beat. She'd spent the morning in bed and had only come to her parents' house for a diversion while Richard helped Dylan fix a door. Dark bags hung under her green eyes, and her handkerchief stayed on the table, stained with brown spots from months of coughing up blood. Carrie offered to play by the couch so Mariah could lie down, but Mariah insisted she'd been "lazy enough" for one day.

"Jacks are good, right darlin'?" Mariah asked Carrie.

"Depends on the—"

May slapped Carrie's hand. "No table talk. She's just trying to intimidate her father."

"Who me?" Mariah said, flashing a smile which showed more exhaustion than she probably realized. "Well, I think I finally gotta good hand, so I'll choose—" A cough interrupted her. She snatched her handkerchief and doubled over, hacking a gurgling, sickening cough.

May closed her eyes, CJ went white, and Carrie offered a quick prayer, wondering how Greg could stand watching his mom get worse every day. Mariah forbade him from finding medical help in other clans. Anymore of this, though, and Carrie would strike out on her own—either that or force her to go to the government hospital in Aurora. Mariah had her citizenship card now. There was no reason she shouldn't get help other than money, but money was overrated anyway. The rest of them managed without.

Once the coughing settled, Mariah looked horribly pale, but she just started where she left off. "I'd better choose hearts. I figure it's always best to choose the heart, right darlin'?"

Carrie couldn't answer. She stared at a smudge of blood on Mariah's chin. "Are you okay?"

Greg's mom grabbed her handkerchief and wiped her mouth again. "Just fine. Tell me, where did Amber and Zach run off to today?"

Typical Mariah, changing the subject away from herself. The longer Carrie knew her, the more she admired her strength. So she followed her lead. "Amber's with Braden, and Zach is at Tucker's, working on their slingshots."

"Slingshots? Like my Gregory's?" Mariah said.

"Yes," Carrie said, managing a smile. Zach had worshipped Greg ever since the baseball game. "I shouldn't have let him go, but he's been fighting me a lot lately. Amber, too." She sighed. "When do they grow out of this snarky stage?"

"Don't ask me," Mariah said. "My boy still hasn't."

Carrie choked back a laugh. Greg definitely had snarky moments.

"I'm afraid," CJ said, "he gets that from a certain grandparent of his."

It took May a second to understand her husband's inference. Then she glared. "Are you going to yap all day, CJ? It's your turn."

CJ winked at Carrie. "See what I mean?"

That time Carrie laughed outright. So did Mariah, which got her coughing again, which extinguished all joy in the room. Mariah's eyes squeezed shut as she struggled to catch a breath. She claimed she never felt pain, but anyone looking at her knew differently.

When she recovered, the only sound in the dim house was the rain hitting the window.

Mariah seemed to notice their worried expressions. "In all serious-ness, Carrie, the best parenting advice I ever got was from this woman right here. Do you remember what you told me, Mama, when Greg and Kendra were teenagers?"

May was still too shaken to respond.

Mariah just squeezed her hand. "You told me to worry less and love more. Remember that, Ma? Worry less. Love more. Great advice, don't you think?"

Soft tears rolled down May's wrinkled cheeks, and Carrie knew May was too worried about the future to care about the past. *Worry less. Love more.* How could Mariah be so calm about her own prognosis? How would May and CJ live without her? How would Greg?

"You'll see," Mariah said back to Carrie. "Love trumps worry every time. Amber and Zach will turn out just fine."

The next hand of cards was silent. Mariah only made it halfway through before she set down her cards.

"I've got a sudden headache," Mariah said. "Do y'all mind if I lie down?"

Carrie looked up in surprise. Mariah never complained about anything. "Of course not. Can I get you something? Pillow or blanket or maybe a drink of water?"

"Nah, I just feel bad deserting you. Not that I was doin' you much good anyhow as your partner."

Mariah pushed her chair back and struggled to stand. Her face went white and her arms shook as she clutched the table. Carrie and CJ both stood to help, but she waved them back. Then, grabbing the wall for support, she inched toward the couch. As she lowered herself onto the cushions, she gasped softly in pain. Stubborn woman.

Carrie sighed. "Actually, I should probably go. I need to get home and make dinner."

"No!" Mariah said sharply from the couch. "You don't wanna head on home with all this rain. Not yet. Play just a bit longer. It'd make Mama real happy."

Carrie wasn't in the mood to get soaked outside and it felt wonderful to spend time with her surrogate grandparents again. She'd hardly seen them since Mariah and Greg moved in—and Greg turned Rottweiler on her. Plus, with Mariah's coughing bouts, May and CJ looked like they needed a distraction.

Carrie gathered the cards. "What do you think? Should we switch to a game of—"

The Trenton's front door swung open and a blast of damp air whooshed in. Greg flew inside, soaked through.

"If I'd known it was gonna rain," Greg said, stomping his feet, "I never woulda gone today."

His brown hair was so wet it looked black, his ratty jeans hung low on his hips, and his light blue UNC shirt clung to his chest in a way that made Carrie blush. When Greg first moved in, the women drooled over his unnaturally good looks—even the married ones. Not Carrie, who struggled to see past his initial rudeness. Now she felt like she had to look away to avoid staring. She hated herself for being so shallow. Looks didn't matter. She would like Greg regardless. Reaching up, she fidgeted with her plain-Jane braid, wishing she'd done something better with her hair.

Greg used the corner of his drenched shirt to wipe his dripping face, and Carrie diverted her gaze again.

"Man, does it ever quit rainin' in Illinois?" he asked.

"Not this time of year," CJ said. "Right, Carrie?"

Greg's eyes snapped up, spotting Carrie at the kitchen table. She waited for a smile of hello, the small one he reserved for her that quirked up on the left side, but it didn't come. Instead he gave her a curious look, probably wondering why she was at his grandparents' house playing cards for the first time in months on the very afternoon he moved out.

Carrie smiled a nervous smile, her own version of 'hi.' That seemed to break him. His lips quirked up.

"How'd it go in town?" his mom asked, settling back on the couch.

Greg slipped off his soaked shoes. "Bad. I was hopin' to talk to Richard about it. He around?"

"No, but he'll be back soon." Mariah closed her eyes again. "Carrie told us it was gonna downpour, so we've been playin' cards. Guess she forgot to tell you?"

"Yeah. Thanks for the warning," Greg said.

Carrie didn't miss the bite in his tone. She shuffled the cards with extra gusto.

Greg walked into the hallway, grabbed a towel from the linen closet, and rubbed his hair, face, and arms, all pale with cold. If she'd known he was going into town, she would have warned him. She'd been tracking weather for six years and could predict storms quite well. Of course, that would have required a conversation.

"I didn't think you were coming back until Thanksgiving," his grandpa said. "How's the new house?"

"Clean. Real clean," Greg said, giving Carrie the slightest nod of gratitude.

She felt the blood drain from her face. He knew. He wasn't supposed to know it had been her because she hadn't just swept and mopped. She'd baked muffins. Like a desperate girl flinging herself at the hot guy next door. Thankfully Greg didn't elaborate. Who knew how his family would exploit it.

May looked up and finally noticed her grandson. Her hearing got worse by the day, and she usually missed half of anything happening in a room. "Gregory, you came back! You're just in time, too. We're playing cards, and Carrie needs a partner."

Carrie stiffened. So did Greg.

No, May, Carrie begged silently. *Don't play matchmaker. Not now.* Greg hated when his grandma threw the two of them together. No, he loathed it. But sadly, May had an accomplice.

"Yes," his mom said from the couch. "I just deserted poor Carrie, so your timing is perfect."

His timing was more than perfect. It was suspicious.

Carrie turned to examine the front window, the same window Mariah had faced the entire game. That 'sudden headache' had been caused by nothing more than seeing her son running up the walk. Greg's mom was every bit the matchmaker May was, only Mariah was usually less obvious about it. But she wasn't even lying down anymore. She was back on her feet, painfully working her way into the kitchen.

Carrie scowled. Terminally ill people shouldn't use their sickness like that.

Greg grabbed a cup by the water bucket. "Thanks, but Carrie's better off on her own. I gotta work on—"

"What?" his mom cut in. "You gotta work on what?"

His eyes flickered to Carrie. "Stuff."

In that second, in that one simple look, Carrie knew. Sasha had been right. Greg had been avoiding her.

Why?

Mariah's chin lifted and her hands went to her hips. She was a head shorter than her son, but more intimidating when she wanted to be. "It's pourin' rain, and you gotta wait for Richard anyhow. So sit, play, and be sociable." She pulled out a kitchen chair for him.

Mother and son stared each other down, looking like twins with their brown hair, green eyes, and rock-hard expressions. Carrie could guess Greg's thoughts well enough: how do you avoid someone when you sat across from them? But unfortunately for Greg, he'd been born into a family of women more stubborn than he was. In the end, he caved.

"Yes, ma'am."

He sat across from Carrie, look of gratitude long gone. Carrie shuffled the deck ten more times, mind spinning. Greg had been her best friend, laughing, teasing, and talking not that long ago. He'd been there for her when Jeff and everyone turned against her. He'd held her together after Jenna's death. He loved her. He almost kissed her—twice.

What did I do?

"Now," Mariah said to Greg, "they're playin' this game called Euchre."

"Never heard of it." He started to stand, but his mom pushed him back down.

"Quit fightin' me," Mariah said. "I don't feel good."

Instantly he went contrite. "Sorry. You wanna lie down again? Or I can take you on home if you need."

"I'll rest again in a bit," she said. "For now, you need to pay attention so you and Carrie don't get creamed."

"CJ and I could be on a team," Carrie offered softly. Then Greg wouldn't be stuck with her. "I don't think May and CJ should be allowed to play together anymore."

"No!" May cried. "You and Gregory have to be partners. You make such a lovely team."

Greg's grandma grabbed their hands and brought them together in the center of the table. Carrie jolted as Greg's cold hand slid around hers, but May just broke into a wide grin, wide enough to show her missing molars. "I'll even let you two table talk all you want."

Mariah chuckled, CJ shook his head, but Greg just looked at Carrie, really looked at her with those piercing green eyes. He didn't retract his hand. If anything, he squeezed hers a little, making her heart jump. There was a hardness to his expression, a new determination, but it wasn't anger, and it wasn't aimed at her.

He motioned to his grandma and said in a voice she'd never be able to hear, "Let's take them down. Let's take them *all* down." Then a light touched his eyes and he smiled. A true, genuine smile.

Finally.

Carrie felt the tension leave her muscles. "Okay."

———— ◆ ————

"There you are, Simmons."

Oliver jerked up, heart pumping. He dropped the sheets of paper behind his leg. "Sir?"

Chief Dario gave him a strange look. "Why are you behind the counter?"

"I'm...filing some reports?" Oliver hadn't meant to say it like a question. He was a horrible liar, but he kept going like an idiot. "I was doing research on a neighborhood in my new area. I...wanted to see the last time it had residents."

"Have Ashlee pull the report for you—assuming you can find her." The patrol chief looked around. "Where did she go anyway?"

The bathroom. Exactly two minutes ago. She usually primped for five. Oliver's time was ticking. "Okay. I'll ask her when she comes back. Thanks."

"Oh, by the way," Chief Dario said, "I'm giving you Jamansky's office. Dump anything you don't want."

Jamansky. The guy Oliver ratted out. He nodded quickly.

"And I'm assigning Portman and Bushing as your new partners."

Oliver went still. "Both? I thought I was getting a new recruit." Someone he could mold. Portman and Bushing were young—too young to be in uniform—but they'd already been trained, informed, corrupted. Plus, there were two of them. *Two!*

"With things escalating in Chicago," the chief said, "I got word that Central Office won't be replacing Jamansky and Nielsen after all. We have to make do with what we already have. That means you get Portman and Bushing starting today."

"Today?" Oliver squeaked. "Sir, wouldn't it be easier for me to keep working on my own?"

The chief of the Kane County Unit eyed him. "Why don't you want a partner, Simmons?"

No one had ever asked him before. He knew he wasn't well liked. If it wasn't for his late father, an old sheriff, he wouldn't have scored the government position after the Collapse. He'd assumed he'd never been given a partner because no one would shed a tear if he disappeared in some sweep gone bad. With this promotion, apparently he was no longer expendable.

"I just know we're short on officers right now," Oliver said. "I-I-I'll be fine alone. Plus, the three of us would have double the territory but only one car. We'd have to work all hours of the day just to cover it."

"And I care because...?"

"Because we'll make mistakes," Oliver said, thinking fast. "Maybe you could give me the dogs instead." Jamansky's dogs were waiting for a new trainer anyway—and dogs couldn't give away Oliver's secrets.

"No. It's a done deal. Portman and Bushing are young and naïve. I expect you to whip them into shape."

With that, Chief Dario walked out of the front office. Oliver should have chased him down and argued further, but he had a bigger task at hand. He checked over his shoulder, saw the bathroom door still shut, and shuffled through the files.

Woodland Drive. Woodland Drive! Where is it?

"What are you doing?" Ashlee said.

Oliver jumped, knocking over a plant. He scrambled to set the plant upright, but it was a fake. No damage done. Carrie would never tolerate a fake plant.

"What is it with you men going where you don't belong today?" Ashlee opened the counter and clomped into the desk area, heels snapping on the tile. Her blonde hair was freshly combed, her red lipstick freshly obnoxious.

"Sorry," Oliver said, shutting the cabinet. "I found what I need." He hadn't, but he couldn't risk her finding out.

She folded her arms. "I was in the bathroom two lousy minutes. You couldn't have waited?"

It was five, and no.

Heading into the common area, he shoved the papers into his back pocket. Unfortunately, Ashlee wasn't done ranting. She'd been a beast to work with ever since David Jamansky's arrest. If she knew the arrest was Oliver's fault, she'd claw his eyes out.

"Paperwork is my job, Officer Simmons," she said. "Next time, let me do it or Mayor Phillips will think I'm useless and have me canned."

She *was* useless. Still, he acted penitent. "Sorry."

Oliver ran through the rain to his car, knowing he'd only accomplished one of three goals. And he'd waited half an hour for the chance to do it. Maybe he would have to pull the fire alarm. Either that or drug Ashlee, because one way or another, he had to get that file.

six

Carrie couldn't believe how serious Greg took cards, like it was another project he needed to tackle. With each new card, he rubbed his clean-shaven jaw as if he held the fate of the world in his hands. They lost the first game ten to three, but halfway through the second, he changed strategies.

"You can't trump Carrie's card," May said.

"Isn't Carrie's strategy to win?" Greg asked. "And we're partners, so any points I take she gets, right?"

"Yes, but it's rude," his grandma said pointedly.

Rude was pushing it, but Carrie had an amazing hand—assuming Greg didn't switch suits. Still, she kept quiet. In spite of May's permission, she and Greg were fiercely obeying the "no table talk" rule. Of course, they'd been obeying that before the game started.

"She'll forgive me," Greg said, and then stole the trick from Carrie.

Carrie reminded herself that the goal was to win, and after another few hands, May and CJ were losing for the first time all day.

As they played, Carrie's thoughts wandered. Greg really was beautiful to look at—Amber's word, not hers. The angles of his jaw. Those thick brows so full of expression. She didn't even know she was an eyebrow admirer, but Greg's dark brows defined his face. His brown hair had dried to a messy thatch that somehow looked stylish. It had grown out some but was still shorter than other men's in the clan who had reverted back to medieval-length hair. Would he ask Carrie to cut his hair again? Back then, she couldn't get him to leave her alone. And now?

Worry less. Love more, she told herself.

Greg played the jack of diamonds, trumping her card. Again.

Carrie huffed. He clearly didn't understand the concept of partners. He just gave her a questioning look as if to ask, *What's wrong?*

You tell me, she wanted to say. One minute he was her best friend, the next, he vanished. Heck, he had no problem avoiding her as she sat two feet away. She needed his advice right now, needed to know how to handle things with Oliver, Sasha, and everything else, but he was as distant as the others.

His perfect brows lowered in true concern, so she talked herself off the cliff. Something was off with Greg, but in all fairness, something was off with her, too. Had been since Jenna's death. She'd never felt so unsteady.

Or paranoid.

She offered a tiny smile which seemed to appease him.

However, it wasn't until the next round that she realized he was actually staring through his cards and not at them. He looked troubled. The longer it went, the deeper the worry lines creased his forehead. Something was bothering him. Maybe he wasn't the lousy best friend. Maybe she was.

The next time he glanced up, she tried to communicate like he had.

What's wrong?

As he stared at her, she saw more of that deep worry. If his grandparents weren't there, she would have asked him what happened in town, but he slipped out a card and stole the next trick.

May threw down her cards. "CJ and I have been partners long enough. It's time for a change: ladies against men."

Carrie looked up, shocked that May's competitive side could outweigh her matchmaking desires.

"Nice try, Grandma," Greg said. "We're not changing partners."

A burst of pride shot through Carrie, pathetic as it was.

"Speaking of partners," CJ said, "have you told Greg about Oliver yet, Carrie?"

Carrie froze. *No.* CJ knew she hadn't.

"What about Oliver?" Greg said.

What happened to CJ breaking the news for her? Things were strained enough between her and Greg. Either CJ was unable to remember his earlier offer or he was content to throw Carrie under the bus.

"Carrie?" Greg said. "What about Oliver?"

Sighing, she told him about Oliver getting a new partner and everything that might entail, including full-time guards or thirty-four people
moving back into his grandparents' house. Greg muttered something
about his day just getting better and better, but he never blamed her
which was a relief.

"Having a partner is unacceptable," Greg said. "Oliver's gotta get out
of it."

"He doesn't have a choice," Carrie said. "It's not like he can tell them
what to do."

"Well, somebody has to!" Greg snapped. "They think they own
everything—everybody. Somebody has to stand up to them!"

Every eye went to him, including his mom who startled awake at his
outburst. Carrie was about ready to drag him from the room and ask what
happened, but he immediately backed down.

"Sorry," he said. "I just meant if Oliver stands up to his boss, he'll
back down. His boss is spineless."

"Yes," his grandma said, "but so is Oliver."

Carrie whirled around. "May!"

"Well, he is," she said unapologetically.

Sadly, Carrie couldn't refute it. Oliver spent half their conversations
apologizing. How would he stand up to the chief of patrols? But if he
didn't, they were stuck living like they had the first year when tempers
flared and sicknesses took Carrie's parents and Richard's first wife.

"Carrie wants to tell the clan at the meeting tonight," CJ said.

"I'd rather she didn't," Greg said.

"Why?" Carrie asked in surprise. Greg always wanted to discuss
things in his meetings. Out-in-the-open was his style, planning for every
just-in-case situation.

It took a moment for him to answer, and when he did, he spoke each
word with care. "After all that's happened, *now* is not the time for things
to look strained with Oliver in any way." His eyes lifted to Carrie's. "The
clan still hasn't forgiven us for what happened, Carrie. If they find out
about this, they never will."

Jeff.

Jenna.

A pit formed in her stomach.

Jeff had insisted Carrie should lead Oliver along for the safety of the
clan, but she refused. Maybe if she hadn't fallen for Greg instead, Jeff

would have simmered down, but he feared Oliver's retaliation. So did everyone else. A jilted, angry patrolman could destroy them in one night, one thought. But Carrie knew Oliver wouldn't.

So did Greg.

But when Greg sided with her, Jeff went nuts. He tried to return Carrie's couch, a symbol of him breaking ties. Carrie still couldn't believe one stupid, ugly, ripped couch had caused so much grief—nor could she fathom why Jeff insisted his pregnant wife help him move it. While the rest of the clan danced oblivious at Mariah and Richard's wedding, Jenna slipped, hit her head, and never opened her eyes again. Jeff went on a rampage, nearly killing Carrie and Greg, plus CJ and Zach who got in the way. Luckily his rifle hadn't been loaded. Luckily Greg talked him down before he found another way to seek revenge. But some injuries went deeper than the skin.

Greg stared at Carrie. The way he had said *us* tugged at her. She wasn't the only one being shunned.

Before Jeff left to find his parents in North Dakota, he claimed Jenna's death wasn't anyone's fault but his own, but that didn't matter. People were blaming Carrie because she chose Greg.

And possibly…

…because Greg chose her, too.

Maybe that's why he'd been avoiding her. Not because he hated her, but because the more time they spent together, the worse it looked. Jenna was dead, Jeff was gone, and Oliver was getting a new partner.

Her throat burned.

Greg.

They stared across the table at each other, lost in a horrible past and a potentially worse future.

Greg broke away first. "This has to get settled quietly—and soon. I gotta head back into town on Monday to clear up some things. I'll track Oliver down and try to convince him to stand up to his boss."

"Actually," Carrie said, "Oliver's coming here Monday. You can talk to him then."

"Why?" Greg asked.

Only then did she realize her mistake. "He's…" She tucked a lock of hair behind her suddenly-hot ear. "He's taking me for a short drive. I guess some trees in town are blooming. He says they're pretty."

It sounded so dumb. Especially as Greg's eyes went wide with shock.

"Is that safe?" CJ asked.

"No!" Greg barked. "It's not. What is he thinking? What are *you* thinking, leaving the neighborhood?"

Carrie shrugged. "He's getting me some temporary travel permits in case we're—"

"With what card?" Greg interrupted. "No. You can't go. It's not safe. Please don't go."

"It's just a quick drive, and I'll be in his car the whole time," she said. "He's a senior officer now, so no one will bother us. I trust Oliver. He would never risk it—risk me."

It was the wrong thing to say.

Greg sat back, arms folded, cards long forgotten. "So he's takin' you to see those trees." The muscles in his jaw worked a moment before he spoke again. "How nice for y'all."

"Zach and Amber are coming, too," she said quickly. "Plus anyone else who wants to. May, do you want to come? You, too, Greg. Then you could talk to Oliver."

"Oh, no," he said. "I'd hate to disrupt your...*view* of the trees. I'll talk to him after your little drive—or maybe before in case he's occupied after."

Greg was jealous.

That was the only way to describe his dark expression. He was jealous of Oliver and their harmless drive that wasn't even a date to see some inconsequential trees. Why? Any time she got close to Greg, he insisted they keep things at friendship. Half the time he threw her at Oliver anyway, hoping to get her citizenship she didn't even want. What right did he have to be jealous when he knew full well she'd chosen him? That, even with everything, she was *still* choosing him.

She wanted to shake him and say, *What do you want from me?*

A knock sounded on the front door. May couldn't hear, CJ couldn't walk, Mariah couldn't sit up, and Greg was too busy scowling to notice. Even though Carrie was the only non-Trenton there, she stood and crossed the room, happy to leave that table.

She opened the door and saw Ron Marino, holding his coat over his head to stay dry. He stepped inside and looked around.

"Are Zach and Tucker with you?" Ron asked, breathless.

"No," Carrie said. "They went to your house after school to work on their slingshots."

Ron shook his head vigorously. "Tucker never came home. He said he was staying after school with Zach, but I was just at your place and they aren't there. Are you sure they aren't here?"

Carrie's pulse leapt. "Yes. I haven't seen either of them since this morning. They must have gone somewhere else. Maybe Dixons?"

Ron's dripping face turned white. "No. I've checked everywhere. No one has seen them since school. I went to all the houses looking for you. They aren't there. They aren't here. I've checked the pond. I've even checked the abandoned homes." He swallowed, looking sick. "I can't find them, Carrie. The boys are gone."

Carrie clutched her stomach. *Zach!*

"How long ago did school end?" Greg asked, joining them at the door.

Carrie couldn't breathe. With the storm, Zach and Tucker wouldn't be trying their slingshots outside. They weren't allowed to explore beyond the neighborhood. No one was.

"Carrie?" Greg said.

The room spun. She grabbed the wall for support.

"I came here," she whispered. "After school, I came to tell CJ about Oliver." Then the rain started, and they'd been playing cards ever since. She pressed her fingers to her trembling lips. "At least three hours," she said. "More like four or five."

Her worst fears screamed in her mind. She could see from the terror in Ron's face that he thought it, too.

The boys had been arrested.

Zach was gone.

She stumbled out into the rain.

seven

Greg blew air on his numb hands to warm up. He'd been searching for Zach and Tucker long enough the rain had stopped, but still no luck. The whole clan was out looking, scouring every house and wet yard. When those came up empty, they expanded the search to the old cornfields and woods beyond the subdivision.

Nothing.

Chris Marino, Tucker's older brother, admitted the boys wanted to test their slingshots on the other side of the pond. Greg headed that direction and beyond, winding down the trail where Terrell traded supplies on the black market. But to no avail. The longer it went, the deeper the pit in Greg's gut grew. If patrolmen had found them, there would be no getting them back.

Soaked and chilled, Greg headed back to report to the others at his grandparents' house. Carrie stood by the fireplace to warm up. Her honey-colored braid hung low, wet like the rest of her. Amber stood next to her with red, swollen eyes.

The second Carrie saw Greg, she rushed over. "Anything?"

"No," Greg said. "Sorry."

Closing her eyes, Carrie hugged herself. "Tell me Zach's okay. Tell me he's fine."

"They're thirteen, Carrie."

"Meaning?"

"They're stupid," Greg said. "They probably wandered off, went too far, and got caught in the storm. If they're smart, they're huddled up under a tree. But the storm's done now. They'll be back soon." Greg waited until she looked up. "They'll be fine. Wet, cold, but fine."

She looked like she wanted to believe him but couldn't quite.

"What if patrolmen found them?" Amber asked.

Greg didn't answer because they wouldn't want to hear. Zach and Tucker would be made wards of the state, shipped off to live in some boys' camp where they'd be raised on propaganda. They'd never see their families again—assuming they weren't brainwashed to give away the location of the clan. Greg thought of those young patrolmen finding young, stupid Zach and shuddered.

"They're fine," he said. They had to be.

"Then why haven't they heard us calling for them?" Dylan Green said. "Maybe they drowned in the pond."

Amber covered her face and started crying. Carrie looked a few seconds shy of passing out.

Greg's temper flared. Whatever animosity Dylan and Sasha Green felt toward Carrie, now wasn't the time to express it. He sidestepped, placing himself between Dylan and the Ashworth sisters. "Maybe you should head over to the fire to warm up that cold heart of yours," Greg said softly.

Dylan had the audacity to look shocked. "What? We should be checking every possibility."

"Tucker's a good swimmer," Ron said.

"Zach, too," Carrie said, looking only slightly relieved. "I just don't understand. Zach knows the rules. Doesn't he know how dangerous it is out there?"

"Do you?" Dylan shot back. "You're leaving next week."

Greg about leveled him. Wisely, Dylan moved a safe distance away, but Carrie's hands flew to her mouth.

"Tucker wanted to go with us," she said. "He wanted to, but I didn't think we'd have room. What if he and Zach went to Shelton? What if…" Her breathing sped up. "What if…"

Greg put a hand on her damp shoulder. "Terrell already checked the path into town. They didn't go that way. Even if they did, Zach and Tucker are smart. They'll hide until it's safe to come back."

"Not if the patrolmen have dogs," Amber whimpered.

Braden pulled Amber into his arms. "They won't," he said, stroking her dark hair. But then he shot Greg a look to ask if that was true.

Greg shrugged.

Carrie noticed the interchange and stared at them without blinking. Without breathing. Her freckled face went from pale to pure white. "We need Oliver," she whispered. "He has a car. He can help us look for them. He even has a map of the area. We need Oliver."

While Greg might not like it, he knew she was right. Oliver seemed to solve everything these days. Plus, if patrolmen had found the two boys, Oliver would have record of it in the station. Not that he could get them back. This wasn't just some flour and chickens like last time.

Carrie looked up at Greg with her big blue eyes, and he nodded before she could ask.

"I'll head back into town and find Oliver," Greg said. With his citizenship, he was the only one who could go. "But he's only in Shelton a couple times a week, maybe less with this promotion. If he's not there, I'll have to wait for him to show up—which I can, but maybe we should search a bit longer."

"Where?" Amber cried. "We've looked everywhere!"

"Except…" Carrie turned to Greg suddenly. "When you and I walked to Ferris, your mom fell, and they sent Zach to find us. He knew the area enough to know where we'd be."

"We haven't checked that path yet," Greg said, nodding.

Carrie took off, sprinting past him for the front door.

"Wait!" Greg said, running after her.

She flew out of his grandparents' house and down the wet sidewalk. Even though the rain had stopped, the air still had a bite to it, chilling Greg in his already-soaked clothes. He hadn't been dry since noon, leaving him in a constant state of chills. Then again, neither had the boys. He sped up. Carrie still outpaced him, darting down Woodland Drive and taking a sharp left next to his new house.

"Zach!" she called.

They ran across fields as wet grasses slapped their clothes. Both of them panted heavily and after a few minutes, they couldn't hold the pace. They slowed to a half-jog.

"Zach!" Carrie continued to shout.

Greg thought about shushing her. Oliver's territory covered most of northern Shelton, but things at the station were in upheaval since the arrest of Jamansky and Nielsen. Who knew what area Oliver had now, or what would happen if those two trigger-happy recruits heard her calling. But he couldn't bring himself to stop her.

"Maybe Zach's bad ankle gave out," Greg suggested breathlessly. "He wouldn't have been able to walk home."

"Yes. They might just be waiting for someone to find them."

"Hold up," Greg said, grabbing her arm.

The path to the Ferris Clan narrowed up ahead, leaving one small deer trail through the center of a patch of pines. In the height of spring, the small trail overflowed with fresh grass and weeds. All of it hung with raindrops. All of it looked undisturbed.

"They didn't come this way," Greg said.

"How do you know?"

"There woulda been a fresh trail. Nobody's been through here, not since the storm." Greg turned full circle to double-check. His and Carrie's trail was obvious, but it was the only one. "I don't think the boys came this way, Carrie. I'm sorry."

Her expression went blank. She stared at the sodden ground and yet saw nothing as her eyes filled.

"Zach..." she breathed.

Greg had never seen Carrie cry. Not really. He wasn't about to start now.

He pulled her in for a hug, encircling her cold, damp body. She kept her arms close to herself, allowing him to envelope her. Even though both of them were freezing, the combination warmed him.

"My parents trusted me," she whispered into his chest. "They trusted me to take care of Zach and Amber, and I've failed." Her voice broke. "I've failed everyone."

Greg lifted her chin. "Hey, you're doin' better than any parents could hope. But you can't give up. Zach's gonna be just fine."

With a blink, a few tears slid down her freckles. "How do you know?"

Greg thought about Carrie's little tomato plant and smiled. "'Cause he's an Ashworth. They're fighters, remember?"

She managed a smile. "Thanks."

Her nose and cheeks were red, and a few tears clung to her delicate lashes. Wisely, he resisted the urge to wipe them away—something too intimate for their friendship. Instead, he pulled her tight against his chest and stroked her cold, wet hair. She had a petite frame even before the Collapse had starved most of America, and he'd forgotten how well she fit in his arms.

Carrie Ashworth was dangerous, even as a friend. Maybe especially as a friend, because he kept letting down his guard. Each time he held her, it was harder to let go. She stayed cuddled up against him, too cold and preoccupied to realize the complete and utter lack of space between them. But Greg noticed.

In another second, he'd forget about Zach completely and do something they'd both regret. So he forced his arms to go slack and stepped away from her. Then he shoved his hands in his pockets and surveyed the area.

His body shivered without her.

Focus. Zach.

"Where next?" he asked.

Carrie looked as clueless as he felt. She looked distressed. Depressed. Defeated. Another hug was definitely warranted.

Focus!

"Let's head back and see if Richard had any luck on the north side," Greg said.

"And if he hasn't?" she whispered.

Greg reached up and brushed a wet lock of hair from her rosy cheek. "You can't lose hope, Little Miss Optimist. It'll be fine. C'mon."

He grabbed her hand and started back the way they'd come, through the thick, wet grass. "My stomach's growling, and if mine is, you can bet the boys' are. I'd bet we see them before too long." If not, he'd seriously panic because one thing he knew was the stomach controlled a man, whether that man was thirteen or twenty-five. "Empty bellies make for lousy adventures," he said. "Just ask my mom. I was a bear comin' north. The boys will be back for dinner. I'd bet my last shoe on it."

When Carrie didn't respond, he glanced sideways. She looked tense but in a different way. He nearly asked why, but then he noticed her gaze flicker down. To his hand which held hers. No, not held. Gripped. Like his life depended on it.

Like he'd just hugged her.

He dropped her hand, reaming himself out. She didn't meet his gaze, knowing he'd grabbed it on accident. In his defense, it only felt natural to hold her hand. Quite frankly, he wanted it back. But she wasn't the type to force her wishes on anybody—least of all him. For once, he wished she wasn't so selfless.

Suddenly, none of it mattered. Oliver. The clan. The future.

He grabbed her cold hand and started off again, only this time sliding his fingers into hers, leaving no doubt about his intentions. In a matter of seconds, her hand went from cold to warm. Somehow that justified it in his mind.

They were nearly to his new house when her hand slipped from his. She sprinted forward. "Zach!" she cried.

Greg trotted after her and saw Zach coming down Woodland Drive, limping his usual limp, with Richard right behind him.

"Look who I found," Richard called.

Carrie engulfed Zach in a hug that almost knocked his scrawny body over. "Where have you been? We've been worried sick!"

Zach pushed her off him. "Quit it. Geez!" He brushed down his red t-shirt. "I don't know why everyone's freaking out. We were just trying out our slingshots."

"Since lunch?" Carrie said. "You've been gone half the day."

"So?"

So? A retort like that would have got Greg a swift backhand growing up. The kid was gutsy, but this wasn't Greg's battle.

"Zach!" Amber yelled, running down the street with Braden right behind her. She descended on her little brother, smothering him like Carrie had. And just like before, Zach shoved her away.

"Quit it! Get off me!"

Carrie folded her arms. "You told me you were going to Tucker's after school. Everyone thought something horrible had happened to you."

"Yeah," Amber added darkly. "I froze my butt off looking for you. You have to do my chores for a month. No, a year!"

Zach rolled his eyes. "Whatever. It's no big deal."

"No big deal?" Carrie's face reddened. "You're not supposed to leave the neighborhood. Ever."

"Why? We're leaving Monday?"

Amber shook her head. "You're such an idiot. That's totally different than—Ow!" she cried as Zach punched her.

Greg grabbed Zach and yanked him back before he could inflict any more damage.

"Enough, you guys!" Carrie said. "Amber, let me handle this. And Zach, that drive with Oliver is in the safety of a car with a patrolman escorting us. What you and Tucker did was so dangerous, it makes me sick. Patrolmen could be searching anywhere, anytime."

"They could have arrested you, buddy," Braden said.

"Arrested?" Amber said, piling on. "They could have killed him!"

"We. Were. Fine!" Zach yelled.

As the three siblings went at it, Greg glanced toward his grandparents' yard. While Zach was surrounded by his sisters, Greg, Braden, and Richard, the rest of the clan huddled around Tucker. All thirty of them. Almost like lines had been drawn in the sand. Carrie's side looked pitifully small.

Greg squinted, noticing something peculiar. He turned back to Zach. "Where'd you say you were exploring?"

Zach stopped mid-yell. "Um. The woods."

"Then why aren't you and Tucker wet?"

Carrie's eyes widened on Zach's shirt. Other than dampness around his shoes, the rest of him was completely dry.

Zach's freckled face went red with guilt. "We just wanted to find a good place to shoot the slingshots. When the rain started, we hid under a tree until it stopped. Then we ran home."

"A tree?" Greg said. "My mom and I spent eight months hidin' in trees. I wish we'd stayed that dry. You wanna try that again?"

Zach's expression hardened. "It was a big tree."

There was more to Zach's story than he let on. He and Tucker found shelter, real shelter, outside of the neighborhood, but Greg didn't press.

"I found them on the other side of Bramman Highway," Richard said.

Carrie's mouth dropped. "Zach! You're never leaving the neighborhood again."

"Whatever. I'm going inside." Zach started across his front yard.

"I mean it," Carrie said, following. "You're grounded. You're not leaving the house except to do chores. Not even Monday with Oliver."

Zach whirled. "What? You can't do that!"

Carrie folded her arms, looking more parent than ever. "I just did. You're grounded for the rest of your life."

Zach shot her a look that, if he'd been a few years older, would have caused the hair on the back of Greg's neck to stand on end. "I hate you."

Carrie jerked back like he'd slapped her.

Stepping forward, Greg put a strong hand on Zach's shoulder. "Hey, Carrie, can I talk to Zach for a sec?"

Carrie hugged herself. "Be my guest. When you're done, send him inside because he's not leaving the house for a long, long time."

eight

Greg led Zach around the side of the Ashworth's house toward the pond. They weaved through the backyard that had once been beautiful and now looked wild with spring growth. Greg's clothes were cold and heavy, the kind of cold that wouldn't go away until he found a warm fireplace—something his new house didn't have. Maybe he'd venture inside after he talked to Zach to see if Carrie had started a fire.

A flock of Canadian Geese floated lazily on the gray surface of Logan Pond, not quite ready to venture out after the storm. Greg stopped just short of the cattails on the shoreline.

"Have a seat," he said.

Zach looked down at the muddy grass. "It's wet."

"So am I," Greg said with a pointed look. "Have a seat."

Zach sat with a grunt. "You're just going lecture me. I thought you were cooler than that, but whatever. I shoulda known you'd be on Carrie's side."

"I'm not on anybody's side." And to prove it, Greg sat next to him, shivering as the cold grass seeped through his jeans. What he would have given for a hot tub.

"Where's your slingshot?" Greg asked. "I wanna see what it can do."

Zach rolled his eyes but pulled it from his pocket. "We didn't know everybody was looking for us. I didn't even think they knew we were gone."

Greg said nothing as he studied the homemade slingshot, a pathetic contraption of two sticks and black rubber scraps. The two sticks formed a rough 'Y', bound together with twine that was frayed and ready to snap. "How good does it work?"

"It doesn't." Zach snatched it and cocked his arm, ready to chuck it into the pond.

"Whoa," Greg said, grabbing it back. "It's not that bad. You just need tubing, maybe some better lashing here around the middle. Mine has two scopes sticking out the top that help me aim. I can help you lash some on if you want."

"I won't hold my breath." Zach dropped his slingshot on the grass like he couldn't be bothered to ever pick it up again.

"So…" Greg said after a minute, "where'd you and Tucker go? The real story this time."

"I already told you."

It was a challenge Greg knew he'd lose, so he let it slide. The two of them watched the tranquil Canadian Geese. Then Zach picked up a rock and hurled it across the surface of the pond, startling the geese to high heaven. The geese raced and cackled away.

"I'm so sick of Carrie," Zach said. "All she does is boss me around. Amber, too. They treat me like a little kid. I hate being stuck here all the time. I hate the stupid rules. Everyone says it's dangerous out there, but it's not. It's fun."

Zach chucked another rock, only this time he threw it parallel to the surface. It skipped four or five times before dropping away, reminding Greg of the time Carrie killed him skipping rocks. Zach had a lot of Carrie in him—at least when it came to looks. Same wavy hair: a mix of blonde, red, and brunette, depending on the light. Same fair skin tone and freckles. But personality-wise, Zach was all Amber. Hot-blooded. Emotional. Greg wondered which of their parents had been fair skinned or which had Amber's darker features. Who had been the stubborn hothead and who was the peacemaker like Carrie.

Greg himself was pure Trenton stock, but part of him worried that he had a lot of his dad in him. The side that made it easy to leave, to walk away and forget everything. The side that nearly sent Greg packing after Jenna's death if Carrie hadn't intervened.

"You know, when I was five," Greg started. Zach groaned, but Greg pressed on. "My dad left. He just up and walked out. My mom had to take two jobs to make ends meet, which meant my little sister and I were alone most the time. I had to become the man of the house. I didn't wanna be. That's just how the chips fell." Greg ran his hand over the wet grass. "A man of the house treats the women of the house with respect. Do you think you treated Carrie respectfully just now?"

"What about *her*?" Zach shot back. "Oliver said I could go."

"Carrie treated you a heckuva lot better than you deserved. If your dad were here, what would he have done?"

Zach's expression tightened with pain. "I don't know. I can't remember him that well."

Zach had been seven when his parents died. Young, but not too young. "I'm guessin' you remember enough. What would he have said if you'd run off today?"

Zach's shoulders fell.

"I thought so," Greg said. "And your mom?"

"Carrie's not my mom!"

"No. But she's the closest thing you've got, and frankly, she's doin' a good job."

Zach chucked another rock. "I knew you were on her side."

"I'm on your side," Greg said. "Why do you think I sent her inside? She was ready to skin you alive back there. I just saved your life, kid. You should be thanking me."

Zach nearly smiled. "Maybe."

Seeing a small window, Greg decided to push. "So I'm gonna be blunt 'cause I think you can handle it. It's time to man up. If you're the man of the house, your sisters should come first before you. Carrie shouldn't have to tell you to do the chickens, it should be done before she's up, and then you should be startin' on her list. No more messin' around in class either. You're lucky to be getting an education."

Zach didn't look thrilled by the lecture, but he didn't argue, so Greg kept going. "Your situation isn't all that different than mine was. I had a mom and a sister to take care of. You have Carrie, who's kinda like your mom, plus Amber to take care of."

"How did your sister die?" Zach asked quietly.

A fair question that twisted Greg's stomach. He nearly sidestepped it, but Zach needed to know the kind of world waiting out there.

"She had asthma pretty bad," Greg said, looking out over the sprawling gray pond. "Last spring she caught pneumonia on top of it. It got so she could hardly breathe. So…my mom and I packed up, left our clan, and sneaked us into a government municipality in Raleigh."

Zach's eyes widened. "What was it like?"

"As bad as they say and worse. The government thinks they're helpin' everybody with these welfare cities, but there are more people than spaces to put them in. Blue cardies slave for every scrap of food—at least those lucky enough to find a job." Greg shrugged. "Once inside the fence, I begged every work farm for a job. I had to get money so they'd let Kendra into the hospital. I lucked out and found a job shoveling leftover chicken parts in a slaughter house."

Zach pulled a face. "Ew."

Greg nodded, remembering the smells and the sounds—mostly the smells. "I worked from sunup until nine or ten at night, depending on how late they'd let me stay. It'd get so I could hardly think straight, but…" His stopped in sudden memory. "In the end, it wasn't enough." His jaw clenched. "It's my fault she died."

"Why?" Zach whispered.

Greg picked up a rock and rubbed it absentmindedly. "One day the midnight shift guy didn't show up, so this other guy and I had to work double hard. Our foreman was a patrolman with a major attitude. A real jerk. He started yellin' at the guy for fallin' behind. The guy was older than my mom, down to skin and bones, and he could hardly lift the heavy buckets on a good day. So I figured we'd work together. I'd help him with his pile, and then we'd work on mine. We were makin' good time, but the patrolman didn't like it. He told me I was stealin' the other guy's work and I should focus on my own. So I did. Until the guy fell behind again, and the foreman clubbed him with a nightstick."

"He hit him?"

"Hard. Real hard." Even a year later, the incident made Greg seethe. "The old guy dropped like a sack, so…I punched the foreman. A lot." Because that seemed to be Greg's answer to everything.

The Canadian Geese slowly worked their way back to the pond, but they flocked to the opposite side, keeping a safe distance from the two of them. A smart move.

"Once they pulled me off him," Greg went on, rubbing his rock, "not only did I get the beating of a lifetime, but they fired me on the spot. They kept all my unpaid wages, and the foreman wrote up a report making it impossible for me to work anywhere else."

"But that's not fair," Zach said. "You were just trying to help that old guy."

"Fair? That's what I'm tryin' to tell you. You live in a protected little corner of the world. Because of Oliver—and only because of Oliver—y'all are safe. But Oliver's not like other patrolmen. If *his* boss found out he was helping us, Oliver wouldn't just get beat up, he wouldn't just get fired, he'd be dead."

Zach's blue eyes went wide. "Really?"

Greg nodded slowly. "Look, I know everything feels all hunky dory here, and you should be able to go wherever you want, whenever you want. But out there," he pointed past the pond, "it's uglier than ugly. You don't wanna be out there. Trust me."

Zach picked up his slingshot and pretended to study it, although his eyes were far from focused. "So what happened to your sister?"

Greg's muscles seized. He flung his rock into the wide expanse of gray water, thinking, remembering, and hating himself all over again.

"When I showed up at the hospital, I begged the doctors to keep givin' her medicine even though I didn't have money. They refused. They cut off her medicine right then." Fury clouded his vision and it took a moment to finish. "She died that night. Suffocated in her own body. My mom and I left the next day and came here."

Zach said nothing which was the nicest thing he could say.

When Greg spoke again, his voice was a whisper. "It eats me every day that I failed my sister, Zach. Every. Single. Day. I was the man of the house, and she died 'cause I was a stupid, hotheaded fool."

"Like me?" Zach said softly.

Greg didn't respond, but the message was implied. And now his mom was dying because he couldn't find her help. What about Jenna? Another hotheaded fight that ended with another death.

Who next?

He glanced over his shoulder. Carrie stood at her kitchen window, watching them from a distance.

Greg shot to his feet and brushed off his jeans. "Look, I gotta go, but I wanted to make sure you understand. Carrie and Amber come first over everything now, even you. Their safety—their happiness—come first."

Safety.

Happiness.

The words tasted bitter after what he'd just done with Carrie, throwing her future—and Zach's—to the wind. But Zach nodded, unaware of Greg's hypocrisy.

"That means you gotta go inside and apologize," Greg said. "Apologize to everybody else for scaring the livin' daylights out of them—just like Amber apologized for the raid. Then you gotta accept whatever punishment Carrie gives you without complaint. And..." Greg waited until he looked up, "you can't ever leave the neighborhood. Ever again."

Zach kicked the grass beneath him. "But that's not fair."

"I know, but you'll do it 'cause it's the right thing."

The right thing. How Greg loathed those words.

"Fine." Zach stood and sighed. "Is that why you hate chickens so bad?"

Greg nodded. "With a passion."

Slowly, Zach headed up his yard for the deck stairs. But before he reached the sliding glass door to his kitchen, he turned back. "It wasn't your fault, Greg," he called. "You didn't know what would happen to your sister. You were just trying to help that guy."

Trying to help.

That was always Greg's justification.

His fists clenched. Zach wasn't the only one who needed to man up.

"That doesn't change the fact that she's dead, and I coulda stopped it," he said. "So go on. And when you're done, tell Carrie I need to talk to her. I'll be waitin' right here."

nine

Carrie headed for the sliding door, still in shock. Zach not only apologized, but he hadn't argued about being grounded or missing the drive, making her curious what Greg had said out there.

But as she slid open the door, something on the kitchen counter caught her eye. She crossed the room and picked up a jar filled with several small branches from a—she sniffed—Bradford Pear? The clusters of white blossom were gorgeous but painfully pungent. Definitely a flowering pear tree.

There was no way Amber would have cut the branches for their house. And Carrie had been with May and Mariah all afternoon. Sasha? But that didn't seem likely.

Then she spotted something else. Someone had scattered a dusting of flour on her counter and, with a finger, drawn a single word into the mess:

THANKS

Carrie broke into a wide smile and looked outside. Greg stood by the pond, waiting for her.

Her heart sped up. Greg brought her flowers. She had the sneaking suspicion they weren't from the neighborhood either. He'd been in town today, saw the same trees Oliver had, and wanted to bring a piece of them back to her. Those trees must be a sight to behold for two men, who cared little about flowers, to take notice.

She thought of how Greg had held her out there, how he'd grabbed her hand without thinking, and her smile grew. No wonder he'd been so angry about her drive with Oliver. He must have sneaked these flowers into her house before cards, before Zach, before everything.

Joy bubbled up inside of her. She hadn't looked in a mirror, and with the rain, she didn't want to. She'd always felt plain with her wavy hair and fair skin. Her clothes were ugly and her body model thin, but at Mariah's wedding, Greg had called her beautiful—stunningly beautiful, even—and she wanted nothing more than for him to still think she was.

Setting her flowers aside, she reached up and undid her braid. Then she finger-combed her damp hair, hoping it would look naturally wavy and not scraggly. With a quick breath, she slid open her kitchen door and made her way down to the pond. Greg's head came up with her approach, but he stayed facing away from her.

"Thank you, Greg. For…" Her mind swirled. "…everything. I think that's the most penitent I've ever seen Zach."

"It needed to be said," Greg said, kicking some mud off his shoes. "And so does somethin' else."

The breeze coming off the pond chilled her still-damp clothes. She hugged herself and bit the insides of her cheeks to keep from smiling. It was strange how many emotions she could feel in a short time.

When Greg faced her, though, his expression was more stoic than she expected. He took in her hair down and wavy, which made her blush. Of course he would notice.

"Can I be blunt, Carrie?"

Are you ever not? she thought, but nodded.

"It's time for you to move on," he said. "I need you to quit lookin' at me like you do, to quit talkin' to me like you do, makin' muffins, and"—his eyes took in her hair again, blowing softly in the breeze—"all of it. I think it's time for you to move on and hate me already."

"Hate you, Greg? I could never—"

"I don't think you and I should see each other anymore," he cut in.

The ground dropped out from under her. "What?"

"I think we should avoid each other as best as we can from now on."

It took a few moments before she was able to regain her composure. "May I ask why?"

He faced the pond again. "Today with Zach was another reminder that you and I could never work—that I shouldn't even consider the possibility. This clan needs Oliver, and Oliver needs you. Zach is…well, Zach feels caged, but Oliver can give you the kinda life you deserve. No more squatting on government property. No more worrying where the next meal will come or fearing for your brother's life when curiosity takes him too far."

She bit her lip, and though she couldn't say it full voice, she said it just the same. "Oliver isn't the only one with his citizenship."

Greg's eyes rose heavenward. "Oh, so now you're gonna accept my proposal? You're killin' me here."

Her face went red hot. "No. I just meant…"

He whipped out his yellow card. "You think this flimsy thing does me a bit of good? I was nearly arrested today, just for walkin' down the street. Two patrolmen stopped me, guns and all."

"What?" Frantic, she searched every inch of him. "Are you hurt? How come you didn't tell us?"

"I'm fine. The point is that even if I wanted to get you legal, and even if the government let us tack you, Amber, *and* Zach onto the family, we can't afford it. Grandpa's broke. Taxes alone, and he's outta money in ten months. Ten!" He kicked a dirt clod, sending it sailing into the pond.

The blows kept coming. She struggled to keep up. "I thought we had several years. Not months."

"That's 'cause Grandpa didn't take into account that this new regime is a bunch of filthy, slimy crooks. When the money's gone, that's it, Carrie. My family's back to where y'all are. No house. No citizenship. Nothin'."

She felt sick. That's why Greg had been so upset earlier. "I had no idea."

"Nobody does. I planned to break the news at the meeting tonight. And now with this whole Oliver partner mess…" He let out a long, weary sigh.

"What about the flower shop?" she said suddenly. Greg had been so excited about his idea before, yet she hadn't heard a word about it since she turned down his idea to get her legal. "You had some elaborate plan about us earning money, buying homes one by one."

"The mayor turned me down flat today. I pitched the whole idea, but he turned me down flat 'cause it's a stupid idea. They were pie in the sky dreams. It's over, Carrie, and we're in serious trouble."

Greg looked defeated, but he couldn't be. Not him.

"No. The mayor just needs time," she said. "I know you can make it work."

"Me?" His eyes narrowed on her. "That's just it. *I* can't do it. I'd need you and Richard and so many things, it just can't work. We're outta money, almost outta citizenship, so it's time for you to move on. It's time for you to choose Oliver already."

She hugged herself, desperate for the gift of words to fight his logic. The more she knew of Greg, the harder she fell for him. Catching glimpses that he felt something for her in return only made the pull stronger. He might try to keep people—her—at a distance, but he had a good heart. Her life would only benefit from having him in it. Same with Zach and Amber's.

Yet the only word she could find was, "No."

He pinched the rim of his nose. "For the love of all that is holy, why can't you quit fightin' me? I'm havin' a hard enough time convincing myself. Even if there was a way to get money, Carrie, I have a citizenship card that can be revoked, a house that can be repossessed, chickens that can be shot, and wells that can be destroyed. Oliver has money, *real* money. He has an income and a house with heat and running water—running *hot* water. He has food he doesn't have to grow or kill himself, clothes without rips, a car, phone, TV, and even a stupid umbrella, *plus* his citizenship. We're a sinking ship, and he's throwing you a life preserver, so take it already and be done with it."

The words flew out of him like he'd rehearsed them. She struggled to keep up.

His green eyes searched hers, pleading for understanding. When he spoke, his voice dropped to a whisper. "Oliver's the good one, remember? You told me yourself. Your perfect man. Braden has the charm, I have the looks, and Oliver has the goodness. He's the good one."

Her perfect man. How she regretted that conversation. What Greg didn't realize—and what it took her too long to notice—was that he had all three: the charm, the looks, *and* the goodness. Only he didn't see himself that way. He only saw the bad, the flaws, the mistakes.

Would he ever forgive himself?

If she was anyone else, she would have grabbed his hand like he'd grabbed hers or wiggled her way back into his warm arms. Maybe if she had a different personality, more forward or flirtatious, he wouldn't be able to brush her off so easily. The best she could do was hold his steady gaze.

"Of course I want all that," she said. "But at what cost?"

"You're doin' it now," he whispered. "Lookin' at me like that. You gotta stop. It's killin' me. Seriously."

She refused to look away. She wasn't trying to manipulate him or whatever he thought she was doing. She was just trying to figure out what was going on in that stubborn head of his.

"You promised to stop pushing me to be with Oliver," she said, "so why are you?"

"I won't anymore, 'cause you're not gonna see me again."

"What do you mean?" When he didn't answer, her heart raced in understanding. "You can't leave the clan." He threatened as much after Jenna's death. "You promised you'd stay."

"I don't have to leave to disappear," he said softly.

He'd already proven that.

Her insides began to shake. She was losing him again, only this wasn't just some wall he was hiding behind. It was an electric fence, with barbed wire and no way to see through—to see him.

"What about being my friend?" she said, losing control of her voice. "My best friend?"

"I'm not sure that's such a good idea anymore."

Pain laced through her. Her flowers. Holding her hand. It didn't make sense. It's like Greg wasn't just fighting against her but against himself, too.

"What happened with Zach that changed you so drastically?" He went from holding her hand to pushing her away within minutes, and she had whiplash.

He kicked the grass softly. "I've been thinkin' about this for a while."

"And my flowers?" she asked.

"A mistake."

The knife twisted deeper, but she held strong. "No. They're beautiful and sweet and perfect and—"

"—a mistake."

"What about holding my hand?" she fought back. Or that hug? Even the way he looked at her sometimes, or how he'd almost kissed her twice. "It's like any time you forget yourself, you...you..." *You love me.*

For the life of her, she couldn't spit it out. "What am I doing wrong?" she whispered.

He sighed. "It's not what you're doing. It's what I refuse to do again. Everything today reminded me that life's too fragile. I've been too careless too many times with too many people. I know what I should do, and I know what I want, but they aren't the same thing. I just…I can't be responsible for ruining any more lives."

"And," she said slowly, "you think you'll somehow ruin my life if you're part of it?"

His jaw tightened. "I know I would, 'cause sometime in the future, there's gonna be a day like today with you, Zach, or Amber. Only one of you will end up dead or arrested, and I'll know I coulda prevented it if I'd just walked away now—if I'd just let you love Oliver."

Reading between the lines had her heart beating much too fast. Greg really did love her. He was just trying to protect her in some crazy, bossy, masochistic way.

Worry less, love more.

Carrie's chin lifted. "Who's to say you won't ruin my life by walking away now?"

He gave a mirthless laugh. "And that's why I can't be around you. 'Cause you say stuff like that, and you look at me with those baby blues, and it makes me forget what I gotta do—what *you* gotta do. So, I'm sorry, but I'm gonna end this before it starts. I'm gonna disappear as best as I can, and I need you to quit fightin' me on it."

He was more than capable. Thirty-four people in one tiny neighborhood and she'd never see him again. But worse, once his mom died, Carrie knew all bets were off. Greg Pierce would skip town as fast as he'd come.

Her pulse pounded, her thoughts raced for something that would stick this time, but he didn't give her a chance.

"If I were you, Carrie, I wouldn't take anybody else on that drive Monday. Use the time to open your eyes and look around—really look for the first time. See the kind of life you could have. Oliver's a good man. He'll be good to you." Greg's eyes took in her hair, her eyes, and every aspect of her face as if taking a last mental picture. He still found something worth admiring in her, and yet he was walking away. "You're lucky to have him."

"I don't want him," she whispered.

He smiled sadly. "You don't know what you want."

Backing up, he started away from her.

"Please," she said. "Don't do this."

"See you around, Carrie." Then he stopped. "No. I guess you won't."

And then he was gone.

———————◆———————

Oliver and the dogs reached the end of the first street and circled back. His two new partners had special training today, giving him the day off of babysitting—or at least it felt like babysitting with how young they were. So Chief Dario insisted Oliver take Jamansky's German Shepherds with him for this sweep.

Pulling hard against their leashes, Bretton and Felix kept up a brisk pace as they swept through the Ferris neighborhood. Trainer Jerry had given Oliver a crash course in dog handling. Oliver had already forgotten most of it, but the dogs seemed to know the drill.

House after house they searched. It wasn't a thorough sweep. Oliver just opened the front door and let the dogs sniff around. If they didn't bark, he didn't search the interior. In his mind, finding illegal squatters was like using a snow shovel to stop an avalanche. The latest report from Washington estimated hundreds of illegal squatters for every one found. Most days their sweeps were useless. The only squatters left in this territory were smart enough to stay hidden.

Thankfully.

After Oliver finished here, he was headed straight for Carrie's. He just had to figure out how to ditch the dogs before their drive. He couldn't take them to the station, not without Chief asking a million questions, but neither did he want them at his house tearing his place to shreds. Yet, he could only picture Bretton and Felix in the backseat, panting, drooling, and smelling Carrie's hair. What if she brought Amber, Zach, *and* Greg? How would they fit everyone?

Home it was. His couch was doomed.

It will only be a short drive, he told himself. Which got him wondering how long was short. Five minutes? Thirty? And what if Carrie brought others? How could he keep them all hidden when he only planned on—

Barking erupted, and the dogs suddenly leaped forward, jerking on their leashes. Oliver tightened his grip as his head whipped back and forth, surveying the area.

"What is it, boys?"

This neighborhood had been deserted for a while, long enough Oliver almost skipped it to make it to Carrie's on time. But the dogs pulled him down the street toward a two-story house with large, white pillars out front.

A movement in an upper window caught his eye. A shadow.

Oliver grabbed his gun while struggling to keep hold of the charging dogs. He saw another shadow in a different window and his stomach leaped into his throat. There were at least two illegals in that house, maybe more. Not good. The squatters could see Oliver, but he couldn't see them.

Not good!

Bretton and Felix barked and snarled, ferocious when they wanted to be. As they reached the yard, Oliver pulled them to a stop and slid up behind a massive tree. He kept his gun up and searched every window. Protocol required him to release the dogs so they could round up the squatters. The leash burned his palm as the dogs jumped and pawed to be set free, but he locked his muscles and grabbed his radio.

"I need backup!" he shouted over the barking. "Are Portman and Bushing back yet?"

"Yes," Ashlee said, "but they don't have a car."

"Get one! I'm on Joshua Drive, northeast section of Shelton. Go fast!"

Oliver peeked out from behind the tree trunk. While dogs were an asset in finding illegals, they were also a hindrance. He couldn't hear anything over their barking. Yet he could sense people watching him. There could be a whole clan holed up in this neighborhood. Chief added this sub to Oliver's route last year after a sweep went horribly wrong. He'd never encountered any sign of life since then, but there could be a roving Bedouin clan, or a new group like Carrie's taking up permanent residence.

For all he knew, it was just some poor trapped animal, driving Bretton and Felix crazy.

He made a rash decision even knowing it could get him killed. He exchanged his gun for his Taser. His coworkers rarely used Tasers since they didn't mind killing a squatter or two. Less mouths to feed. But

Tasers could only fire around 30 feet. As much as he didn't want to, he had to get closer anyway.

Pulse hammering, Oliver peeked around the tree trunk and watched for what felt like an eternity. No more shadows in the upper windows. The people—or animals—would have already jumped him if they wanted an altercation. Maybe. And if they had guns, he'd already be dead.

Maybe.

With a ragged breath, he convinced himself to act more patrolman and less Oliver Simmons. His hands still shook as he inched away from the tree. When all stayed shadow-less, he broke into a sprint, letting the dogs drag him toward the porch.

Oliver pressed up against the bricks next to the front door. The dogs climbed the door to get in, making him wish they could tell him who or what he was up against. Based on their loud agitation, he guessed it wasn't just some raccoon.

He glanced down the street. *Come on!*

This was Karma. Jamansky and Nielsen used to run his backup. Oliver squealed on them, and now his life was left up to ditsy Ashlee's ability to find a car for his inexperienced, acne-ridden partners.

The leashes burned his palm. Barking filled his ears. Still, he held strong. The front door stayed closed. Windows, too. Bretton and Felix couldn't get inside unless he let them in.

His boss was right to give him partners. As much as it would complicate his life—and Carrie's—he was getting too old for this.

When the pain became unbearable, he let go of the leashes. The dogs jumped, barked, and climbed the front door. Oliver stayed pressed to the brick, so they ran back and forth in front of the house, looking for another way in.

A sudden shout broke out over their barking.

"Hey, pig!" a man yelled. "You have thirty seconds to leave before we start shooting!"

Oliver's stomach lurched. Either that was one amazing talking raccoon or he was in serious trouble.

ten

The dogs took off around the side of the house for another way in. One of these days, Oliver wouldn't make it home after a sweep. He hoped it wasn't today.

"Show your cards," Oliver yelled to the illegal, "and you won't be harmed!" Straight out of the handbook. The squatters wouldn't have cards, though. They never did.

Back pressed to the brick, he could sense the movement inside. Could hear shuffling. He kept his Taser up and scanned the corner of the house, the street, the neighborhood, braced for an ambush. They could have stationed people anywhere.

"You're surrounded!" Oliver shouted, which was true if he counted the dogs. "I advise you not to resist arrest. I—we—don't want to harm you!"

The bricks tried to scratch off what was left of his hair as his head whipped back and forth. Then he heard a yelp. The dogs' barking turned to sudden whining. Behind the house, Bretton and Felix had been attacked.

Oliver was a dead man.

The sunlight suddenly dimmed overhead. He looked up in time to see an object—huge—fall from a second story window. His reaction time was slow. It hit him squarely on the head, knocking him flat on his stomach.

Pain exploded everywhere. Head. Neck. Back. Fog clouded his thoughts as the heavy object covered him. He blinked, vision blurring, and tried to think through the haze. He took in the size and shape of the object. A door. They'd dropped an interior door on him.

Oliver spotted a flash of gray sneaking out the front door. Tennis shoes. He shoved the door off and whipped out his Taser.

"Stop! Don't move!" Oliver called.

The man took off, leaping from the porch and sprinting down the sidewalk. Oliver fired. Two probes shot through the air and hit the back of the man's thigh. The man lurched up with a scream and then dropped. Hard.

Head pounding, Oliver dragged himself to his feet and looked for other illegals. He saw no one. Hopefully, this guy was it.

Rubbing his neck, Oliver checked on his captive. The man moaned and convulsed as his muscles shook with electric shocks. He was a skinny guy, maybe mid-twenties, with a thick red beard and black hoodie.

Keeping the Taser trained on him, Oliver said, "Roll onto your stomach. Face down."

More pained groans, but the man didn't roll over. Oliver wasn't even sure he heard him.

A few years back, he made the mistake of being compassionate during the moaning phase. He waited too long to cuff the illegal and got a stiff elbow to the jaw. But he had backup then. Jamansky wrestled the guy down until they could cuff him.

Now he had no one.

The probes, still attached to the man's thighs, were ready for more electricity if needed, yet Oliver suddenly felt vulnerable as he remembered something. He'd seen two shadows. Not one. Where was the person who had dropped the interior door on him—or the one who took out the dogs? They could have a whole army in there.

"Roll over!" Oliver shouted, frantically scanning the house. "Now! Face down."

The guy didn't roll until Oliver raised his Taser. Then he flopped onto his stomach and pressed his red beard to the cement.

Barking erupted again from somewhere. One of the dogs—Bretton—charged up from around the back of the house. He sprinted to the squatter on the ground and barked in his face. The man cowered which was too much movement for Oliver's comfort.

Oliver knelt next to him and cuffed his hands behind his back. "You're under arrest for trespassing on government property and assaulting an officer. Are you alone?"

The man glared at Oliver through narrowed, murderous eyes.

"Who's in there?" Oliver tried anyway. "Your family?"

The bearded guy didn't answer, but his eyes did. With a pained look, they flickered back to the front door. So who was it? A buddy? Girlfriend? Then again, it could have been the guy's sumo-sized brothers. Someone strong enough to rip a door from its hinges and toss it out the window.

Oliver had to get out of there.

Ignoring the pain shooting down his neck, he straightened and waved the Taser. "Now stand up. Slowly. We're going to walk to my car." Four very long houses away.

The guy got to his knees, but that's all he managed with weak muscles and cuffed hands. Or…that's what he wanted Oliver to think. Oliver saw his fists clenching. The effect of the Taser was wearing off.

"Up now!" Oliver roared.

Bretton ran circles around the man, waiting for the signal to tear his arms off. The guy struggled to his feet, shoulders hanging in defeat, but the look he gave Oliver was pure hatred.

"Now walk," Oliver said. "To my car. Nice and slow."

The guy took two steps forward and then suddenly spun. Head down, he charged Oliver.

The dog and Oliver reacted at the same time. Bretton went for the guy's arm. Oliver squeezed the Taser and fired off another charge. The man screamed and dropped as more electrical impulses shot through his body.

Doubling over, Oliver heaved huge gulps of air. What was that guy thinking? Oliver's head pulsed in time to his heartbeat. The man cried full-on sobs as his body convulsed. The whole time, Bretton kept his jaw clamped on his arm, unaffected by the Taser while waiting for permission to snap the guy's bones in half.

"Bretton!" Oliver shouted. "Komm! Komm!"

Obediently, Bretton released the guy's arm and trotted to Oliver's side.

The man ended up in a fetal position, whimpering on the cement. He wasn't harmed, at least not badly. Just incapacitated. But with a second charge, he wouldn't be able to walk for an hour. Oliver would have to drag him to the car. Four houses might as well have been four miles.

When the crying died down to whimpers, the man looked at Oliver again. "Is that..." he huffed, "the best you've got? Why not just...kill me!"

Oh, please no. Why did Oliver always get the fighters?

"I'd advise you not to resist arrest, sir," he said. At least not more than he already had.

Red beard pressed to cement, the man looked at the German Shepherd and bared his teeth. Then he let out a low growl.

Bretton went nuts, barking and snarling.

"Sitz!" Oliver screamed. "Sitz!"

Bretton obeyed unwillingly.

"Are you crazy?" Oliver yelled at the man. "That dog can rip you to shreds." The guy was lucky Oliver remembered a few commands.

"Live free..." the man whimpered, "or die."

Oliver froze. "What did you say?"

Cheek to sidewalk, the man shouted, "Live free or die! There are things far worse than death!"

A chill ran down Oliver's spine. It's the third time he'd heard that quote during an arrest. Last time, he looked it up. The squatters were quoting John Stark, a Revolutionary War general. The eerie thing was that each arrest had been in different cities. Either the illegals had independently stumbled upon the same quote—even though they had no access to computers or libraries—or they were uniting.

Oliver's head pounded.

It wasn't just Chicago anymore.

"I refuse to live in one of your prison camps," the man continued, voice growing stronger with each word, "so just kill me already!"

"I don't want to harm you," Oliver said, meaning every word.

"No? You just want to rip me from my wife and two-week-old baby. You just want to turn me over to slave away in some work camp for the rest of my life. Where's the harm in that, huh pig? I was born a free man, and I will die a free man!"

Oliver glanced over his shoulder, having only heard the part about a wife and a new baby. His gut twisted with guilt. Was it true?

What would Carrie say if she saw him right now?

He heard an engine. A patrol car sped down the road. His new partners spotted him and screeched to a stop in front of the white-pillared house. They ran out and yanked the man to standing.

"Do you want him in our car or yours, sir?" Portman asked.

Sir? Oliver still wasn't used to the title.

"I don't know." He shook his throbbing head to clear it. Then he glanced down at his watch. 2:24! He was late. "Yours if it's alright. Can you take him in and start his paperwork?"

"Sure," Portman said.

"Oh, and take him to Sugar Grove, not Shelton," Oliver added.

Portman looked at Bushing. "Do we get credit for the arrest, sir?"

Oliver was too tired to argue. He had a migraine the size of Texas and a growing goose egg on the back of his head. "Yes. Fine. Get it started and I'll be there later. I'm late right now."

"Late for what?" Bushing asked.

Oliver wanted to kick himself. He'd said too much, but his seniority made them too nervous to press. His young partners pushed the red-bearded man into their backseat. Once the door shut, Portman came back.

"Are there others, sir? Should we do a final sweep of the area?"

The red-bearded man jerked up, horrified, confirming what he'd said. He really did have a wife and baby inside that house. The other shadows. The man ran to deflect Oliver, sacrificing himself to save his young family. And now he stared at Oliver, pleading for mercy.

"No," Oliver said. "He was alone. Thanks for taking him in."

"Sure," Portman said. "And sir, you should probably take care of that."

"What?"

He motioned to Oliver's head. "Branch to the forehead?"

Oliver reached up and felt a warm, sticky liquid trailing down the side of his face. Blood. Great. He gingerly felt around to gauge the size of his wound. "A door, actually. Does it need stitches?"

Portman shrugged.

Just his luck. He was late to Carrie's and bleeding to death. If Carrie had a phone, he could have called her. Then again, if it wasn't for Bretton, he might not have made it to Carrie at all.

Oh, no! Oliver whirled around, remembering Felix who still hadn't emerged from the backyard.

"I'm missing a dog," he said. "I'll catch up later."

He took off and ran around the back of the house. Hopefully, the guy's wife wouldn't think he was coming back for her and drop another door on his head.

He found Felix on the back porch, whimpering. His hind leg was twisted awkwardly. Bretton rubbed his nose against Felix's and whimpered along with him. And yet, over the two dogs, Oliver heard a far more disturbing sound. A sound coming from inside.

A baby. Crying.

There was something distinct about the cry of a newborn, a tiny wail that wavered with pitch. That mother was probably frantic to silence her baby. By duty, Oliver should go inside and take both. He probably could with little resistance.

As much as he needed the numbers to fill his quota, he couldn't do it. But that didn't alleviate his guilt. Not arresting her might as well be a death sentence since she and her baby would be on their own to defend themselves, hunt for themselves, hide, and just plain survive.

The baby continued to cry.

"I'm sorry," he whispered to the house. Then, careful to keep Felix's broken leg steady, he picked up the dog and carried him to his car.

eleven

Amber didn't share her sister's love of the outdoors. Just the opposite, which made planting days absolute torture. At least on harvest days, she got food. All she'd get today was muddy clothes, elephant-like skin, and broken, dirty, farmer-girl nails.

They planted the early crops a few weeks ago. Those were a few rows over. This morning they were planting the rest, as in the entire garden which was large enough Carrie called it a field. Amber called it a mud pit. Beans, squash, corn, and who cared what else.

Because of the delay in planting, food stores were low, so several men left to hunt, including Braden. But a bunch of women skipped out, too. Mariah had thrown up blood an hour ago, so May took her inside. Fair enough. But the others? Sasha said she couldn't help because of the little boys, even though Carrie used to weed with Little Jeffrey and Jonah all the time. But was Amber allowed to make an excuse? No. All day long she would turn dirt. If she was lucky, she'd get to rake in dried goat manure, but that was only if she was lucky.

Of course if she was truly lucky, a rock would flip up, hit her between the eyes, and incapacitate her for the rest of the day. Then Braden would have to kiss her forehead to make it better. Obviously her lips would be hurting, too. How could he resist that?

Carrie stopped digging. "What suddenly cheered you up?"

"Move your shovel over the next time I bend over," Amber said.

"Why?"

"I need you to flip a rock up and render me unconscious for the day."

Carrie shook her head and sank her shovel into the next six inches of dirt. Only five thousand more to go. "Sometimes I wonder if we came from the same parents. I know you don't like planting, but don't you enjoy the fresh air at least?"

"Excuse me?" Amber cried, pointing to the smelly milk goat. "What do you call that?"

"A blessing."

Amber rolled her eyes. They lost one goat in the raid back in March. As soon as Butterscotch stopped giving milk, Braden's family was out of a job, and Amber's bland diet would drop another notch. But she wasn't about to be side-tracked.

"I hate the cold—and don't say it isn't; my fingers are about to fall off. I hate the dirt, it's ruining my nails. I hate digging. I hate seeds. I hate everything about planting. If I ever get my own house, I swear I'll never have a vegetable garden, a flower garden, or anything else plant-ish. I'll move to Arizona where I can have a yard full of dirt."

By the time she finished, Carrie was laughing. "You and I couldn't be more different."

"Well, there's the understatement of the…" Amber trailed off as a movement in the distance caught her eye. She went up on tiptoes and grinned. A few men strode out of the woods. Braden was up front, looking very masculine carrying whatever small dead animal he'd shot. Very cave-man-kill-wildebeest. Greg and Terrell were next, hauling a large deer by its feet.

Carrie stood next to her. "Finally," she whispered.

With summer around the corner, Braden spent more time outside, giving him a nice tan and sun-kissed hair. He looked like California personified.

Amber stretched up taller to see and be seen. Funny thing, Carrie did the same. The three men headed for the Trenton's backyard where they would skin and gut the animals. Amber had to get out of digging before then. The smell and sight of animal guts always made her feel faint. Then again, fainting might be less painful than a rock between the eyes.

"When did Braden start shaving?" Carrie asked.

"Saturday," Amber said. "I told him his beard was itchy."

Carrie turned slowly. "Just how much have you been kissing?"

"Ah," Amber sighed dreamily. "Not enough."

"Amber," Carrie said, "you better be careful. You two can't be—"

"Please." Amber held up a hand. "I know more about men than you do." As if Braden would let it get that far anyway. "Now I can't decide if he looks better with or without. What do you think?"

"Without."

Amber grinned. "Of course you do. Greg doesn't have a beard."

Carrie shot her a dark look. "Neither does Oliver."

"Ew. You just ruined it for me."

Reaching up, Amber shook out her long, dark hair and waited for Braden to notice. She even put a hand on her hip to look more feminine in spite of the mud caked everywhere.

"You know," she said, "Greg's the one who taught Braden to shave with a knife. Man, I wish I could have seen that."

Carrie sighed and went back to digging.

"By the way," Amber added, "since Zach is grounded, can Braden go on the drive with us today?"

"No."

"Why not?"

"Because I said so."

Amber hated that reply more than she hated planting days. "Whatever. I'll just tell Braden he can come."

"No, you won't," Carrie said. "Braden wasn't invited."

"Then I'll ask Oliver if he can go." Oliver didn't like Amber— especially since that raid mishap in March. But he wouldn't turn her down. Oliver never turned anyone down. "Oooh. Maybe he'll teach me and Braden how to drive."

"Amber," Carrie said in the sternest voice she could manage, "stop or you won't go either."

Carrie needed to make better threats. She needed Amber on that drive more than Amber needed to go. Nobody wanted to be stuck alone with nerdy Oliver for that long, not even Carrie.

The other dirt diggers left to see what the men had killed. Amber stayed because Braden broke from the group and headed straight toward her. Her pulse quickened.

She waited for him to look up and smile, but his head stayed down, watching the ground. The closer he got, the lower his head hung, which bugged her. She spent extra time that morning brushing her dark hair one hundred times to make it glow. The least he could do was notice. When he was within twenty feet, he still didn't glance up. He just kept walking, holding that stupid dead furball.

And that's when she saw.

He wasn't wearing his red bracelet.

She should have waved, hollered, or shouted a greeting, but the dejection washed over her. Fifteen feet. Ten. Not a flicker of his eyes. Nothing.

As Braden walked past her—close enough she could have punched him—his crooked smile finally broke through.

"Heya, Gorgeous," he whispered.

Pathetic what two little words could do to her. She melted into a smile—not that he noticed. The jerk still hadn't so much as glanced her direction, and he didn't the rest of the way inside of the Trentons.

Amber threw her hands in the air. "Why does he do that to me? He knows I hate his games. One of these days, he'll be chasing me and not the other way around."

"He already does, or didn't you notice how he took the long way around? By the way, don't dig in this area," Carrie said, kneeling next to a tomato plant she babied like it would sprout gold. She drew a large circle around the stem. "I'll pull the weeds myself."

Amber cared even less about digging than she had two minutes ago. She stared down at Braden's footsteps in her newly-turned soil, at her red bracelet without a partner. Sometimes she wondered if he was just putting up with her until he met someone else—*if* he ever met someone else. Heat built behind her eyes as all of the insecurities of a sixteen-year-old hit her full force. Not tall enough. Not pretty enough. Not anything enough.

Carrie stood and put an arm around her. "Braden is crazy about you. Believe me, you could have it a lot worse. If you had eyes in the back of your head, you'd see him in May's kitchen, staring at you right now."

Amber spun. Braden stood by the kitchen window, but he wasn't looking at her. His head was turned, talking to Greg. Worse, he was laughing. Probably at her. Probably telling Greg about the ugly bracelet.

"That's it!" Amber said. "I can't take anymore. I'm done with Braden forever!"

Carrie's expression turned suddenly cold. "That's enough, Amber. Seriously. Cut the drama and get back to work before I double your chores."

Amber turned. "Geez. What's your problem?"

"I'm sick of you complaining about Braden, the garden, and all of it. The guy you love calls you gorgeous to your face and stares at you behind your back. What more could you want?"

Amber's shoulders lifted. "I don't know. More."

Carrie folded her arms. "Braden is as uncomplicated as it gets. Why can't you just be happy?"

"Why can't you?" Amber shot back. "Man, what has you all peeved today? I thought planting day was your favorite day of the year."

Carrie instantly sobered. "It is. I'm sorry. I should be happy. I should."

But Amber didn't miss her glance back toward the Trenton's. Greg stood next to Braden, but the second he saw Amber, he moved away from the window. Amber's own guy problems were suddenly forgotten.

"Oh, my gosh. You love Greg. For real, though." She'd teased Carrie about him before, but she thought it was just a passing crush. Now it was all making sense. "But he doesn't like you back. He went the long way around the garden, and now you're ready to bite my head off."

Carrie's blue eyes turned into unflattering slits. "You don't know anything, so shut up."

Amber's mouth dropped. She and Zach weren't allowed to say 'shut up.'

Greg no longer stood by the window, but that didn't stop Carrie from checking for him.

"Oh, come on," Amber said, laughing, "I saw you stretch up tall so he'd notice you. But it's okay." She put a hand on Carrie's arm. "I won't tell anyone. I promise."

Carrie yanked free. "You also promised to never bring up the subject again."

"If it makes you feel better, I'd be in love with Greg, too. In fact, I'm in love with him for you. He's amazing, super hot, and the way he saved you from Jeff was—"

"If you don't stop talking right now," Carrie said, "you're not going today."

"Man. You've got it bad." Amber grinned. "Does he know?"

Carrie dropped her shovel. She turned and started out of the garden, past the early crops, past May's well and Butterscotch. Shocked, Amber watched her. When it was clear she wasn't turning back, Amber shouted, "Carrie, wait. I'm just teasing. Come back!"

Carrie kept walking. Out of the garden. Out of the yard.

"Carrie?"

But Carrie didn't stop. She just left. She walked out of May's backyard on planting day.

Her favorite day of the year.

———— ◆ ————

Oliver's nerves were fried.

He'd cleaned up some since the attack. Thankfully, the laceration above his brow was on his left side facing the car window so Carrie might not notice. It was too early to bruise but his head throbbed like mad.

He dropped Felix and Bretton off with Trainer Jerry so they could recover. If only his troubles had ended there, he might have enjoyed the rest of his day. But when he came back around the front office, Ashlee handed him a large envelope to deliver to one of the local citizens. One look at the name and Oliver had felt sick ever since.

As if that wasn't enough, he couldn't get that illegal man's wife out of his head. He'd dreamed up every face for that woman, ending with Carrie's. That could be her someday with Greg's—or whoever's—baby, and Oliver just destroyed her life.

By the time he made it to the Logan Pond subdivision, he could hardly think straight.

Mrs. Dixon and her twins strolled down the sidewalk. The boys waved excitedly at Oliver because they weren't old enough to realize who he was or what he was about to do.

twelve

Greg heard Oliver's car heading to pick up Carrie. He stopped digging as a pang of jealousy shot through him, though for more than the obvious reason. He missed the pull and speed of his old Ford—of any car. The ability to decide one minute he was hungry and be home with pizza and a Coke ten minutes later.

Pizza...

His stomach growled. He knew better than to think of old food. Grabbing his shovel, he went back to working on the Dixon's well.

The well behind Carrie's hadn't taken this long. Of course, Carrie hadn't complained about the location and made him start over three times. He'd also had more help. Some guys offered to help after the hunt, but Greg turned them down. He wanted to be alone today.

Carrie and Oliver's first date.

Hopefully after this one, it would get easier.

A few minutes later, Greg saw a movement and a tall guy in uniform came striding around the side of Dixon's house.

"There you are," Oliver said. "I've been looking for you."

Greg's temper flared. "Why? Did Carrie send you?" No matter how much she might want Greg to join them on the drive, he vowed to stay away from her. Four days and holding strong.

"No. I have something for you," Oliver said.

"Oh." Greg's muscles relaxed, but only for a second. Then he remembered the other beef he had with the patrolman. "By the way, what makes you think you can keep Carrie safe today? Just because you— Whoa!" he said, interrupting himself as he got his first good look at Oliver. "What happened to your face?" He had a huge gash over his left eye which was already swelling to something ugly. That wound was fresh, plus the other scratches on the side of his face. "Run face-first into a tree?"

Oliver reached up and tenderly touched his wound. "A door, actually. Bad day."

"No kiddin'." Shaking it off, Greg resumed his tirade. "What makes you think you can keep Carrie safe on this drive? The chance of her getting arrested isn't worth seeing some trees. Not in a million years."

"I have it all worked out," Oliver said.

"With fake travel papers? As if that'll work."

Oliver's eyes narrowed. "I'm not stupid, Greg. Give me a little credit."

That pulled Greg up short. "Not travel papers? Then how?"

Oliver swallowed and looked away. "None of your business."

Greg stared at him, piecing more together than he wanted to. "You got Carrie papers, fake *citizenship* papers? Just for some drive?"

"Yes. No. Not exactly. Aren't you...?" Oliver fidgeted with his uniform. "Aren't you coming with us?"

It took Greg a moment to answer calmly. "No."

The gash over Oliver's brow rose, but Greg was too distracted. Oliver forged fake citizenship for Carrie. Or...maybe the papers weren't fake. Was it possible...? Greg stopped the thought cold. No. Oliver wouldn't.

Would he?

No way.

Oliver wouldn't draft a marriage license without Carrie's permission. Except...it was just paperwork, a little red tape to ensure her safety, linking her permanently to a patrolman through marriage. She couldn't get safer than that. Amber and Zach would be included, too, since families of patrolmen were granted citizenship.

It was brilliant actually.

But thinking of Carrie's name on a marriage license—especially without her knowledge—twisted Greg's stomach with rage. She'd turned Greg down when he suggested the same thing, and she *liked* him.

"Does Carrie know about this?" Greg asked.

Oliver turned white. "No, she can't. I'll tell her when it's right, but not now. This is just for her safety, nothing more. Please." Oliver cowered as if Greg might strike him. "I know you two are together. Don't hate me."

Carrie was married.

Greg wanted to scream at him for doing it behind her back, knowing how betrayed she would feel. A yellow card—no, not even a yellow card. A green card. One citizenship level higher.

Mr. and Mrs. Oliver Simmons.

Greg tried to talk himself into the idea. This was good—at least, good for Carrie. If Oliver was smart, he'd do everything in his power to make it a valid marriage, with love, affection, white picket fence and all. Little golden-haired Carries running around the house.

Suddenly Oliver looked older than Greg remembered, balder than he remembered, and far more awkward. Oliver might keep her safe, but how would he ever make her happy when he could barely look her in the eye?

Greg leaned against his shovel and took several slow breaths.

It's done, he told himself. *Let it go.*

Let her go.

He waited until he trusted himself to speak. "Carrie and I aren't together."

Oliver's eyes popped open. "But I thought...I mean, Carrie made it sound like—"

"Can I be blunt?" Greg interrupted.

"O-kay..." Oliver said, leery.

Greg thought about Kendra and Jenna's deaths to solidify his decision. "Go for it with Carrie today. Give it your all."

It took a moment before he regained the ability to speak. "May *I* be blunt?"

"Always."

"What's wrong with you?" Oliver blurted.

Greg smiled a little. "Plenty, but what specifically did you have in mind?"

"Why are you constantly pushing me to be with Carrie when it's obvious there's something going on between you two? Are you playing some kind of game with me? Making fun of me?"

Greg's smile faded. "No."

"Then why are you so insistent I make a move with Carrie when it seems like you already did?"

Greg grabbed his shovel and sunk it deep in the hole. "You're better for her."

"Yeah, but still..."

Ouch. The guy could have at least hesitated. Everyone knew Oliver was better for her—everyone, that is, but Carrie.

"Suffice it to say," Greg said, "she and I won't work, so go for it. And none of this wishy-washy stuff from my mom's wedding. She didn't even know that was a date."

Oliver scowled at him which looked painful given the current state of his face, but Greg plowed on.

"And another thing, you've gotta get out of this whole partner thing. We can't handle another—"

"Partners," Oliver corrected softly. "I have two of them. And it's too late. It's a done deal. We do our first sweep through the neighborhood on Saturday."

"What? No way! This new promotion gives you more say than ever, so get out of it. Tell your boss whatever you have to. Having partners will ruin everything."

"As if I don't know that?" Oliver snapped. He pinched his eyes closed. "Look, I don't have time for this. I'm late getting Carrie, and I'm not in the mood for one of your lectures, Greg. Need I remind you that I was in high school when you were in diapers? I came to talk to you, not the other way around!"

Greg's jaw dropped at the uncharacteristic outburst. "Wow. You really must have had a bad day." He set his shovel aside. "Alrighty. What's up?"

Oliver's demeanor changed in a heartbeat. He went contrite as he pulled an envelope from his uniform, a thick envelope that suddenly took all of his attention. "This."

"What is it?"

Instead of handing it over, Oliver's grip tightened. "I'm sorry, Greg."

Something inside Greg stirred. Something close to panic, although he wasn't sure why. He leaned sideways to make out the hand-written script on the front:

Gregory Curtis Pierce
541 Denton Trail
Shelton, Illinois

"I didn't know mail services had been restored," he said. And who knew he lived here anyway? Not his old girlfriend. And nobody else cared about him.

"They haven't. That's why they asked me to deliver this to you."

They.

The word made Greg's muscles clench. It's just that Oliver looked paler than usual, and Greg hadn't received a single letter since the Collapse. A voice in the back of his head shouted that he should have seen this coming, which was ridiculous, because he didn't even know what *this* was.

He held out his hand. "Give it to me."

Oliver didn't. "I'm sorry, Greg. I didn't realize...I mean, I should have, but when you got your yellow card, I didn't know this would happen. You won't believe me because you think I want you out of Carrie's life—which I kind of do—but you said yourself that you and her aren't even—"

"Oliver!" Greg snapped. "Give it to me."

Oliver straightened in his green uniform, looking more patrolman than ever. Then he handed over the large, yellow envelope.

Greg slid his finger under the lip to break the seal and slipped out several sheets of paper. The first was typed on a crisp white paper with the seal of the United States of America in the upper left corner. Greg studied that seal like his life depended on it, knowing the second he read the words below, he couldn't unread them.

His eyes betrayed him.

Printed in bold letters across the top of the page were five words:

ORDER TO REPORT FOR DUTY

thirteen

Greg went numb, but he forced himself to keep reading:

ORDER TO REPORT FOR DUTY

THE PRESIDENT OF THE UNITED STATES,

TO: Gregory Curtis Pierce ,

GREETING:

Having submitted yourself for the purpose of determining the place and time which you can best serve the United States in this present emergency, you are hereby notified that you have been selected for immediate government service.

Report to the following training facility, Naperville , of the county of DuPage, Illinois , at 8 am on May 26th . From and after the day and hour named, you will be a servant in the service of your beloved United States.

United We Stand.

President Bennett Rigsby

Greg couldn't move. Couldn't think. "Does this mean what I think it does?"

"I'm sorry," Oliver said again.

In other words, yes.

Greg's name and information had been hand-written in, but everything else looked formal. Official. Binding. He took a slow, steadying breath.

"So...I'm being drafted? Are we at war?"

"Sort of," Oliver said.

"With who?"

"Ourselves."

Understanding hit. "The smoke," Greg said softly. "Chicago."

Oliver nodded. "The southern half of Chicago proper is in ruins."

Greg quickly flipped through the other papers: a map to the training facility, packing list, rules. Still, he struggled to process it. "So they're recruiting me to the army?"

"Either the army or they might train you to become...a...um..." Oliver swallowed.

"For the sake of my sanity," Greg said, "spit it out!"

"A patrolman."

All coherent thoughts stopped for the space of three seconds. Then Greg burst out laughing. "Oh, this is rich. They wanna make *me*, of all people, a patrolman?"

"Or a soldier," Oliver said. "They're short on both."

Greg stared at him. "This is seriously happening?" He'd spent every day since the Collapse loathing President Rigsby and his new regime, and now he was being asked to serve them? No. To become one of them?

A green cardie.

Greg shook his head. Oliver might be able to stomach it, but he never could. "They can't force me to serve."

"Yes. They can."

"I'll run," Greg said, heart racing. Richard was taking care of his mom now, and Carrie needed him out of her life anyway. "I'll just disappear. What can they do?"

Oliver pointed. "Look at that envelope, Greg. It has your grandparents' address on it. They know where you live—where your family lives. Your mom. Mr. O'Brien. You're all tied to the same household. If you don't show up for training next week, they'll come looking for you. And if they can't find you, they'll arrest them. Or worse."

Greg went cold.

There was only a handful of people left in the world that he cared about. Going AWOL was a death sentence to every one of them. But even worse, the clan was dependent on his grandparents for survival. If Greg wanted to run, he had to drag thirty-four people with him. Not just adults either. Young kids. Babies. The elderly.

Maybe we should run, he reasoned. Ten months and they were broke anyway. Only...they'd never be able to feed that many people on the run. He and his mom had nearly starved coming north, and that was two of them. What about shelter in the winter? Clothes? Water? In ten months, they could still hide in one of the other houses, post guards, and make it work. And deep down, he knew if they ran out of money, Oliver would step in and help. His grandparents' house was still the clan's best chance of survival.

He reread the words, stomach tight with dismay. *ORDER TO RE-PORT FOR DUTY.*

May 26th. Ten days.

"So we're in a civil war," he said, still struggling to come to terms with it. "People are finally fighting back, so the government's drafting me to fight illegals here as one of you or else in the army to fight a war I've never heard of until today." He shook his head bitterly. "That's a mighty fine choice they're givin' me." Although he already knew what he'd choose. He'd rather fight official wars than destroy a single clan like the one he lived in.

"You don't get to choose," Oliver said. "They choose for you."

"Of course. Tell me I at least get a say in where I'm assigned. That I'll come back here when all is said and done?"

Oliver was quiet far too long. "I'm sorry, Greg."

Greg glared at him. "If you say that one more time, you're gonna end up with another black eye."

Flipping through the papers, Greg searched for a loophole, anything. "How long is..." He cleared his throat. "How long is training?"

"Last I heard," Oliver said, "four months."

His mom would never survive that long. He promised to stick around until she died, but he would miss it, miss her, miss everything! All with no promise of return or survival.

"Wow, thanks for the heads up," Greg said darkly. "Thanks for suggesting I get my yellow card. So far, it's helped me waste Grandpa's money, read the latest propaganda, and now..." He couldn't finish, because now he'd be trained to kill. Not some foreign enemy overseas. They'd train him to kill his own people.

Americans.

This was because he visited Mayor Phillips. It had to be. Greg knew about those patrolmen working the black market, and the mayor wanted him gone.

"Can I injure myself?" he asked. "Blind myself? Somethin'?"

Oliver didn't answer, which was answer enough.

"Well, there's one bit of good news," Greg said bitterly. "This clears the way now for you and Carrie, doesn't it?" The clan would be thrilled, too. No more Greg causing issues.

Oliver's face reddened. "You think I'm happy about this? I didn't know they were actively recruiting, Greg."

"Yeah, you look real shook up."

Oliver's gaze dropped to the grass long enough for Greg to feel guilty. This wasn't Oliver's fault. It wasn't. There was no reason to kick the messenger.

ORDER TO REPORT. ORDER TO REPORT. The words kept echoing in his mind.

In a way, Greg would make the best patrolman. He'd lived life as an illegal. He'd lived in two different clans in two different states, escaped a municipality, and spent eight months traveling north, eluding patrolmen right and left. He knew all the tricks squatters used to become invisible. He could probably quadruple their monthly quota for arrests.

But his mom...

Carrie...

The defeat washed over him. "How far away is the training facility?"

"Twenty-five miles, give or take," Oliver said. "I...I can give you a ride if you want."

"Oh, no. You've done plenty already."

Stung, Oliver frowned. Greg ignored him. Twenty-five miles on foot was far, but not impossible. A two-day walk or four-day round trip.

"Do I get home leave?" Greg asked, and then immediately shook his head. Who was he kidding? They'd never let him leave for an hour, let alone four days to visit some sick mother they wanted dead anyway.

"I don't know. I didn't go through training this new way."

"Well, aren't you the helpful one," Greg muttered.

"Apparently not." Oliver glanced over his shoulder. "Look, I have to go. I'm late picking up Carrie and the others, but I wanted to let you know that I am really, truly, honestly, and thoroughly sorry about this."

Which might have made Greg feel better if the guy didn't act like this was a death sentence.

"Yeah," Greg said, waving him off. "Go on your drive. Enjoy the rest of your life," white picket fence and all.

Oliver's expression turned dark, darker than Greg had ever seen. "In spite of what you think, Carrie doesn't want me. She never has. This will only make it worse."

"How?"

"Because she has double the reason to hate the government—to hate me. This is an opportunity for you, Greg. You're about to get the only things I had to offer her: a house, money, car, security. So before you hate me too much, know that your letter doesn't do me a bit of good."

Shocked, Greg glanced down. This wasn't just a draft notice. It was a letter of employment, an offer of a steady income. A green card. Freedom for his mom, his grandparents, and, if he wanted, Carrie. If he could just survive long enough to get assigned somewhere, he could even take the rest with him, all thirty-four of them. He could become an Oliver for them. No need for some stupid farmers' market that wouldn't work anyway. This was a real job. Real money.

Carrie.

Oliver shook his head. "I knew it. I knew that you loved her."

"You can't tell her," Greg said urgently. "I won't tell her about your papers, and you can't tell her about mine. I get the right to tell her in my own time, my own way."

"As if I'd want to!"

Greg studied Oliver's green uniform with beige tie and gold stripes, his gun belt, and the huge gash above his eye. The guy rarely smiled and usually looked a few beats shy of the suicide watch. But maybe Greg could pull it off. Serve. Fight. Get money. Fix things with the clan, Carrie, and everything.

Except…

…he'd have to swear allegiance to Rigsby. *United We Stand.*

In the army or as a patrolman, Greg would be killing his own people. And either way, he wouldn't be here when his mom died.

"You don't understand," Greg said. "I can't do it. I can't be one of you." Not even for Carrie.

"Unless you want to get your family tortured or killed," Oliver said, voice rising, "you'll be whatever they tell you to be. Not every 1930's German wanted to be a Nazi."

That sparked a memory in Greg. The memory knocked the air from his lungs. Any last hope he felt dissolved into nothingness.

Back in Raleigh when they tied him up and beat him to a pulp, they'd given him a gift. His back and upper arm, now scarred, held irrefutable evidence of his rebellion. They branded him, hoping to hold his insubordination over his head forever, hoping he'd have to beg for every scrap of food for the rest of his life. But he and his mom escaped. They beat the system and never looked back. He'd never told anybody about the scars on his shoulder or back, not even his mom, but if anybody saw his branding number, he'd never survive training let alone what waited for him after. His mom would outlive him. Or worse. Because once they killed him, they'd punish anybody with ties to him.

"What's wrong?" Oliver asked, noticing the sudden change.

The world swirled and Greg's knees went weak. He leaned against his shovel, picturing his mom whipped, beaten, and locked up. Going was a death sentence to her and the clan, but so was not going.

"There's gotta be a way out. There has to be." Greg looked up. "Please. You gotta help me."

"Me? You've got it backward." Oliver pointed to the fresh wound on his face. "If *you* find a way out of this, let *me* know, because after six years of pure torture, I never have!"

Oliver stormed away without a backward glance.

Greg was still staring at his crisp white letter when he heard Oliver's car pull out of the neighborhood with Carrie inside.

fourteen

"What happened to your head?" Carrie asked as Oliver pulled out of her driveway. His cheek facing her had several small scratches, but that wasn't what concerned her. She leaned forward to see the nasty gash above his eyebrow that he'd tried to hide from her.

He turned further away. "I…ran into a door."

"You must have hit it pretty hard," she said. "Does it need stitches?"

"It's fine."

She leaned forward, yet he stubbornly kept it turned away.

The others hadn't come—she hadn't let them—which made it just her and Oliver on this drive. She would have been nervous if she wasn't so distracted by his injuries. As he pulled onto Williams Drive, the first non-Logan Pond street, she searched the road up and down. Everything looked deserted, so she said, "Can we stop for a minute?"

"Oh. Yeah. Sure." Without any other cars around, Oliver stopped right in the middle of the road.

"May I please see your head?" she asked.

When he didn't budge, she grabbed his chin and turned it toward her. Startled, he flinched back and stared at her. His reaction startled her, too. They never touched. She nearly let go of his chin, but she was too determined. Gently, she urged his face toward her.

Then she gasped.

The cut looked deep with dark blood threatening to ooze out. "Oliver, you just got this. What really happened?"

His small, gray eyes studied her with so much sadness, it made her heart ache. "I ran into a door," he repeated softly.

It bothered her that he wouldn't tell her. Who would attack a quiet, sweet guy like him? How did he get away? And more importantly, what kind of life did he really live? Bad enough he hid the truth from her.

She turned his chin every which way, studying the wound. "I think you need stitches."

Grabbing her hand, he gently lowered it. "It's fine, Carrie."

He held her hand a moment too long, held her gaze an extra second, and her nerves prickled. She lowered her lashes as her cheeks warmed.

Muttering an apology, he put the car in drive and started down the road. The silence felt heavy, so she focused on the scenery. After six years, riding in a car felt familiar and foreign at the same time. The hum of the engine. The slight jarring with every bump. She and her family used to take Sunday drives, and she soaked up all of the spring colors: pink flowering peach trees, white dogmas and pears, and lime-green buds sprouting on everything else.

Yet the tiniest things brought back the past with a vengeance. Rikard Elementary where her mom ran a dozen fundraisers. Maren Stephen's house on the corner. Zio's Pizzeria. Banks. Stores. Everything was broken down, boarded up, and abandoned like the town had prepared for a massive hurricane and never returned.

"I figured it would be bad, but this…" She was at a loss for words.

"You really haven't seen Shelton since the Collapse?" he asked.

"The first few years we wandered out of the neighborhood to visit different—" she almost said *clans* but caught herself. Sometimes she forgot Oliver was a patrolman. While she trusted him with her clan, he made a living arresting others. "—places. But we always took the backwoods, not the roads."

"Sugar Grove looks a little more alive since patrolmen live there. We even have our own stores."

"Stores?" She hardly remembered what that was like.

They passed Frank's Hardware where her father spent every weekend for a year trying to finish their basement. Now that basement was empty and abandoned.

"Sometimes," she said, "it feels like we've returned to caveman days of growing food and finding shelter, only unlike cavemen, we don't have a clue what we're doing."

"That's not true. I've always admired your clan's resourcefulness."

She smiled. Only Oliver could find something to admire in enemy territory.

They wound further from her neighborhood on a direct route for Main Street. Oliver swerved here and there, dodging potholes that had probably been there for years. They didn't pass a single car, which she expected. Fuel was another commodity no one could afford. It was like driving through a ghost town, and yet she realized Shelton might not be as dead as it looked. Other clans could be surviving, just hidden from view. There had to be at least a few if Oliver still had a job. The thought encouraged her and she started searching for different signs of life. In the process, she spotted something in the far distance, a dark wispy trail in the sky.

"Is that smoke?" she asked.

Oliver followed her gaze and nodded.

Leaning forward, she tried to gauge where it was coming from. Not Chicago. She'd heard about the smoke there, but this was coming from the south and it didn't seem like just a simple fire.

"Do you know what it is?"

For a moment, it didn't seem like he'd answer. Then he said, "There have been a few disturbances lately. That's probably another one."

Her eyes widened. What kind of disturbances caused fires large enough to be seen from miles away?

"By the way," he said, "my partners and I are doing our first sweep through Logan Pond on Saturday. So…yeah."

"Partners?" she repeated. "You have more than one?"

"Two, but I'm in charge, and we only have one car between the three of us, and it's my car, so that's good. I think I can keep them away from your neighborhood other than for sweeps. Hopefully, it won't disrupt things for you too much. You shouldn't have to post guards, at least not yet, so if you don't hear from me, you can assume you're safe."

Safe. Carrie always felt safe with Oliver.

Maybe that was the problem.

She thought about what Greg asked her to do: open her eyes and see what Oliver could offer her. But after two seconds she huffed. Greg thought he knew everything. She knew who Oliver was, who Greg was, what life might entail with either man, and she'd made her choice. It was time for Greg to get over it.

Oliver slowed down. "Here we are."

For a second time, he stopped in the middle of the road, this time at the head of Main Street. A thousand more memories slammed into her: homecoming parades, exploring the eclectic shops with her mom, snacking on cookies from the bakery with her siblings. There was so much to drag her back into despair, and yet she smiled. Broadly.

Overshadowing the boarded-up buildings was the most gorgeous display of spring she'd seen yet. Tree after tree stretched down both sides of Main Street, loaded with white blossoms. The trees grew straight and tall, hiding the abandoned shops, cars, and trash-lined sidewalks. It was even more breathtaking than she remembered.

Seeing the trees made her think that all wasn't lost in the world—or with Greg. He'd seen these and wanted to bring a piece of them back to her. That had to mean something.

"Mind if I roll down the window?" Carrie asked.

"Go ahead."

She put her head outside to soak up the sun. The scent of spring, so clean and fresh, brought more warmth to her soul. She had a few branches back home that smelled horrible and were losing their blossoms, but they meant the world to her. She was half-tempted to jump out and grab more.

Then she caught sight of something, a small building on the far end of Main Street and her heart swelled. "Can we drive down there?" she asked.

"Sure."

As Oliver started rolling forward, she leaned every which way to see through the mass of blossoms. Not that she needed to read the sign to know. She only mentioned Buds and Roses once in passing to Greg, one of those silly dreams she never expected to happen, but then Greg came up with a whole plan to make it a reality.

What happened with the mayor that turned him from ambitious dreamer to giving up on everything, even her? The farmers' market was still a great idea. They just had to find a way to make it work. They could sell chickens, eggs, vegetables, and even seeds. Of course, they'd need a bigger garden. They barely had enough room as it was. Maybe if they got a male goat, they could breed Butterscotch and—

A sudden movement caught her eye. A man ran out of a building down the block, waving his arms frantically over his head at them. Carrie jolted as she saw the green uniform.

A patrolman.

Instinct took over. She dropped in her seat.

Oliver slammed on the brakes. "What is he doing here? They were supposed to go to Sugar Grove!"

Carrie's heart pounded so hard it felt like it might beat right out of her chest. She couldn't see anything scrunched down, but had the patrolman seen her? He'd been fifty yards away, easily in viewing distance. Was he coming toward them?

Go, go, go! Carrie wanted to shout.

Oliver looked as scared as she felt, but he just waved to his coworker, a stiff, forced wave. Then he let his foot off the brake and turned left, pulling down the first side street.

He drove too slow for her frantic nerves. He should have been speeding away whether she had fake travel papers or not. One wrong move and she'd lose Amber, Zach, and everything that mattered to her.

She couldn't breathe.

Go!

Oliver turned down another side street before he glanced down at her. "I'm sorry, Carrie. They weren't supposed to be here."

"Is he following us?" she asked, adrenaline still surging through her veins.

He checked his mirror and his grip loosened on the steering wheel. "No. Sorry. I just panicked."

He panicked? Carrie's whole body shook. Slowly, she crawled back up into her seat and checked for any sign of life. The streets here looked dead.

"Who was that?" she asked.

"One of my new partners."

"Did he see me?"

"I hope not—I mean," Oliver amended quickly, "I don't think so. I'm sorry I startled you. He just surprised me, that's all." His eyes flickered to her. "Carrie, you know you're completely safe, right? That I'd never let anything happen to you?"

In theory. She felt stupid for doubting him, ducking and hiding like a child, but what if his new partner followed them? What if he became curious about the woman in Oliver's front seat? Her pulse struggled to resume its normal pace. Too many years hiding.

"Do you want to head home or keep driving?" he asked.

They were winding through old vintage homes with enough trees in bloom to remind her of why they'd come. Checking once more behind them, she forced herself to breathe normally.

Oliver would keep her safe. He always did.

"Maybe we can go a little farther," she said. "Then I should get home to—"

A loud beeping cut her off. She jumped, and her heart picked up right where it left off.

"What is that?" she cried.

"Sorry. This will just take a minute." Clearing his throat, Oliver pressed a button on his dashboard. A speaker crackled to life.

"Yes?" Oliver said.

Technology. A car phone.

Carrie clasped her hands tightly in her lap, begging herself to calm down. She just felt so out of place, so out of practice with real civilization.

"Sir," a man shouted over the speaker, "why didn't you stop? I was trying to wave you down!"

"What's wrong?" Oliver said. "Why are you in Shelton?"

"We have a situation with that illegal you arrested. He's going nuts, sir. We need you to come back right now."

Over the static, Carrie heard a man yelling in the background.

When Oliver spoke again, anger colored his voice. "I told you to take him to Sugar Grove."

"He completely freaked out in the car! We wouldn't have made it that far. Please, sir. You have to come back. We don't know what to do with him."

Carrie pieced it together. The gash above Oliver's eye. Oliver hadn't run into a door. That illegal had attacked him.

Worried, Oliver glanced at Carrie. "I'll be there in twenty minutes."

"No, sir. Now! The guy is trying to—" More yelling cut him off, this time from someone else. It sounded like utter chaos in the patrol station. "We think he's trying to kill himself, sir."

"What?" Oliver shouted. He slammed on the brakes, sending Carrie flying into her seatbelt.

"He's already knocked himself out once, sir, bashing his head against the wall. Now he's going crazy, screaming nonsense. Do we have your permission to shoot him?"

"No!" Oliver shouted. "Whatever you do, do *not* shoot him!"

"We don't know what else to do!"

"I'll be there in twenty minutes," Oliver said. "Just wait."

"He won't be alive in twenty minutes, not if he has anything to do with it. You have to come back now, sir! Please!"

Oliver looked at Carrie again.

"Go," she mouthed. She'd just duck down on the floor in the parking lot or hide somewhere else. Her hands shook in her lap, terrified of being spotted again, but she clenched her fists. A man's life was at stake. *"Go!"*

Oliver gave her a pained look and she could see him debating. Then he shook his head. "Don't do anything," he said into the speaker. "I'll be there in twenty minutes."

"But, sir! You can't—"

Oliver punched the button, ending the call. Then he pressed the accelerator to the floor and sped down the road.

"I can hide," Carrie said. "You can go back. I'll just hide."

"No. It's not safe. I promised I'd keep you safe."

He took the next turn at full speed. She grabbed the door to keep from flying off her seat.

"Then drop me off here and I'll walk," she insisted. "I can take the back trails home. I know the way."

"No. No. No! I have to get you safe."

She tried to argue further, but he didn't hear, so she held on and watched the road fly by too fast for her comfort. Her stomach wasn't used to speed and it turned end over end, threatening to empty itself.

By the time he screeched into her driveway, Carrie was ready to jump out, but he grabbed her arm. Not hard, but any contact from him was unexpected.

"There's something I have to tell you," Oliver said. "Something about Greg. He'll kill me for telling you because I swore I wouldn't, but he already hates me, and I have the feeling he's not going to tell you, and you deserve to know what could happen to him—or rather, what's about to happen to him."

fifteen

Oliver sprinted into the station. It was quiet. Too quiet.

He slid to a stop.

Portman and Bushing carried the red-bearded man by the feet and hands, dragging him out of the holding cell. The man's ear and right side of his head were bloody, his shoulder twisted out of its socket. The face behind the red beard looked ashen gray.

He was dead.

Desperate, Oliver searched his body and saw two dark spots on his chest. "I told you not to shoot him!" Oliver yelled.

Bushing, his nineteen-year-old partner, turned with red-rimmed, angry eyes. "We did him a favor, sir. He was going to kill himself one way or the other, and he was making a mess of it."

Oliver looked around. The cement floor and walls in the holding cell were smeared with blood. His stomach pitched, and he didn't see anything else after that. He grabbed his desk to keep from losing it.

"Why didn't you stop?" Portman asked.

"You were to obey my order," Oliver said, sidestepping the question. "I told you not to—"

Portman dropped the bearded man with a thud. "Why wouldn't we shoot him? These rebels are dangerous. He was shouting nonsense about burning the whole country down."

"He threatened to kill President Rigsby, sir," Bushing added. "What would you have had us do?"

It sounded more like a test of Oliver's loyalty than an actual question. Bushing and Portman were young, too young to be shooting illegals or questioning Oliver's authority. So Oliver used his seniority to say exactly what he wanted.

"How was *he* a threat to Rigsby? He couldn't even walk when I left him."

"Sir!" Portman straightened, standing erect in his new uniform. "We followed protocol. With all due respect, why aren't you?"

Oliver stared at the dead man. At the young husband and father.

When it was clear he wasn't going to answer, his young partners dragged the body the rest of the way outside. All Oliver could think was that he couldn't save both of them: Carrie and the man he didn't even know.

His migraine spiked.

As he turned to find some ibuprofen, he caught sight of something in the holding cell, something dark red. Four words had been finger-painted onto the furthest wall. The man's dying words, painted with his own blood.

Live free or die.

Oliver was still staring at those four when he heard his chief's voice boom just outside.

"Don't leave that body out here, for crying out loud! You want every citizen writing complaints? Take it around back until I can get Sanitation to dispose of it." Chief Dario swore loudly. "Idiots!"

Oliver forced his eyes down to the blue carpet only to see more dark smears of blood.

"What in the world is going on, Simmons?" Chief Dario said, storming inside. "There's blood everywhere!"

"I'm not sure what happened," Oliver said, "but I plan to find out."

"How do you not know? Aren't those *your* partners dragging that body out?"

Oliver realized his mistake too late. His head pounded like a bass drum, and he could hardly think straight. But then he remembered. "The squatters attacked the dogs. I had to take them to Trainer Jerry." Oliver hoped his boss didn't verify the timing.

Suddenly the chief grabbed his arm. "What happened to your head?"

"It's fine."

"It better be!" the chief snapped. "When I told you to train your partners, this is not what I had in mind. If they're going to shoot someone, tell them to do it before the rebel makes a mess of my station. Why was that man even brought here? He should have been shot the second he attacked you."

"I Tasered him, sir."

That was the wrong response. The chief stabbed a finger at him. "You know protocol. I don't want another incident like this happening again. Am I clear, Simmons?"

Oliver nodded, sufficiently chastised.

Chief Dario turned and caught sight of the same four words painted on the wall. He swore louder. "Get the clean-up crew in here, stat!"

"Yes, sir."

As he left, Oliver dropped into his desk chair. He made the call to Sanitation and then held his throbbing head in his hands. He wondered how he could have handled everything better. With the man. With Greg. With Carrie. Oliver closed his eyes, wishing for a deep sleep that could erase the whole day, every last second of it.

When Portman and Bushing came back in, Portman glared at Oliver as he headed to the bathroom to clean up. Young Bushing just went to the closet and grabbed the mop.

"Leave it," Oliver said tiredly.

"I can at least clean up the worst of it, sir," Bushing said.

"I said leave it!" Oliver snapped. Guilt seized him and he took a deep breath. "Sorry. Sanitation will be here soon. They'll take care of it."

Bushing stared at him with a look that was small and childlike. He was close in age to Braden Ziegler and looked like he belonged on a tractor, not with a gun. Even Oliver, who was old enough to be the kid's father, felt too young and inexperienced for this.

"Why don't you take a break," Oliver said. "I'll file the paperwork."

Bushing nodded and bowed out, leaving Oliver alone at last.

He pulled out all of the right forms. Ironically, dead squatters required more paperwork than live ones. He didn't know the guy's name, but the government still wanted to know how he died, why he died, and whether it was caused by disease, rebellion, or something else. Oliver refused to write down rebellion knowing the reaction that would garner with Chicago in flames.

Oliver stared at the papers for a long time, not working, just thinking as his mind swirled from the man, to Carrie and Greg, to the man's wife, and then back to the look on Carrie's face when he told her about Greg's recruitment. That would torture him for a long time.

So would the sound of that baby's cry.

Live free or die.

His headache grew into an all-consuming pain which spread down his neck and back. Even his wound throbbed with each heartbeat. Maybe he should get it checked out, but government doctors took too much effort. And time. And money.

Gingerly, he leaned against the wall and closed his eyes.

He didn't know how much time passed when he heard a noise, shouting and shuffling from just outside the station. The cleanup crew. Only they were being awfully loud about it.

Standing, he stretched his back and then moved to where he could see the front doors. A blur of black swarmed outside, men yelling orders. Definitely not Sanitation. They wore uniforms like Oliver's, only theirs were pure black.

"Are those federal patrolmen?" Portman asked, coming back into the room.

"Yes, but why are they in Shelton?" Oliver wondered aloud. "Did you report that squatter as a rebel?"

"Not yet. Did you?"

"No." And even if he had, federal patrolmen couldn't have come that fast.

"I hope they don't see the body," Portman said. "We left it on the side of the building."

"Hopefully covered," Oliver said.

Portman looked sheepish. Oliver's headache tripled.

The shouting grew as the federal patrolmen stormed inside. In an instant, it was a blur of black blocking Oliver's view of the front office. Oliver heard Ashlee cry out in surprise, and he exchanged a worried glance with his partners. But instead of checking on things, he moved toward the holding cell, desperate to block the blood-smeared motto that was sure to get their whole precinct fired.

"What is the meaning of this?" he heard Chief Dario shout over the chaos. "What are you doing? Let go of me!"

Oliver sprinted for the front office. He was just tall enough to see over the heads. Federal patrolmen had grabbed Chief Dario and shoved him against the wall, cheek to plaster. The rest stood back, guns ready, watching the chief struggle to free himself.

"Alphonso Dario," a new voice said, "you're under arrest for imped-ing a federal investigation."

Oliver's blood ran cold at the sound of that voice. It was familiar, but he couldn't quite place it. How did he know that voice?

Ignoring the pain in his back, he stretched up taller to see. He spotted a thick shock of blond hair and jerked back.

No. It couldn't be.

It couldn't.

Terrified, yet curious, he jumped to see better. Mayor Phillips stood in front of Chief Dario, for some reason a part of this arrest. But that's not who had Oliver's mind racing out of control. Next to the mayor stood a man Oliver planned to never see again in this life. A tall, blond patrolman. David Jamansky.

The guy Oliver ratted out.

Months ago, Chief Dario refused to believe his own patrolmen could be involved in illegal trading, but Oliver showed him the logs from the raid on Carrie's neighborhood. The last Oliver had seen Jamansky was in that dark neighborhood where Jamansky threatened to kill him if he didn't return the supplies. Jamansky and his partner had been rotting in a heavily-guarded prison ever since.

And now the feds were arresting Chief Dario.

Oliver backed up. That couldn't be Jamansky out there, because if that was, Oliver was a dead man.

He slinked into a corner, looking for a door, a window, anything, as the federal patrolmen removed Chief Dario from the building.

"Sir?" Bushing said. "Are you okay?"

Before Oliver could answer, the flood of federal patrolmen swarmed the back room.

"Which one is he?" one of them called.

David Jamansky sauntered back, taking his own sweet time. Unlike the federal officers, he wore his green uniform, the one identical to Oliver's. He scanned the room and found Oliver in the corner. His eyes narrowed. "The older one there. Escort those two young ones out while I take care of that one."

The federal patrolmen jumped into action. Half escorted Portman and Bushing outside. The others grabbed Oliver and slammed him against the wall. Pain exploded in Oliver's already-sensitive skull. Confusion. Dizziness. Something warm oozed down the side of his face.

The federal patrolmen held him tight as Jamansky walked up to him, smiling the kind of smile that made Oliver's skin crawl.

"Officer Simmons," Jamansky said in a sing-song voice. "It is *so* good to see you again."

Sweat poured down Oliver's face, mixing with the blood. The guy had the looks of an actor and the ferocity of Attila the Hun.

"You're looking good, Simmons. But wait. What's this?" Jamansky reached out and fingered the two gold bands on Oliver's arm. "You betray me, and that scumbag Dario gives you a promotion?" In one swift move, he ripped the gold bands from Oliver's sleeve. Then he tried to press them to his own arm. They flopped right off, but he smiled anyway. So did Mayor Phillips.

Mayor Phillips.

Still pinned to the wall, Oliver suddenly understood. Jamansky and the mayor had been working the black market together, padding both of their pockets. Mayor Phillips had been the one to spring Jamansky from prison, and now the mayor would help Jamansky slit Oliver's throat.

"Too bad about Chief Dario," Jamansky continued. "Interfering with a federal investigation is a major crime."

Federal investigation?

As if reading his mind, Jamansky said, "Mayor Phillips assigned me to infiltrate the black market and run an undercover investigation. Years of hard work, and Chief Dario blew it all to smithereens. Isn't that right, Mayor?"

Mayor Phillips nodded, looking almost bored. The mayor was twice Jamansky's age, even older than Oliver, yet Jamansky seemed to be running the show, scheming up some ridiculous story no one would believe, most of all Oliver. It didn't escape Oliver's notice that Jamansky's former partner hadn't returned with him. Neither Jamansky nor the mayor seemed concerned about that.

"So let's be honest," Jamansky continued. "You also had a hand in my arrest, didn't you, Simmons?"

I'm dead. I'm dead. I'm dead.

Oliver's knees would have given out if the officers in black didn't have him pinned in painful, vice-like grips.

When he didn't answer, Jamansky lunged. His fist swung wide and slammed into Oliver's gut. Oliver grunted as the wind flew out of him. He couldn't breathe. Couldn't double over. He stayed pinned, gasping for air which didn't come.

"Answer me!" Jamansky screamed.

Oliver's vision darkened. The world faded in and out. He needed air!

Then he dropped. The federal patrolmen had loosened their grip, allowing him to fall to his knees and finally catch a breath.

Jamansky crouched next to him. "I spent a lot of time in that prison cell, thinking about you, Simmons. I bet you didn't know that. It gave me time to wonder if perhaps you were just an innocent bystander in Dario's mess. Maybe he just used you as his pawn. In fact, I'm impressed you stood up to me and Nielsen. I always took you for a coward, but what you did, that showed guts. However..." Jamansky's voice lowered and his expression turned murderous, "you nearly ended my life, and so now I own you. Now that I'm back, I'll need someone to do my every bidding. Do you understand? You cough the wrong way, and you'll only wish they hauled you off with Dario today. *Capiche?*"

If Oliver didn't have Carrie and her clan to protect, he would have willingly followed the chief out those doors. But on the floor, head bleeding, lungs burning, he couldn't think to do anything but nod.

Jamansky straightened and motioned to the others. "You can leave. I have command of this station now."

"Do you still need me, Chief Jamansky?" the mayor asked.

Chief.

Oliver closed his eyes, ill.

"No, I'm all set," Jamansky said. "We'll meet in the morning about the new changes."

As the mayor left with the others, Jamansky looked down at Oliver. He gave him a last kick in the ribs. Not hard, but Oliver still cried out in pain.

Jamansky smiled. "I have the feeling you and I are about to become best buddies, Simmons. What do you think?"

The word *slave* came to mind.

Jamansky offered him a hand up. Oliver looked at him like he'd gone mad. Using the wall, he pushed himself up. Every part of him screamed with one pain or another. As he stood, he caught sight of the bloody words in the holding cell. Maybe the red-bearded man hadn't been so crazy after all.

Jamansky followed his gaze. "What is that?" His voice turned shrill. "Why is that in *my* precinct?"

"A squatter from today," Oliver said. "The cleanup crew is on their way."

"Those rebels will *not* take over my area! Not on my watch. Where did you arrest that squatter?"

Oliver couldn't hold himself up anymore. He fell onto his chair. "The Ferris neighborhood. He was the only squatter I saw in the house, though," Oliver amended, which was technically the truth.

"Burn it."

"What?"

"Burn the house down," Jamansky said. "They're burning our buildings, so you'll burn theirs. *You.* Not *we.* Hear the distinction?"

He heard it but didn't understand. Burning homes wasn't allowed. The government had confiscated those homes after the financial collapse. They were government property now. Oliver wasn't allowed to burn government property, not even if rebels were sighted. But Jamansky would make him do his dirty work, knowing if Oliver balked, he could throw him into the same traitor's cell as Chief Dario.

"Report to me when it's done." Jamansky patted Oliver's cheek like a grandmother would pat a child. Then, whistling to himself, he walked out to find his new office.

Oliver couldn't move but hot blood pulsed through his veins. Burn down the house? He didn't even know where to start. And what if that woman and her baby were still there?

He stared at the dark red words on the wall. *Live free or die.* His mind supplied the rest of the saying. *There are things far worse than death.*

A fine sentiment with one huge, glaring problem:

The dead can't help the living.

sixteen

Carrie waited. Two days and then five, she waited for Greg to tell her. She saw more fires, each closer than before. Each was a slap in the face that Greg was heading out into that madness. But Oliver said Greg wanted to tell her in his own way, so she waited.

She made herself available in private places: early in the morning in her yard or late in the evening in his grandparents' garden. He lived across the street from her. She knew he could see her. A few times, she caught him watching her from an upper window, but he didn't come. She told herself it was okay. He'd tell her when he was ready. He would.

Except he didn't.

Saturday, when the clan packed up all of their things and scrunched into May's for the first sweep with Oliver's partners, Carrie tried to catch Greg's eye. The Trenton's house was stuffy and full with people and summer bearing down on them. She spent time all evening talking to Greg's family, but anytime she headed his way, he disappeared.

Now it had been a full week without word. The only thing making it tolerable was she hadn't heard a single whisper about his recruitment from anyone else. In a clan as small as theirs, news like that would have circled a dozen times.

She wasn't the only one Greg wasn't telling.

But an hour ago she did the calculations. Greg had to walk to Naperville, a two or three-day trip. Which meant he'd be leaving any day—any minute—to make it in time. He was just going to up and leave without a single goodbye. The pain sliced through her.

"Hi, Kristina," Carrie said at the Ziegler's door. "Have you seen—"

"Amber isn't here," Kristina interrupted. "She's with Lindsey, but don't ask me where. If you find them and Braden's with them, will you send him home?"

"Sure." Only Carrie wasn't looking for Amber. "Have you seen Greg?"

"No. Why?" Kristina looked suspicious. She hadn't been as close to Jenna as Sasha had been, but she was still part of that married group, the one now shunning Carrie.

"No reason. Thanks."

Carrie got halfway down the porch when she suddenly turned back. "Kristina, I'm sorry about how things have been lately. I know times are hard—and possibly getting harder—but I want you to know that I never meant to hurt anyone." Carrie hugged herself. "Especially Jenna."

"I know you didn't mean any harm." The rest was implied: *But that doesn't change anything.*

"I miss Jenna," Carrie said quietly. "I wish things hadn't happened like they had. I wish I could change how they turned out."

Kristina's expression softened. "Jenna's death wasn't your fault, Carrie. You shouldn't blame yourself."

Then why was everyone else?

Carrie sighed. "Do you think Jeff is okay?"

They both scanned the neighborhood as if they could see beyond to where Jeff walked, trekked, and searched for his parents in North Dakota. He could have been arrested, dead on the road, or halfway there, and they would never know the difference. And yet, he'd been banished for attacking fellow clansmen.

"I'm praying he makes it back to his boys," Carrie said. "And…back to us."

Kristina looked surprised by that. Carrie and Greg had taken the brunt of Jeff's violence, but Carrie still wanted him back. He belonged in their clan. His little boys needed him.

"Me, too," Kristina said, and some of the coldness melted between them.

Carrie gave a quick wave. "I better go. If I see Braden, I'll send him home."

Then she trotted down the street, heading for the front of the sub to Mariah and Richard's house. Terrell said Greg was with Niels chopping wood, but he hadn't been there and he wasn't working on Dixon's new well either. Greg couldn't hide forever—or he could after he left for training, but she refused to let him run away before he even left.

His mom's house was the last place he could be. Carrie hadn't tried there yet because Mariah seemed to sleep more these days. Carrie hated to disturb her. There was a chance Greg hadn't told his mom yet.

No.

Greg would have told Mariah right away. He told his mom everything. The whole clan probably knew, but he'd sworn them all to secrecy.

The bitterness was eating Carrie alive. Even if she and Greg had no romantic future together, he was still her friend. She deserved to know and she deserved to hear it from him.

Richard and Mariah lived in the farthest house next to the North Entrance. Carrie didn't knock on their front door. Instead, she pressed her ear to the door, doubt creeping up on her. What was she thinking, barging in on Mariah right now? Surely this was the last thing they—

Richard walked down the stairs and spotted her through the window. He pulled open the door with a smile. "Hello, Carrie. What can I help you with?"

"Have you seen Greg?" Carrie asked softly in case Mariah was sleeping.

"Yeah, he's upstairs with his mom. Come on in."

Of course Greg was here. He'd spend every last minute with Mariah before saying goodbye—possibly forever. And Carrie wanted to intrude on it for what? Her wounded pride? Her broken heart?

"That's okay," she said. "Can you tell Greg to find me when he's done?" He never would, but she had to try.

"Nonsense. Come on in," Richard said. "Mariah will want to see you, too. Just head upstairs. They're in the last bedroom on the right. I'll be up after I rinse these out."

Carrie noticed the blood-stained rags in Richard's hands. "How is she?"

The joy faded from Richard's face and he sighed. "She'll be happy to see you."

Carrie tiptoed upstairs, determined to sneak right back out if Mariah's door was shut. But the last door hung wide open. Greg sat next to his mom's mattress on the floor, back to Carrie, Yankees hat pulled low over his face. Mariah was speaking behind closed eyes. One of her legs was propped with pillows, which didn't make sense. Mariah's problems had always been lungs and stomach, not legs. Maybe it was spreading, whatever *it* was.

"...could be a good thing," Carrie heard Mariah say. "All's not lost. You gotta quit worryin' so much. You're gonna give yourself ulcers."

"I can't, Ma," Greg said softly.

Mariah coughed into a fresh rag, leaving her voice raspy. "Yes, you can. I'll never forgive you if you don't."

Greg's whole body stiffened. "How's it fair to say somethin' like that? At a time like this?"

She smiled. "It's not, but it helps my cause, doesn't it?"

His head lowered further.

"Come on now," Mariah said, reaching to him. "I say you're wrong, you know you're wrong, so quit fightin' me. Legality is overrated. It's not too late, so you can't give up."

Give up. The words twisted Carrie's gut. Greg didn't think he was coming back.

"Ma..." he said tiredly.

She patted his knee. "In this world, you gotta fight to be happy. Even when it seems hopeless, you keep fighting. Fight and win."

Fight. Another word that made Carrie ill. Greg was heading to a place where fighting was the only way to survive, where war and revolution permeated every moment.

Greg shifted slightly, putting his profile in Carrie's view.

She gasped.

He had a beard. A new one, but still.

Hearing her, he jumped and whirled around. She'd startled him, sneaking up on him for a change, but she hadn't meant to. She just couldn't believe what she saw. His clean-shaven look was the first thing she noticed when he moved in. Every other clansman stopped shaving after the Collapse. Too tedious and difficult. But Mariah told Carrie that Greg hadn't missed a day shaving in six years, not even in all their times when they barely had food or a place to sleep. But now dark stubble trailed his angular jaw.

He really was giving up.

Carrie struggled to breathe. This couldn't be happening.

His eyes narrowed on her, solidifying what she already knew. She shouldn't have come.

Backing into the hallway, she worked to make a quiet escape.

"Hey, Ma," she heard Greg say, "I'll be right back. Try to sleep for a bit. We'll leave after you rest up."

Leave? Greg was taking Mariah with him?

"Wait," Mariah said. "Did I just see Carrie?"

Mortified, Carrie stepped back into view. "I'm so sorry. I didn't mean to bother you. I came to talk to Greg, but I'll just wait for him outside."

Mariah waved her in. "You're not bothering anybody. Actually," she said with a warm smile, "Greg and I were just talkin' about you."

"You were?"

But before Carrie could rewind the conversation, Greg shot to his feet and stormed over to her in the doorway.

"Who told you?" he whispered. "Grandma?"

Carrie's own temper kicked in. "No. *May* didn't. Why didn't you? I've waited all this time thinking—"

"Oliver!" Greg spat his name like an expletive. "I shoulda known he'd break his promise. How far out of the neighborhood were you when he told you?"

Her chin rose. "Oh, no you don't. You don't get to be mad about this, Greg. Why didn't you tell me?" She took in his dark scruff and her voice broke. "You weren't going to, were you?"

His eyes softened with guilt. "I wanted to, but it only woulda made things harder. I promised to stay away from you, Carrie, only unlike Oliver, I actually keep my promises."

"Even the stupid ones?" she challenged.

"Hey, y'all," Mariah called from her mattress on the floor. "Don't kill each other just yet. I wanna chat with Carrie first."

Carrie moved past Greg and knelt next to his mom's mattress. The sight of Mariah was enough to distract her. She looked significantly worse than she had a few days ago. Her cheeks were sunken and the circles under her eyes were so dark they looked like bruises. The rest of her looked gray.

Wincing, Mariah shifted to face her, careful to keep her leg propped.

"You alright, darlin'?" Mariah asked.

She wanted to know if *Carrie* was alright? Carrie refused to answer such a pointless question and instead asked, "What can I get you? Do you want some water? Can I get more pillows from my house?"

"Nah." Mariah patted her hand. "Just take care of my boy for me."

Carrie's breath hitched. It sounded like a dying mother's wish.

Maybe it was.

Mariah's gaze went to Greg in the doorway. "I begged him to tell you, but he's stupid. Real stupid. Real, real, real—"

"Ma," Greg cut in, "I'm gonna talk to Carrie downstairs. Try to sleep, alrighty? We'll leave in a bit."

Carrie took the hint and followed Greg out of Mariah's room. Before he closed the door, Mariah called, "Remember what I said, Greg. Fight and win."

With a grunt, he shut her door.

"Where are you taking your mom?" Carrie whispered, following him down the hallway. Hopefully a doctor, though Carrie couldn't imagine how without a car, money, or time.

"I gotta take her into town to renew her yellow card," Greg said.

"In her condition? She doesn't look like she can stand, let alone walk all the way to town."

He stopped on the third step down. "What choice do I have? What choice do I have in *anything*? What choice does anybody have anymore?" Swearing, he whirled and threw a fist against the wall.

Stunned, Carrie watched him.

Greg's fist stayed on the wall, looking ready to pound it over and over again. But then his shoulders drooped, his eyes closed, and his head fell against the wall.

Silence descended on them like a heavy weight. Carrie studied his new beard and the defeat in every inch of his body, and her heart broke a little more.

"When do you leave for training?" she said softly.

"First thing in the morning," he said into the wall.

Her eyes filled. "Why didn't you tell me, Greg?" They could have had a week together.

The entryway fell silent. He just stood on the third stair, head against the wall, making Carrie feel shut out all over again.

"If this is just a way to get money," she said, "it's not worth it. We'll find another—"

His head snapped up and he pointed at his mom's closed door. "You think any amount of money would tempt me to leave right now? I'm going because I have no choice, Carrie. Not a single one."

"Then we'll figure something out. We'll—"

"Do what? Survive how? Live where?" he asked.

But you could die.

The words lodged in her throat.

"Then we'll take in May and CJ," she tried. "We'll hide all of you so you can stay."

"And let the patrolmen come in and rip out the garden? Shoot the chickens and burn down the house? What about government raids every week? Where will y'all hide if I go AWOL?"

"In the woods."

"With dogs that can follow your trail?" He shook his head. "I've gone over and over this. Every option leaves thirty-four people arrested or dead. It's me or them, Carrie." He sighed long and deep. "It's gotta be me."

Her heart cried, *No!* but part of her knew he was right. She just couldn't accept that Greg would be one of them, someone like Oliver, who arrested illegals and lied about running into doors.

She hugged herself. "Who else knows you're leaving?"

"I told my grandparents a little bit ago," he said. "When you showed up, I figured my grandma ran straight to your house."

"No one else? Why?"

"I didn't wanna be here when they threw the party."

"Greg!" she cried as softly as she could. "How can you think anyone wants you to leave? Don't you know what you mean to the clan?" *To me?*

He didn't respond. He did nothing but stare blankly down the stairs.

Carrie stared at Mariah's closed door. Greg's mom wouldn't survive four months. She might not even survive four weeks, and Greg just had to walk away.

"I'm sorry," she whispered.

He followed her gaze and his whole body went rigid. "Don't. Don't bring it up. Don't say it. Don't think it. Don't mention it—mention her. There's nothin' I can do." He sank down on the third stair, head in his hands. "Absolutely nothing."

If Carrie was any other person, she would have put an arm around his shoulders. Instead, she sank down and sat next to him on the stair, searching for some way to comfort him.

Richard walked into the entry way, clean rags in hand. But one look at them blocking the way up, and he turned right around.

Greg didn't even notice.

In the silence, Carrie studied the back of his light blue UNC shirt, remembering something Mariah once told her. Something about the day Kendra died. Greg showed up to the Raleigh hospital that day limping, bruised, and utterly defeated. Even now Mariah didn't know what had happened with his foreman. Something bad enough he hadn't taken off his shirt in front of his mom—or anyone else—since.

"What did they do to you in Raleigh?" Carrie whispered.

He pursed his lips as if wondering whether to tell her. Then he reached over his shoulders and pulled up his t-shirt, exposing his entire muscled back.

Carrie's hands flew to her mouth.

seventeen

Carrie couldn't breathe.

Greg's back was covered with crisscrossed, raised scars, like he'd been whipped. Zach said they punished him for speaking out in defense of an older man, but they whipped him for it? It seemed so cruel, so...medieval.

It took her a second to find her voice. "How could they do that to you?"

"Oh, that's not even the best part," Greg said. He dropped his t-shirt and lifted his sleeve, exposing his upper arm and shoulder. Another scar, this one circular and more defined, only it was raised and tinged pink. An old burn. It was about the size of her fist and shaped like a symbol: a circle with a diagonal line through it, like the kind of circle in a *No Smoking* sign. Only this diagonal line crossed out a single, solid star.

Squinting, she noticed numbers tattooed into his skin below the crossed-out star. Identifying numbers.

"They branded you," she said, barely audible.

Greg had been whipped, branded as a traitor, and watched his little sister die in the space of a few hours. All for standing up to the evils he was about to join.

He dropped his sleeve. "If they see these during training, who knows what they'll do."

Kill him.

Because he hadn't just been punished and marked. He ran. He and his mom escaped. He only had a yellow card because Oliver faked some ID numbers. There was no faking his way past those scars.

Here she was worried about what would happen to him *after* training. He might not even survive the first day.

"You can't give up," his mom had said. *"Even when it seems hopeless, you keep fighting. Fight and win."*

Carrie pinched her eyes to block the sudden flood of emotions, but over and over her mind screamed, *Don't go!*

He leaned forward on his stair, elbows on knees. "Even if I can keep all this hidden, what do I do? Arrest people like us? Brand other traitors? I'm scared that even if I manage to make it back here alive, it's not gonna be me anymore, you know? I'm scared they're gonna get into my head and mess with it. That I'll become one of them and want to hurt people like us. I'm scared I'm gonna forget who I am—who we are."

Greg had never been scared of anything. It terrified her.

She wanted to offer to write, but there wasn't any mail service. No phones. She couldn't visit. She couldn't do anything.

"You won't forget," she whispered.

His eyes flickered back to her. "What makes you so sure? You haven't been in their clutches before. You haven't read their propaganda or watched the guy next to you become a robot just to stop the pain."

"Because you're a Pierce." She smiled sadly. "They're fighters, remember?"

It almost came, that tiny smile he saved for her. But then his face fell. "That's what they want. Fighters. Killers."

"You can't give up," she said urgently. "Hide your scars and follow the rules. Do whatever is necessary to stay alive. Please don't give up."

He gave her a strange look. "Who says I'm givin' up?"

"Your mom and"—she pointed at his face—"that."

"Ah." He scratched his dark stubble. "You once asked me why I shaved. Well, I wanted to look like a patrolman." Her eyes popped open and he nodded. "Ironic now that I'm gonna be one, but squatters look too obvious, too homeless with their scraggly beards. I figured if I was ever spotted by a patrolman, they'd assume I was one of them. My mom and I—and Kendra, when she was around—needed those extra seconds of uncertainty to make a run for it. I wanted to look like one of them, and now…and now…"

And now he probably couldn't grow a beard fast enough. That beard was his way of fighting back, of telling himself he wouldn't become one of them. Even his hair peeking out of his Yankees hat was longer than she'd ever seen.

"So…you're not giving up?" she said carefully.

It came. Another tiny flash of a smile. "Nah. I've never been smart enough to quit while I'm behind."

A burst of hope shot through her. He could do this. He could survive. And knowing him, he'd take down half the government in the process.

After a minute, he nudged her arm, reminding her how close they sat on the stair. "So how'd you like the view of the outside world?" he asked. "I never heard how the drive went."

"The trees are beautiful." She smiled. "Thank you for bringing a piece of them back to me."

"The blossoms stink. Sorry. I didn't know."

She laughed softly, trying to keep her voice down so Mariah could sleep. "Yes, but they're beautiful. I love them."

"Well, I figured you should get to see them—even though they nearly got me arrested."

She turned. "That's why you were almost arrested?"

"Yeah. Hope they were worth it."

"Are you crazy? Nothing is worth you getting arrested."

"Wow," he said with a roll of his eyes. "Way to kill the romance."

She startled. Was that what his gift had been? There was no reason for her face to go hot, but it did. Romance. She lowered her head to hide behind her thick hair.

Greg reached up and lifted her chin to study her cheeks. "Man, I'm gonna miss this."

He meant his uncanny ability to make her blush, but part of her longed for him to mean more—that he'd miss *her*. Because she would miss this, too. The two of them alone, talking, friends again, him finally letting his guard down, dropping a wall or two to let her inside.

His hand fell away from her chin and he faced the stairway again. "So…Oliver didn't happen to divulge anything else, did he?"

"Like what?"

"That'd be a big fat *no*. Oliver! That guy and I are gonna have a little talk. Or…not." His thick brows pulled down. "This whole leavin' thing really stinks."

"Yeah."

And just like that, the brief happiness fled.

Greg suddenly faced her on the stair. "Listen, Carrie, when I start gettin' money—which had better be soon 'cause that's the only good thing to come from this—I'll find a way to send it back to you. Maybe you can use it to buy supplies or even convince my mom to see a doctor. Who knows? If I can survive long enough, we might be able to save up enough money to buy another home, maybe even get a few more people legal."

"Your plan," she whispered.

His face lit up. "Yeah. Not exactly your flower shop, but this might work better—or at least faster. Even if we can only buy one other home, my grandparents could abandon theirs and then maybe I could...I might be able to..."

"...come back," she finished.

His eyes locked on hers, and she felt it, felt the connection, the possibility between them. Did he feel it, too, care about her like she cared about him? Would he come back to her or just come back? She didn't know, but she lost herself in the depth of those green eyes, in the flecks of gold and the possibilities. She could have sworn he was leaning toward her, but with a blink, he sat back and faced front.

"It's a long stretch, but we might be able to pull it off. Until then, can you do somethin' for me?"

"Anything," she said.

"Make sure my mom, Richard, and my grandparents head into town by the 15th of every month. They're gonna need help gettin' there. Wait," he said with a sudden scowl, "you don't have a card yet. What am I thinkin'? You can't take them."

"No, I'll do it," she said quickly. "I can stay hidden. I promise to take care of your family while you're gone, Greg." It was the least she could do.

"Thanks." He scratched his dark stubble. "Man, what I'd give for a car right now."

"Can Oliver drive you to Naperville? Or even into town today with your mom?"

"He offered," Greg said, "but I turned him down."

"Why?"

"'Cause I'm stupid, remember? Real, real, real stupid. But it's fine. I'm a good walker. If only my mom was. I'm thinkin' about carting her around in Old Rusty. Think it'll work?"

"Terrell's old supply cart? Maybe," Carrie said, "or if that's too cumbersome, you can take our water wagon. It's smaller, but she should fit."

"That'd be easier. If only that could get me to Naperville faster. I'd take anything at this point, car, motorcycle, horse. I'd even take Butterscotch if she'd let me ride her."

Carrie sat up. "What about a bike?"

He nodded slowly, considering. "I could make the trip in an hour or two on a bike. That's plenty of time to get home and back in the middle of the night. If I hide it in the woods, they'd never even know I had it." He turned. "Why? Grandpa said we didn't have any left. Is there one?"

Carrie's heart raced, and for more than just the possibility of seeing Greg again. He'd used *home* to describe this place which only solidified it in her mind. He belonged in Shelton, and one way or another she would make sure he came back.

"No." She smiled. "We have two."

———◆———

Dust flew everywhere, sparkling in the light streaming through the garage windows. Terrell Dixon, the supply guy, would freak once he saw his OCD organization undone, but Greg had to find those bikes.

"Bikes are valuable on the black market," Carrie said, "which is why we're down to two. But I'm scared of your reaction when you see them."

"Why?" Greg asked, moving an old computer monitor.

With another box flung aside, Carrie uncovered the first one. It was pink with purple stars. Wincing, Carrie said, "Amber got it for her seventh birthday. It's smaller than I remember."

No kidding. The handle bars barely reached Greg's thigh.

"Where's the other one?" he asked.

After another minute, they unearthed a boy's bike which was slightly larger, but not large enough for Greg's adult body. Not great, but still faster than walking. The tires on both were flat, the boy's was missing a seat, and neither had chains. Greg pulled the purple sparkly seat off Amber's old bike and twisted it onto the other. Then he stood back, unsure what to do about the missing chains or flat tires.

Carrie searched through more boxes. "I know they had chains a few years ago. Where did they go?"

Greg pulled the tires apart to examine how much patching they needed. But when he opened the first, he grunted. He grabbed the second, third, and fourth tires with the same result.

"Any idea where the inner tubes are?" he said.

Carrie turned slowly. "You're kidding, right?"

"Wish I was." He had a pretty good idea where at least one ended up. Zach and Tucker's slingshots. He rubbed the grease from his hands. "Any luck on the chains?"

"No." She tore through boxes like a madwoman. "Maybe Terrell knows where they are."

The sun streamed through the windows with a yellow afternoon glow, reminding Greg of his limited time. The township office closed at five, whenever that was. Even with a wagon, it would be slow moving his mom.

"It's no use, Carrie. They're not here. Even if we had chains, they're probably bent or broken, and we still don't have tires. I'd never make it work in time."

"No. They have to be here," she said, still rummaging.

Greg pulled off his Yankees cap and wiped his forehead. "Look, I gotta go, but it's fine."

Another box. Another pile. Only she'd already searched those ones. She was just moving in circles.

"Carrie." He grabbed her arm and pulled her back. She looked up at him, cheeks flushed from work. "Even if I had a bike," he said, "that training camp is gonna be a fortress. They're never gonna let me leave, not even at night. It was a one in a million chance, but it's fine."

She didn't look fine. She looked devastated, and he could have kissed her for it.

"I should go," he said again.

Her downcast eyes stayed on his t-shirt, and his conversation with his mom resurfaced. Guilt tugged at him.

"You know," he said, "when I swore to stay away from you, I never dreamt karma would play this kinda joke on me. I'm sorry I didn't tell you, I just…" He pictured her name on a marriage license and stopped himself from saying more. "I just thought it was for the best."

She nodded, though her gaze stayed down. "Zach will be devastated when he finds out."

"I'll leave my baseball so he can use it. He can have my slingshot, too. And here. Give him this."

Greg took off his Yankees hat, brushed Carrie's honey-blonde hair back from her face, and situated his hat on her head. The vision unexpectedly pleased him. Her hair looked nearly gold as it curled out from under his hat, and the hat's navy color brought out her beautiful blue eyes—eyes that suddenly had him pinned.

His resolve to stay away from her lasted all of a week. A lot of good it did him. A lot of good it did *either* of them.

"I should go," he said again. "My mom's probably awake now." He said the words, yet his feet stayed put. He'd never been good at goodbyes.

"Just out of curiosity," he said, "how much of that conversation did you hear back there?"

She peeked up at him through her lashes. "Not much."

He doubted that. His mom had lectured him about giving his relationship with Carrie a chance. She didn't care about marriage licenses or what Oliver had that Greg didn't. She said Richard had plenty of reasons to hold back from loving her, but he hadn't.

"Worry less. Love more," she had said. *"In this world, you gotta fight to be happy."* Even when Greg insisted there was no guarantee he'd make it back to Shelton—or Carrie—she said life didn't come with guarantees. *"So you keep fighting. Fight and win."*

Fight to be happy. Advice given at the most inopportune time. Typical of his mom.

And yet...

If he could survive four months of training, get over his qualms about the new government, and find a way to make this position work to his favor—army or patrolman—he could become an Oliver for Carrie, minus the whole *"I'll take Oliver's goodness"* aspect. The thought scared him. Scared and intrigued him, which was stupid. There were too many *ifs* to think about anything beyond the next few days.

Only...

Carrie looked so dang cute in his hat. A stray lock of hair escaped his attempt to tuck it back. It curled next to her soft cheek, begging to be brushed aside.

He shoved his hands in his pockets. "I really should go."

Those huge blue eyes stayed on him, and his mom's words rang in his ears.

Fight.

Suddenly, he straightened. "Look, Carrie. I don't know if I'll be able to come back or if I'll even live past—"

"You will," she cut in. "I know you'll find a way to come back to us."

There was so much trust in her voice. She had more faith in him than he'd ever had in himself, which solidified his decision.

"If I make it back, and if I try to give you a chance—I mean, try to give *us* a chance," he said, suddenly fumbling over his words, "will you give Oliver a chance while I'm gone?"

She gave him a strange look, probably wondering why, the second he said he'd give their relationship a chance, he asked her to do the same with another guy.

"No," she said simply.

"Carrie…" He nearly told her about the marriage license, except Oliver hadn't specified how he got Carrie legal. Those papers could be something else. Even if it was as Greg suspected, she might not care. Just because she rejected Greg's marriage proposal, didn't mean she would reject Oliver's. With freedom within her grasp, she might jump on the citizenship wagon—which she should. Greg just didn't want to be around to witness it.

But if she did still choose Greg after everything, he never wanted her to doubt her decision. She needed to do it with her eyes wide open. She needed to know what kind of papers had her name on them and *then* make her choice.

Something warm brushed his hand. He jolted when he realized what it was. Carrie was reaching for him. Carrie Ashworth, his introverted, self-conscious friend who hadn't initiated a thing in her life, had brushed her fingers across the back of his hand. From any other girl, it was the equivalent of flinging herself at him.

His resolve melted, and his hand answered her plea, lacing his fingers through hers.

While his body was hers, his mind refused to yield.

"C'mon. Oliver will be good to you. He's the good one, remember?" Oliver had the goodness. Braden had the charm. Greg had the age and good looks. Three men to make Carrie's perfect man. At the time, he'd been thrilled she found anything appealing about him. Now his part seemed pitifully small.

"Greg, when I said it took three men to make my perfect man..." Her lashes lowered. "I hope you know that's not true anymore. I'd take *your* goodness, *your* charm, *and* your looks." She blushed right through her freckles. "You keep telling me Oliver's the good one, and he is. But so are you."

He stiffened. "No, I'm not. I'm no Oliver."

"No, you're better. A little crazier and harder to figure out," she added with a tiny smile, "but better because you're willing to give me up to keep me and my siblings safe. You're willing to give yourself up to keep this clan safe. You were even willing to stand up for a factory worker you barely knew to keep him safe. And when Jeff attacked me..." She paused, voice tightening. "When I thought Jeff was going to kill me *and* Zach, you made us safe and then gave Jeff his freedom to keep him safe, too." Her eyes finally met his, blazing with intensity. "So, yes. I'll take your goodness. I'd take it all, and I'd take it in a heartbeat."

"And you think *I'm* crazy?" he said, shocked.

Her blush deepened. "It's true."

Greg wanted to argue, but the way she looked up at him...those words...

Carrie Ashworth was pure light: her hair, her skin, the sun streaming in on her soft lips. That chin of hers was lifted, practically begging him to lean down. She was the most kissable woman he knew—not that he had any way of knowing for sure. But those lips begged to be explored. Appreciated.

But if he kissed her now, her heart would close off to Oliver completely. It wasn't fair to do that to her, not with her, Amber's, and Zach's futures on the line.

Not with the chance Greg wasn't coming back.

Reaching up, he slipped off his Yankees hat, letting her hair spill over her shoulders. Then he cradled her face, leaned forward, and pressed his lips to her soft forehead. It was a safe, friendly goodbye kiss, the kind even Oliver would approve of. Maybe not, but Greg approved of it. His mom would, too.

She closed her eyes and leaned into him. The pull to her was strong and his arms wound around her petite waist. He held her for a long time as his mind tripped over itself, racing toward the future. If he could pull this off, if enough things fell into place and his luck finally turned, he could change her life for the better. Not just hers, but the entire clan's. It was the only thing that made leaving bearable.

He pressed her cheek to his chest. "Take care of them for me," he whispered into her hair. His mom. His grandparents. All of them. "Take care of yourself, too."

"You, too." She leaned back and looked up at him. "Come back to us. To me."

"I will." Because one way or another he was done letting life—and the government—steal people from him. He was ready to fight back. Fight for happiness. "I promise."

Though it took effort, he released her. Then he reached up, brushed the hair back from her face—purposely missing that stray lock a second time—and placed his Yankees hat back on her head, knowing this moment would keep him company long after he left.

As he started to leave, his feet turned back suddenly. "Can I come see you tonight?" The words left his lips without permission, but he didn't retract them. "Maybe after my mom's asleep?"

She smiled a radiant smile. "I would like that."

For some reason, her response surprised him, but he beamed with pleasure. "Meet me by the pond just after dusk."

"I'll be there."

Greg didn't know if he could resist her a second time—or if he should even try—but he took control of his feet and trotted out of the garage, grinning the whole way.

eighteen

"Did you kiss her?"

Ignoring his mom's question, Greg knelt on the weeds. "Is it still just the one leg, or is the other one actin' up now?"

His mom folded her arms. "I'm not answering 'til you do."

At least she was sitting in Carrie's water wagon now. The first half of the trip, she refused to be "dragged around like a baby." Heaven forbid the woman accept some help. So he'd kept an arm around her waist and listened to her wheeze as she limped into town. The whole time he pulled the wagon behind them, rattling and begging to be used. But her mind was stronger than her body, and she slowed fast.

Each time they stopped to rest, she took longer to get back up. Richard offered to come and help, and maybe Greg should have taken his offer. But Greg wanted time alone with his mom, so Richard hadn't pressed.

With each passing moment, the sun dipped lower in the western sky. He had no idea what time it was, or if the township offices had already closed and this whole trip was for nothing.

His mom watched him, still waiting for an answer. Anytime she wasn't walking—or wheezing—she had enough energy to pester him about Carrie. She was the nosiest woman he knew, at least next to his grandma. The mother/daughter duo could pry information like the best-trained spies, but he refused to bend.

"You ready yet?" he asked.

"Greg," his mom said pointedly. "Did you kiss Carrie?"

"None of your business."

She smiled a slow, tired smile. "Good boy."

Ruthless.

That was the last information she was getting.

Besides, if she knew he hadn't kissed Carrie—not really kissed her—she'd ream him out, and there was no need for that. He was scolding himself plenty. That vision of Carrie in the garage was intoxicating. He was anxious for their dark walk around the pond where they could steal a few more minutes of privacy before he left. She'd be cold and he'd need warming up, too. He pictured her chin lifted, her lips slightly parted, and...

His mom was smiling at him. Grinning, actually.

He stood. "We better go. How about you ride for a bit."

"Not a chance. Help me up."

Greg put an arm around her shrinking waist. Once her legs were steady under her, they started off. Her breathing went downhill faster than she did, and she was raspy by the time they made it to Shelton. Each of the short cement steps up caused her to wince, but the doors weren't locked, and the clock on the wall read 4:43pm.

They'd made it.

Like Greg figured, Ashlee was waiting for them, fake grin and all. He'd planned to come tomorrow on her day off, but such was life.

Ashlee waved from behind the counter where she was busy helping another man and woman with some paperwork. The three of them chatted like best friends while Greg helped his mom to the nearest metal chair. Once he eased her down, she rubbed her legs, relieved to be off her feet.

"You okay?" Greg asked.

She waved him off, too tired to respond.

The older couple turned to leave but spotted Greg and his mom in the corner. "Are you two new in town?" the man said, striding over to shake their hands.

"Moved in a few months ago," Greg said warily.

"Welcome. I'm Aaron and this is my wife, Liz. Where do you folks live?" he said, eyeing his mom with a look of concern.

Greg shifted to block his view. "North of here."

He purposely kept it vague, but Ashlee, being the ditz she was, spilled the specifics anyway. "Oh, they live over in the Logan Pond subdivision. Have you met May and CJ Trenton?" Ashlee asked.

"I think I met them awhile back," the man said. "With everything going on, we citizens should stick together."

Greg nodded. "Nice meeting y'all."

Taking the hint, the couple left Greg and his mom alone with the blonde vulture behind the counter.

"Good afternoon, Mr. Pierce," Ashlee said, smiling. "So nice to see you and your...your..." Her words trailed as she got her first good glimpse of Greg's mom. Her fake smile faded into a look of pure horror. She thought Greg had fabricated his mom's illness.

Seeing Ashlee's reaction confirmed his fears: his mom was declining too fast to last four months of training.

His mom straightened with considerable effort. "Help me stand."

"Stay," Greg ordered. "I'll bring the paperwork to you."

She shot him a dark look. "I'm not dead yet. Help me up."

Stubborn woman.

"I'm so sorry you had to come in, Mrs. Pierce," Ashlee said as they worked their way over. "So sorry. I wish there was an easier way."

His mom leaned against the counter, eyes closed to catch her wheezy breath. "It's Mrs. O'Brien now, but no worries. The fresh air...it..." Another wheeze. "Clears my lungs."

Ashlee shot Greg a worried look. He glared back. What right did she have to feel sympathy when she was the reason they were there in the first place?

"Can we sign her stuff quick?" Greg said.

"Yes, of course. Let me scan your card, Mrs. O'Brien. Now that you're married, we'll also need to change your name on your paperwork and issue you a new card."

His mom realized her mistake the same time Greg did.

Mrs. O'Brien.

"Can't we update her information next month?" Greg said in exasperation. If she even lived that long. "We're in a real hurry."

"I don't know." Ashlee glanced up at the camera in the corner. "We really should—"

Greg sidestepped, blocking the camera. "Next month. Please."

It took a moment, but Ashlee nodded. With a half-hearted smile, she scanned his mom's card in her little device and then did the same with his. "When do you leave for training, Greg?"

He froze. "What did you say?"

"Your training." She smiled at him. "I can't wait to see you in uniform."

He stared at *You-can-just-call-me-Ashlee*. Greg had thought Mayor Phillips signed him up because Greg found out about the black market mess, but the handwriting on his envelope had been distinctively female.

Ashlee's.

Hot blood coursed through his veins. "It was you," he said. Ashlee submitted his name for service because he wouldn't give her the time of day.

"What?" She feigned innocence even as she backed up.

His mom grabbed his hand. "Let it go."

Ignoring the warning, he said, "Don't play dumb. Why'd you submit my name?"

"It wasn't me," Ashlee said. "I swear. But this is a good thing, Greg. Just think. You'll be bringing peace and harmony back to our country. You'll be protecting citizens like me and your mom, like those citizens you just met. You'll get money and your green card, and, and, and you'll be fighting the rebels."

I am a rebel! he wanted to scream.

Clueless, Ashlee's courage seemed to return. She leaned over the counter and lowered her voice. "You could even take your mom to the doctor," she whispered, as if his mom had gone deaf with her cancer.

He refused to speak to *You-can-just-call-me-Ashlee* after that. She didn't deserve his civility.

They'd nearly finished the paperwork when a shout echoed in the front office.

"You again?" a man yelled. "What are you doing here?"

Greg turned as a light-haired patrolman strode out of the back hallway. Every muscle in Greg's body stiffened at the sight of him. It wasn't the first time Greg had seen this patrolman, but he assumed it would be the last.

David Jamansky stormed into the front office, eyes darting back and forth between Greg and Ashlee.

"So this is what you've been doing while I was gone, Ash?" Jamansky yelled. "Running around with this creep? I told you to stay away from him!"

Ashlee and Jamansky looked like twins with their light hair and lean bodies, but Ashlee wasn't cowed by her brother's outburst. She knew he was nothing but a puffed-up bully.

"Oh, calm down," Ashlee said. "Greg's only visited me a few times while you were gone, but it's been great, hasn't it, Greggy?" She ran a finger along her collar bone and let out a sultry sigh. "Oh, what encounters they've been."

Jamansky went red with rage.

Greg gaped at her. Was she trying to get him killed? The day he met Ashlee—the day he got his yellow card—David Jamansky about leveled him just for talking to her. Since then, Greg not only helped Oliver frame Jamansky for working the black market, but when Jamansky came for Oliver, thirsty for blood, Greg hid Oliver in the clan. Now he couldn't figure out why Jamansky was here instead of rotting in prison. Which begged the question, where was Oliver?

Dead?

Greg tightened his grip around his mom's waist. "Let's go," he whispered.

"Not so fast," Jamansky said, jumping in front of them to block their escape. Startled and already wobbly, Greg's mom stumbled back and fell against the counter. She yelped in pain, but Greg caught her before she tumbled the rest of the way to the floor. Jamansky didn't even glance at her. He glared daggers at Greg. "I wasn't done talking to you!"

Rage surged inside Greg. The patrolman had at least one gun, a nightstick, a Taser, and the ability to end their lives. Greg had nothing but clenched fists and a yellow card that should have protected them from this kind of abuse.

His mom leaned against the counter, wheezing and struggling to breathe. If she started coughing, things would go from bad to worse.

Fast.

"You okay, Ma?" Greg asked.

Jaw tight, she managed a nod.

It took every ounce of Greg's will power to keep from leveling the patrolman. Fights like this got people killed. He had to stay calm.

"We were just leavin'," Greg said through gritted teeth.

He turned to help his mom and that was his mistake. Jamansky grabbed his arm, spun, and wrenched it behind Greg's back. He slammed Greg's head down on the counter.

Pain sliced through Greg's skull. His mom screamed. So did Ashlee. Jamansky ignored them both to press an elbow in Greg's spine.

"You don't leave until I say you can leave, Greggy," Jamansky hissed in his ear.

Greg's mom alternated between crying and coughing, but he couldn't see her with his cheek smashed to the counter.

"Ma?" he called, frantically searching for her. She wasn't where she should be, which meant she'd fallen. Jamansky had knocked her over. "Ma?"

Her crying turned to choking sobs. "Leave...him...alone!"

"Shut up or you're next!" Jamansky yelled down at her.

That did it. Too many loved ones hurt. Too many freedoms stolen. Greg had two choices: comply or fight. He knew which he should choose. But if he didn't do something fast, his mom wouldn't live long enough to appreciate his compliance. His blood pumped with fury, but he forced his muscles to go completely slack.

"David," Ashlee said, running around the counter to him, "these people came in to renew their citizenship. That's all. I was teasing about Greg. I've barely seen him. He's done nothing wrong!" She tried to pull Jamansky away, but his elbow dug into Greg's back. "Leave him alone!"

"Shut up, slut!" Jamansky roared. "If you'd just—"

Greg made his move. With a single step back, he dropped his shoulder and rammed it into Jamansky's chest.

Caught unaware, Jamansky stumbled back. His grip loosened and Greg was free, but Greg didn't stop. He kept barreling back until Jamansky went down as hard as his mom had.

Jamansky was only on the floor a second before he jumped to his feet. Greg was ready. He swung fast and sunk his fist into Jamansky's gut. But before he could get another punch in, Jamansky whipped out his gun and leveled it at Greg's nose.

Greg's fist froze mid-air.

More screams erupted behind him. His mom was growing hoarse, but he didn't dare check. Fear clawed at him as he stared down the barrel of that gun.

The two men heaved deep breaths, each braced for the other to make the first move. Five seconds. Ten. Then it became apparent that Jamansky wouldn't shoot. Not here. Not over something so ridiculous.

Regaining control, Greg glanced over his shoulder. Ashlee had crouched down next to his mom, trying to calm her down, but his mom couldn't quit coughing. Already her sleeve was splattered with blood as she coughed into it. She'd be vomiting soon if Greg didn't end this.

Now.

"We're leaving," Greg said, still breathing heavily.

Without waiting for Jamansky's approval, he turned and headed back to his mom.

"Stop!" Jamansky yelled.

Greg kept going. He was getting her out of there before any more harm was done. He wouldn't be cowed, but he was done fighting.

"Unless you want her dead," Jamansky shrieked, "you will stop right now!"

Out of the corner of Greg's eye, he saw Jamansky change aim, lowering the gun to his mom's head.

"No wait!" Greg said, whirling. "Stop. *Stop!*"

"Why?" Jamansky said. "Looks like I'd be doing her a favor."

Hatred surged through Greg so vile he could taste it. His mom was too engrossed in her own problems to realize she had a gun aimed at her. Greg sidestepped, hands high, placing himself between her and Jamansky.

"Leave her out of this," Greg said. "She's done nothin' wrong. What do you want from me?"

"To never see your face again," Jamansky sneered.

"Done. I'm leavin' in the morning. I've just been drafted and I'll be gone for good."

Jamansky snorted. "You expect me to believe that?"

"It's true, David!" Ashlee said from the floor. "I saw the papers myself."

"Shut up, whore! Not another word from you." Then Jamansky turned and shouted, "Simmons! Get your scrawny butt out here!"

Oliver entered the hallway that connected the patrol station to the township office. The second he took in the scene—Jamansky's gun trained on Greg, Greg's mom coughing up blood on the floor—his face went white. Greg wanted to warn him to keep a poker face. Oliver couldn't recognize them, not without making things worse.

"Yes, chief?" Oliver managed to squeak.

Chief? Greg wanted to scream. What was happening?

"I want this punk detained," Jamansky said, waving his gun at Greg. "Lock him up."

"No!" Greg's mom cried, tuning back in. "You can't..." More coughs sputtered. "You can't arrest him."

"Mrs. O'Brien," Ashlee said, sounding near to tears herself, "please calm down. You're coughing up blood."

"Do it!" Jamansky yelled at Oliver.

Panicked, Oliver's gaze flickered to Greg before going back. "Sir, may I ask why this man—"

"I said do it!" Jamansky bellowed. "Now!"

Oliver pulled out his metal handcuffs and started for Greg. "Feet apart, sir," Oliver said. "Hands behind your head."

nineteen

Greg was too stunned to react.

In a blink, Oliver had cuffed Greg's hands behind him. But with the click of the lock, Greg's brain kicked back in. Oliver tugged on his arm, urging him toward the holding cells. Greg dug in his heels.

"Stop!" Greg shouted. "You can't arrest me!"

"Stop fighting," Oliver hissed softly. "You'll only make it worse. Let me handle this."

Something animal raged inside Greg. His mom was on the floor, and if he didn't show up on time to training, the government would make his family—and the clan—pay. Not to mention, how would his mom make it home without him? "No. I've gotta report for service!" He writhed, trying to see Ashlee. "Tell him!"

Ashlee leaped up and ran for Jamansky. "He's telling the truth, David. Greg was just drafted for service. He leaves in the morning. I wrote the papers myself."

Jamansky whirled on her. "I told you to stay out of this!"

She folded her arms, expression full of loathing. "When are you going to wake up and realize that I hate you? This here, this situation just solidifies it. I'll never take you back, so get it through your thick, idiotic skull! We're through!"

Jamansky's eyes widened. So did Greg's.

Ashlee and David Jamansky might look like twins, but they weren't siblings. They were dating—or had been. And Jamansky thought Greg had been messing around with her.

"Like it or not, Ash," Jamansky barked, "I'm back now, and there's nothing you can do about it."

"Yes, I can." Her chin lifted. "If you detain Mr. Pierce, you'll be interfering with national security. I'll write the report myself. Do you really want the feds back here, snooping around? Greg has to report for duty on Thursday, and as Chief of Patrols, it's your job to make sure he gets there. So what's it going to be?" Her eyes narrowed. "Your pride or your badge?"

Jamansky glared. "If he doesn't have to report until Thursday, then I can detain him until Thursday."

"No," Greg said, jumping back into the conversation. His hands were cuffed behind him and Oliver still held his arm, but Greg wrenched forward. "I don't have transportation. It'll take me at least two days to walk. I planned on leavin' first thing tomorrow—maybe even tonight just to be safe—but if you detain me and I don't arrive on time, I'll report this precinct for interfering with national security."

"As if they'd listen to you," Jamansky scoffed.

He had a point. Greg was a nobody, soon to be lower than dust once they saw his scars.

"Maybe not," Ashlee said, "but they'll listen to me."

"You wouldn't dare," Jamansky said.

"Try me."

For a second, it looked like Jamansky might strike her. The two of them stood in a lockdown standoff. Oliver kept a firm grip of Greg, mute and utterly useless.

In the end, Ashlee caved first. "You're mad at me, David, not them. So let them go. If you want to know the truth, Greg wouldn't give me the time of day. There. Are you happy?"

"My son is innocent," Greg's mom added, still crying. She shifted as if to stand, but her leg gave out and she fell back on the floor with another cry of pain. Tears streamed down her pale cheeks. "Please, please let him go. He'll be gone tomorrow."

Jamansky breathed heavily, eyes darting from person to person before resting on Greg again.

Greg held his breath, praying for mercy.

"Let's hope they put you on the front lines and you're killed off early, Greggy," Jamansky finally said. "Just to be clear, even if you survive long enough to get a badge, you will never work in Shelton. I never want to see your face again. My precinct is and always will be full. Capiche?"

Nostrils flaring, Greg forced himself to nod.

Oliver finally spoke up. "Sir, I can escort this citizen to Naperville on Thursday if you'd like. That way we know he has reported for duty."

"No. Take him now," Jamansky said.

"What? No!" Greg cried, eyeing his mom.

Jamansky waved his arm. "Get him out of my sight. I want him out of my precinct, out of my town, and I want him out now. He can sleep outside the gates. Keep him cuffed until you're there. In fact, leave the cuffs on. They'll find a way to break them off."

Blinding panic shot through Greg. "But I haven't packed yet!"

Jamansky laughed a dark laugh. "You don't need anything where you're going."

"At least let me get my mom home. She can't walk without help." Greg tried to yank free, but the metal cuffs dug into his skin. "Just let me get her home, and I'll leave from there. You have my word. Please. She can't walk!"

"Then she shouldn't have come!" Jamansky yelled. "Get him out of here."

"Sir," Oliver said, "I can drop off his mother before I escort him to Naperville."

Jamansky's gun rose again, only this time aimed at Oliver. "So help me, Simmons, if you say another word, I'll blow your brains out. Get your partners and get him out of here. Now."

"Yes, chief."

Oliver called for his partners, and the two young patrolmen who had stopped Greg on the street came running. Each took an arm and dragged Greg toward the front doors.

Greg twisted and writhed. "Wait. At least let me say goodbye." Every labored breath of his mom's was like a punch to his gut. He would never see her again. His foot caught hold of the door jamb and locked strong. "Let me say goodbye!"

"David," Ashlee begged, "you can't do this. Let Greg say goodbye."

Jamansky didn't even look at her.

"I'll give you what you want!" Ashlee yelled.

That caught Jamansky's attention. He held up a hand, stopping the three patrolmen, and slowly turned. "Everything?"

She looked disgusted, but her jaw tightened with determination. "Yes, but only if Greg gets to say goodbye *and*...you let me drive Mrs. O'Brien home. In your car. Now." Ashlee held out her hand. "Give me your keys."

The only sound in the office was Greg's mom crying and wheezing.

"This better be sincere, Ash," Jamansky finally said, digging out his car keys. "No more games."

"It is." Ashlee snatched up the keys.

Jamansky motioned to Greg. "Fine. You get one minute. Not a second more."

Greg didn't know why Ashlee was on their side, especially after how he'd treated her, but he was forever grateful. His mom would make it home alive.

Out of the corner of his eye, he saw Oliver giving him a wide-eyed, terrified look. A warning of some kind. Before Greg could decipher it, his young partners dragged Greg across the room and shoved him toward his mom. Hands still cuffed, Greg landed hard on his knees.

He felt helpless kneeling in front of her, hands bound. He couldn't help her stand. He couldn't even wipe the tears streaming down her hollow, gray cheeks.

"I'm sorry," his mom cried between raspy sobs. "I-I'm so sorry."

"Ma," Greg whispered, "you gotta calm down. It's fine. I'm gonna be fine, and so are you. Ashlee will make sure you get—" He stopped in sudden dread, realizing why Oliver was freaking out by the door.

Ashlee couldn't take his mom home.

Not with a neighborhood full of illegals who weren't expecting them. People would be outside. Ashlee would see them, report the clan, and Jamansky would obliterate every last one of them.

"Ma," Greg whispered, "Ashlee can't take you. She can't."

"I know. It's fine. I'll just..." She paused to shift positions. Even that much movement made her cry with pain. "I'll get out of it. I'll take the wagon and rest when I need to. You just take care of yourself."

Greg's chest seized up seeing her like that. It was happening again. Kendra first. Now her.

His eyes burned. "I love you, Ma."

She scowled. "Don't say it like you're never gonna say it again."

He might say it again, but she might not hear it again.

"You gotta wait for me," he said. To die. She had to wait. She'd fought her disease for eight months to make it to Illinois, and she'd fought ever since. She was a Pierce. She was a fighter. Then again, so was Kendra, but this time Greg wouldn't buck the system. He'd play by the rules and become a soldier or whatever they told him to be. He'd get her help. But she had to fight long enough for him to make it back. "You gotta wait."

Her eyes swam with tears. She reached up and laid a shaking hand on his cheek. "I love you, son."

He wanted to yell what she had—*Don't say it like you're never gonna say it again!*—but his throat constricted. She hadn't promised to wait. She hadn't even tried.

A few hot tears slipped from his eyes. "I know."

She managed a tiny smile. "Just remember that whatever they—"

"Times up!" Jamansky barked. "Get him out of here."

The two patrolmen yanked Greg back and away.

"Wait," Greg said. "Wait!" He wasn't done. She was in the middle of something. But they dragged him out of that building faster than should have been possible. He kept thrashing, desperate for a last glimpse of her. For a last word. But suddenly it was blue skies and fresh air.

She was gone.

"Put him in my car," Oliver said.

His young partners shoved Greg in the backseat. Greg landed hard on his elbow, having no other way to break his fall. Then one of the patrolmen moved to get in beside him, and the other opened the passenger door.

"What are you doing?" Oliver said. "Go back inside and assist Chief Jamansky."

"But, sir," the older one said, "I think Chief wants us to go with you."

Oliver grabbed the passenger door and slammed it shut. "Go! That's an order!"

Without another word, Oliver stormed around to the driver's side and got in. His partners jumped on the sidewalk to get out of the way as he threw the car into reverse.

Greg might have been thrilled, but Oliver's bravado came two minutes too late. His mom's fate was sealed. She'd never survive the next hour, let alone the next four months. His head hung. His eyes burned red hot.

"I'm sorry, Greg," Oliver said as he backed up.

"You're sorry? Sorry!" Greg shouted.

He leaned forward, wishing his hands weren't cuffed so he could reach through the safety cage and claw him. "Do you realize what's gonna happen to her if she walks home? Or the clan if Ashlee drives her home? How could you let Jamansky do this to her—to us?"

"Sit down!" Oliver yelled back. "I can't think, and my partners are still watching."

Oliver drove at a slow pace down Main Street, past the trees which had finished blooming and Carrie's flower shop, driving slow enough to drive Greg mad. He sat back, fists clenching behind him. His mom would die out on those cornfields entirely and utterly alone. No one would even know why they never came back.

Greg searched his door for a handle. None. But the window didn't look too thick. He could kick it out.

"How is Jamansky even here?" he asked, sliding over to where he could bust out the passenger-side window. "How is he the new chief?"

"Mayor Phillips sprung him from prison," Oliver said. "They've been working the black market together this whole time, so they arrested Chief Dario to get him out of the way."

"Not you?"

"No. Jamansky owns me now and he knows it."

"Obviously! She's gonna die!"

Oliver ignored his outburst. He clutched the steering wheel and checked his rearview mirror again. "Not yet. Not yet," he said to himself.

Greg glanced behind them. Oliver's partners had disappeared inside, which meant Oliver was watching for Ashlee and his mom to emerge, heading for Jamansky's car. Greg watched, too, desperate for a last glimpse. But then they cleared a bend and the township office slipped from sight.

Oliver slammed on the brakes, sending Greg sliding into the metal barrier. Then he jumped out and opened Greg's door.

"What are you doin'?" Greg asked.

"Get out."

"Why? It's too late!"

"No, it's not." Oliver rustled some keys from his pocket. "I'm taking your mom home. I'll make sure she gets there safely. Now stand up and turn around."

"What? How?" Greg asked even as he stood.

"If she's walking, I'll find her on the trail and drive her the rest of the way. If Ashlee's driving her, I have to stop them before they get to Logan Pond. I don't know how much time I have, so you have to make a run for it. You'll have to walk to Naperville on your own. Turn around."

Greg stared at him for one heartbeat. Then hope sprung in his chest.

"What excuse will you give Ashlee?" he asked, turning and offering his hands.

Oliver unlocked his handcuffs. "I don't know."

Greg rubbed his wrists. The skin was raw and burning, but he barely noticed. "Tell Ashlee my mom can't walk upstairs. Her bedroom's upstairs, so you need to carry her. Whatever you say, make sure Ashlee doesn't tell Jamansky."

"I know, I know, I know! I have to go if I'm going to catch them. If Jamansky spots any of us—including you—we're all dead."

"Don't worry. I can disappear," Greg said. "Go!"

Oliver nodded and pointed down the road. "Head south for a long time, find the expressway and go east."

Not the greatest directions now that Greg didn't have the map that came with his draft notice, but he didn't care. He'd figure it out.

"I owe you big time," Greg said.

"Then I expect you to pay up. Which reminds me," Oliver said. "The rebellion's motto is *Live Free or Die,* but the dead can't help the living, so don't be stupid. No getting yourself killed. Everyone here is counting on you coming back, especially your mom and Carrie. So for once in your life, shut your mouth and play by the rules so you can make it back here alive."

"Deal." Greg reached out and shook Oliver's hand. "Same goes for you."

Oliver nodded. "See you soon."

"Let's hope."

Then Greg took off running, feet slamming against the pavement. He heard Oliver get in his car and peel away.

Just like that, Greg willingly sprinted away from Shelton, his mom, Carrie, and six years of freedom. By force, he had to trust the fate of everybody and everything he loved into the hands of somebody else.

All so he could become the next David Jamansky.

twenty

Oliver sped down the residential roads. He hit the brakes before Union Street and peered down toward the patrol station. Jamansky's car was gone, which meant Ashlee coerced Mariah to go with her. Oliver pressed the gas to the floor, flying past old vintage homes.

How far had they gone? Would Mariah convince Ashlee to drop her off early? What if Mariah fainted, and Ashlee decided to do the kind, citizenly thing and drive her all the way home?

Oliver had to find them.

At each side street, he checked through for Jamansky's car. He pushed 50mph in what used to be a 25mph area. When he ran out of side streets, he sped back to the main road. By then, he was out of the main part of town, dangerously close to the neighborhoods on the northern outskirts.

Then he spotted it, a green patrol car up ahead with CHIEF printed on the back. Oliver sped up and flipped on his lights without his siren. It only took a moment for Ashlee to notice and pull over.

Jumping out, Oliver ran up to her car.

"Officer Simmons?" Ashlee said, rolling down her window with wide, terrified eyes. "What are you doing? I thought you were driving Greg to Naperville."

"Change of plans." Leaning down, he checked on Mariah in the passenger seat. Her hand was over her chest and her face was clenched as if in great pain.

"Where?" Mariah wheezed loudly. "Where's Greg?"

"Your son is walking to Naperville, Mrs. O'Brien. He'll be fine."

Somewhat relieved, Mariah lay back against the seat, but Ashlee nearly jumped out of her skin.

"What?" Ashlee said. "Why?"

Oliver wanted to explain—especially to Mariah—but she looked like death and he still had a part to play. As a dutiful officer, he wasn't supposed to know Greg or his mom any more than the average citizen.

"Mr. Pierce was gravely concerned about his mother," he said. "He's worried that, even if she makes it home, she won't make it upstairs to her room. She needs to be carried, and he didn't think you could handle that, Ashlee." The whole thing sounded like the convoluted lie it was, but he went on. "So I dropped him off on the outskirts of town and came to find you. Do you think I did the right thing?"

Without a single hesitation, Ashlee nodded vigorously. "Yes. Mrs. O'Brien isn't doing well. I'm scared she broke something when she fell. Maybe a hip or leg. It's bad. Portman and Bushing had to carry her to the car."

A chill ran through Oliver. He took in her appearance. Her skin was not only deathly white, but moist and clammy. Her breaths were loud and labored, and something was off with her eyes, like she was seeing, but not clearly.

Ashlee went on. "She kept saying she could make it home, but I'm really scared."

"I'll take it from here."

Oliver ran around and opened Mariah's door. Taking her trembling hands, he helped her stand. She was only up a second before her legs buckled. She screamed. He caught her by the waist and did his best to carry the bulk of her weight, but every step caused her to cry out. Ashlee hopped out and grabbed her other arm.

Oliver cursed himself for not pulling up right alongside Jamansky's car. It was only twenty feet, but it felt like forever with Mariah in so much pain.

"Where are you hurt, Mrs. O'Brien?" he said, no longer caring what Ashlee heard or how familiar it might sound.

"My—Ah!" Mariah gasped with another step. "My hip."

Oliver stressed about holding her so firmly around the waist, but he didn't know how else to help her walk. Ashlee opened his passenger door and he eased Mariah inside. She was a sobbing, wheezing heap by the time he got the door shut.

Ashlee looked up at Oliver, tears smearing her mascara. "How are you going to get her inside?"

"No idea," he said honestly.

"I can follow you there if you want," Ashlee said. "I can't help much, but I can help some."

Which was a sweet offer if there wasn't an illegal clan waiting for them. Thinking fast, he said, "I'm sure her husband can help me move her."

"Maybe you should take her directly to the hospital," Ashlee said. "Something is seriously wrong with her."

He considered that. Mariah had her yellow card, and she needed help, more help than she'd get in the clan. "Good idea," he said.

"Gosh, I'm shaking like crazy," Ashlee said, clasping her hands. "We barely got her to the car. I was freaking out, wondering how I was going to get her inside her house. Thank you for coming back, Officer Simmons. I don't know what I would have done."

"Thank you for stepping in," he said, meaning every word. "I don't think she would have made it home, but I know..." He wasn't sure how to say it without making both of them uncomfortable, but he wanted it said anyway. "I know it was a sacrifice."

"David's a jerk," Ashlee whispered. More tears leaked down her cheeks.

Oliver nodded, feeling sorry for her. No one should be stuck with David Jamansky, let alone a second time. Pretty selfless for a woman he'd pegged as self-absorbed.

"Oh well." She wiped the mascara from her eyes with a sad smile. "We would have ended up back together eventually. We usually do."

True. As dysfunctional a relationship as Oliver had ever seen.

"What should I do now?" Ashlee asked. "David won't be expecting me back yet. And what about you? You're supposed to be driving Greg to Naperville, but the hospital will take longer than an hour."

"Just kill some time," Oliver said. "I'll figure things out on my end. Thanks again."

He got in his car but didn't immediately drive. Mariah's eyes stayed closed and her chest heaved with every breath, but the breaths were no longer dry and raspy. They sounded wet and bubbly, making his stomach churn. Blood was smeared across her chin.

Her eyes fluttered open. She looked at him as if she wanted to say something but it would hurt too much. In the end, she reached over and patted his arm.

"You're welcome," he said in understanding. Then he pulled onto the road.

"Mrs. O'Brien, do I have your permission to take you to the hospital? The nearest one is in Aurora and I could..."

He trailed off as she shook her head. Her eyes closed, but her head kept on shaking.

"Are you sure?" Every instinct, including the hairs prickling on the back of his neck, told him she was at death's door.

It took effort for her to form the words. "Home. I want...home."

"But the hospital can help you. They'll have pain medicine and they can find out what happened when you fell. If you're worried about money..."

He stopped as tears poured down her face. Her wheezing picked up. The last thing he wanted was for her to start coughing again.

"Okay," he said. "I'll take you home."

He wanted to speed, but the roads were horribly unkempt with potholes, and every movement caused her to cry out. So he drove carefully until they made it to the North Entrance and Richard O'Brien's house. Oliver started to pull into Richard's driveway, but Mariah waved a hand.

"Not here?" he asked.

With effort, she pointed down the road. He had no idea where she wanted to go, so he drove slowly. Once he turned onto Denton Trail, he figured it out. She wanted to go to her parents' house.

As he pulled into the Trenton's driveway, Carrie came out of CJ's garage, wiping her hands on her jeans.

"Hi, Oliver. I didn't expect to see—" Carrie stopped short. "Mariah? What happened?" Frantic, she searched Oliver's car. "Where's Greg?"

Oliver jumped out. "Long story. Where's Richard?"

"I have no idea. Probably back at his house," Carrie said.

Too far. "Help me get her inside."

Mariah could no longer bear any weight. Oliver tried to lift her legs out of the car, but her nails dug into his shoulder as she cried out.

Oliver had heard enough.

"I'm sorry, Mrs. O'Brien," he said. Then he bent down and scooped her up. She hardly weighed a thing, but she writhed and screamed, making it difficult to keep hold of her. "So sorry," he said.

Through her jerky movements, she nodded. She knew he had to get her inside somehow.

"Help me find her a bed," he said to Carrie. "Then I'll explain everything."

———— • ————

Carrie stared at Mariah's sleeping form, grateful she'd finally slipped into a deep sleep. The small candle flickered in May and CJ's bedroom, having burned most of the night. It was down to a stub, but Carrie was too exhausted to grab another.

Richard had taken the first shift with Mariah, and Carrie took the next. Now CJ and Richard slept on the living room couches while May slept next to her daughter on the king-sized bed. Carrie sat on a chair, too overwhelmed to do anything but stare.

Greg. Mariah. The new patrol chief who nearly destroyed their lives.

With the house silent other than Mariah's labored breaths and May's snores, Carrie kept reliving the day, the month, the years. Too many deaths. Too many losses.

Her emotions felt raw.

Mariah's skin looked pasty white under the yellow hue of the candle, resembling Jenna's before her death. It seemed like she'd broken her hip in the fall, but they had no way of knowing for sure.

Through the pain, Mariah had struggled to keep her characteristic brave face. Anytime she wrenched back, May went into a tizzy. So Carrie finally urged May from the room, telling her they should find Mariah some food.

When they'd entered the kitchen, Carrie had been shocked to see Oliver still there. His visits usually only lasted a few minutes, and she'd been back in the bedroom with Mariah for some time. Yet Oliver crouched next to the fireplace, heating up water with CJ.

None of them spoke as they had worked, so Carrie heard it perfectly: heart-wrenching sobs filled the back bedroom, like a wounded animal. It was as if Mariah could only put on a brave face for so long, for so many people. Being alone with Richard, she finally allowed herself to fall apart. Greg had been stolen right in front of her. She was dying. Kendra was already dead. May and CJ would be alone again. So would Richard. Not to mention, the physical agony of a body rejecting this life. The sounds had cut Carrie to the core. Thankfully May was too deaf to hear. But CJ heard.

So had Oliver.

Standing, Oliver had nervously brushed off his hands and said he needed to get back to the station. Carrie had excused herself and followed him outside. By his car, she tried to thank him for all he'd done for Mariah, but he shrugged it off like he usually did. But if it wasn't for Oliver...

A small moan escaped Mariah's lips, bringing Carrie back to the candlelit room. She dipped a cloth in a bowl of cool water and sponged off Mariah's damp brow.

The door creaked behind her, and Richard tiptoed in. His graying hair was disheveled and wisping out of its ponytail, and his eyes were red with sleep and tears.

"Has she woken again?" Richard whispered.

"No," Carrie said. "I think she's finally settled down."

Nodding, he sat at the foot of the king-sized bed and rubbed Mariah's legs. "Goodness," he breathed. "What a day."

Carrie agreed, feeling weary to the bone.

After a minute, Richard looked at Carrie. "I can't tell you how pleased Mariah was that Greg finally kissed you. It actually brought a smile to her face amidst the pain. She has such hopes for you two."

Heat flooded Carrie's cheeks. How did Mariah know about that?

"Greg didn't kiss me," she said softly. "I mean, not really. He wouldn't have even if he wanted to." It was the third time she'd expected it, felt her heart flutter in anticipation and then drop when it didn't happen. A kiss on the forehead, as sweet as it had been, just wasn't the same. If things hadn't happened in town, Greg would have met her out by the pond. They would have walked and talked for who knew how long. Maybe then? Her stomach flipped at the thought, but just as fast, she was shaking her head. Maybe not. She was starting to think she knew nothing about men—Greg in particular.

Richard frowned. "What do you mean, he wouldn't have even if he wanted to?"

"Oliver."

"Ah. So my stepson hasn't given up that obsession?"

"Nope. Still going strong." With no end in sight. She dipped the cloth in the water and rung it out.

"Well," Richard said, "love wouldn't be any fun if it came easily."

"It came easy enough for you and Mariah," Carrie noted.

"I know. I was just trying to make you feel better."

Carrie laughed. She couldn't help it. The late hour—or early hour, rather—along with everything else was causing wild fluctuations in her emotions. May stirred at the outburst but rolled onto her side and fell back asleep. Mariah didn't budge. It seemed wrong to joke about anything right now, but it also felt wonderfully light. Carrie appreciated Richard's attempt at a distraction.

"In spite of how it might seem sometimes," Richard said, watching the sleeping women with fondness, "my stepson has a good head on his shoulders. Greg has seen the ugliness of the world even more than we have. You can't blame him for wanting to protect you from it."

A picture of patrolmen dragging Greg handcuffed out of that office made Carrie shudder. What would happen when he reached Naperville and they realized who he was—what he'd done?

She squeezed the water from the washrag and wiped Mariah's brow again. "Greg needs my support now more than ever. Even if Greg was right—which he isn't—I still wouldn't pursue things with Oliver. Oliver has a gentle soul. A failed relationship would only hurt him more than if I never allow it to happen in the first place. I don't want to crush him, if that makes sense."

"I can respect that. Frankly, I think that's why Greg held back with you for as long as he did."

She turned. "Really?"

"Yes. Greg mentioned to me once about his concern that he might, I believe his word was, 'squash' you. With your soft-spoken nature, you and Oliver are more similar than you might realize. But you stood up for yourself well enough with Greg. Perhaps Oliver would like the same chance."

She gave Richard a strange look. That almost made it sound like he agreed with Greg.

He lifted his hands. "My apologies. I didn't mean to intrude."

"No. Not at all. Just…" Why hadn't she ever given Oliver a chance? He was fifteen years older than her, which was odd but not horrible. The two of them struggled to carry on a conversation longer than two minutes. How could a relationship develop if neither person had enough gumption to take the lead? Maybe that was their problem. She and Oliver were *too* similar.

"Do you think this civil war can help things for us?" she asked. Because if citizenship wasn't an issue, Greg could no longer use Oliver as an excuse. "Do you see things ever going back to how they were?"

Richard sat back on the bed, pensive. "It's hard to imagine our side gathering enough support to make a dent in Rigsby's new system. We only have a few ways to protect ourselves and even fewer ways to communicate with others like us. Unfortunately, I think this civil unrest will only complicate life—at least, in the near future."

A depressing thought.

"Will you lose your citizenship if..." She caught herself too late, but Richard didn't seem to mind. His citizenship was tied to Mariah's by marriage. What happened when she was gone?

"I doubt there's an easy way to find out without getting myself arrested. Honestly," Richard said with a sigh, "I don't mind going back to illegal status, especially after what happened today. I've lived my life, Carrie. I'm content to spend the remainder of it in Logan Pond. But are you? Are your siblings?"

Frowning, she studied the ragged rise and fall of Mariah's blankets, contemplating the price of freedom. Would Mariah say it was worth it? Would Carrie's parents? How about Jeff or Jenna? More importantly, would Oliver? Carrie had a hard time thinking his life was happier or easier simply because he had citizenship and money.

But how could she think it was worth it to stay in Logan Pond as she studied Mariah's skinny, gaunt face? Mariah looked like a body finished with this life, and it killed Carrie to think that it might not be that way if it wasn't for horrible citizenship games.

Carrie's eyes filled with hot, silent tears.

Richard laid a hand on her arm. "I'm sorry, Carrie. I've overstepped my bounds again. I just think that if your father was here, he'd say you couldn't go wrong with either man. Then again, he'd also say you're free to choose neither of them. Just because Greg and Oliver love you, doesn't mean you're obligated to love them back."

The mention of her father brought another wave of emotion. And memories.

She'd forgotten how close Richard and her dad had once been. After the Collapse, when the clan was thrust under May and CJ's roof for months, the two became friends. Richard's first wife, Sherry, was first to get sick. When she passed, Carrie's dad helped Richard through the grief. So when tides turned and it was Carrie's mother on her death bed, Richard stayed by him the entire time.

Of all the nights in Carrie's life, she wanted to forget that one. But being back in this room, Richard sitting where her dad once had, Mariah lying where her mom once had...

It was too close, too raw. The memories assaulted her. She clutched Mariah's cold hand, unable to look at Richard or Mariah again for fear she'd see her parents instead.

"Your father," Richard went on gently, "might also tell you that just because he and your mom chose to live here as illegals doesn't mean you have to. You're free to choose your own future, Carrie. I know your parents would understand. They would be proud of who you have become, of all you have done for Zach and Amber, and they would trust you to decide."

Her breathing sped up and she struggled to hold back the flood of tears. How could she date a patrolman when patrolmen had destroyed the lives of so many people she loved—even today? How could she consider leaving the clan after her parents sacrificed everything to keep their children out of the government's claws? Maybe that's why she'd never considered Oliver before, because, in a way, it was a slap in her parents' dead faces.

The room felt hot with emotions, and as rude as it was, Carrie longed to have her parents here instead of Richard and Mariah. She ached for their advice, their comfort, their arms around her. It wasn't fair they'd been taken so young. Then again, it wasn't fair that she was here with Mariah instead of Greg.

No, she realized suddenly. None of them should be there. Carrie and her parents, or Greg and his. They should all be sleeping in their own homes and beds, alive and happy without thought of citizenship, war, or death.

"Apparently, I don't know when to stop," Richard said. "I'm sorry."

"No, I appreciate your thoughts. Are you going to be okay?" she asked in return. He would have no one to go home to. Again.

His glistening eyes went back to his wife of less than a month. "I will be. We all will be because that's what she wants."

They grew silent, each listening to Mariah's soft wheezes as their thoughts carried them to the deep places where the soul longs for privacy.

After a few minutes, Richard nudged her. "For the record, though, my vote is still for Greg. Entirely selfish reasons. It just feels like you're already part of our family."

Family.

The word wrapped around her like a blanket. She may have lost her parents, but May and CJ virtually adopted her afterward. And Richard and Mariah felt more like parents than anyone.

Richard couldn't have said anything kinder, because sitting in that candlelit room with May, CJ, Mariah, and Richard all a breath away, Carrie didn't feel like an intruder or even a good friend. She felt like family.

Their family.

And she knew that, no matter what happened with Greg, she always would.

twenty-one

Mariah didn't make it to sunrise.

She woke with a jolt sometime after Carrie nodded off to sleep. A gurgling sound erupted, and Carrie grabbed a bucket. Richard rubbed Mariah's back until the vomiting stopped. Then he and Carrie helped ease her back down.

Mariah stared up at the ceiling for a long time after that. Not speaking. Just staring. When she finally broke the silence, her voice was barely a whisper in the candlelight.

"Tell Greg…sorry."

Carrie's eyes filled. Only Mariah would apologize for dying.

"Of course, love," Richard said, rubbing her hand.

Mariah stared upward several more minutes. Then her eyes widened as if in sudden amazement. "Kendra…" She paused for a ragged breath. "My girl."

Carrie was tempted to follow her gaze upward but knew she'd see nothing. Richard's eyes overflowed, but he forced a bright smile.

"You give Kendra a big hug from her new stepdad, alright?"

Mariah's pale features lit with joy. She closed her eyes and her breathing came easier after that. Too easy and far too spread out to sustain life.

Carrie's heart plummeted. When Greg asked her to take care of his family, this wasn't what she'd envisioned. Not so soon. Not like this. Amber would deliver water to them, and Carrie would bring Mariah flowers and as many dinners as Richard would allow. Yet twelve hours after Greg left, Mariah was slipping away. Greg would be devastated when he found out that things in town had pushed his mom over the edge—or how close he'd been to being there with her himself.

Twelve hours.

Richard stood. "I think it's time. We should probably wake up May and CJ."

Mariah coughed a few more times, but her eyes never opened again. With May and CJ holding one hand, and Richard and Carrie clutching the other, her breathing stopped with a long, final exhale.

———— ♦ ————

Greg crouched behind a patch of trees near the outskirts of Naperville, ignoring the overall ache of his muscles. If he had calculated correctly, the sun had been up for an hour, which meant he still had time before check-in. The air already felt muggy and humid. After two and a half days of walking and rain, his smelly clothes clung to him, but he focused on the scene ahead.

The training facility looked like a compound, an old prison with double fences ten feet high, topped with razor wire. One gate led inside and was guarded by at least six armed men. The surrounding area had been cleared of trees and brush, making it difficult to get close enough to fully scope out the rest.

His stomach growled. That's what two days and three squirrels did to a man. Scrawny squirrels at that. Part of Greg wished he hadn't left his slingshot with Zach so he could have scored a few more meals. He'd been left to set traps, a skill he'd never perfected. Thankfully, water had been plentiful with yesterday's downpour.

Though it killed him to admit it, it was a blessing he left Shelton when he had. The trip took longer than expected. His body was in decent shape but unaccustomed to that much distance on foot. The first day he'd been stopped twice by patrolmen who had enough time to hassle him, but not enough time to give him a lift. After that, he steered clear of the main roads, which cost him more time and mileage. He'd taken a wrong turn somewhere outside of Aurora and had to travel half the night to make it here in time. Now his feet ached with massive blisters from walking in rain-soaked shoes.

To say he was in a foul mood didn't do it justice. He was wet, exhausted, chewed from mosquitoes, and still fuming over events with Jamansky. Coupled with two lousy nights of sleep and the fact they'd drafted him in the first place, he felt like tearing a tree to shreds. Or…destroying a government compound.

With a deep breath, he reminded himself to play by the rules. Dead people can't help the living. Survival was his new goal—although not necessarily his own survival.

A car pulled down the road and stopped just shy of the compound gates. It wasn't a patrol car, just a normal, boring sedan. Two people got out, an older and younger man, maybe father and son. The son hefted a bag over his shoulder and they hugged. Then the son walked through the gate. A few guards approached and pointed him toward a small building.

Seemed easy enough. Walk up. Give them your card. Hope they don't shoot. Still, Greg stayed low, cherishing his last moments of freedom.

A twig snapped to his right. More rustling, and he made out footsteps. Several of them too slow and loud to be animals. He spotted splashes of blue and orange moving through the trees. The people stopped just inside the edge of the woods twenty yards from where Greg crouched. They weren't talking loud, but in a place like this, they might as well have been shouting.

"—not sure how long," one guy was saying.

"It looks pretty guarded," another answered. "Do you think they'll let me keep my gun?"

"If we survive that long."

Greg jerked up. That last voice had been higher. Female.

The government was drafting women?

He squinted but couldn't see through the thick brush, so he crouched low and crept closer. He stopped ten yards away.

Two guys and a girl watched the compound, either late teens or early twenties. Like Oliver's partners, they looked too young to fight. Either that or Greg was just getting old. The last encounter with Jamansky and his mom had him feeling much older than twenty-five. The three of them all had meat on their bones and no rips in their jeans. Even their shirts had plenty of color and thickness to the threads. Yellow cardies. The girl's shirt was neon orange and reflected off the trees, making Greg roll his eyes. Subtle.

They never once looked over their shoulders or scanned the woods. Even the guards could have looked up from their posts and spotted them easily on the edge of the woods. Definite yellow cardies. Each of them carried bags with their belongings. Not only did they have *things* to pack, but they actually had *time* to pack.

Greg hated them.

It wasn't fair. He knew that. The next few months would be kinder to him than them—assuming he lived that long. But it was people like those three who didn't know what it was like to starve, hide, sleep in the rain, or wear the same clothes day in and out. People like them would become haughty, unfeeling patrolmen like David Jamansky.

Greg looked down at his own light blue UNC t-shirt. If this training compound was anything like Raleigh's Third Municipality, the government would confiscate and burn it. He'd planned to leave his lucky shirt home along with everything else he cared about. If it weren't for his condemning scars, he'd leave it here in the woods and go shirtless. But, like so many other things, his lucky shirt was another victim.

So was his luck, apparently.

Another engine sputtered and a small green bus rumbled toward the gate. Two dozen people climbed out. Those ones didn't have the clothes or demeanor of the yellow cardies next to him—or the age. They were older and dirtier with matted hair, blank expressions, and matching factory uniforms. Blue cardies. They didn't look scared. They hardly looked alive. Six years of living under the government's thumb had beaten the life out of them. He was surprised how many middle-aged men were in the group, plus several women. The group shuffled toward the front gate.

Greg watched those women, noting how many were older. His pulse leapt with a horrid thought. The government wouldn't recruit his mom, would they? No. Ashlee knew how sick she was. Then again, Greg wouldn't put it past Jamansky. Revenge of the worst kind. He went numb with dread.

"That group won't last long when the fighting starts," the dark-haired guy said with a laugh.

"If that's the kind of people they're recruiting," the girl said, "we're all dead. The illegals will conquer us before the real fighting starts."

Considering Greg crouched less than ten yards away from them, he figured the blue cardies had a better chance at survival. Blue cardies at least knew how to survive.

The girl slid her arm around the dark-haired guy's waist. "It's 7:42, Ethan. We better go."

He brushed some hair from her cheek. "Who knows what's waiting for us down there—what's waiting for you, Meg? Don't go. We'll lie and make up some story about you getting sick. Please just go home."

"I'll be fine," she said. "Come on."

Greg watched the young couple walk toward the compound, hands entwined. He felt sorry for them. It was bad enough Greg was here. He couldn't imagine bringing Carrie with—

His thoughts jolted him for a second time.

Carrie.

His mom wasn't a likely candidate for service. One look at her and they'd know. But Carrie had papers now. She was young and perfectly healthy. She could be recruited anytime. Next month. Next week. Only she was too sweet and quiet to be thrown into this pack of wolves.

He prayed that, as the "wife" of a patrolman, she'd be exempt from service, but knowing how Jamansky had it out for Oliver, Carrie could easily end up with a target on her back.

Greg could hardly think straight.

Carrie.

His mom.

Where did it stop?

He strode out of the woods at a furious pace, wanting nothing more than to speed up time and get this over with.

By the time he made it to the guards, the three yellow cardies had disappeared inside the compound. Greg pulled out his yellow card and handed it to a Tongan guard who had to be 6'4" and over 400 pounds. The guard crossed Greg's name off a list and tossed his yellow card into a box. Greg eyed the overflowing box, figuring that was the last he'd see his citizenship card.

Good riddance. That card had been nothing but trouble.

"Where's your bag?" the beefy guard said. "All bags much be searched."

"I didn't bring one."

"Why not?"

Greg glared up at him. "I wasn't given the option to pack."

The guard snorted a laugh. Then he motioned Greg toward a small cubby and another beefy guard. "Search him."

Greg obediently walked toward the corner, where he spotted another box, this one filled with piles of discarded clothing. His muscles seized. He figured somebody would see his traitor's mark at some point, he just didn't think it would happen within the first minute of captivity. He wanted to grab hold of his lucky shirt and never let go.

"Everything off," the second guard said, mindlessly tapping his nightstick against his leg.

Stalling, Greg held his arms out wide. "As you can see, I'm unarmed. Check for yourself."

"Nice try. Everyone is strip-searched. No exceptions."

The second guard not only had a decent-sized nightstick, but a large assault rifle hanging off his shoulder as well.

Heart thudding, Greg pulled on the corner of his shirt, taking his time in hopes of prolonging his life. But as he did, he caught sight of a flash of orange. Right on top of the box was a neon orange shirt. The girl's shirt.

"Everybody is strip-searched?" Greg asked, scanning all of the guards. Every single one was male. "What about the women?"

"Best part of the job," the guard sneered. "Now move!"

Rage surged through Greg as he stared at that shirt. Oliver told him to play by the rules, but too many played the game and still lost. At some point, somebody had to cry foul.

In one swift move, Greg yanked off his shirt. Even if it was the last act of his life, he wanted the world to know he wasn't part of this. He was here by force only. With a traitor's crossed-out star on his arm and whip scars on his back, he wanted everybody to know that if they didn't watch *their* backs, he'd make them pay. For his sick mom. For his dead sister. For Carrie and his starving clan. The list was endless, including the girl with a neon orange shirt Greg had never even met.

The guard circled Greg. "Interesting." Then he turned and called, "We've got ourselves a rebel!"

In an instant, six guards swarmed into the small enclosure.

"Thought you'd sneak in undetected, did you?" the Tongan asked. "Thought you'd stick the system?" He motioned to the others. "Hold him."

Guards grabbed Greg, and the beefy guard swung fast. The nightstick slammed into Greg's stomach. The pain was blinding. The wind rushed out of him.

"Didn't bring a bag. Said you weren't armed to get out of the search. Clever," the massive guard said with another swing.

The black metal slammed against Greg's jaw. Greg's head snapped back, world exploding with light and agony.

"The boys inside will have a hay day with you. They won't kill you, but you'll wish they had. Protocol gives them—and us—the right to break you, starting right now. By the time we're through with you, you won't even remember the word *revolution*. Welcome to Naperville."

Greg saw another flash of black. He tried to duck, tried to shrink, but there was nowhere to go. The nightstick smashed into the side of his skull.

Everything went dark.

twenty-two

"Hey," Braden said, "what are you doing here?"

Amber startled, heart jumping in her chest. Braden stood in front of her on the grass. She felt stupid he'd found her here. The clan cemetery sat in a quiet corner of the neighborhood. There was no reason for her to sit in the shade and play with the grass by her parents' graves. That's something Carrie would do. At least Amber wasn't crying. Of course, that was also something Carrie would do.

"I had to take Richard some noodles." Amber had been distracted ever since. If she went home, Carrie would give her more chores. "What are you up to?" she asked, noting with pleasure that he wore his red bracelet.

Braden smiled. "I was bored. I finished work so I came looking for you. Mind if I join you?"

"Do I ever?" She fluttered her dark eyelashes up at him, hoping to look appealing.

Laughing, he sat by her on the grass. She immediately leaned into him to solidify the connection, loving the feel of his warmth, even on a hot, humid day.

"I feel bad," he said, studying Mariah's grave. "I didn't know her that well."

He misunderstood her visit to the clan cemetery, but she didn't correct him. She studied Mariah's fresh plot of grass. Wilted flowers lay next to the rock that acted as her headstone.

"She was always nice to me," Amber said. "Even when everyone else hated me after that raid, she was still nice."

Without meaning to, Amber's gaze wandered back to her parents' graves. During Mariah's funeral, she'd had the overwhelming desire to stay behind and talk to her parents like she used to. In the lonely months following their deaths, Amber had sat under this same tree and chattered away. Mostly she talked to her mom, but sometimes her dad, too, especially when Zach and Carrie drove her nuts. She hadn't been here for a while. She hadn't even talked to them today. But the shade, the warm grass under her fingers felt too good to leave.

She frowned. She really was turning into Carrie.

Rocks marked her parents' graves like Mariah's. Each one had three letters scratched into their sides: TGA and LLA. That's all that was left of her dad and mom, chicken-scratched initials on ugly rocks. Their voices, even their faces, were fading from Amber's memories. Time had become her enemy.

She brought her knees to her chest. "Is this going to happen to all of us?"

"What, die?" Amber felt Braden shrug. "I guess eventually."

That's not what she meant. Not exactly.

She counted rock after stupid rock. Eight graves. It should have creeped her out to know people's bones lay beneath her, but what bothered her most was thinking that they'd started with forty people in their clan. One fifth of them were now dead. If she counted Jeff and Greg as MIA, that number rose to one-fourth gone in six years.

How depressing was that?

"I meant," she tried again, "are we all going to die young? Die early? Die...*here*?"

Braden stiffened. "You won't die young."

"But I could."

"But you won't."

"But I *could*," Amber insisted. "All of us could."

Before he could argue, she heard some rustling off to the side. A flash of red darted through the patch of woods behind them.

"Zach?" Amber called.

More rustling before Zach and his friend Tucker emerged in the small cemetery.

"Oh, hey. Hi," Zach said, breathless. "What are you guys doing here?"

"What are *we* doing?" Amber asked. The cemetery wasn't anywhere near where those boys should be.

Tucker lowered his guilty eyes and Zach's freckled face turned red. They looked at each other, searching for a lie Amber could see coming a mile away.

"We, uh…lost something," Zach said. "We were trying out Greg's slingshot, but Tucker shot the rock too far. We lost it."

"You lost a rock?" Amber challenged.

"Yep. Bye!" Zach said. Then the two scrawny teens took off down the street.

Amber didn't know where Zach had been, but she could guarantee he didn't want Carrie knowing.

Maybe there were some bribery possibilities.

"Zach thinks we live in a cage," Amber said. "Maybe he's right. The older I get, the smaller it feels. I mean, Richard's been widowed twice in this same, stupid neighborhood, in that same, stupid house. How bad would that be?"

"It would be the worst thing ever," Braden whispered. "But it won't happen to you. I won't let it. I promise."

Surprised at the gravity in his voice, she turned. Braden's face was inches away, perfect turquoise eyes looking more depressed than she felt. She reached up and smoothed the tanned worry lines between his brows.

"Okay," she said happily, as if he could change her fate with a simple promise.

Having him that close with the soft breeze keeping them company was too tempting. Anywhere his arm touched hers, she felt a current under her skin. She tilted her chin up, begging for a kiss. Clueless, Braden sat back and raked a hand over the grass. She huffed softly. How had he missed that hint?

"What would they do if I volunteered?" he asked after a minute.

"Who? Volunteered for what?"

Braden's mouth twitched, but he didn't answer.

The words finally registered. She turned sharply. "Volunteered for what?" she demanded.

His shoulders lifted. "For service. Like Greg."

"Are you nuts?" she cried.

"I don't have a citizenship card," he said, still stroking the grass, "but maybe the government is desperate enough that they'll take illegals. I've seen five more fires since that one in Chicago. Things must be bad."

"Exactly! That's why Greg didn't want to go." Her eyes narrowed. "We hate the government, remember? Why would they recruit illegals when they're trying to *kill illegals?*"

He was silent too long. "It could...get us out of this cage."

Us.

The word distracted her momentarily. Did he mean *us,* as in him and her, or *us,* as in the entire clan? But thinking of him fighting—on the wrong side—sent a chill down her spine.

"You're crazy," she said. "I'm not letting you go."

His turquoise eyes rolled. "As if you could stop me."

She whirled on him. "Why are you talking like this? The government doesn't even know you exist, Braden Ziegler. For good reason."

"Which is why I'd have to volunteer."

"No!" Her insides shook like an earthquake. "It's bad enough Greg left. We don't even know if he made it to training, or if he's dead, or if he's killing other people like us. You can't volunteer. You just can't."

"But Oliver helps—"

"Oliver's an idiot!" she shouted in exasperation.

His jaw, still cleanly shaven—which she suddenly hated—tightened to a hard line. She didn't want him to look like a patrolman. She wanted him to look like—and forever be—a squatter.

"Stop it, okay?" she said. "You're scaring me. Let's talk about something else. In fact..." She jumped to her feet and brushed off her jeans. "Let's see what Maddie and Lindsey are up to."

She held out a hand to help him stand, but he continued to stare up at her. He wanted to keep talking about this madness, about him volunteering to die, but she kept her hand out, waiting for him to take the hint. They were leaving that stupid cemetery and the subject. They were going to find his sisters and pretend they never had this conversation.

He took her hand and stood but dropped it the second he was up. "Actually, I think my dad needs some help. I better go. Catch you later, okay?"

It would have been okay if he hadn't told her he was bored when he showed up, if he hadn't dropped her hand like it disgusted him, and if he hadn't refused to kiss her—or look at her—now.

"Fine. Yeah. Sure," she said.

Seething, she marched down the sidewalk. Braden didn't know what he was talking about. Volunteering to join the enemy, to kill people like them? Was he insane? Luckily, the government was on her side. They'd arrest him before they'd let an illegal join their cause. Braden wasn't going anywhere. Thankfully.

Sometimes their cage didn't sound so bad.

———— ◆ ————

From the time the sun was up, Carrie sat by her window, watching the empty house across the street. It had become her routine: sitting, thinking, and watching the sun's first rays touch Greg's empty house. Two weeks of this. Lame, but she couldn't seem to stop.

She was proud of herself for sitting on her ripped green couch. It took a while to do that much after Jenna's death, and only after a stern lecture from Amber.

"That couch was ours before you ever gave it to Jenna," Amber had said. *"Mom and Dad used to read to us here. It's the last thing we have of theirs, so sit down!"*

Now Carrie spent the first few minutes of every day wondering if Greg made it to Naperville, wondering how he had adjusted to being back under government rule, wondering what he looked like in a green uniform, gun attached to his hip, aiming at who-knew-what.

Had they noticed his scars yet? Punished him for it? Killed him for it?

How long before he found out about his mom—or would he?

The ache of missing Mariah hadn't dulled yet. May was too heartbroken to let Carrie forget for long. And try as she might, Carrie couldn't squelch the fear that Greg had followed his mom—and far too many others—to the grave.

But once the sun was up, she forced herself to get moving. Life pushed her through the days and weeks.

With Greg gone, she'd expected Zach to mope around, but instead he helped more and fought less, all with Greg's slingshot hanging from his back pocket. Somehow, she'd neglected to tell Zach that Greg also left a NY Yankees hat for him. It lay smashed under her pillow, which made her the most pathetic female on earth, but she didn't care. Zach got the baseball and slingshot. The hat was hers.

Possibly forever.

After teaching school, Carrie packed up some muffins and wandered the neighborhood for the newest blooming flowers. She cut several branches of purple lilacs from behind Kovach's house, letting their sweet aroma enliven her. When Greg asked her to care for his family, she'd planned to take Mariah flowers every day as an excuse to check in on her. Now it only seemed right that May be the recipient.

Carrie knocked on the Trenton's front door. When no one answered, she let herself in.

CJ lay on the couch, snoring. May wasn't anywhere to be seen, but Carrie guessed she was in her bedroom napping as well. Greg's grandparents slept more than they ever had, but people dealt with grief differently—which explained why she'd hardly seen Richard in the last two weeks.

Quietly, she made her way into the kitchen and set the corn muffins on the counter. Then she exchanged the old flowers in the jar for the fragrant lilacs. Lilacs were May's favorite, and Carrie hoped they'd lift her spirits.

She puttered a few minutes, refilling their water bucket and hand-washing their dirty dishes. She thought about peeking in on May, but the house seemed so peaceful. Plus Rhonda Watson was in the backyard, hoeing the garden. The Watsons were in charge of the crops, but knowing how much Carrie loved it, they'd relinquished some of the responsibility to her. Carrie slipped out the back door.

Rhonda's head came up. "Hi, Carrie. How are you?"

The question implied more than typical concern. "Good enough," she said truthfully. "How are the tomatoes?"

"Dry." Rhonda shielded her eyes from the bright sun. "Everything is. We might need to do a water line if it doesn't rain soon."

Carrie sighed. The new crops were still small and tender, making them susceptible to drought. Even her prized tomato plant looked droopy. So far this June had been hotter than any others Carrie had charted. They could spot-water a few plants from May's well, but they didn't want to risk the well running dry either. But a bucket assembly line would bring water all the way from the pond to May's backyard, a three-house journey. The clan hated bucket assembly lines, but they couldn't afford to lose more crops.

"Maybe we can organize it for tomorrow if it doesn't rain," Carrie said. "We can tell everyone tonight."

"Is there still a meeting tonight?" Rhonda asked.

"Yeah. At least, I think today is Thursday." Oliver hadn't stopped by since Mariah's death two weeks ago, and the days were blurring together. People were stressed that he hadn't returned, but Carrie insisted he was just busy with his partners. He'd warned her that he might have a hard time stopping by.

In a short time, it felt like she'd lost three of her best friends: Greg, Mariah, and Oliver.

"Oh. Sasha said we might not have the adult meetings anymore," Rhonda said, striking the ground again with the hoe. "She doesn't think we need them."

"What?" Carrie said sharply. "Why not?"

Rhonda shrugged.

Carrie couldn't believe it. Greg started the weekly adult meetings as a way to implement his new plans.

"But we need those meetings now more than ever," Carrie said. "We're in the middle of Dixon's well and have two others to dig. Plus the barricade needs work. And now that Mariah's gone..." The words choked off. Greg's fourth idea was to find medical help in other clans. It was the only idea the clan voted down. But his third idea, consolidation, still needed work. "Now that Mariah's gone, someone needs to tell Richard to move into the cul-de-sac. And what about—"

"Whoa, Carrie," Rhonda said. "Calm down. I was just telling you what Sasha said. I'm still fine to meet every week."

"We need to."

Carrie didn't know why she was so defensive. They were Greg's ideas, not hers. But with everything else falling apart, the least they could do was keep things progressing at home.

As she knelt to weed the carrots, something in the back of her mind nagged at her, telling her they could do more. She thought about Greg's fifth plan, the one only she knew about. The farmers' market, a way to earn money. There had to be a way to make it work. But how? Illegals like her had no business being in Shelton. Yet the thought wouldn't leave her alone.

Two rows later, she had it. The solution. By the time the sun lowered in the western sky and the adults congregated in May's living room, she'd resigned herself to make it happen. Even if it went against clan rules to do so. For the first time in weeks, she felt a tiny spark of hope.

twenty-three

"Thank you all for coming," CJ said to the hot, stuffy room. They opened all the windows, but people still fanned themselves.

Carrie was disappointed Richard hadn't come. He knew Greg's ideas better than her and should have taken over the adult meetings. While she understood his mourning, she hoped he didn't become the hermit he had been before Mariah moved in. Poor CJ sat on a chair up front, too tired to stand and lead the meeting.

CJ asked for updates, and Rhonda reported on the water bucket line. That went over as well as Carrie expected.

"Still no Oliver?" CJ asked.

Carrie shook her head. "No."

"Great," Sasha said from the back of the room. "What if there's another raid he hasn't told us about? I think we should start posting guards again."

Before Carrie could argue, Sasha's husband Dylan spoke up. "I agree. We can't take a chance on this. Not after all that happened between Carrie and Oliver—or even with Mariah and Greg in town. There's just too much in the air to go weeks between hearing from Oliver. Guarding is safer until Oliver returns."

There were groans around the room—the men hated around-the-clock guarding—but no one disagreed. Reluctantly, Carrie nodded as well. Better safe than sorry.

"In that case, Dylan," CJ said, "make a schedule and let everyone know when they're up."

Dylan didn't look thrilled, but he nodded.

Terrell stood next. "I'm meeting with Barry tomorrow. What supplies does everyone need?"

Without mentioning her reasoning, Carrie requested bike chains and inner tubes, which earned her strange looks. Terrell said he'd try but not to get her hopes up. The rest of the supplies only took a few minutes, and then the room fell silent. Normally Carrie didn't mind the silence, but tonight she couldn't bear it. She'd been churning on Greg's fifth idea all day—actually a combination of the fourth and fifth—and with a quick breath, she took the plunge.

"I have a proposal," Carrie said, standing to face the room. A wave of nervousness washed over her. Greg's fourth idea had already been turned down, and he never presented the fifth for good reason. She glanced at the empty wall where Greg used to stand and decided that if he couldn't be here, at least his ideas could.

"I think we should revisit Greg's idea to contact other clans," she said. "I know it was voted down, but a lot has happened since then."

"What's the point in finding help now?" Sasha said bitterly. "It's too late for Mariah and Jenna."

It was like a punch to the gut. Carrie couldn't believe she could be so blunt and unfeeling. Luckily May had stayed in her bedroom for the meeting, and the clan's widowers, Richard and Jeff, weren't there either. But poor CJ stared down at the carpet.

"Who knows when the next person will get sick, Sasha," Carrie managed calmly. "But finding medical help wasn't Greg's only reason to reach out. I think maybe we could..." She clasped her hands, wishing for Greg's ability to speak his mind without fear. "Maybe we could start a farmers' market, a trader's guild of sorts for illegals like us."

People stopped fanning themselves to exchange surprised glances.

"They already have it," Terrell said. "It's called the black market, and in case you forgot, Barry owns it."

"But that's just it," Carrie said. "This wouldn't be one guy extorting prices and padding his own wallet. This would be an open exchange, free for anyone who wanted in." Only instead of having it in town like Greg hoped, they'd start smaller with illegals in a place they could control. "Just think, we could trade food, seeds, clothing, or even educational stuff, like medical knowledge or our books."

"You want to give away our books?" Rhonda cried in dismay.

"Maybe not. But then again, we could trade them for other books. I don't know." Carrie hated to say it, but Greg would want her to anyway. "With how things are going in Shelton, Oliver's been able to help us less and less. This might help us become more self-sufficient. Maybe we could hide each other if times got tough or there was an inconvenient raid. Plus, we need to find a source of income if we're going to keep May and CJ legal. Who knows? If we could ever earn enough, we might be able to buy another house from the government and get a few more people legal."

Someone snorted a laugh, probably still Dylan, but Carrie had already turned to Terrell, the supply guy.

"What do you think?" Carrie asked.

Terrell sat back in his chair. "It sounds nice in theory, but I'm telling you, Barry will go ballistic if he finds out we're cutting into his profits. He'll quit trading with us and everyone else."

"Then maybe it's time to shut Barry down," Carrie said in frustration.

Soft gasps sounded around the room. Barry got them supplies they couldn't produce like sugar, salt, matches, shoes, and ammunition. And yet, Barry's demands got higher each time, and CJ's garage wouldn't stay stocked forever.

Greg loved the shock and awe effect. Carrie wished she felt the same, but she kept her chin up.

"Well, why not?" she said softly.

"So..." CJ said, stroking his long, white beard, "where do you propose we hold this farmers' market?"

"We could invite people here, maybe even outside of your garage."

Dylan leaped to his feet. "Have you lost your mind? Have you forgotten why we broke ties in the first place? Even guarding with guns, people still tried to walk off with our stuff."

She hadn't forgotten. One guy hung around longer than the others. For months he tried to sneak back, testing different ways to raid their stash. It wasn't until Jeff almost blew his head off that he left for good.

"Not worth it," Terrell added. "We can't have others see our supply stash. Not with us down to two guns."

"Then maybe we meet in the woods like you do with Barry," she said, thinking aloud. "Maybe every Tuesday we meet at a designated place or something."

More shaking heads, so she went on desperately. "At least consider it. This could solve several problems. Don't you want to know if other clans survived, especially with a civil war brewing?"

Her fellow clansmen looked as if they could spend the rest of their lives in isolation. It was like, after six years, they'd forgotten how to interact with others.

"At some point," she said, raising her voice to be heard over the heated discussions, "CJ's garage will be empty and his money will be gone. If things have to change eventually, why not now?"

More complaints, but she noticed a few others, like Braden and his parents, nodding and considering her proposal—Greg's proposal.

CJ held up his hands to silence the adults. "I think this deserves consideration. I think we should all take some time to ponder the implications of reaching out. We can discuss it next week in more—"

"No!" Carrie interrupted. "I'm sorry, CJ, but I don't think we should wait. Please. We still have time." She couldn't bear another week of doing nothing more than surviving. Between Greg and Mariah, Jeff and Jenna, she felt the clock ticking like a time bomb. "What happens when another person gets sick? Do you realize one-fifth of our original number now lies in our cemetery?"

That got their attention and mouths dropped. Like her, people hadn't stopped to do the math.

"There has to be help out there," she said. "Like my mom's friend, Gayle Harrison. She was—"

"—nothing more than a medical paper pusher," Terrell cut in. "Look how she messed up Zach's ankle. No, I'm telling you, branching out is a bad idea. Barry won't like it."

"Who cares about Barry!" Ron Marino said. "We need to do what's best for our clan."

Others nodded in agreement, and Carrie felt a flash that it might work.

"I suppose with that," CJ said, "it's time to vote. All in favor of contacting other clans say 'Aye.'"

It was too hard to tell if they had a majority, so CJ asked for raised hands. Carrie counted every one while Terrell, Dylan, and Sasha glared at her. When she reached ten people, she exhaled in relief. Usually things passed by a wider margin, but ten was enough.

Carrie's insides bubbled with joy. Greg's ideas had passed.

"Great," Terrell muttered. "Barry's going to kill us—kill me. Literally."

Carrie ignored him. "Okay. Where should we start? Which clans might still exist?"

"Ferris," CJ said. "Perhaps the folks in Oakwood?"

With a little work, they came up with seven. According to Barry, two of those had been caught by the government, but hopefully the others were still alive and willing to trade.

"Five," Carrie said. "That's great. Maybe we should send a small group out to explain what we have in mind and see which ones are interested."

"Yeah, but who's going to make first contact?" Sasha asked. "Whoever it is, I hope they don't get shot."

Carrie's hand flew into the air, the first to volunteer for the diplomatic mission. Unfortunately, her hand was the only one. "Come on," she begged. "They'll remember us."

Still no one.

"Who was the last person in contact with others?" CJ asked.

Every eye went to Terrell.

Terrell shook his dark head. "Oh, no. You're not dragging me into this. My neck's already going to be on the line. "

"It only makes sense for you to go," Ron Marino said. "You know the trading business better than anyone."

"Which is why I was opposed! Illinois is headed into a civil war, and you want to traipse around the back woods and trade carrots?" He folded his arms. "I'm not having anything to do with this. I'm not."

Carrie swallowed. "Someone else, then? Anyone?" She'd go alone if she had to, but she really, really, really didn't want to.

"I'll go," someone said from the kitchen.

Carrie turned and smiled. Richard had slipped inside May's without her noticing.

"And Terrell will go, too," Richard added, "because he's the best and because he's absolutely correct. This area is headed into a civil war, which means things are going to get worse for us. We need all of the resources we can get. Who's to say Barry won't be found and caught? And then what? Carrie's right," he said, giving her a proud look. "We need options, and we need them now."

Terrell's wife, Jada, elbowed him. "Come on. Barry doesn't have to know."

Terrell's black eyes rose heavenward. When they lowered again, they narrowed on Carrie. "Fine. But if I go, I'm in charge. When I say hold back, we hold back, and if I say we belt our voices to the world, then you two better back me up."

Carrie couldn't help but grin. "Of course."

Terrell pretended to be fierce and mean, but really he was a big soft teddy bear. Even more, he was a salesman. Between him and Richard, she knew they'd make it work.

"Okay," she said. "How soon should we leave? You're meeting with Barry tomorrow, so maybe after—"

"Oliver's here," Rhonda Watson interrupted.

As one, the room turned to the opened windows as Oliver's car pulled into CJ's driveway.

"Finally," Carrie breathed.

Oliver got out of his car and headed up the sidewalk. CJ waved him in. "Come on in, Oliver!"

Oliver never let himself in, so Carrie climbed over the people and opened the front door. "Hi, Oliver," she said, still beaming. "I didn't think you'd be able to make it today."

"Yeah, sorry. I couldn't get away this morning." With a nervous look, Oliver surveyed the group of adults. "Sorry to interrupt your meeting."

"It's fine," Carrie said. "We were almost done."

With the discussion still lingering in the air, she was tempted to ask if there were other clans in the area. But the fact that he and his coworkers still did sweeps in Shelton told her enough.

Oliver cleared his throat. "I'm scheduled to do a sweep here again on Monday with my partners. We should be by just after sunset. So...yeah."

"Thank you for letting us know," CJ said. "I suppose that means no guard duty?"

Dylan and the other men looked relieved by that.

"Would you like to come inside for a bit?" Carrie offered.

"No, I should get going," Oliver said, backing onto the porch.

The last Carrie had seen Oliver was the evening Mariah died. Too much had happened since then for him to just leave.

"Mind if I walk you out?" she asked.

A light touched Oliver's gray eyes. "I'd like that."

twenty-four

Carrie and Oliver stood next to his patrol car as the sun descended in the western sky. A stiff breeze had kicked up, attempting to lower the sticky temperature.

"Any word from Greg yet?" Oliver asked.

"No," she said. Not that she expected differently, but that didn't make it easier. Questions plagued her day and night.

Oliver leaned against his car. "Don't worry. He's a smart guy who knows how to survive. He should be fine—assuming he controls his sharp tongue. Although that is a big *if,"* he added with a tiny smile.

She mirrored his smile. Greg seemed like an off-limits topic between them, yet Greg and Oliver were friends, too. They watched out for each other. And her.

If she could control the universe, Oliver wouldn't love her. Then she, Greg, *and* Oliver could stay friends. Sometimes she felt like dumping the notion of love altogether, especially after her talk with Richard. She refused to string Oliver along on the off-chance something sparked between them. She'd wait for Greg as long as it took. Hopefully Oliver didn't feel the same way about her. But the thought of a tri-friendship, the possibility that one of them didn't end up heartbroken…

Oliver studied her with a long, sad expression. He knew she was thinking about Greg. She ached to tell him to move on, but maybe there was no one else left. Maybe she was the last single woman he knew.

"How is Mariah doing?" Oliver asked softly.

The ground dropped out beneath Carrie. She struggled to breathe. Oliver didn't know. He left before Mariah took a turn for the worse. He didn't know, and she had to tell him.

Just like she'd have to tell Greg someday.

"Mariah is..." Her throat constricted. "She's..."

"Oh, no. I'm so sorry, Carrie. I wondered if she had, but...but I hoped she hadn't." His shoulders fell. "When?"

She blinked rapidly to stave off a flood of tears. "A few hours after you left."

Oliver looked horrified. But just as fast, his jaw tightened and his face went red. "I'll kill him," he whispered so quietly she wasn't sure she heard right. Except his expression matched his dark words. Then he seemed to catch himself. "Sorry. I shouldn't have said that. But if you knew my boss..." He ran a hand over his bald spot. "And Greg doesn't know?"

She could only shake her head.

The sun dusted the western sky with pink and orange. The colors blurred in her vision. She faced the evening breeze to cool her flushed skin.

Don't cry. Don't cry.

"I'm sorry, Carrie. I'm sorry about all of it. Very, very, very sorry." He moved to touch her arm but retracted at the last second. "Will you be okay?"

"Yes." She sniffed. "It's May and CJ that I worry about. And Richard." And more than anyone, Greg. Not only that his mom had died while he was gone, but knowing it was caused—in part—by what happened in town. Greg already blamed the government for so much. What would he do when he found out? "I just wish there was a way to let him know."

"I could try to get a note to him. I mean, I doubt they'll let me—they usually keep those places locked down—but maybe if the letter looked official?" He shrugged.

"Could you?" she asked. "That would mean so much to his family."

He nodded. "I'll try."

May's front door swung open, and the adults streamed out. Terrell saw them by Oliver's car. "We gave up waiting for you," Terrell called.

"Sorry," Carrie called back. "We'll talk after you get back from..." She nearly said Barry's but remembered Oliver beside her. "When you get back. Richard and I can come over Saturday."

"Sure. I look forward to it," Terrell said with heavy sarcasm.

He and the others started for home.

Oliver straightened. "I better go, too. I'll try to come next Thursday morning, like usual. It's just hard to get away. I pick my partners up from their house and drop them off after our shifts. It's been crazy."

"It doesn't have to be Thursdays," she said. "You're welcome to come anytime."

"I am?"

She gave him a strange look. "Of course. I like it when you visit."

He stopped moving. Stopped blinking.

Heat rose to her cheeks and she turned back to the sunset. Poor Oliver had no self-esteem whatsoever, especially when it came to her. "You know, you've become my calendar just by visiting on Thursdays." She found a little courage to smile at him. "As long as you don't mind me asking what day it is, come anytime."

"I don't mind. Today is June 9th and the time is..." He checked his watch. "8:54. No, wait. 8:55."

She laughed softly. "Perfect."

"But won't it make the others nervous if my car drives in here on a different day? I already worried about coming tonight instead of this morning, but I didn't know what else to do with the upcoming sweep."

"Oliver..." She looked up into his long, kind face wishing again for the gift of words. "You're part of our clan now. I hope you realize that."

He stiffened. "No, I'm not."

"Yes, you are. Especially after..." Emotions swirled inside her, catching her unprepared again. "Especially after what you did for Mariah. You're part of us now, so visit as often as you like."

"As often as I like," he echoed. His gray eyes studied her as if to ask, *How often do* you *want me to visit?*

Carrie dropped her chin and let the soft breeze blow her hair to shield her. She would have said as often as he wanted, but after that conversation with Richard—and Greg—she couldn't. She loved Oliver as a friend. Why wasn't that enough? If only Greg had really kissed her and ended the debate once and for—

Her gut clenched with a sudden thought.

That kiss.

Greg's goodbye.

Telling his mom about a kiss that wasn't even really a kiss. Richard saying how Greg had held back with Carrie. What Greg said in the garage about them, about Oliver. Dot by dot, piece by piece things slammed into her, and it had her heart racing with dread.

Richard thought she and Oliver had the same personality. Soft-spoken. Crushable. And Greg said he'd *try* to give their relationship a chance when he got back.

Try.

Which meant…

Her stomach twisted further.

She was Greg's Oliver.

She was his friend, even a close friend, but a friend nonetheless. He was trying to love her because his grandma and mom wanted it. It was his dying mother's wish. So he kissed Carrie on the forehead and lied to his mom, all while trying to convince himself—possibly unconscious-ly—that it was what he wanted, too. It was the same type of kiss Carrie might give Oliver.

Try.

Like people wanted her to do with Oliver.

She was Greg's Oliver.

Her legs felt weak, and she leaned against Oliver's car. She should have known. She wasn't Greg's type—not flashy or flirty enough—just like Oliver wasn't hers. From the beginning, Greg begged her to fall for the patrolman instead, probably to alleviate his own guilt because if she loved Oliver, his dying mother could have no complaints about him moving on.

Devastation rolled over Carrie.

Oliver gave her a probing look, waiting for an answer to a question she hadn't even heard. Blinking, she said, "Sorry, what?"

"Are you sure you're okay? You look…ill."

She was. Horribly.

Oliver loved her while Greg was *trying* to love her. The difference was a stab to the heart. So why was she fighting it? Why did she keep choosing the man with the most potential to hurt her? She wasn't even the type of girl to chase guys, and yet she'd been chasing Greg like mad, desperate for his attention like a pathetic puppy dog.

She looked up at Oliver. Oliver, with the small, kind eyes, dark, thinning hair, crisp, green uniform, and shoulders hunched protectively toward her. She loved Oliver, but was it enough? Did it even matter anymore?

His forehead wrinkled, looking even more concerned.

"I'm fine," she answered. "I just…"

She took another breath, feeling the shift in her mind.

Oliver.

Not Greg.

But the second she thought it, her heart sank, her limbs began to tremble, and the next words just blurted out of her.

"I love Greg."

Oliver paled. "What?"

Blood rushed to her cheeks. She hadn't meant to say it—she hadn't even meant to think it. Looking up at the darkening sky, she wished away the words. She'd never said them aloud, not even in her own mind. And yet…Greg could be dead somewhere, locked up somewhere, never returning, coming back tomorrow, or unable to truly love her in return. But that didn't change anything. Steeling her nerves, she did the last thing she should do.

She said it again.

"I love Greg. I'm so sorry, Oliver, but you need to know." And more than anything, she needed to say it. "I'm sorry if that hurts you." She was even sorrier for herself, knowing how much it hurt to love someone who was *trying* to love you back.

"I know you do," he said with a sad smile. "It's okay, Carrie. I appreciate your honesty."

Though he tried, he couldn't quite hide the pain in his eyes. She shouldn't have told him, but the honesty felt so liberating.

Clearing his throat, he looked around. "I better go now."

As he grabbed the door handle, the next round blurted out of her.

"The thing is, I kind of love you, too. I mean, I think I might, but I don't know for sure, and I really don't want to hurt you, and I know saying this probably does, but…"

Stop talking! she yelled at herself. But thinking of Greg forcing himself to love her, to not have been open with his motivations—whether consciously or not—hurt deeply. She couldn't do that to Oliver. She wouldn't force herself to love anyone or force them to love her back. Let the chips fall where they may, she would have full disclosure with everyone. Even if she lost both men.

Oliver's expression looked a few seconds shy of a heart attack. "You what?"

The guilt engulfed her. She told Richard she didn't want to hurt Oliver, yet she managed to say the two worst things within seconds: she loved Greg but she kind of loved Oliver, too. Despair and hope in the same breath.

"I count you as one of my dearest friends," she whispered. "I love you, but it's different than it is with Greg, and I don't know if that means anything, but...but..." The words stopped flowing, and her gaze dropped to her hands. "I just wanted you to know."

He didn't breathe for a full minute. When she stole a peek up at him, his eyes were wide in shock. He was only able to manage one word.

"Okay."

Silence smothered them. The words replayed over and over in her mind: *I love Greg, but I kind of love you, too.*

Was she insane?

One of them needed to break the silence, but neither could. That's why they needed Greg. Someone who could plow on and crack a joke, poke fun at their social ineptitude, or even bluntly force the conversation onward. In her mind, the ball was in Oliver's court, so she stared down at her clasped, trembling hands, waiting.

"Okay," Oliver whispered to himself. "Okay, okay, okay."

Another minute, and then he straightened. "I think you know...um..." He shifted. "I think you know how I feel about you, Carrie. I mean, I think you know. And I'm sorry because I can't *not* feel that way. I've tried, but it hasn't worked. But...I think you know."

She nodded, overwhelmed and humbled.

"Okay." He took another deep breath. "Okay, okay, okay."

He loved her, and she kind of loved him back. So where did that leave them? Turning, he opened his car door and got in. Apparently, that left them nowhere. But he didn't leave. He stared at CJ's garage for several heartbeats before he rolled down his window.

"See you soon?" he said with a timid smile.

She tried to smile back. "Okay."

Long after his car disappeared and the sun slipped behind the horizon, Carrie still stood on May's driveway. She had no idea when Oliver would be back or what that would mean for them when he returned. But regardless, she was glad she had said it. Full disclosure. Even if she lost both men.

"Okay," she whispered to the wind.

twenty-five

"Up! Get up! Hurry!"

Greg felt groggy until something—or rather, somebody—smacked his face. Hard.

With a grunt, Greg peeked an eye open. A dark shape hovered close to his spot on the top bunk. Lopez looked terrified like he usually did. But it was still dark in the long, sleeping barracks, and Greg was too tired to care why Lopez's anxiety had kicked in so early. His thoughts lingered with his dream. Burying his face in his pillow, he worked to return to the girl next door.

"Get up!" Lopez said, shaking him. "It's late!"

Greg glanced at the clock. 5:42 AM. He shot up without thinking and slammed his head on the ceiling. Stupid bunk. Rubbing his scalp, he said, "Why'd you let me sleep so long?"

"Be glad I woke you when I did," Lopez said. "Are you sick or something? It's usually you dragging me out of bed."

Greg didn't answer as he jumped down and threw on his green standard-issue shirt. His head pounded from the ceiling and lack of sleep—he got maybe two hours.

In the last few weeks he'd learned that the men slept soundly, having pushed their bodies past capacity during the day. They ran until they threw up, sat in class—or propaganda hour as he called it—until they couldn't think straight, and shot guns until they could split hairs. All with a constant stream of yelling that insisted they weren't fast enough, smart enough, or good enough to stay alive.

It wore the body out.

But last night Greg laid awake long after lights out, thoughts swirling from person to person: his mom, wondering how she was recovering; Oliver, wondering how Jamansky was torturing him; the clan, wondering if they'd already abandoned his plans; and Carrie, wondering—all too obsessively—if she was still Carrie Ashworth or if she was Mrs. Oliver Simmons yet. Or…if she'd kept Greg's hat.

Most of training had been a blur. His new sergeant hadn't said anything about his traitor's scars, although Greg got more than his fair share of beatings. Just last week, three guards cornered him, kicked him to bits, and called him rebel scum. He came out of it bruised but not broken. Typical. But his commanding officer never breathed a word of Greg's past, making Greg wonder if he even knew. Still, Greg kept his back and arm hidden as much as possible in the tight quarters.

In the space of a few weeks he learned that President Rigsby was a genius who must be worshipped, toilets were never clean enough, push-ups were never repentance enough, and the only acceptable response was, "Sir, yes, sir!" But most importantly, he learned that nightsticks to the head never got less painful.

Their sergeant hadn't told them when or where they would be assigned: as patrolmen on the home front or in the army to handle the "small incident" which gained momentum by the day. Greg even heard whispers that yellow and blue cardies were joining the illegals, hoping to undo everything Rigsby had destroyed in the last six years. Greg would give them all standing ovations if it wouldn't mean another nightstick to his head—or retribution for his family.

All in all, training could have been worse.

They got three full meals a day with plenty of protein so they could bulk up. A fine prospect considering half of them were starved wisps when they had arrived. Variety in the diet was also a nice change. Greg ate hamburger for the first time since college. Peanut butter, too. And every day he took a shower so hot it burned his skin. He'd learned the new laws—which they no longer labeled as 'emergency'—and when you could and couldn't perform a search on full-fledged citizens. All good stuff to know.

If he could get out.

Lopez eyed Greg as he pulled on his socks. "Where did you go last night?" Lopez asked.

"Don't know what you're talkin' about," Greg replied.

177

Grunting, Lopez smoothed his bed sheets. His cheek had swollen something ugly overnight after taking a hit yesterday when he'd fallen behind on a run. He was in his early thirties with two kids and a wife, a blue cardie from a municipality in Rockford who wanted to be there as much as Greg did. Lopez had good reason to be afraid. Greg wasn't in the mood for a morning beating either. He laced his heavy black boots in record time.

Around midnight last night, Greg had given up on sleep. Hugging the wall, he sneaked past forty snoring guys and down the stairwell. It was the first he'd wandered, the first he'd broken a rule. He didn't even know where he was headed until he got there. With methodical caution, he reached the only unguarded door to the outside, a kitchen door leading to the refuse bins.

Propping the door open with a spoon, he hopped a fence behind the garbage bins and spent the next few hours exploring the massive training grounds. Every section of electrical fence pulsed and hummed in the darkness. Even if he could overcome the electrical issue, the fence was ten feet high and looped with barbed wire. And behind the first fence was another just as daunting. He might as well be in a vault. But he hadn't given up. Crouching near the front gate, he watched the guards to see if they ever dozed off. They never even blinked let alone snoozed, downing coffee by the gallons to stay perfectly alert all night long.

Finally, Greg gave up. He sneaked back in and crawled into bed. He'd slept fitfully after that, all two hours of it. His eyes burned with exhaustion.

Lopez wasn't an idiot. He continued to watch Greg.

Once dressed, Greg made his upper bunk, straightened his things, and stood at attention in time for his commanding officer to come down the line at exactly 5:45AM.

"Good morning, ladies," the sergeant said. He'd greeted them the same way every morning. He wasn't particularly tall, but he had a massive chest and bulging arms. As he strolled down their sleeping barracks, he checked uniforms, overall appearances, and the tightness of their sheets.

He stopped in front of Greg, examining him with a dark eye. "I thought you were going to shave that beard, soldier."

"Sir, yes, sir," Greg said. He was the only one who hadn't shaved off the scragglies since arriving. He couldn't tell if his commanding officer liked that about him or not because every day the guy told him to shave, and every day Greg obediently said, "Sir, yes, sir," yet never so much as looked at a razor. So far, he hadn't been beaten for showing up scruffier than the day before.

So far.

But the sergeant eyed him longer than usual today. Long enough Greg squirmed in his standard-issued boots. Today might be the day of forced obedience—or abject humiliation.

Greg still hadn't decided which way to play the game during training: weak and dumb to fly under the radar, or smart and strong to climb the leadership ladder in the off chance they'd give him freedom—and money. So far, he'd done neither. He'd gone the quiet route, socializing with nobody, speaking only when required, and being the most obedient soldier in all of Illinois.

Except the beard.

He was the first to show up, the first to run, the first to finish the run, and the first to clean anything required—and then some. His body, already used to manual labor, adjusted quickly to the rigors of training and he stood straighter than any other guy. His sergeant could have no complaints about his behavior.

Except the beard.

Greg didn't blink as he held the sergeant's gaze. He didn't know the guy's name since they were only allowed to call him "Sir, yes, sir!" But he wore a perpetual scowl and his meaty arms looked like he could snap somebody's neck.

"We don't allow barbarians on our side!" the sergeant yelled in Greg's face. "That's the illegals' job. Are you trying to look like an illegal? Like an enemy to the United States of America?"

"Sir, no, sir!" Greg wasn't *trying* to look like anything but who he was.

"Then I'd suggest you shave, soldier."

"Sir, yes, sir!" Greg barked, knowing full well he wouldn't. He wasn't even planning to trim his beard.

His sergeant turned and shouted to the room. "Today we will break your bodies. Are you ready, ladies?"

As one, the room yelled, "Sir, yes, sir!"

The sergeant started to leave but then stopped. He backed up a few paces and eyed Greg again. When his hand slid to his nightstick, fear crawled down Greg's spine. Greg hated being a coward even on the tiniest level, but pain had a perfect memory. His head pounded in anticipation of the bruises he could feel coming.

"I want you in my office," the sergeant said. "Zero nine hundred hours."

Every eye left their rigid spots to stare at Greg. This was a change in the routine they had followed with exactness since they'd started. This was different, and in Greg's limited experience, different wasn't good. He could see the pity in their eyes. Maybe he'd lose the beard after all.

He was proud of himself that his voice didn't quiver when he answered, "Sir, yes, sir!"

twenty-six

The sergeant leaned against his desk, arms folded, eyeing Greg like a piece of rotting meat.

Two other men stood against the back wall. Greg had never seen them before, and his sergeant didn't introduce them. They weren't dressed like guards, plus they were too old and pudgy. Both wore uniforms: one with several medals on his chest, and the other in a uniform like Oliver's, only pure black. Greg guessed this was some sort of informal court marshal. Seemed over the top for not shaving. Or…maybe he hadn't been as sneaky last night as he thought.

Great.

Greg stood stiffly, feet shoulder-width apart, hands clasped behind his back. Sweat beaded on his forehead that had little to do with his rigorous morning drills. Over the last few weeks, a guy would disappear from time to time—usually those who fell behind or mouthed off. If the government sent them home, it was in a body bag. As long as they punished him and not his family, he could handle this. He could.

"What's the deal with the beard?" his sergeant finally asked.

"I just prefer beards, sir," Greg lied. In truth, he detested them. Too itchy and hot, especially this time of year. But he kept his gaze snapped straight ahead over the heads of the two other officers.

Bad mistake.

He saw the fist a moment too late. A moment too late and a moment too soon. That was the worst part, knowing what was coming and not being able to dodge, roll, and throw a punch in return. His sergeant's fist swung high and smashed Greg's bearded jaw.

Pain. Lights. The usual.

Vision swimming, Greg shook his head. *The dead can't help the living,* he chanted to himself. He wouldn't fight back.

He ran his tongue over his teeth to make sure he still had all of them. When the room stopped spinning, he planted his feet and stared straight ahead again. It's amazing they got anybody to do anything with regular beatings. At least this had been a fist. He detested nightsticks.

The other two men hadn't budged, but Greg's sergeant sat back against his desk, rubbing his fist. Greg hoped he'd broken a few fingers.

"Show them your marks," the sergeant said.

"Sir?" Greg said, not sure if he'd heard right or if his ears were still ringing from the blow.

"Shirt. Off. Now."

So this wasn't about last night or stupid beards. It was a thousand times worse.

His sergeant knew.

Greg eyed his nightstick and two guns, and then multiplied them to include the other men's weapons. Heart thumping, he unbuttoned his outer green shirt but left his tank on. His sergeant motioned for him to turn so they could see his shoulder. Greg obeyed, hoping that would be the end of it. A crossed out star with ID numbers on his upper arm was plenty.

The officer with the medals grunted. The officer in black just scowled.

"Now the rest," his sergeant said.

Greg gritted his teeth, pondering the value of playing by the rules if it still got you—and your loved ones—killed. But he shed his tank top.

"Turn."

Reluctantly, Greg faced the wall. He'd only seen the criss-crossed scars on his back a few times, having avoided mirrors since the incident, so he wasn't sure exactly what they saw. Whatever it was, everything went silent behind him.

Every muscle in Greg's body braced for the next blow, fully expecting it to be fatal. His mind raced with the million things he'd hoped to do before he died. That flower shop. Kissing Carrie. Telling his mom he loved her. Kissing Carrie again. A lot.

"Care to explain?" his sergeant said after a full minute.

Stalling, Greg said, "May I put my shirt back on first, sir?"

His sergeant nodded.

Greg took his time dressing, giving him a few seconds to figure out how honest to be. They already knew he was a traitor. The entire Raleigh incidence was probably in some file somewhere. His sergeant seemed like a no-nonsense kind of guy, so Greg answered honestly.

"I punched a patrolman, sir."

"Your foreman if I'm correct," his sergeant said.

Greg was grateful he'd gone the honest route. "Sir, yes, sir."

"Did he deserve it?" the older officer in black asked.

An interesting question. Yet as Greg remembered that day in the chicken factory, watching that older man drop, the rage simmered like it always did. Greg never saw if the guy recovered or if he ended up with his own set of scars.

"I wouldn't have punched him if he didn't, sir," Greg said tightly.

The sergeant didn't seem to appreciate that. "Insubordination is not tolerated in my unit!"

It wasn't tolerated in Raleigh either, which is why Greg had the scars he did.

The sergeant pushed away from the desk and circled Greg, spending a long time studying his beard. "Where have you been since you escaped Raleigh?"

"Hiding."

"And how did you get to Illinois?"

"I walked, sir."

The sergeant stopped in front of him. "You walked all the way from North Carolina to northern Illinois?"

"Sir, yes, sir."

His eyes narrowed. "How did you get your yellow card with that kind of record?"

Either Oliver forged fake numbers or Ashlee was too ditsy to check what was in his file. "I'm not real sure, sir."

"You're honest, Pierce. I like that. Continue to be and you might live to see another day." The sergeant stood back. "Why the beard now?"

"I just really like beards, sir," Greg said again.

The sergeant's eyes narrowed to dark slits. "You dare lie to me after I complimented your honesty? You didn't have a beard on your yellow card issued in March. That pathetic scruff you have now can't be more than a month old. So let me ask again, and you better think twice before you answer. Why the beard now?"

Greg scrambled for a response that wouldn't get him shot.

Smelling blood, his sergeant leaned close. "Why are you really here, Pierce? What are you after? How long have you been involved in the rebellion?"

That took Greg back. "Not a single day, sir. I hadn't even heard about it until just before I came to training."

"Then how do you know about the program?"

"What program, sir?"

"Do not lie to me!" the sergeant roared.

Greg saw a flash of black. The nightstick. Instinct took over. He ducked low, spun, and caught the nightstick mid-air, ripping it clean from his sergeant's hand. Then he whirled.

A voice screamed in his head. His mom. Carrie. The entire clan. If he fought back now, they'd pay the ultimate price.

He clutched the nightstick over his sergeant's cowering head. It took every ounce of willpower to keep from slamming it into that skull like it had been slammed into his countless times. Considering all the men who'd taken a beating with that very nightstick, considering Jamansky had nearly arrested him and his mom for doing their citizenly duty, considering President Rigsby and every other corrupt official who preyed on the American people, Greg had more than enough reason to lash out.

But he didn't.

His fingers released their grip. The nightstick dropped to the floor with a clank. Then Greg snapped back to attention, hands clasped behind his back, pretending like he hadn't disobeyed the unofficial order to hold still for beatings. Pretending like he hadn't stolen his commanding officer's weapon and threatened him with it. Pretending like he didn't know what the consequences would be.

"Oh, he's mine," the man in black said.

Greg didn't have time to process what that meant, because his sergeant jumped in front of him, veins bulging and eyes wild with rage. "You dare attack me?"

There was no good way to answer that, so Greg didn't.

His sergeant whipped out a different weapon. Something cold, hard, and metallic. He rammed a pistol under Greg's chin. "I'll ask one more time," he huffed, "and you will answer truthfully or you'll get a bullet through your brain. Where did you hear about the program?"

Terror flooded Greg's veins. Carnal, blinding terror.

"I don't know a thing about any programs, sir!" Greg shouted. "I swear."

He tried to ease back from the gun under his chin, but the sergeant just dug it further into his skin.

"What about your sick mother? Your grandparents? Will they back up your story if I bring them here for questioning, even under coercion?"

Coercion.

Greg felt the world drop out from under him. But only for a moment. Then his body filled with fury. If the sergeant brought his family here, if he even looked at them the wrong way, Greg would slit his throat.

The sergeant waited for a response.

Gun still digging into his chin, Greg's fists clenched and nostrils flared, but he told himself to breathe.

Just breathe.

"My family would answer the same, sir," he said through gritted teeth. "We know little about the rebellion. Our only goal, our only knowledge for six years, has been basic human survival."

"Then why the beard now?"

Greg had little chance of surviving this answer, but if he was dead anyway, he might as well go down with a fight.

He looked him directly in the eye. "'Cause I don't wanna be here. Looking like a squatter is a reminder to myself of who I am and"—his gut tightened as he thought of Jamansky—"who I refuse to become."

He steeled himself for the bullet. Would they send his body home or bury him in a mass grave? Would his mom forgive him for his insubordination, or would they punish her and his grandparents next? Another death on his shoulders. It seemed like no matter what he chose, they lost.

The sergeant glared at him for a long, tense minute. "I knew there was rebel blood in your veins. I could see it in your eyes." Yet the gun dropped enough Greg felt like he might have a chance.

The skin below his chin stung.

"There you have it," his sergeant said to the others. "A professed traitor with major attitude who pretends to abide by the rules while deep down he'd love to see us all cut to pieces."

The man with the medals held up his hands. "He's too much for me. I'm out."

With that, he left the room. That left the man in black. He was older than the sergeant by a decade, but not as sturdy. Yet something in his expression made him more intimidating. He studied Greg with open curiosity.

Standing tall, Greg finally realized what the two men represented. The army or the Patrol Unit, some program they assumed Greg had been vying for. Only the army just walked out on him.

The commander in black, the patrol leader, waved a hand in some signal.

The sergeant grinned and whispered in Greg's face, "Good riddance."

Greg closed his eyes.

Sorry, Ma.

But the sergeant returned the gun to its holster. Greg fought the urge to double over and heave gulps of air. Instead he stayed rigid and alert. Just because the gun was gone didn't mean he was out of hot water.

"Follow me, soldier," the commander in black said.

Greg's nerves tingled with a new foreboding. As much as he hadn't wanted to be in basic training, he had the premonition he didn't want to follow that guy out the door. But he trailed the older man down the long hallway and outside into the bright sun.

"Today is your lucky day, Pierce," the man said as they walked at a brisk pace. "You're being reassigned."

"May I ask to what group, sir?" Greg said.

"Mine."

Greg figured that much.

The training field faded behind him as they headed across the huge compound toward a square building he'd been told to never enter. For all he knew, he was being taken in for government testing and they'd turn him into a human pin cushion.

"What about my things?" Greg asked. Not that he had much back in the sleeping barracks. His UNC shirt had already been confiscated, and they could have everything else.

"You won't need your things where we're going."

The man in the black uniform stopped abruptly and turned, forcing Greg to stop, too.

"I'm taking a huge risk with you, Pierce. Prove yourself to me, and maybe, just maybe, you'll live past this training. But first, you have to prove that you deserve this."

Deserve what? Greg wanted to ask. Instead, he said, "Sir, yes, sir!"

twenty-seven

Oliver wasn't sure how he'd explain the extra miles to Jamansky, but he flew down I-88, grateful for an hour without partners.

He glanced at his odometer. The training compound in Naperville was farther than he remembered, which meant he'd underestimated the distance for Greg. Hopefully Greg made it on time. Hopefully Greg made it at all.

Slowing, Oliver pulled up beside the massive fence. He leaned against the steering wheel and watched the groups of trainees working out inside of the massive compound. Sergeants barked orders that carried across the hot, humid day. Oliver felt sorry for them.

He scanned the sea of green for a guy of medium height and short brown hair. Greg. After a minute, he gave up and drove to the front gate. A group of guards played poker inside the attached building. As soon as they saw him, one stood.

"Card," the guard said.

Oliver wasn't thrilled to hand his green card over knowing Jamansky could trace his activity, but he didn't have a choice.

After the guard swiped it, he handed it back. "What do you need?"

"I have a message to deliver for a trainee," Oliver said.

The huge guard grunted. "No mail in and no mail out."

"I'm aware of that, but this is urgent," Oliver said. "I was specifically ordered to deliver it here."

The guard eyed the small envelope in Oliver's hand. "What kind of message?"

"Not sure," Oliver said, hoping his feigned innocence would give the letter more clout. "I'm not privy to that kind of information."

"Give it to me."

Oliver expected as much and handed over the sealed envelope. The guard tore it open and pulled out the official Shelton Patrol paper. Oliver kept the message short, making it read more like a telegram than a letter:

Gregory Curtis Pierce:
M. passed.
Cond.

M could stand for *Mother* or *Mariah,* and *Cond.* could stand for a lot of things besides condolences. The whole thing was a stretch. Even if they delivered it, Greg still might not understand. But Oliver didn't dare write more knowing it would be seen. He hadn't signed it either.

"Alright," the guard said, folding up the paper. "We'll see what we can do."

That was better than Oliver hoped. "Thank you. I'll let my commander know."

As Oliver walked away, he glanced over his shoulder. The six guards went back to their game, opened envelope on the edge of their table.

———— ◆ ————

Carrie clutched the stick and drew another line in the dirt behind Terrell's house, this line perpendicular to Main Street. "This is Union, and I think this road is Baker. There's another neighborhood off to the left here," she said, adding another line, "but I'm not sure how it's shaped. I've just seen it from the main road."

Terrell took the stick and added a few roads of his own. "Jada's friend lived in a sub over there. It's pretty big."

"So is that a potential?" Richard asked.

"No," Terrell said. "If I remember right, a bunch of yellow cardies clumped into that neighborhood to stay close to town."

"Maybe we could include yellow card holders in our trading," Carrie said. "They might have better things to trade."

"And risk them turning us in for a reward? No thanks." Terrell drew a curvy line south of the abandoned golf course. "Beyond that, Oakwood is over this way. Or maybe more like this…"

They kept scratching what they could remember of Shelton in the dirt. By the time they finished, they had ten square feet of a detailed map. Not bad without any reference.

Richard stroked his graying goatee. "Where should we go first?"

"I know you don't think my mom's friend knows much about medical stuff," Carrie tried for the thousandth time, "but Gayle and I talked a few years ago and she might—"

"Is this a social visit or a business venture?" Terrell said pointedly.

"Business," Carrie relented.

What did he have against the Ferris Clan anyway? They'd interacted with them the most over the years. Something must have happened with Terrell and Frank, their leader. But she'd promised to let Terrell take the lead, so she clamped her mouth shut.

"Then I suggest we go to the biggest clan first," Terrell said. "That's Oakwood. What was their leader's name? Mitchell...?"

"Mitchell Cheng," Richard said. "Short, pushy guy."

Carrie nodded. He'd yelled at her once for dropping a box of sugar rations.

"So," Richard said, taking the stick, "if we start with Oakwood, which route do we take? Perhaps we should cut through the old cornfield behind the river. That would keep us out of the patrol areas."

"Yeah," Terrell said, "but that puts us next to the main road. Too close for my comfort."

"May I?" Carrie scratched a new path in the dirt. "My dad and I once cut through this other neighborhood on the way to Oakwood. I think that's the fastest." She shrugged. "Plus we could check that neighborhood we weren't sure about."

"That's good enough for a start." Terrell stood and brushed off his jeans. "I'll go grab the rifle."

Carrie's head snapped up. "You're bringing the rifle?"

"Yes. No discussion. I'll be back in a minute. Maybe two, since I better say goodbye to Jada and the kids in case we don't come back."

As Terrell trotted inside, Richard shook his head. "I've never seen him this nervous."

"Me neither," Carrie said, which worried her. Terrell knew more about this than anyone.

She followed Richard up around the side of the Dixon's house to wait in the front yard.

"How are you holding up?" she asked.

It took Richard a moment to answer, and when he did, he tried to smile. "Well enough. It's amazing how quickly I had become accustomed to having someone around the house again, but I suppose I'll adjust back to the quiet soon enough." He shrugged off the loneliness. "Thank you for all the meals, by the way. They aren't necessary, but they've been delicious." He put an arm around her shoulders. "I do know how to cook, though, so no more, alright?"

She shrugged without committing.

Richard took in their sprawling neighborhood. "How about you? Did you have a nice visit with Oliver?"

"Yeah, I guess." Although she still hadn't figured out what *okay* meant.

Carrie heard knocking on a window. Turning, she saw Little Jeffrey Kovach's face pressed to Terrell's front window. She broke into a wide smile. Little Jeffrey left the window and a second later, Terrell's front door flew open. The three year old came barreling straight for her, fists pumping. She scooped him up, twirled him around, and squeezed him close.

"How are you, Jeffrey?" she said. "I've missed you so much."

"Good."

He squirmed to be let down. She set him back on the grass and ruffled his dark curls, so much like Jenna's.

"Find any good bugs lately?" she asked.

He dug through his pocket and fished out several assorted bug skeletons: ladybugs, centipedes, and a few "doodlebugs" as Greg called them. Seeing all those crumbling bodies gave her the jitters, but she smiled anyway. "Wow. That's great. Why are you here?"

On cue, Terrell came outside with Jada and Sasha. Sasha carried Jonah on her hip and scowled. "Jeffrey, you're not supposed to go outside without telling me."

"Look!" Little Jeffrey said, pointing. "Carrie!"

Carrie nearly picked him up and hugged him again.

Sasha noticed his enthusiasm and softened. "I know. Hi, Carrie. Thank you for the water."

"What water?" Carrie asked, even as her cheeks went hot.

"My water buckets that are filled on my porch before I wake up. It's been very nice."

Embarrassed, Carrie could only nod. At least Sasha wasn't mad.

"I was thinking," Sasha added, "that I should use your well from now on since it's closer. You should, too, Jada. At least until your well is finished here."

Carrie tried to mask her shock. Was that Sasha's way of apologizing, of letting Carrie back in? Sasha was the mother hen of the marrieds. Jada looked equally surprised but nodded.

"Terrell says you're headed out right now," Sasha continued. "Think it will work?"

Carrie looked down at the boy whose only toys were dead bugs. Even if this new plan took years to set up—or to see benefits from—Little Jeffrey and the other kids deserved a better future. It was up to them to make it.

"I guess there's only one way to find out," Carrie said. "Are you ready, Terrell?"

Getting to Oakwood had been the easy part. They traipsed through thick woods and across an old cornfield that had once supplied their clan with grain but had since returned to its natural habitat. They passed two different neighborhoods, watching and creeping around the perimeter to check for signs of life—specifically gardens. When both turned up empty, they kept going.

It seemed like a different town Carrie had driven through with Oliver. Instead of seeing the outside shell of an egg, they explored the inside. Same place, different perspective. The only time Carrie felt nervous was when they crossed roads. It made her feel too exposed. But Terrell was overly cautious and had a sixth sense about where to go, when to hide, and when to enjoy the scenery.

But when they reached Oakwood, it became obvious Oakwood wasn't an option. Hiding in a small corner of the neighborhood, they could see that the yards, while far from perfect, were maintained, and children ran freely between houses, children dressed in clothes without rips. Children with shoes on their feet.

Either the government turned this neighborhood into green card housing, or yellow card holders had banded together on their own and found a safe place to live.

Either way, Terrell refused to find out. They turned and headed home.

twenty-eight

Greg held the .45 pistol with both hands and fired off a shot. Another hole busted through the center of the paper man's chest. The next station required him to lie flat on his stomach and shoot a moving target.

Loud background noise roared in his giant headphones, making it sound like he was in the midst of a battle zone. Only it wasn't cannons and gunfire. People screamed, women and children. Commander McCormick wanted more than great shooters. He wanted soldiers who could shoot straight in the middle of chaos. But the cries for help sounded real enough that Greg's nerves were strung tight. To calm himself, he envisioned Carrie bringing flowers to his mom, the two of them chatting like school girls. Then he found the small red dot in the paper man's chest and obliterated it.

He glanced at the next station, did a double-take, and laid right back on his stomach to perfect the current one. The paper man flew back and forth in front of him. Greg aimed over and over, enlarging the hole in the guy's chest as the war zone sounded in his ears.

It was crazy how quickly he'd become accustomed to technology again. Headphones. Real guns. Even small things like air-conditioning, ice cubes in his drinks, and the computer tracking his progress to the hundredth percent. He was up to 93.23% accuracy. Not bad considering the short time he'd tried this subcompact. All of his training until this unit had been with full assault rifles, but he liked pistols better and this Glock in particular—even better than his slingshot back home. It felt more natural in his hands.

Maybe too natural.

He still wasn't positive what this small unit was training for, but he and the other twelve guys hadn't mixed with anybody else in the compound. They all wore black like Commander McCormick. The uniforms looked heavy and bulky but felt lighter and more breathable than his former green garb. Technology again. Greg's hunch told him they were on the path to becoming patrolmen, and yet he doubted even Oliver had this kind of specialized training. They'd spent a full day on survival skills alone, starting fires with wet wood, collecting drinkable water, and finding shelter in a storm. Greg could have taught the classes better than the teacher. Why would a patrolman like Oliver need to know that?

Somebody kicked his leg softly. Commander McCormick.

Greg jumped to his feet, pulled off his safety goggles and earphones, and stood at attention. The world went silent until his ears adjusted to the normal sounds of the firing range.

"Why are you still on this station, Pierce?" Commander McCormick asked. "You're supposed to move on."

Greg stole a glance sideways. Oshan had finished the next station a few minutes ago, leaving it vacant. But when Greg caught sight of the target, his stomach churned again.

"I haven't perfected this one yet, sir."

Commander McCormick eyed the gaping hole in the paper man's chest. "We don't have time for perfection. Hit the target and move on. 80% accuracy is good enough. Understood?"

Without answering, Greg bolted his feet to the floor.

In his teen years, he'd played plenty of video games, even violent ones he shouldn't have, but the next station felt different. Wrong on many levels. The next paper human was half the size of this one and the undeniable shape of a child, maybe three years old. Like Little Jeffrey. The child was poised in the act of running after a ball in the yard.

All Greg could think was: *What's wrong with these people?*

He should have asked as much, but sadly, he liked Commander McCormick. He hadn't planned to. He wanted to hate everybody and everything here, but McCormick treated the thirteen of them like fellow comrades in arms, like they not only had strength but brains as well. If their group ever went to real combat, Greg figured they'd watch each other's backs, the commander included. McCormick had a sense of humor, reasonable expectations, and Greg even sensed a layer of contempt when he spoke about President Rigsby, as if McCormick thought the President was some punk kid running rogue. Greg liked that. He was the kind of commander Greg could envision following into battle.

But still…

A child?

The soldier behind Greg, a guy named Burke, tapped his gun impatiently, waiting for his turn to shoot the moving paper man.

Greg set his gun on the table. "I've found my weapon, sir. With my accuracy, I believe I've mastered target practice. I'm ready for the next task."

McCormick scowled. "You've not mastered it until you finish all of the stations."

The station after the child was a paper outline of a bird in flight whirling across the dark background. The targets were getting smaller and faster. The last one was probably a dime whizzing through the air. Greg could have hit them all with his slingshot, maybe even with this new Glock. But a kid? Unlike the outline of the adult male which had the circular target on the chest, this red dot was where the child's face would have been, directly between the eyes. It was beyond disturbing. Greg couldn't escape the picture of Little Jeffrey running from some patrolman someday. Would that patrolman really shoot him? What happened when that patrolman was Greg? Suddenly the station felt less like target practice and more like a test of loyalty or obedience. Probably both.

His new commander eyed him, waiting.

It's just paper, Greg told himself.

Stepping up to the station, he put the earphones back on, cringing against the sudden roaring chaos. He unfocused his eyes until the paper child was nothing more than a blur of white. Unfortunately, that made the red circle on the head disappear.

You're a Pierce, Carrie whispered from his memories. *They're fighters, remember?* She insisted he wouldn't forget who he was and that gave him the courage to change aim. The bullet slammed into the wood to the left of where the paper child's ear would have been.

McCormick folded his arms. "Again!" he shouted over the screams in Greg's ears.

Greg raised his Glock. This time he missed on the right side.

"Again!"

Greg went back to the first spot. Any closer and he could have pierced the child's ears.

"Pierce!" McCormick yelled, growing angry. "Again!"

By now, the other guys had stopped to see what caught the attention of their commander. Greg stood, arms straight in front of him, ready to give in. It was just paper. But within the chaos in his earphones, he heard children screaming. Something was seriously wrong with these people.

Out of the corner of his eye, he saw the next target. Turning slightly, he blew a hole through the bird's head. Stepping down the line, found the next target, a small moving dot as he predicted, and shot a hole through the center of that. Once finished, he set his gun down, took off his headphones, and stepped back.

"I'm done, sir."

"I am *not* amused," McCormick said, seething. "Why haven't you followed protocol?"

"I shot to the best of my ability, sir. I believe even within the required 80% accuracy."

Greg saw the tiniest flash of emotion. Respect maybe? At least he hoped the commander hated President Rigsby enough to loathe this part of his job. Whatever it was vanished in the blink of an eye.

"How stupid do you think I am, Pierce?" McCormick snapped. "Why did you purposely miss this target?"

Greg's mouth set in a firm line.

The muscles in the commander's neck tightened. "I asked you a question, soldier?"

"I didn't think it necessary, sir."

That was the wrong response. McCormick whirled and motioned to the next guy. "Burke, show him how it's done."

"Sir, yes, sir."

Burke had no problem shooting the paper child between the eyes and making Greg look like a fool. And deep down, Greg felt it.

Commander McCormick turned back to Greg. "Now you."

Greg stared at the target. *It's just paper. Just paper.*

And yet…

It wasn't.

He stood at strict attention. "I did the best I could, sir. If you have a complaint with my performance, maybe I shouldn't be in this group."

The second Greg said the words, he regretted them. This group was a thousand times better than the last. He felt like a person again and not just a robot trained for blind obedience—at least not until this moment. He didn't want to lose this group, this reasonable commander, but neither would he blast a hole through a child's head, regardless of the reason.

"Perhaps not," his commander said darkly. Then he moved. It was a tiny flick of the hand, but the message was delivered.

As one, Burke and three other guys jumped Greg. They got in a few punches before Greg reared back. He shook off one guy, dropped, kicked, and brought down another. Somebody got him in a headlock, and another guy punched his ribs. The world spun, his lungs burned, but Greg grabbed the guy's arm, lifted his legs, and kicked another. Then he dropped hard, swinging the guy behind him up and over his back, dropping him with a thud.

Burke came up, fists swinging, nose bleeding, when McCormick jumped between them.

"Enough!" McCormick shouted. "I said enough! Pierce, follow me. The rest of you, finish up!"

Breathing heavily, Greg stayed down, ready for the next attack. When it didn't come, he wiped his mouth, hand coming back red and bloody, and followed McCormick out of the firing range.

twenty-nine

Pulse roaring, Greg trailed McCormick into his office. He hadn't been beaten since he'd changed units a few weeks ago. The old bruises were gone, and he'd almost forgotten what they felt like. Now his left side was tender and throbbing. They better not have cracked a rib. His upper lip felt swollen and tasted bloody.

The second the commander entered his office, he whirled on him. "Why wouldn't you shoot that target?"

Greg refused to answer. McCormick already knew. Plus Greg couldn't forgive him for ordering that attack.

Swearing loudly, the commander yelled, "It's your job to obey me, regardless of the task!"

"By shooting a child?" Greg challenged.

"By obeying a direct order!"

"Technically, you never ordered me to shoot that child." He refused to add *sir* to the end of his sentence. Any respect he had for the commander fled three minutes ago. But based on the commander's reaction, he was surprised smoke didn't come out of his ears.

"You think you're cute, Pierce?" the commander hissed. "You think you're funny?"

Greg glared right back.

Swearing again, McCormick stormed over to his office door and slammed it shut, rattling the windows in the room. That was expected. But locking that same door, locking himself and Greg inside, wasn't. Greg felt suddenly uneasy. When McCormick sat on the corner of his desk to appraise Greg, his expression had done an about-face. In an instant, he almost looked friendly. Amused, even. And Greg went from uneasy to downright terrified.

"Take a seat, Pierce."

"Sir?" Greg said, too shocked to call him anything otherwise.

"Pull up a chair. I want to have a frank discussion with you, but you're far too defensive. So sit. Relax. Breathe."

McCormick motioned to a chair off to the side. Glancing at the locked door, Greg grabbed the chair. He sat rigidly in front of his older, pudgy commander, unsure how else to present himself. Sitting made him feel weak and unprepared for whatever was coming.

"How's the lip?" McCormick said.

Greg wouldn't have answered, but the commander gave him an arched look, daring him to stay silent.

"Fine," Greg said coolly.

"Where else did they get you?"

"I'm fine."

McCormick's expression hardened. "That's not what I asked."

"Ribs," Greg said.

"Any broken?"

Greg took a slow, deep breath. It hurt but not unbearably. "No."

"You mean, no, *sir?*"

Greg ground his teeth. "No, sir."

"Good."

Good? Greg wanted to yell. *You ordered the attack!*

His commander regarded him another moment before he clasped his hands on his lap. "Alright, Pierce. Here's the deal. You and I are not having this conversation. Anything we discuss will be kept to this office. Am I understood?"

Greg nodded warily.

"Good, because I think you're ready."

"Ready for what, sir?"

"The program."

Greg's eyes widened. The last he'd heard about a program was in his former sergeant's office, the first time he'd seen Commander McCormick. Greg still hadn't shaved, giving him a thick, dark beard which he loathed, but he figured this new program with thirteen guys was what his sergeant had meant. Apparently not.

"Which is…?" Greg asked.

"I'm going to make you one of my special operatives in a new program created by the federal government."

That didn't answer Greg's question, at least not completely. "And I'll be…?"

"You'll be doing clan infiltration."

It took Greg a second to understand. "You want me to spy? On illegals?"

"We prefer the term infiltration, but yes. This program is an experiment of sorts. You won't just be watching the illegals. You'll live as one of them. President Rigsby requested our unit take the lead on this since the civil dispute started in Chicago. I'm determined not to let him down."

Greg's mind raced. He would be living in a clan again, only trying to weed out the revolutionaries. He should dread this assignment, but he was too excited with possibilities.

"Do I get to choose which clans I infiltrate?" he asked.

"You really hate that beard, don't you?"

Greg dropped his hand, realizing he'd been scratching his beard. Recent nervous habit. "Yes, sir."

"Well, it works for where I want you, so you'll have to keep it a while longer. We've been running the program for a few months, but unfortunately, it hasn't gone well. I've already lost several men, so I'm changing my strategy."

"Lost?" Greg repeated.

McCormick nodded soberly. "I can't just have any person on this assignment. Since its inception, I've been searching for a specific kind of trainee. Yellow citizens who come in here don't know how to hide or blend in. Blue citizens are too beaten down to strike out on their own. Green citizens are arrogant and even more clueless about how to hide and survive—plus they're trigger happy. It would be like asking a pit bull to blend into a herd of deer.

"Ideally, I'd have someone who has lived as an illegal, who knows how to hide, blend in, and become invisible. But as you know, recruiting illegals is next to impossible. Any we manage to catch either swear allegiance to the rebellion or pretend not to and switch mid-assignment, causing more grief than they're worth. But I've found a way around that with you, Pierce. You've lived life as all types of citizens, am I correct?"

Greg was stuck on that one phrase: *I've found a way around that,* and Greg found a new reason to hate the commander. True illegals didn't have loved ones back home with names and addresses plastered on citizenship cards.

Greg was tempted not to answer, but they already knew his past. "I only lived as a blue cardie for a couple weeks in Raleigh, and I received my yellow card just a few months ago. The rest of the time, I've lived as an illegal. I haven't owned a green card yet."

"We're issuing you a green card tomorrow," McCormick said, "only it's better than typical green cards. It will grant you special clearance to things other green card citizens don't have. Speaking of which, if you ever run into any problems, or if you're accidentally arrested, flash your new card and it will alert me immediately."

It was coming too fast. Greg couldn't keep up.

McCormick clasped his hands again. "So this combination, this past of yours, puts you in a unique position that, quite frankly, I'm going to exploit. But..." His voice lowered and he leaned closer. "It's not just your position and your past experience that put you here. It's your view on the rebellion."

That he wanted to join it? That didn't make sense.

Greg thought back to the firing range and nodded slowly. It really was a test, only not the type he thought. And somehow he'd passed. "You didn't want me to shoot that paper kid."

McCormick eyed the locked door. "Again, this conversation never happened, Pierce. But no, I didn't. I agree with many things the President is doing to handle this civil dispute. However...there are a few areas in which the President and I disagree."

Greg nearly leapt from his chair. *I knew it!*

"I'd like to preserve freedom for our citizens, safety for all involved at the same time we preserve human dignity. So I need someone on this mission who still has a conscience, who won't go blasting through the illegals with a search and destroy mentality just because we're at war. The President might feel differently, but in my view, these rebels were American citizens six short years ago. We need to take out the worst of them, and then we'll be able to restore peace."

Preserve human dignity, Greg repeated to himself. Had anybody in Rigsby's regime ever uttered those words?

He caught himself returning to the dangerous territory of liking Commander McCormick.

"So I've been waiting for someone with the skills, strength, and background I need," McCormick continued. "But more importantly, I've been searching for someone who knows when enough is enough. I've trained over fifty men. Do you know how many refused station number four?"

Greg shrugged.

"You," McCormick said. "Others initially refused, but the second I pressed, they gave in."

Greg almost had, too. Now he was glad he hadn't.

Maybe.

"What will my duties be, sir?" Greg asked.

"Get in, assess the situation, find out how involved each clan is in the rebellion, and then report back to me. We'll take it from there."

Greg would be an informant. Not great, but not horrible either. It beat serving on the front lines where he'd have to kill illegals, rebel or not, adult or not.

McCormick stood and started pacing his office. "The fact that you've been branded a traitor will only add to your credibility. It's perfect, really. If any rebels suspect you're one of us, flash your scars and let them know how much you hate us. You wear your hatred like a badge. They won't suspect a thing."

A pit formed in Greg's stomach. The commander really was going to exploit his past. Get in, chant some anti-Rigsby rhetoric, flash a scar or two, and single-handedly bring down the rebellion. Nobody would suspect a thing. President Rigsby would probably reward Greg for it, too. With little effort, Greg could propel himself up the political ladder, earning money, titles, and power.

He scratched his beard to remind himself of who he was and what he refused to become. They branded him for a reason. He wanted nothing more than for the new regime to topple until it was ashes. There had to be a way to work this new position in the rebellion's favor. Knowing he'd be the one to decide which clans were harmless or not, which were targeted or not, meant he could sway things whichever way he wanted. He just had to do it in a way which wouldn't get his family killed.

Up until this point, he'd had one goal in life: save his loved ones.

Now he had two.

One way or another, he had to save the rebellion.

As he considered this, his fat lip pulsed, reminding him of the practice room. His eyes snapped up. "With all due respect, sir, if you've been waiting for somebody to refuse that station, why give the order for the attack?"

McCormick smiled. "Your fellow comrades are heading to positions of authority. You didn't follow an order. They needed to see it punished. As far as they're concerned, you're in here getting a verbal lashing. Officially I'm placing you on probation with the understanding that one more issue will land you in prison. That way, when I send you on this mission, they'll think you've been locked away for good."

Greg nodded slowly. So not even McCormick's guys would know there were spies, ensuring less chance of exposure.

"What happens to the others once they finish training, sir?" he asked. The ones who shot the fake three year old.

"They'll become federal patrolmen," McCormick said. "Technically, that will be your title, too, just assigned under this special operations umbrella."

Greg eyed the commander's black uniform. "And...what's the difference between federal patrolmen and regular ones?"

"So many questions," McCormick said. He paused as if debating how much to say. "The short answer is that federal patrolmen aren't restricted to laws the same way regular ones are. They aren't restricted to Illinois either. They go wherever Rigsby needs them. You walked from Raleigh to Illinois, giving you experience in several states. I'm sure Rigsby will exploit that soon enough, but not until I'm through with you. For this particular assignment, you'll stay in this area. We believe the center of activity is coming from a group of clans on the southern outskirts of West Chicago, ten or so miles north of here."

North.

Not quite northwest, but close enough that he'd already hatched a plan. If there was any wiggle room in this new assignment, he'd sneak home and check on his mom, maybe see Carrie, and warn his own clan of government spies.

"And if I refuse this assignment?" Greg asked.

McCormick grabbed a file from the desk with Greg's name typed across the top. He didn't have to open it for Greg to understand the threat. It held the names and information about his family. "You won't."

"Thank you for the opportunity, sir," Greg said numbly.

"Don't thank me yet. I'm counting on you to be smarter than the others who haven't made it. This isn't going to be easy. Don't let me down and don't come back in a body bag."

Greg nodded. "How soon do I leave?"

"You and your partner will leave on—"

"Partner?" Greg cut in. "Sir, I can handle this on my own."

McCormick gave a mirthless laugh. "You might be the perfect fit, but I don't trust you, Pierce. Not one bit. I'm guessing a guy like you could turn invisible and disappear on me in a flash—or worse, undermine everything we're doing. No. You'll have a partner every second of every day. Your partner, Lieutenant Ryan, is one hundred percent loyal to me and this cause. The two of you will be virtually linked at the hip, so don't get any ideas."

Greg felt his hopes plummet.

How could he swing things in a clan's favor with some guy following his every move? How could he sneak home and warn everybody?

"Lieutenant Ryan has infiltrated other clans with great success," McCormick said. "You're in good hands. I'll inform Ryan that we've spoken, and the two of you can work out the details with the goal of leaving by the end of the week. You'll be living off the land, traveling with little more than the clothes on your back, but I have a feeling you're more comfortable that way. Once you and Ryan sketch out a rough idea of how to attack this thing, get back to me for final orders." He reached out to shake Greg's hand. "I expect big things from you, Pierce. If we don't nip this skirmish in the bud, we could be on the brink of a second civil war. You'll be doing your country a great service."

That was what he was afraid of. "Sir, yes, sir."

"Good. Now go back to your quarters with your tail between your legs. You've been severely chastised for disobeying a direct order."

It wasn't hard for Greg to look downtrodden as he left. Until he met this Ryan guy, he had no way of knowing what he was in for or if he was about to do exactly what McCormick hoped he would:

Sway the war in Rigsby's favor.

thirty

Oliver hovered over the map of Shelton with his two young partners, explaining why he had organized the sweeps like he had. The map was laminated so they could mark days and times with erasable marker, but no matter how they mapped out next week's schedule, it was too much area to cover, even if they worked eighteen-hour days.

"What if we fit the northern part of Sugar Grove in on the same day as Shelton?" Oliver said. "Then we don't have to…"

He trailed off as David Jamansky walked in.

"What's going on here?" Jamansky said, eyeing the maps. "Why are all of you standing around? Get to work!"

Oliver gripped the marker. After everything, it was all Oliver could do to speak civilly to the chief. Oliver was older than Jamansky by eight years. He should be the commanding officer, not the other way around.

"We're just going over our areas, chief," Portman said, "calendaring our next week."

Jamansky pointed out a spot in Sugar Grove. "Those are my old areas. I had them whipped into shape, so you better take good care of them."

Oliver nodded. His whole body felt on fire with a need for revenge. It had been this way for a month. He couldn't endure much more.

Jamansky pointed to a far corner of Shelton. "When is this section being patrolled?"

"That's what we're trying to figure out, sir," Bushing said. "So far there aren't enough hours to—"

"No sections are to be ignored!" Jamansky snapped. "Do you have any idea what's happening in the country right now?"

Bushing ducked his chin. "Sorry, sir. Yes, sir."

Oliver kept a firm grip on that marker, breathing deeply to keep from punching his arrogant boss. There had to be a way to extort that arrogance. Thinking, Oliver searched the map, thinking. Jamansky hated him almost as much as he hated Jamansky. But Jamansky hated Chief Dario even more. Maybe even enough to…

"Sir," Oliver said, "Portman and Bushing thought that maybe we should split up." His partners' heads snapped up with terror at being mentioned, but Oliver plowed on. "They say we could cover twice the area in the same amount of time, but…but I think it's too dangerous. Chief Dario said the three of us should stay together to stay safe. He gave me explicit orders never to work alone again."

"Safe?" Jamansky said. "Are you a sissy girl, Simmons? What happened to you doing patrols on your own?"

"It's just that with everything going on," Oliver said, keeping his eyes downcast while his insides jumped with possibility, "it's not safe for me to be alone."

Jamansky leaned across the table and yelled in his face. "This is no time for cowards, Simmons!"

"Sir, yes, sir," Oliver said softly.

"Portman, Bushing," Jamansky barked, "from now on you two are together. Simmons, you work alone. No more complaining about hours or covering all of the sections. I expect your jobs to be done with accuracy, like I did mine. Am I understood?"

Outwardly, Oliver worked to look dejected while inside he did a back flip. He was alone again.

"What about a car?" Portman asked. "We all share one right now."

"Not my problem," Jamansky said. "Use Simmons' car when he's off duty or walk to your patrols for all I care. Just figure it out."

That might complicate things, but Oliver was too thrilled to let it change his mood.

He'd won.

"Portman and Bushing," Jamansky said, tracing a line on the map, "you now have the northern quadrant. Simmons, you take the southern."

In a flash, Oliver's joy disappeared. Shelton was in the northern quadrant. Logan Pond. Carrie. Oliver couldn't lose Shelton.

Think. Think!

Using the same strategy, Oliver moved around the table and lowered his voice. "Thank you, chief. I've had that upper quadrant for the last six years. It's deader than dead. I'm anxious to try a new section. Maybe I'll actually reach my quotas now."

Jamansky turned slowly, eyeing him through dark slits. "Unbelievable. How did you get a badge?" Without waiting for an answer, Jamansky went back to the map. "It seems Simmons here has been slacking in his duties. Portman and Bushing, you're on the southern quadrant. Simmons, that northern section better become the best-behaved area in all of Illinois. I better not hear of one more rebel slipping through your fingers. Am I understood?"

Oliver bit the insides of his cheeks to keep from smiling. Jamansky was a fool. A complete and arrogant fool.

"Sir, yes, sir," he said.

———————— ◆ ————————

Amber hated to admit it, but she missed Braden. Since the cemetery, she'd been giving him the cold shoulder, waiting for him to apologize. But he hadn't come, and lately it felt like he was the one giving her the cold shoulder and not the other way around. The longer it went, the more she missed him.

"I'm just going to find him," Amber told Carrie.

Carrie cracked an egg into the bowl. "Okay, but maybe you should think before you go storming over there. It sounds like you have some apologizing to do."

"Me?" Amber cried. "I'm the one who's mad, remember?"

"Yes, but you said yourself you're not entirely sure why you're mad. Plus, sometimes you aren't exactly…well…" Carrie cracked another egg.

"Perfect?" Amber offered. Because she already knew that.

"I was going to say *nice.*"

Amber about burst a vein. "Excuse me?"

"You can be kind of bossy," Carrie amended quickly. "At least sometimes. Maybe you should focus on being nice."

Amber huffed. She hadn't been bossy in the cemetery. She'd been right. Braden was a fool to want to volunteer. Someone had to tell him.

But…she really did miss him.

"Fine. Whatever," she said. "I'll be the bigger person and apologize first." Then she'd prove how mature she was.

She found Lindsey first, delivering milk to Sasha and the little boys. But when Amber asked where Braden was, Lindsey snapped at her.

"Why should I tell you? You only talk to me if you want to know where Braden is," Lindsey said. "I thought we were best friends, but I guess not. Find him yourself."

Amber's initial response was to fight back, but she thought about what Carrie said. *Sometimes you aren't exactly...nice.*

"I'm sorry, Linds," Amber said. "I'll be better, I promise. But right now I really need to talk to Braden. Do you know where he is? Please? Please, please, please? I'll file your nails and cut your hair and rub your—

Lindsey held up her hands. "Alright. He's chopping wood behind Kovach's, but you better be nice to him." Another glare. "He's been in a bad mood lately."

Again with the nice?

As Amber walked, her temper kept creeping up. Braden was in a bad mood?

Be nice, be nice, be nice, she told herself.

She crept around the side of Kovach's house and spotted Braden, chopping wood. Gratefully he was alone. His shirt was off, and his tanned, muscled back sparkled with sweat in the sunshine. He wasn't wearing his bracelet, but then again, neither was she.

"Hi, Braden," Amber called nicely.

He startled and spun around.

"Oh. Hey, Amber," he said. Then he turned back and swung the ax again.

She wanted to sidle up next to him, get a better look at him without a shirt, see his crooked smile, his turquoise eyes, and a hundred other things, but she didn't dare with that swinging weapon.

Be nice.

"Want some help?" she offered. Not that she knew anything about chopping wood, but if he wanted to teach her...

"No, thanks. I got it."

He shimmied another piece of wood onto the chopping block and took another swing. Hard and violent. Splinters splayed everywhere. Turning the wood, he swung again, harder.

The silence stretched between them, more oppressive than the summer sun.

"So…" she said, "how have you been?"

"Fine. You?" Another swing.

Tears sprang to her eyes. *Horrible. Depressed. Lonely.* "Fine," she lied.

"Good."

He didn't sound mad at her, but neither did he sound madly in love. He sounded like a guy who couldn't care less where she was or how she felt. Just another clansman.

He worked another minute before she couldn't stand it any longer.

"I don't know what I did to make you so mad," she blurted, "but I'm sorry. I know I can be a pain, and bossy, and a jerk, so I apologize. I just want things to go back to how they were. I miss you."

"I'm not mad," he said, still working.

Then why wouldn't he look at her?

She watched his tanned, sweaty back, waiting for more explanation. It didn't take long to know it wasn't coming. After another minute, she backed up and silently left the Kovach's backyard.

Braden didn't even notice her leave.

Or the tears streaming down her cheeks.

thirty-one

Burke and the others wanted to 'cheer' Greg up that night. Ironic considering they'd been the ones to give him the bruises. Of course, Burke had a nasty gash of his own from Greg's kick, so Burke called it even. Greg called it idiotic. But he let them drag him out of the barracks, across the compound toward a small building Greg hadn't noticed before. The inside was poorly lit with loud music, the smell of liquor, and scantily clad women entertaining officers. Greg started to turn around, but Burke grabbed his arm.

"You need this," Burke said, dragging Greg toward the bar. "We all do."

"No, I need to sleep," Greg said. And to think. He also needed to figure out how to infiltrate a clan without getting shot, how to not jeopardize the rebellion, and how to sneak home with a partner attached to his hip.

"Come on. It's not that late. You need to lighten..." Burke trailed off as a leggy blonde waltzed past, hips moving in time to the music. She gave Burke a seductive wave, which made him sigh. "Why didn't they tell us about this place before?"

Greg grunted angrily. Two minutes of pounding music and he had a migraine. But he sat at the bar and ordered a simple drink, determined to be quick and get back. Burke sat next to him, but the other guys ditched them for better prospects.

Greg swirled the ice in his dark drink, loving how it clinked in his glass. Nobody else appreciated ice like he did, or how each bubble of carbonation floated to the surface. He took a sip and wrinkled his nose.

The drink was more sugary than he remembered. It also burned his throat more than something so benign should. Then again, all he'd had to drink since the Collapse was water and goat's milk. This was—

"Too strong?" a woman said, sitting on the stool next to him.

His gaze flickered sideways. The dark-haired woman wore a low cut dress with curves showing everywhere. She also wore way too much makeup. He swirled his ice again without answering.

She grabbed his glass.

"Hey!" Greg said.

Holding it close to her nose, she sniffed and then took a sip. "Just double checking," she said, handing it back.

Her red lip prints lined the rim of his glass, making him wonder why he'd let Burke talk him into coming. Greg set his glass aside and motioned to the bartender. "Another Coke?"

"Get into a fight today, handsome?" the dark-haired woman asked over the blare of the music.

Burke snorted a laugh and answered for Greg. "You could say that. This guy decided he was too good for training, so we convinced him otherwise."

The woman appraised Greg's bruised cheek. "Maybe you should have hit them back."

Again, Greg refused to answer so Burke did.

"How do you think I got this?" Burke said, turning to show her the other side of his face.

"Nice," the woman said with a laugh. She nudged Greg. "I like you already."

Unamused, Greg finally looked at her full on. She was older than him, maybe early thirties. She wore four-inch heels and a tight black skirt which showed too much of her long legs. She had far too much confidence for his taste, not to mention the ease of somebody who'd tossed back a few too many drinks. One of her dark brows rose, almost in an invitation, fully aware of his scrutiny.

Greg turned back. The bartender handed him another Coke. This time the carbonation didn't burn so badly when Greg took a sip.

"Recovering alcoholic?" the woman asked. "Going dry? What's the story on the soda?"

No story. He just wanted a clear head, and the extra sugar, caffeine, and carbonation were plenty. Plus, his dad had been an alcoholic. So maybe there was a story, but she'd never hear it.

She leaned forward to speak to Burke, dark, curly hair spilling over the counter in front of Greg. "Your friend isn't very chatty, is he? Maybe we should convince him to order a real drink. Get him to loosen up so we can get acquainted."

Make it stop, Greg begged silently.

Times like these made him miss Carrie and her un-pushy, un-pretentious personality. Burke was plenty single. Kinda ugly, but more than willing to give this woman whatever she wanted—and then some.

"Good luck. I already tried," Burke said. "Believe me, this guy is wound too tight."

"Is he married?" she asked.

Burke eyed Greg's left hand. "Don't think so."

"Engaged? Not into girls?" She frowned. "I usually have better luck than this."

Greg pushed back from the bar. "I'm gonna turn in for the night," he said to Burke. Then he worked his way through the pulsing crowd.

He didn't realize the woman had followed him until he was nearly outside. She grabbed the corner of his black uniform, pulling him to a stop.

"Hey," she said, "I didn't mean to scare you away. I just think you and I should be friends. What's your name?"

"Not interested," Greg said, trying to step around her.

She laughed but blocked the door. "You're feisty. I like that. But I have a little secret for you." She leaned closer, close enough he could smell the alcohol on her breath. "I already know your name, Gregory Curtis Pierce."

Great. He glared at Burke through the crowd.

"Excuse me," he said, sidestepping. She matched his step, making it impossible to get past without plowing her over, which he was about ready to do.

"I'm not letting you leave yet, Gregory Curtis Pierce," she said. "Don't you even want to know my name? After all, I'm your new wife."

The poor woman was too drunk to know which way was up. Greg worked to keep his voice calm. "In case you missed the other fifty hints, I'm not interested."

With that, he double-backed for the bar, hoping for another exit. He didn't even make it two steps before somebody grabbed his arm and spun him around. Hard.

"That's no way to treat your new partner, is it?" the woman said darkly, keeping a surprisingly firm grip on his arm.

"Partner?" Greg stiffened. "What do you mean?"

Dropping his arm, she held out her hand with a returning smile. "I'm Isabel, your new partner. Commander McCormick told me I could find you here."

"You're who?"

"Lieutenant Isabel Ryan. McCormick said he told you about me, or has that Coke already gone to your head?" she added with a wink.

Ryan.

Isabel Ryan.

"Oh, no," Greg said. "No way." He wasn't going anywhere with that woman, let alone living as partners for who knew how long.

"Out of my way," he said again, forcing his way past her.

He stormed outside into the humid evening and straight across the grounds to the commander's office. Isabel followed, four-inch heels clicking on the pavement. Greg threw open McCormick's door without knocking.

"This," Greg said, pointing back at Isabel, "is not what I agreed to."

His commander eyed Isabel in her tiny getup. "You're welcome."

Greg shook his head. "I'm not doin' this. I'm not. Find yourself another puppet."

He whirled around to leave, but Isabel leaned against the door, long tan legs crossed at the ankles. "Come on, Gregory Curtis Pierce," she purred. "That's no way to treat your new wife."

Wife. So that wasn't some drunken detail?

Greg spun back to McCormick. "Either I go alone or you find somebody else."

"You're not going alone," McCormick said, setting his paperwork aside, "and my niece is the best we've got."

"Niece?" The blows kept coming. The two looked nothing alike. Isabel had a middle-eastern darker look while McCormick was whiter than Canadian-white.

McCormick's niece.

No wonder why he trusted her.

"With all due respect, sir," Greg started, "I—"

"—don't have a choice. She's your tether, Pierce," McCormick said pointedly. "Your very firm handcuffs. You make one wrong move, and I'll know within seconds."

"Probably faster," Isabel said, winking at Greg again.

"However," McCormick added, "with the two of you married and her pregnant, you should be able to garner enough sympathy to weasel into any clan. She'll be injured as well. Maybe you could bruise her up a little to make it convincing."

Married and pregnant. And bruised, no less.

Greg's anger kicked up a notch, but instead of flying off the handle which only caused issues, he took a deep breath and chose a rational approach. "Sir, may I speak with you alone?"

"No."

"Fine. I wish no disrespect to your niece, but she looks like a tramp and smells like a spy. She's not illegal clan material."

"Should I take that as a compliment?" Isabel said. "Handsome here knows how I smell."

"Everybody does!" Greg snapped. "Your hair reeks of shampoo, your skin smells of government soap, your nails are perfectly clean, and your hands"—he stormed over and picked up one to show her uncle—"have no calluses. Plus you weigh too much."

For the first time, anger flushed Isabel's face. She yanked free. "You think I'm fat?"

"You're healthy, which is my point." Greg turned back. "She doesn't look like somebody who spent the last six years on rotten corn and stale potatoes. She looks like a spy, sir. Are you trying to get me—us—killed?"

The commander rose slowly, eyes small slits of fury. "Do you really think I'm that inept, you arrogant SOB? Lieutenant Ryan has infiltrated four clans already and done so without detection. She can out-shoot you, outrun you, and out-perform you in every other way, including blending into these clans. Believe me, she doesn't always look this good."

"Excuse me!" Isabel cried in dismay.

Greg ignored her, but the fact that she'd already infiltrated four clans eased his anxiety. Some. But only for a second.

"Sir," Greg said, "it's still a huge risk. This whole thing is just a—"

"Show him your mark," McCormick interrupted.

"What?" Greg said.

"Show him," McCormick said to her.

With a shrug, Isabel raised the sleeve of her tiny black getup, wincing as she did so. Her upper arm and shoulder were red and inflamed, burned in the shape of a crossed-out star.

"Pretty, huh?" Isabel said, stroking it. "I hear you have a matching one. Hurts like mad, but I guess this makes us twins."

Even after she dropped her sleeve, Greg continued to stare at her arm, horrified. That scar was permanent.

He stepped back from both of them. "What is wrong with you people?"

"It was her idea. Brave girl." McCormick crossed the room and circled his niece like a vulture. "It will come in handy, making it look like you were marked together."

For the first time in Greg's life, he was at a loss for words.

"As I said, she's far more qualified than you are, Pierce, so I'd suggest you start groveling before she levels you and I assign you to shovel manure for the rest of your life." McCormick stopped in front of Greg, eyes set in a hard challenge. "Or do I need to bring in your sick mother to help you remember your manners?"

Isabel walked forward. "No groveling necessary, Uncle Charlie. Greg is just concerned for my safety. It's kind of cute, actually." She slid her arm into Greg's. "We make an excellent couple, don't we?"

A couple. Living together in whatever circumstances these clans thrust on them. Sharing tents, blankets, and who knew what else.

The shock wore off, and Greg yanked free of her grasp. "Fine," he said. "Go run a couple miles without showering, dig some holes to ruin those nails, climb a rope for some decent calluses, yellow your teeth—or better yet, knock out a few—lose twenty pounds and maybe some hair, and *then* I'll agree to this insanity."

Isabel crossed her fingers over her cleavage. "I swear to be sufficiently disgusting when we leave. Who knows? You might even like me better that way." Her dark eyes softened in an attempt to be seductive.

"She's better than she pretends to be," McCormick said, reading Greg's mind.

Isabel straightened, looking suddenly business-like. "*She* is standing right here, so if you men are done playing, it's time to work. We have paperwork to fill out, immunizations to get, maps to scour, and supplies to pack."

"Pack?" Greg said in exasperation. "Need I remind you that we can't exactly waltz into these clans with suitcases and a valet? The only thing I came with was my lucky shirt which was confiscated the second I walked through the gate. You've got no idea what it's like to live as a squatter. Commander, you brought me here 'cause you said I know how illegals live, and I'm tellin' you that this…" Greg motioned to Isabel, head to four-inch-heels, "will not work!"

Isabel cocked her head. "You have a lucky shirt?"

Greg threw his hands in the air. "I'm done. I'm done!"

"Now wait. Did it look like"—Isabel crossed the room and grabbed something from under her uncle's desk—"this?"

Greg spotted the light blue wad. He lunged. "Give me that."

Isabel whipped out a small gun from somewhere hidden in her tight getup and gave him a wicked grin. "Say please."

Greg slid to a stop, staring into the end of her small pistol, calculating just how crazy this dark-haired chick was.

McCormick rubbed the bridge of his nose. "Pierce, if I give you back your lucky shirt, will you shut your trap and cooperate? There can't be any room for mistakes. This polar ice cap between you two has to melt and it has to melt fast or you'll both wind up dead."

"Which will it be, honey buns?" Isabel said, waving his shirt in one hand and her gun in the other. "Come on. You could be really, really rich."

Rich. Greg whirled. "How much do I get paid?"

McCormick scowled. "You get paid in years added onto your life."

"Come on, Uncle Charlie," Isabel said. "Tell him."

McCormick folded his arms over his round stomach. "You'll get paid for every mission—*after* each mission—the equivalent of four month's salary for a normal patrolman. I'm hoping you'll be in each clan less than two weeks, so it's decent money."

That was more than decent. Greg could start sending money back. His mom could finally see a doctor. The clan wouldn't starve. They might even be able to buy another home.

"Fine," Greg said. "Give me my shirt."

thirty-two

"Oliver's here," Terrell said, looking up from their dirt map.

"On a Monday?" Carrie stopped to listen for his car. She'd seen him twice since their *talk*, but only on Thursday mornings and he'd stayed two minutes each time. Their conversations were more awkward than ever. But now it seemed like he'd taken her suggestion to stop by another time. Either that or something had happened.

News from Greg?

Her heart jumped, and she brushed the dirt from her hands. "I better go see what he wants."

"We'll meet outside of CJ's first thing," Richard said. "I have a good feeling about the Watercrest Clan."

Carrie hurried around the side of Terrell's house. Even with her hair pulled up, sweat beaded up on the back of her neck from the long, hot day in the garden. She was in no state to see anyone.

Oliver's patrol car sat in her driveway, but he wasn't at her front door. He was still sitting in his car. She waved as she jogged down the sidewalk, but he didn't see her. When she reached the driveway, she knocked on his car window. He jumped a foot. Then he scrambled to shove some papers in the glove box.

"Hi, Carrie," he said, rolling down his window. "I didn't see you."

The car's air conditioning blew out the window toward her. It felt heavenly. "Sorry. I didn't mean to startle you," she said.

"You didn't. I mean, you did, but it's fine." He brushed down his beige tie. "Sorry. I was just looking at something."

"No problem. How are you?"

"I'm good. Really good—really *well*. I mean, I'm doing well."

Are you sure? she nearly asked, even more concerned he'd shown up on a Monday night. He seemed extra nervous. His thumb tapped his steering wheel at a racehorse pace.

"Did you..." Her gut clenched for the worst. "Did you hear anything on Greg's note?"

"No, but I didn't expect to."

That was better than bad news, but she still worried about how Greg had reacted to his mom's death in a place where he couldn't do anything about it.

She waited, wondering what had him so preoccupied.

"I don't have partners anymore," Oliver said.

"What? That's wonderful! Wait, is it wonderful?"

A smile lit his small gray eyes. "Yes."

No more partners. She couldn't believe it.

"What happened?" she asked. It seemed like there was more work than ever for patrolmen since every few days she spotted new fires.

"My boss hates me," he said simply.

A strange reply. She couldn't imagine anyone hating Oliver. But when no further explanation came, she returned his smile. "Well, I'm glad you're free now."

His brows shot up. "Free?"

"Um...partner-less?"

"Free," he echoed.

He stared straight ahead at her garage door, thumb tapping the wheel again. Each second of him avoiding her felt like an hour. He didn't have partners, but he was obviously stressed about something.

"Carrie," he said after a minute, "I was wondering if, uh..."

His gaze snapped back to her garage door. More thumb tapping—this time with both thumbs. Oliver wasn't the type she could pressure into talking, so she kept waiting. The cold air blew out his window, and she stood as close as she dared, stomach clenched for the worst. Whatever it was, it wasn't good.

Finally, he looked up at her. "Do you eat?"

"Do I eat?"

He winced. "Sorry. I mean, do you *like* to eat? You know, dinner?" With a huff, he looked around. "Never mind. I'll see you later."

Like a light bulb turning on, she understood. Oliver didn't have bad news. He was asking her out. Her first reaction was to turn him down, but he deserved better. Oliver loved her, and Greg was *trying* to love her.

"Actually," she said quickly, "I love to eat."

"You do?"

She smiled. "Yeah."

It took another moment of him staring straight ahead—she could practically see him talking himself into it—before it blurted out of him.

"Would you like to go to dinner with me, Carrie? I know I have no business asking you, but I would really like you to eat with me. I understand if you want to say no, and I won't mind, but if you want to, would you mind coming with me? In the car? To a restaurant to eat"— his face scrunched as if in actual pain—"sometime?"

Oliver Simmons was adorable if nothing else. The poor guy was petrified, sweating bullets even though he sat in perfect air conditioning. He was waiting for a rejection which, of course, she wouldn't give.

"I'd love to," she said.

The color drained from his face. "You would?"

"Yes." But then reality hit her upside the head. "Except I can't go to a restaurant. It's too public. Can I make you dinner here instead?"

"No, no, no. I've got it all worked out. There's a tiny restaurant far from here where patrolmen usually don't go. Plus," he glanced at the glove box, "I still have that thing, those papers from before that would keep you safe. That is…if you want to."

Was that what he'd been staring at? Her travel papers?

Obviously he knew more about the laws than she did, so she shrugged. "Then I'd love to, although it's been so long since I've been to a restaurant—to anywhere public—I'm not sure I'll know what to do with myself."

It was another minute of him staring without blinking before he said softly, "It's more a cafeteria than anything, but…but we can pretend."

"Yes we can," she said, warming up to the idea.

"Yes. Great. Okay." And suddenly he was off again. "My only day off is Saturday. Is this Saturday okay? If not, we can go another—Oh, wait!" he said, interrupting himself. "I have training until late Saturday. Maybe there's another time, like Wednesday, but it would have to be during the day, like lunch or something? Or we could…" He scratched his receding hairline. "Oh, man. I should have thought this through first. I didn't think you'd say yes."

She smiled. "How about now? Have you eaten dinner yet?"

"Now?"

"If you have time. If not, we can try another day."

"I can go now," he said. "Can you?"

"Yes," she said, biting back a full-on grin. How was a man in his position scared of a simple, illegal girl like her?

He glanced down at his clothes and then around the neighborhood. Sasha sat on her sidewalk with the little boys, probably searching for bugs. Rhonda Watson was on her front porch, fanning herself. Oliver didn't seem to notice any of them.

"I have to run a small errand first," he said. "Could you maybe go in, say, thirty minutes?"

Her stomach did another flip. This was really happening.

"Sure," she said. "That will give me a chance to clean up."

"Okay. I'll be back, okay?"

"Okay."

As he pulled out of her driveway, he smiled larger than she could ever remember seeing. She did, too, although a flock of butterflies battled in her stomach. She rubbed the back of her neck and felt her dirty sweatiness. Her dingy-yellow work shirt was filthy, her nails were awful, and the rest of her was sticky. But thirty minutes wasn't enough time to haul in water for a bath, let alone air-dry her hair.

Dashing inside, she threw on her less-ripped jeans and her mom's blue blouse. Then she stepped into the bathroom for a washrag. The second she caught sight of herself in the blue blouse, thoughts of Oliver fled, and Greg filled her mind. He once told her to wear this blouse to his mom's wedding because it 'brought out her eyes.' Greg insisted Oliver would love her in blue, and maybe Oliver had, but she loved the way Greg had looked at her that night, how he'd called her 'beautiful.'

"Quite stunning, actually," he had said.

Frustrated, she dipped the washcloth in the bathroom water bucket and did her best to clean up. Then she pulled the elastic out of her hair and grabbed a brush.

"What are you doing?" Amber said, standing in the bathroom doorway.

"Doing my hair," Carrie said. Or at least trying to tame her honey-colored locks after a long windy day.

"Yeah, but why?"

Carrie almost didn't say but she had nothing to hide. "Oliver is taking me to dinner."

"He what?" Amber scowled. "Why the heck did you say yes?"

"We're just going to dinner." And she felt nervous enough without Amber pestering her. "Oliver said I'd be perfectly safe. I trust him."

"That's not what I meant. Why are you going out with *him*? You don't even like him."

Carrie shot her a dark look. Amber had been a beast ever since her encounter with Braden. It didn't help that she kept seeing him—seeing but not speaking. The curse of living in a small neighborhood.

"Just because you don't like Oliver," Carrie said, "doesn't mean I don't."

"Yeah? Prove it. What do you like about him?"

"What do I like?" Carrie repeated.

"Yes." Amber folded her arms. "What do you like?"

Stalling, Carrie admired herself in the mirror. Her mom's blue blouse definitely brought out her eyes. How was she supposed to eat if her stomach didn't calm down? She pulled the brush through her thick hair with hard strokes.

"I like that he's kind and always thinking of others," Carrie said. "He risked his job to help Mariah, a woman he barely knew. I also like how he ponders something before he speaks and how he—"

"Fine," Amber cut in. "You respect him, but you don't love him, and I swear you don't even like him, at least not enough for a date. Feeling sorry for someone isn't a good enough reason to date them."

Carrie turned. "I don't feel sorry for Oliver."

"Yeah, right."

"Look, I don't have time for this," Carrie huffed. "Please let me finish getting ready. He'll be back any minute."

She walked into her bedroom and knelt in front of her basket to find a pair of socks that weren't too holey. Amber followed, unable to take a hint.

"I can prove that you don't like Oliver." Carrie rolled her eyes, but Amber just broke into a wide, mischievous smile. When she spoke again, she said one word and one word only.

"Greg."

Heat rose up Carrie's cheeks.

"I knew it! So…" Amber's expression turned victorious, "what do you like about Greg?"

Clamping her mouth shut, Carrie dug through her basket. Then she pulled on each sock as if it required her complete and utter concentration.

"And that's why I know you don't like Oliver," Amber said gently. "Because you can talk about him. You can't even talk about Greg."

"I'm not twelve, Amber," Carrie said. "I can talk about Greg."

"Really? Then what do you like about him?"

"What do I like?"

"Yes. What. Do. You. Like? I *dare* you to say it."

Sitting back on her heels, Carrie thought about Greg's ability to say what he wanted when he wanted and exactly how he wanted. She loved his relationship with his mom and his ideas for the clan. There was his confidence, his sense of humor, or his ability to take any situation and improve it. She even liked it when he teased her—most of the time—plus he really was something to look at. There was the moment he'd saved her and Zach without a single hesitation, or how he looked at her, called her stunning, held her close, and a million other things. But for the life of her, she couldn't seem to utter a single one.

"Carrie, Carrie, Carrie." Amber walked over to the corner and picked up Carrie's pillow off the floor. A blue Yankee's baseball cap laid there, flat and smashed, convicting her.

Carrie's mouth dropped. Amber knew she slept with Greg's hat under her pillow. Amber, the biggest gossip in the world. Maybe Carrie really was twelve. Mortified, she wanted to crawl under a rock.

"Carrie," Amber whispered, "why are you going out with Oliver when you're obviously in love with Greg?"

"I don't know, but I am, okay?"

"And how would Greg feel about you going?" Amber waved the hat around, torturing Carrie with the memories of receiving the hat *and* what Greg asked her to do afterward.

Crossing the room, Carrie took it from her. "This date was Greg's idea, okay?"

Amber's brows furrowed. "Why?"

To alleviate his own guilt. So he didn't have to *try* anymore.

Carrie rubbed the rim of the navy blue baseball cap. It was darker than her blouse, but she was tempted to wear it to dinner anyway. Instead, she tossed it in her basket in the closet, determined to give it to Zach once and for all.

"Please don't tell anyone I had his hat under my pillow," she said.

Amber's countenance darkened. "I haven't yet, have I? You know, if you'd actually talk to me once in a while, I wouldn't have to sneak around trying to figure out what's going on with you. I wouldn't feel like an idiot all the time."

"I talk to you," Carrie said defensively.

"About what? Chickens? Getting water? I tell you everything about Braden, but you won't tell me anything about Greg." Amber's dark eyes suddenly filled with tears. "We're sisters, remember? We're supposed to stay up late at night giggling and crying about boys. I swear something's up with you and Greg, but you won't tell me, and now you're going out with Oliver, and nothing makes sense, and you don't even care that you don't confide in me."

"Amber…"

Face flushed, Amber hugged herself. "I feel like you don't even like me. Nobody does. Am I really that awful?"

Carrie wrapped her arms around her sensitive sister. "I'm sorry, Amber. I'm just a private person, that's all." And strangely, the only one she'd ever opened up to about her love life was in Naperville and possibly never coming back.

Tears fell down Amber's olive cheeks. "But we're sisters."

"I know. I'm sorry. Honestly, I could use your advice right now because I'm impossibly confused, and I think I might be messing everything up."

"So…there *is* something going on with you and Greg?"

"Maybe." Only she'd never be able to explain it in a few minutes. "But I'm really late right now. Can I explain it later? I promise to tell you everything."

Amber's beautiful eyes glistened. "Can we talk after your date?"

Carrie smiled. "We'll stay up late giggling and everything."

"I won't hold my breath," Amber said, but then she nudged her playfully. "Hey, want me to 'smoke' your eyes for you?"

Amber had lined Carrie's blue eyes with charcoal for Mariah's wedding—which Oliver *and* Greg had noticed. But right now going into public, Carrie didn't need more attention. She needed to blend in, to be invisible. "No thanks. By the way, how long have you known Greg's hat was under my pillow?"

"Probably since he gave it to you. Or did he give it to you?" Amber's hands flew to her mouth. "Carrie, you little devil, did you steal it?"

Carrie's cheeks felt hotter than the room. "No. Greg gave it to me before he left. Well, he gave it to me to give to Zach. I sort of forgot to pass it along."

Amber threw her head back with a laugh. "I love it. Does it still smell like him?"

"Okay, you're done." Carrie grabbed her arm and escorted her to the doorway. Maybe opening up was a mistake.

Amber stopped at the top of the stairs. "You know, I love seeing you this way, Carrie."

"What way?"

"Totally whooped. You shouldn't go tonight. It's not fair to you, Oliver, or Greg. I might not know much, but I've seen the way Greg looks at you. He likes you."

"Please," Carrie begged. She couldn't hash this out anymore, especially not now. "I'll explain everything later. I promise."

As Amber left, Carrie's head fell against her bedroom door. She stared at Greg's hat in her closet, wondering if she was doing the right thing. Wondering what advice her mom would give right now if she was here. Wondering if any part of Greg loved her on his own without urging from *his* mom. Wondering so many things her head hurt.

Whatever state her hair had been in was as good as it was going to get because she heard Oliver's car pulling down the street.

Her time of wondering was up.

thirty-three

McCormick's guy dropped Greg and Isabel off a few miles from their first destination on the outskirts of West Chicago. From there, they were on their own. McCormick had contacted patrol precincts in the area and ordered all government sweeps to be suspended until further notice, giving Greg and Isabel plenty of leeway to do what they needed.

"Get in. Assess. Move on," McCormick hammered into them. Usually with the follow-up of, *"Oh, and don't die."*

Comforting.

In Greg's mind, this was a suicide mission. The rebels weren't stupid. Then again, neither was McCormick.

This morning, the commander pulled Greg aside for a final warning. *"If you pull any stunts or if anything happens to my niece—and I mean, if a single hair on her head is touched—I will make you pay for the rest of your life. You, your dying mother, your grandparents, and anyone else you've ever cared about. I will cut them in pieces. Slowly. Right before your eyes."* He had patted Greg with a smile. *"Bring both of you back safe and you and I will stay friends."*

Greg and Isabel carried two bags each: a ratty old backpack with smelly clothes and normal squatter things, and a heavy duty bag with guns, maps, radios, green cards, first aid kits, and plenty of stuff that was sure to get them killed. They planned to bury their second bag in the woods outside of each clan.

After rushing around to pull things together and getting enough immunizations to warrant an African safari, Isabel had sufficiently 'squattered up.' She braided her dark hair in a messy do, and she smudged dirt over her clothes and face in a natural, living-in-the-backwoods way. Her nails were hideous, and her clothes looked like they'd been washed in the Amazon. Smelled like it, too, which was good. She still had more curves than the average starving illegal, making her look like a woman who'd recently fallen on hard times, but hopefully with her experience, nobody would know the difference. Greg was just happy to be back in his UNC shirt and ratty jeans, feeling more like himself than he had in six weeks. He hadn't showered in a few days and, combined with a beard he detested, that was all he needed to 'squatter up.'

Admittedly, his impression of Isabel had improved. She could shoot a gun like nobody's business, and in the brief moments she dropped the seductress act and talked strategy, he'd seen real potential. She was skilled. Intelligent. But annoying as all get out.

She talked non-stop as they followed an overrun deer path, making Greg appreciate the peacefulness of his walk north with his mom. Isabel told him every detail of her life. She also invented a story for them as a couple, how they'd met in college—University of North Carolina—at a sports bar where she waitressed. But when she ventured into some story about how they'd been captured and branded, he chimed right up. They fought for the next mile. Greg didn't want to be a bully about it, but neither did he want to end up dead.

A stream wound lazily through a field to the side. Greg stopped. "We better drink up while we can."

"Oh, so now you want to drink?" she said. "Good plan, although I can't let you get too plastered."

Unamused, he said, "We should also eat our last good meal. Probably bury our stuff now, too. That big tree over there's a good marker."

"I think we're still a ways away," she said. "We'll want our things more accessible."

"If they're smart, they're posting guards closer than McCormick thinks. I say we set up base here."

Isabel put a hand on her ample hip. "I'm the expert and senior officer on this mission. Are you ever going to trust me?"

Refusing to answer, he splashed cool water on his face. It felt heavenly after—

He jumped as something slid onto his thigh. Isabel squeezed his leg with a suggestive smile. "Well, are you?"

"Don't touch me," he said, swatting her away.

"Brrrr," she said with a mock shiver. She tried to sidle up to him, but he jumped to his feet and moved further upstream. "You know you're going to have to warm up to me at some point, handsome. Otherwise, we'll never convince anyone we're newlyweds."

"Newlyweds considering divorce," he muttered. Making sure she kept her distance, he leaned down for another drink from the stream.

She watched him for a long moment. "What's her name?"

"Who?"

"The girl back home who has you wrapped around her little finger."

He didn't want to say, but maybe she'd back off if he did. He wiped the water from his beard. "Carrie."

"Is she pretty?"

Yes, only in a way a dark-haired seductress wouldn't understand. Because Carrie wasn't just beautiful, she had quiet dignity. She was self-respecting and other-people-respecting, too. She didn't play games other women did, and he liked that. Loved it, actually. Plus, her blue eyes drove him—

Greg stopped his thoughts before they ran away from him. Thinking about Carrie was too painful. For all he knew, she and Oliver were happily married and living in government housing. A lot could happen in a month and a half. The thought churned his stomach.

Straightening, he glanced around. The sun was lowering in the sky but was still hotter than he thought Illinois sun could be.

"You ready?" he said. "We should head out so we have time to scope out the first clan before nightfall."

"I'll take that as a yes." Isabel shouldered her two bags as she fell in line beside him. "So tell me about this Carrie. How long have you two been together?"

"Not long enough."

Greg meant to say it under his breath, but Isabel laughed. "Ah, I'm sorry you're stuck with me. With any luck, you'll see your precious Carrie soon. Just impress my uncle on these missions, and he'll let you do whatever you want. I always do."

He mulled that over as they traipsed over a railroad track. Was that where he was headed? Isabel's unabashed freedom? How much betrayal would get him a pass home? Was it worth ratting out some rebels to see his mom again? Carrie again? Or was it already too late for both of them?

"By the way," Isabel said, "my guy is named Pete. Thanks for asking."

Surprised, he glanced sideways. Isabel Ryan seemed like the type to have forty guys, not one. Plus, he figured something that like would have come up in her tortuously-long life story.

"Y'all dating?" he asked. "Engaged? Married?"

"No." Her large, dark eyes lost some of their sharpness. "Pete's dead."

"Oh. Sorry," Greg said, unsure what else to say.

She nodded and for a time, the only sounds were the soft chirps of nature and their tennis shoes rustling the grass. It explained some of her recklessness with life—and men. At some point, a person stopped caring what the future held when the only thing worth living for was gone.

Part of him, narcissistic as it was, wondered if Carrie would tell the same story some day: *I loved a man once. He's dead now.* She did love Greg once. He was just selfish enough to hope she still did.

"Pete could make me laugh anytime, anywhere," Isabel continued softly. "I miss laughing."

Greg couldn't remember the last time he'd made Carrie laugh. She'd smiled plenty of times, but laughed? Carrie deserved more laughter in her life, and he vowed that if he ever made it back, he'd make her laugh again. Assuming she wanted him to.

Assuming she was still in Logan Pond.

Isabel grabbed his arm, pulling him to a stop. "Don't tell Uncle Charlie about Pete. He doesn't know."

"Why?"

"Because…" She chewed her bottom lip. "Pete was an illegal. I met him on one of these missions."

"Seriously?" No wonder she hadn't mentioned him. "How'd he die?"

Starting off again, she hugged herself even though it was plenty hot. "This spring, my uncle planted me in a clan with this real jerk of a partner, some arrogant sharpshooter. We were only there a month, but it was long enough to fall head over heels in love with Pete. When the government came into arrest everyone, Pete didn't run. I warned him. The night before I told him who I was and why I was there. I told him what was coming and that he should run. But he just looked at me like I was the devil." Tears streaked her face. "I've never seen anyone look more betrayed."

Her voice trembled, and it was a moment before she continued. "Pete stormed off, but I thought he'd listened. The last I saw him, he was charging a federal patrolmen. The patrolman took aim and…" A shudder ripped through her. "It was over before I could blink. He died hating me. I destroyed the lives of everyone he loved. I didn't even get to say goodbye or explain anything. He hated me." She wiped her nose. "I hated myself, too. Still do."

"So why are we here?" Greg asked suddenly. Not the most empathetic thing to say, but the thought was screaming in his mind. *Isabel loved an illegal!* "You wanna destroy more lives like Pete's?"

Those dark, watery eyes turned on him. "No. I want to help these people. Millions of illegals are starving and dying, but instead of letting us help, they're turning violent and killing others, innocent citizens who follow the laws. You should have seen the kids in Pete's clan. No shoes and down to skin and bones, but no one cared. Well," she said, "I care. If these clans won't come peacefully, they leave us no choice but to acquire and relocate them where they'll be protected and their children will live to see adulthood."

"Acquire? Do you even hear yourself? Most clans are doin' fine. They're only fighting back 'cause the government won't leave them be. Rigsby doesn't want to help illegals. He wants to make them slaves."

Her countenance darkened. "That's traitorous talk."

"Yeah? Well, guess what?" He yanked up his sleeve. "My mark is real. By force and force alone, I'm here. This game of Rigsby's with card systems and so-called *emergency laws* is ugly, repulsive, and still leaves millions dead. So forgive me if I don't jump on your pretended savior bandwagon. I'm here 'cause I've got a virtual gun to my head. Don't ever forget that."

She shook her head. "What did we ever do to you?"

Words escaped him. Did she want to see his back? His sister's grave? The list was far too long, so he settled on the most pressing offense. "You're not the only one who didn't get a goodbye."

She rolled her eyes. "So what? You didn't get a sweet sendoff from your girl? At least Carrie doesn't hate your guts. At least she's still alive, waiting for your return."

"I wasn't talking about Carrie," he said bitterly.

Isabel's brows rose in another teasing look. It was amazing how fast she could jump from emotion to emotion. "Just how many girls do you have? Shame on you, Gregory Pierce. You're a total player but refuse to let me play." She batted her dark eyes. "Was it something I said?"

"I meant my mom," he barked. "The last I saw her, she was on the floor of our township office, sobbing uncontrollably and coughing up blood, all because of one of your patrol bullies. She's sick, dying of some kinda cancer, but one of *your* guys ripped me out of her arms— literally—before I got a goodbye. She couldn't walk. She couldn't move. I don't know if she made it home. I don't even know if she's still alive. I know nothing!"

Isabel's face fell. "I'm sorry. No, really. I am."

His fists clenched along with the rest of him, but she wisely let the subject drop and fell silent.

Finally.

The desire to make a run for it overwhelmed Greg, only unlike all the other times, he didn't fight it off. They walked five minutes before he had it planned.

"Look," he said, "there's no point waltzing into camp right now. People are more relaxed in the evening. They might be more open to two newbies. Plus, illegals like us look for shelter toward night anyhow. I say we watch this group until dusk and then make the approach."

"Alright," she said.

No fight. That surprised him.

Another minute passed. Greg scratched his hot beard like he was thinking on the cuff. "In fact, I'd feel more comfortable if we watched them for a full day. With the rebellion heatin' up, people will be more skittish than ever about lettin' folks into their clan. If we watch them for a full day, we'd know who's the leader and how to spin our story. We could go in just before dusk tomorrow."

"Another day?" Isabel fixed him with a flat stare. "What are you scheming, Pierce? Don't forget I have radios that are being tracked by McCormick as we speak."

He stiffened. Homing devices? That would have been nice to know. Still, he could pull it off.

"I wanna leave," he said point blank. "I wanna go home for a day."

"What?" she shouted, loud enough it echoed off the trees.

230

Greg shoved a hand over her mouth. "You scout out this clan while I'm gone,"—and keep both locater radios—"and I'll be back tomorrow afternoon in time to go in."

She swatted his hand away. "You're crazy."

"I'd be gone just one day, and then I'll finish the mission." He'd run all day and night if he had to. "Then I'll commit to do whatever you want. No more fighting."

"*Anything* I want?" she asked with an arched brow.

Women like Isabel got their way, especially with men, but he'd deal with the fallout later. It was worth it to go home even for a few hours. But when he opened his mouth to answer, another word left his lips.

"No."

She rolled her eyes. "That's what I thought. How would you even find your way home? Or back here?"

"I came a thousand miles on foot. Believe me, I can find my way."

"So you want to leave your sweet pregnant wife to visit your old girlfriend. Talk about a slap in the face."

"To see my mom," he corrected. "I don't even know if she's still alive, but if she is, I'd like the chance to see her and say goodbye." Seeing Carrie would just be a bonus. "I'll beg if I have to."

"I'm guessing a guy like you doesn't beg often." She folded her arms. "What's in it for me?"

Adrenaline coursed through him. She was actually considering it. He'd only been gone six weeks. His mom could have survived that long. She still had six weeks in her. She had to.

"A chance to redeem yourself," Greg said. "To prove to Pete—and yourself—that you're not the horrible, brainwashed person he died thinkin' you were. That you still have a heart."

It was a low blow, but she chewed her bottom lip, pensive. "And...you'd be back when?"

"How far are we from Shelton?" he asked, perched on his feet to make a run for it.

"Maybe ten miles."

Twenty miles roundtrip. It would be hard, but he could do it. Maybe Carrie had fixed a bike or he'd find Oliver and snatch a ride back. Either way... "I'll be back tomorrow afternoon. You do the surveillance now, and I'll be back in time to go in tomorrow night. No more fighting you."

Looking around, she studied their surroundings. He could barely hear over his pounding pulse. Carrie. His mom. But then her countenance fell.

"I can't. I'm sorry, Greg. I just can't."

"If you had a chance to say goodbye to Pete," he pled, "wouldn't you take it? C'mon. It's my mom."

She swallowed and looked away. "I can't. I'm sorry. My uncle would kill me and I just don't trust you enough."

"Please. I'll do anything. What do you want from me?"

"To stop asking." She turned away from him. "Listen, the sooner we do this mission, the sooner you can get home to your mom—and your precious Carrie. So let's go."

Isabel started off at a brisk pace. Greg clutched his bags, defeat consuming him. He'd been so close. So, so close. She didn't try to talk to him, and he refused to speak to her. It was pure silence the rest of the way to the first clan.

thirty-four

"You look…" Oliver said at Carrie's door. "You look great."

Carrie smiled with a blush. "Thanks. You, too." She'd never seen him wear anything but his green uniform, but he'd changed into a black polo and khakis. The clothes made him look different. Younger. More relaxed. More…attractive even, which made her more nervous.

Oliver pulled out a small bouquet of wildflowers from behind his back. "Here."

"Oh. They're beautiful." Flowers in every shade. She held them close and inhaled the scent of summer. She smiled in disbelief. His errands were to change and pick wildflowers?

"Here," she said, "let me put them in water. Come on in."

He entered but stayed by the front door. As she walked into the kitchen, she searched around for something. Her only jar was still occupied with dead branches which had dropped their white blossoms long ago. She hadn't tossed them out though—another pathetic sign she was twelve years old. Filling her own drinking cup with water, she took her time arranging the wildflowers to calm her nerves.

It was just dinner.

Just dinner with Oliver.

"I like your house," he said, looking around as if he'd never seen the inside, as if he hadn't been through many times for government sweeps. Besides her ugly green couch and the card table that served as their kitchen table, her house was empty and the carpets hadn't been vacuumed in years, but she thanked him anyway.

Amber walked downstairs. "Hi, Oliver. Wow. Don't you look nice? And my, those flowers are beautiful, aren't they, Carrie?" She joined Carrie in the kitchen with a wink.

Carrie shot her a warning look. Her sister had never been nice to Oliver before. Opening up to Amber was backfiring already.

"The noodles for dinner are in the fridge," Carrie said. "I'll be back later."

In an instant, Amber sobered. "You'll be back before dark, right?" she asked softly. Amber hated the dark, especially in summer when they went without candles because of long daylight hours.

"Yes. Make Zach finish cleaning the chicken coop. It looks terrible."

"Will do." Amber plastered on another fake smile. "Have fun!"

Feeling jittery, Carrie followed Oliver to his car. He opened the passenger door for her and Carrie slid into the artificially cooled air. Even the seat was cold, and she snuggled in.

"I didn't know you still used your fridge," Oliver said when he started up the car.

"Oh, yeah. It's still good for storing food. In the winter, we use ice from the pond and the insulation works pretty well," Carrie said. "The rest of the time, we use it like a pantry. It keeps the flies off of things."

"Oh. That's smart," he said.

It didn't feel smart, but she appreciated him not pitying her. Between her lack of electricity, holey shoes, and everything else that felt dirty and ragged, there were plenty of things he could scoff at, but he never did.

As they pulled out of the neighborhood, she felt every eye watch them. This was more than a little drive. She was heading into civilization with real people and real places. So she used the opportunity and searched every side road and home for signs of illegal life. Tomorrow she, Terrell, and Richard would set out again, hopefully with more luck. Everything looked dead as they drove, but it helped clarify the location of a few neighborhoods. And then the houses were gone and it was nothing but road.

There were some people you could sit with in silence and feel at ease. Oliver wasn't one of them. Or maybe she wasn't one of them. Either way, the drive seemed to stretch. When they pulled onto the old highway, it solidified the feeling: she was leaving Logan Pond.

"Where are we headed?" she asked.

"South Elgin, if that's alright," Oliver said.

"Sounds great." Carrie and her mom used to go there for a craft fair every year. Absentmindedly, she wondered how far Naperville was, but she didn't dare ask. She was pretty sure it was the opposite direction anyway.

As they neared South Elgin, Carrie saw the first signs of life. People walked the streets. Not homeless illegals like her. Not even patrolmen. Normal-looking people with clothing that wasn't stained, ripped, or hanging on all-too-skinny bodies. At first there were a few random people sporadically strolling down the sidewalks with grocery bags or strollers, but with each passing block, the number increased. And then she saw cars. Real, regular cars.

"Is South Elgin a government municipality?" Carrie asked, even though those people looked too rich for blue cardies. Her nerves tightened.

"It's a new chartered city," Oliver said. "An experiment of sorts. It used to just be government workers and their families, but last year the government asked yellow card holders to move here, offering incentives to relocate, so it almost feels normal here. For the most part, there aren't restrictions here like a blue card municipality would have."

"Like fences?" she asked.

"Yeah…" he said carefully. "And other things."

A vague answer, but she didn't press. Other questions swirled in her mind. How often did Oliver come here? Would Greg eventually live somewhere like this? How did these people earn money to live, eat, and drive cars? It was like the Collapse never happened here. A couple crossed the street in front of them, holding hands and laughing like they didn't have a care in the world. Maybe they didn't, but South Elgin felt a million miles away.

Three patrolmen strolled out of a corner store, and a wave of panic swept over her. She shrank down in her seat, feeling horrifyingly vulnerable. Oliver or no Oliver, travel permits or not, one wrong move and she'd be arrested. Life in prison. No more Amber and Zach.

Oliver pulled up to a curb. "Are you okay?"

He had parked next to an old diner with *Harvey's Deli & Cafe* painted bright red on the window. It looked cute and quaint and… She peeked back and couldn't see the patrolmen anymore, but a different patrolman leaned against the deli, finger in his gun belt, cigarette hanging from his mouth. He glanced at Oliver's car—at her—and her pulse pounded so hard she felt it in her ears.

Oliver leaned forward and peered at her all scrunched in her seat. "Carrie…um…do you want to go home?"

He hadn't even noticed the patrolmen. Of course he hadn't. He was one.

He put the car in reverse, but she grabbed his arm.

"Wait. Sorry. I just…" She worked to breathe slowly.

His eyes softened. "I have your papers in my pocket, Carrie. Do you want to see them? I-I-I've been meaning to show them to you anyway. You need to see them."

"No, it's fine. I trust you." *I do, I do, I do.*

But why?

He arrested people like her and they went to prison forever.

"I promise I'd never let anything happen to you," he said gently. "But…but I understand if you want to go home."

"No." Carrie took a deep breath. "I want to go in." And more than anything, she wanted to stop being afraid. Oliver was giving her a gift tonight, a gift to remember what it was like to live a normal life.

"I'm better now," she said, sliding back on her seat. "Let's go."

———◆———

The second Zach passed the open door, he knew he was in trouble. Amber looked up from her mattress.

"Where do you think you're going?" Amber asked.

"That's for me to know and you *not* to find out," Zach muttered. Then he took off, racing down the stairs two at a time.

Amber chased after him and caught his red t-shirt, yanking him back before he could escape out the front door.

"Wanna bet?" Amber said. "I'll tell Carrie you snuck out while she was gone."

"Wait! You can't tell Carrie. Please. Just let me go. I'll do anything."

"Anything? Hmmm…" Amber tapped the side of her head, expression turning evil. "My chores for a month, including Richard's water buckets."

"No way! Carrie will know something's up."

"Not if you do them when she's in the garden. A month," Amber said, holding out her hand.

"A week," Zach countered.

"Three."

"Fine." Zach shook her hand. "But if Carrie finds out, you have to pay me back and do my chores for that long."

"Fine."

Zach didn't trust his conniving sister, but Carrie wouldn't be gone forever. He raced out of his house, past a bend in the trail by the cemetery, and straight to the meeting place. Tucker was already there, and he looked mad.

"What took you so long?" Tucker snapped.

"I had to finish the chicken coop," Zach said, starting off at a fast pace.

"If they've already left," Tucker said, "I'll kill you. We missed the last two times because of your dumb sister."

It hadn't even occurred to Zach that they might miss the whole thing. He'd be doing Amber's stupid chores for nothing. "We better run."

They did, whizzing past bushes, beyond the weird, double-trunked tree, and over Bramman Highway. Zach ran until his lungs burned and his legs felt like rubber, but he didn't slow down.

When they reached the black fence, they stopped, gasping for air. Then they watched the opening of the old barn.

"Be there," Zach whispered between heavy breaths. "Still be there."

Crossing the last of the distance, they ducked down and shimmied in through the old animal door where chickens or cats used to enter. It was dark inside the barn. Once Zach's eyes adjusted, he and Tucker crept past the old stables and climbed the rickety ladder to the loft. The loft was darker than the rest of the barn, especially with the evening sun.

"Hey?" Zach called softly. "Hello? It's Zach and Tucker."

"Where have you guys been?" a girl said. Her voice came from the usual corner. Zach squinted and made out the group of six or seven teenagers. He couldn't help but smile.

"When you didn't show up last week," the blonde girl continued in her whiny voice, "we thought you guys chickened out."

Zach didn't know why she was the ringleader. Nobody liked her. He couldn't even remember her name—nor did he ask her. His eyes scanned the group and spotted the only other girl there. The girl with the long, black braids, and dark, mysterious eyes.

Delaney.

With a start, he saw Delaney smiling at him. Heat rushed up his neck, and he smiled back. As she slid over and patted the spot next to her, Zach knew he would have done two months of Amber's chores for a chance to be here.

He crossed the loft and took the open spot, making sure his knee touched Delaney's.

"Sorry," Zach whispered to her. "We'll be here next time."

Delaney's shoulder bumped him playfully. "You better be."

———— • ————

Greg spotted signs of life before they reached the first campsite. Brush matted down where people had walked. Trees cut for firewood. Creeping silently, he and Isabel inched as close as they dared.

Unlike other clans, this one wasn't squatting in houses. They lived in two dozen tents in the middle of nowhere under the thick canopy of woods. Exactly where McCormick said they'd be—which made Greg's skin crawl.

He scanned the camp of illegals milling about. They were the Bedouin type. If Greg and Isabel didn't make a move soon, the group could be gone by tomorrow.

"If they're part of the rebellion," Isabel whispered, "there will be obvious signs. They'll be heavy on weapons and have more adults than children—usually more men than women."

Three men stood on the outskirt, rifles drooping in their arms. Guards. Greg figured they hadn't seen much action in a while because they hardly scanned the woods. Several other men moved through the camp, a few women, and only one kid Greg could see, maybe nine or ten years old.

Rebels.

His gut clenched. Could he really do this, become the ultimate traitor?

Isabel unzipped her supply bag and packed away her radio. "They seem mild enough. I say we go in now."

Still miffed from before, Greg said, "Go ahead, but I'm not goin' in until tomorrow night."

She glared at him. "Are you always so stubborn?"

He sat on the moist ground and leaned against a tree trunk. "It's gonna be a long night. Might wanna settle in. It looks like rain."

"I bet you don't treat Carrie like this."

The comment stung. There was a time he'd treated Carrie worse, but he let it slide. "I'll take the first watch. Or you can, and I'll find a spot to bury the—"

A sudden snap of twigs brought Greg's head around. Another shift and somebody jumped out of the woods behind them. In a flash, Greg was staring into the barrel of a rifle.

"Who are you?" a man barked.

thirty-five

Greg and Isabel's hands shot into the air.

"Who are you?" the man shouted again, waving the end of the rifle a foot from Greg's face. He had brown shaggy hair and a beard to rival a Neanderthal.

"We're Greg and Isabel Pierce," Greg said, standing slowly, hands high. "We're alone."

His eyes narrowed. "Why are you sneaking around these woods?

Greg's supply bag was at his feet and he nudged it under the nearest bush. He didn't dare check to see where Isabel's bag was. "We saw your camp. We're just lookin' for shelter actually. We weren't sure if y'all are friendly or not, or open to passersby, so we wanted to watch for a bit to be sure."

"Why?"

"To see which side of the rebellion you're on," Isabel said. "We're looking for others like us, people who want change, and we were told to come here."

A bold response. Even the guy seemed surprised by her direct answer. He glanced over his shoulder where more people came crashing through the woods. Greg took advantage of the distraction and kicked his bag the rest of the way under the brush, keeping his gaze snapped upwards and hands high.

"How do we know you're not government spies or something?" the man asked.

A chill ran down Greg's spine, and the lie he had rehearsed suddenly stuck in his throat. But without missing a beat, Isabel lifted the sleeve of her ratty t-shirt and showed her mark.

"Live free or die," Isabel whispered.

She looked at Greg, and Greg followed suit, hating himself for it.

By then, five others had surrounded them, men who looked ready to swoop in for the kill. They were dirty, thin, and yet hardened with years of strife. These were survivors, and they survived for a good reason.

"How did you get those?" one of them asked, a big guy with gray streaks running through his beard. "Yours looks new."

"It's a long story," Isabel said. "Lower your rifles and we'll explain."

"No." The first guy's grip tightened on his rifle. "Explain first."

———— ♦ ————

Oliver felt like an idiot. He spent the first few minutes apologizing for the atmosphere, and the next few apologizing for the food. The deli wasn't as nice as he remembered. The floor was sticky and the air buzzed with flies. Maybe if he'd had longer to plan, he could have come up with a better option. Luckily, Carrie didn't seem to mind. She fingered the paper napkins, stroked the salt shakers, and stirred the ice in her glass as if she'd never seen anything so wonderful. But she seemed most interested in the TV in the corner, glancing at it every few minutes. Oliver tried to put himself in her shoes, experiencing all of this for the first time in six years.

They sat in a red booth in the corner under the ambiance of cheap fluorescent lights and cigarette smoke. A few other patrolmen sat around with their coffee—guys Oliver didn't know. The rest of the patrons looked normal enough and uninterested in Oliver and his date, which was as he hoped.

Because tonight, Oliver would tell Carrie about the papers.

He nearly had in the car but chickened out. But now he would, over burgers and fries. He would. He had to.

But not yet.

Oliver tried to keep the conversation going, small talk that seemed to fall flat. He asked about her parents and she asked about his. A horrible topic considering both sets were dead. So he asked about her hobbies, and she found out he had none. The longer they talked, the more pathetic he felt. He should just tell her.

"Do you like your burger?" he asked.

"Yeah, it's great," she said. "I'm surprised they have tomatoes this early in the year."

Her eyes strayed to the TV again, but his stayed on her. The soft waves of her hair, her blue, round eyes watching the anchorwoman reporting on the hurricane in Virginia.

"PBS?" Carrie asked.

"Yeah. It's the only station that survived."

"Wow. That looks awful."

The footage cut to President Rigsby addressing a large blue card municipality in Norfolk, promising more help, supplies, and food for the hurricane victims. The usual rhetoric. Oliver didn't trust the news anymore. Too many stories of devastation with President Rigsby coming to the rescue. For all he knew, the hurricane footage was from twenty years ago since he doubted anyone had that kind of food or clothing resources now, even the government.

"I can't believe he's still president," Carrie said. "He looks a lot older than I remember. I guess he's aged."

"We all have," Oliver muttered.

He hadn't meant for her to hear, but she laughed anyway. "True."

Oliver wanted to kick himself. Carrie was fifteen years younger than him, which meant she'd been in her late teens when the Collapse hit. He'd been in his early thirties, making their date feel suddenly creepy.

"It's so easy to forget that life keeps going outside of Logan Pond," she said. "It's like I've..." Her voice trailed off as the anchorwoman switched stories.

"In the latest on the Midwest Uprising," the anchorwoman read, *"more fires erupted overnight on Chicago's west side. President Rigsby promised the new task force will be ready to join federal troops within a week. The numbers haven't been released yet, but according to the White House, the size of this task force is large enough to tip the scales."*

The news feed cut back to Rigsby addressing a different crowd. *"These illegals will be brought to justice,"* he said, stabbing the podium, *"as will all who oppose the liberty and freedom of the American people. America will be great again. United We Stand!"*

People in the background—unseen as usual—started chanting, *"United We Stand! United We Stand!"*

The light faded from Carrie's eyes.

Oliver couldn't believe it either. Why would they send new soldiers out with such little preparation? Were they that desperate?

One word hung in the air between them: Greg.

Greg was part of that new task force.

Oliver thought about shutting off the TV. Instead, he said, "Do you want some dessert?"

Without hearing, she continued to watch the screen until the anchorwoman switched stories again.

"Sorry," she said, finally turning back. "It's just so strange to watch TV again. Is it…" Her eyes lifted to his. "Is it really as bad as it sounds?"

He shrugged. His latest training was all about ways to spot signs of the rebellion. After the red-bearded man, Oliver figured it wasn't too hard. "We've seen some activity in this area," he said honestly.

As if reading his mind, she asked, "Whatever happened to that squatter you arrested? The one who was freaking out on our drive?"

"He…" Oliver paused, hating himself all over again. "He died."

"What? No. How? I know he attacked you, but…" The rest of her sentence was implied. *But did you have to kill him?* It pained Oliver that she thought he would.

"He was dead before I got back," he said quietly.

Carrie paled. "Oh, no. It was my fault. Your partner wanted you to go back. If I hadn't been with you, that illegal wouldn't—"

"No!" Oliver said firmly.

She flinched at his outburst, and heat rose up his neck. He never raised his voice, especially not with her.

"It wasn't your fault, Carrie. It was mine." Every last bit of it. "When my boss found out, he…" His voice dropped. "He made me burn the guy's house down."

She flinched back. "Why?"

"The man was part of the rebellion. My boss wanted to make an example of him. Only I…" Oliver begged himself to shut up, but part of him was desperate to unburden his soul. "I didn't know how to burn a house down. I did a horrible job, only getting the garage and part of the main floor, but still…"

Carrie stared at him, her expression close to horror. Suddenly he saw himself how she did. A patrolman.

The enemy.

They both tried to eat after that. Oliver pushed some fries through his ketchup, but he no longer had an appetite. He kept reliving that day over and over, wondering how he could have saved that—

Something out the window caught his eye.

He dropped his fry, splaying ketchup on his polo. He grabbed a napkin, wiping his shirt frantically while watching three men approach his car. He recognized two of the three, even though they weren't in uniform.

Why were they here? his mind screamed. Had they followed him? Probably not since both Jamansky and the mayor looked surprised to see his car. If they came inside and saw him with Carrie, he'd be in huge trouble. Carrie would be, too.

"What is it?" Carrie asked. "What's wrong?"

Jamansky searched the sidewalk and surrounding shops for Oliver. And then, from Oliver's worst nightmare, he turned toward the deli window. Oliver twisted in his seat and pretended to study the far wall at the same time he searched for a back exit.

"Are you okay?" Carrie asked.

His pulse quadrupled. No back exit. Only one door out. And it swung open with the tinkling of a bell. The three men entered, and Oliver felt time slow down.

This couldn't be happening.

Jamansky spotted him in the far red booth and scowled—his usual greeting. Mayor Phillips spotted him, too, and then said something to Jamansky.

Jamansky leaned sideways for a better look.

Oliver knew the moment David Jamansky spotted Carrie because his eyes widened to huge, hungry circles. When he looked at Oliver again, his face split into the kind of dark, menacing smile that made Oliver's pounding heart stop.

No, no, no, no, no, Oliver begged.

If they asked for Carrie's card, he'd have to show them her papers and pray it was enough. But if they saw her address, if they knew what he'd done—if *she* knew what he'd done—no amount of citizenship could stop the chaos which would ensue.

"Do you know them?" Carrie whispered, noticing the group eyeing her like sharks.

"I-I-I work with them," Oliver stuttered as he raced through every option, including breaking the window and making a run for it. "The tall one is my boss."

Her face went white. "Greg. Mariah," she whispered.

He nodded. "They're not supposed to be here. I purposely came here to be away. They're not supposed to be here!"

Oliver peeked over his shoulder. The three men waited to place their orders. The third man he didn't know was as old as Mayor Phillips, but David Jamansky, who was closer in age to Carrie, just smiled sweetly at them, letting Oliver know he was on the hunt.

Oliver whipped back around. He and Carrie were basically done eating. If they left now, they might be able to sneak out with little questions.

"Do they know that I'm not"—Carrie's breaths came faster—"legal?"

"No." At least, he prayed they wouldn't guess. Patrolmen weren't allowed to associate with illegals. They shouldn't suspect her lack of citizenship. He could say Carrie was his sister, but Jamansky knew he didn't have one.

Think!

"Just ignore them. You're safe," Oliver said, begging himself to believe his own words. Carrie had papers now. They couldn't touch her. Except…a sweaty, pale face made him look as guilty as he was.

Stupid papers or not, she didn't belong in his world. It was time he stopped pretending—

A hand landed on Oliver's shoulder. "Officer Simmons?" Jamansky said with a broad smile. "What a surprise to see you so far from your patrols. What brings you to South Elgin this evening?"

"Chief. Mayor Phillips," Oliver said in a voice bordering a squeak. He didn't bother introducing himself to the third guy because Jamansky had already turned his gaze on Carrie.

"Introduce us to your lady friend, Simmons," Jamansky said.

Oliver took a quick breath. He could do this. He thought about making up a name for her, but if they asked for her papers, they'd know he lied.

"Um…this is Carrie," Oliver said.

"Nice to meet you, Carrie," Jamansky said warmly, reaching out a hand to her. "I'm David Jamansky, Chief of Patrols. I'm Oliver's boss."

White and still terrified, Carrie looked at Oliver as if to ask for permission. She knew what Jamansky was capable of—what he'd done to Greg and Mariah. She looked as excited to shake that hand as she'd be to pet a rattlesnake. Oliver didn't know what to tell her. They assumed she was legal, which was good, but Jamansky wasn't just here to torture Oliver. His eyes roamed over young, beautiful Carrie with far too much interest.

Carrie shook his hand. "Nice to meet you, David," she said softly.

As she shook the other men's hands, Jamansky leaned down and pretended to brush something from Oliver's shoulder. "Looking good, Simmons," he whispered. "Where'd you get the shirt?" Before Oliver could answer, Jamansky straightened. "I didn't think Officer Simmons had a sister. Are you his cousin?"

Again, Carrie checked with Oliver for a clue of how to answer, but he was useless. Nearly mute. Ready to pass out.

"No," she said. "Just a friend."

"Really?" Jamansky shot Oliver a look, wondering how a guy like him was on a date with a girl like her. Then, to Oliver's complete and utter horror, David Jamansky slid onto the red bench next to her. "Well, let's get acquainted then."

thirty-six

"Did you like your food?" Jamansky asked Carrie, all cozied up to her.

Oliver stared down at his plate. This couldn't be happening.

"Yes, it was good," Carrie answered, although she politely slid as far from Jamansky as the small booth allowed.

"The food here is…well…" Jamansky grimaced exaggeratedly. "Let's just say I don't like to eat here. We were headed to a nicer place when we spotted Oliver's car. I'm disappointed my buddy Ollie brought you here. You look like you deserve better, Carrie."

The comment implied more than the food, and the mayor and the other guy snickered.

Oliver went stiff with fury. If he was any other guy, he would have leveled Jamansky by now. As it was, his fists balled under the table. Jamansky had Ashlee, but it wasn't enough. It never would be. Jamansky wanted to prove he could steal a girl right out from under Oliver's nerdy nose.

Thankfully, everything in Carrie's demeanor spoke abhorrence. Oliver was glad he'd told her what Jamansky had done. He wanted her to know the kind of man he really was.

The introductions were finished, no papers had been requested, and so Oliver pushed his plate away.

"Are you about done, Carrie?" he asked. She had a few bites left of her burger, and she'd barely touched her fries, but she nodded quickly, looking only too relieved.

"Good," Oliver said. "We should go."

Without any acknowledgement, Jamansky swung an arm up over the seat back behind her. "So Carrie, I thought I knew all the pretty girls in this area. Where do you live?"

That did it.

Oliver shot to his feet. "I'm sorry, Carrie. I didn't realize what time it is. It's getting late. We really should go."

"Oh, goodness," she said, pretending to check the clock behind her. "I promised my sister I'd be home by now. Excuse me, David."

Jamansky didn't move. "Your sister can wait. We were just getting acquainted. You were about to tell me where you live. Here in South Elgin? Or do you live closer to Officer Simmons?"

Oliver dropped back on his red cushioned seat feeling like he was about to lose his dinner. Carrie looked panicked. He gave her the tiniest shake of the head, begging her to say anywhere but Shelton.

"Um…north of Campton Hills," she said.

Oliver's gut unclenched an inch. A perfect answer.

"Ah," Jamansky smiled at her. "And how did you come to know my *older* employee?"

Oliver grunted angrily. "We met when—"

"I asked her!" Jamansky barked. Then he turned back to Carrie with another swagger smile. "Yes?"

Her hands twisted in her lap. "Oliver and I have been friends for years. Our dads were friends years ago. They were cops together." Her blue eyes darted from person to person. Her words were tight with lies, but the others didn't seem to notice. "I haven't seen Oliver for ages, so we wanted to catch up."

She couldn't have answered better if Oliver had fed her the lines. If Carrie's dad had been a cop, she would have clout in the government now. Maybe enough Jamansky would back off.

Jamansky didn't.

"Interesting. So you and my buddy Ollie are just friends, huh?"

"Yes," she said, "but if you'll excuse me, David, I really did promise my little sister I'd be home before dark." She scooted a little. "Do you mind?"

Though it took a moment, Jamansky shifted out of the seat and stood, clearing the way for her to exit the booth. He took her hand again, only a little friendlier than a handshake. "It was lovely to meet you, Carrie. I hope to see you around again."

She nodded but didn't return the sentiment.

Oliver whipped out his wallet, dropped some bills on the table, and stepped toward Carrie. But Jamansky shifted sideways, purposely blocking Carrie from Oliver's reach. The mayor laughed. So did the other guy.

Oliver was done.

"Move," Oliver hissed at Jamansky. "Now."

Jamansky gave a last menacing smile to let Oliver know this was far from over, and then he stepped out of the way.

With all three men watching, Oliver took Carrie by the arm and led her outside. He opened her car door and screeched away from the curb, barely able to think straight enough to drive.

They rode in silence while Oliver relived it over and over. Even with papers, he couldn't believe he'd been so reckless. He vowed never to take her anywhere again. She belonged in Logan Pond.

Not with him.

He sped down the road, hoping to get her home faster.

"Oliver?" she said.

It was just that after seeing her so fascinated on their drive through Shelton, he wanted to show her more of the world. He wanted her to know that there were still happy places and—if she chose—she didn't *have* to stay in Logan Pond. He'd given her a gift of freedom.

"Oliver?"

Although Carrie didn't know it yet, she had options now. She could wander and shop and eat in towns like South Elgin. But the last thing either of them needed was David Jamansky sniffing around—which he would now because that's what Jamansky did.

Oliver cursed himself for the hundredth time.

"Oliver," she said firmly, grabbing his arm to catch his attention— which it did. "I'm fine. You're fine. It's all fine. Please don't worry about it. Dinner was very nice. Thank you."

He should tell her. About the papers. But he was scared of her reaction, and technically they weren't fully processed yet. They still needed a signature—her signature—and then it would take at least another week for it to be official.

For her to be legal.

And free.

He was tempted to tear up the papers and be done with the whole stupid idea in the first place. He dreaded what she'd think once she found out he'd done it without her permission. Yet...even if she never spoke to him again, she'd still be safer than not having a card at all. Those papers were her ticket to freedom, Zach's freedom, Amber's freedom, and they all deserved to know.

Once they reached her driveway, Oliver parked the car and ran a hand over the bulge in his pocket.

"Thanks again, Oliver," she said. "It was nice to remember what life used to be like—or what it still is for some people. Can I repay you?"

"No," he said adamantly. Not only was she dead broke, but he had been a fool taking her. "Dinner was my gift. I wanted to pay for you."

"I meant"—she tucked a lock of hair behind her ear—"can I make dinner here for you next time?"

He went numb. "Next time?"

"Yeah. When did you say your day off was?"

He swallowed a few times. Blinked, maybe. He couldn't believe she was still talking to him let alone asking him out in return.

"Um. Saturday?" He said it like a question because he was an idiot. How was she supposed to know his day off? "Except...except I have training during the day in Joliet, so it would have to be later."

Carrie smiled. "Okay. Dinner here Saturday night. I don't have a lot of choices, but I can make soup or noodles. Which do you prefer?"

"Carrie..." he said softly, "you don't have to do this."

"Yes, I do. You've done so much for me—for all of us." Her chin dropped and in the fading light of day, she played with a string on her blue blouse. "It would be nice to do something for you for a change."

He immediately stiffened. "You don't owe me anything." If that's why she'd said yes today, if that's why she wanted to make him dinner... He looked her directly in the eye. "What I do, I do because I want to. Not because I expect anything in return. If you're just being nice or trying to repay me somehow, I just, I just..." He couldn't find the words. "Please don't."

She cocked her head. "Oliver, I *want* to make you dinner. Is that so hard to believe?"

"Yes."

She smiled. "Well, you'll just have to get over it because right now I want to know if you want soup or noodles."

250

Stunned, he stared at her. She stared back with those huge eyes, looking lovelier than any woman he could imagine. He couldn't think up a single food he wanted because all he wanted was her. Not in a bad way. Not in a creepy way either. Just in a long-term kind of way, in a way he knew could never happen.

Done with his cowardice, he felt the wad in his pocket again, but that was only part of the story. The full paperwork, including the spots that needed her signature, was in his glove box.

"May I?" he asked. Then he leaned across her seat, reaching for the glove box.

Carrie jerked back, eyes wide, cheeks paling. When he realized why, his face flushed with mortification. She'd misinterpreted his leaning.

She thought he was going to kiss her.

"No, wait," he said. "I was just grabbing something from the…" The word slipped his mind, and he made the mistake of looking at her lips. "I-I'm sorry. I didn't mean to lean into your space."

Your space?

Idiot!

"No, you just startled me, that's all." She brushed down her blouse with a tight smile. "It's fine."

Fine?

His stomach flopped. She thought he was going to kiss her, and she said it was fine.

Was it fine?

Had she just given him permission?

Without meaning to, he glanced at her soft, pink lips again. Even in the fading sun, he could see a lovely blush settle on her freckled cheeks as if reading his mind. But she didn't back away, and she didn't bolt out the door.

She loved Greg, but she kind of loved Oliver, too. That's why he was here. That's why he'd asked her out. To see what could happen, and now it was happening. While he was an idiot in many ways, he wasn't dumb enough to waste a chance like this.

A chance at those lips.

Pulse racing, he did something he had wanted to do for years. He reached up—slowly so she had plenty of time to slap him—and cradled her warm cheek, stroking her skin with his thumb. Even that much of her sent chills down his arms.

Her soft lashes lowered, and she leaned into his hand.

That was invitation enough.

His heart hammered in his ears, drowning out all other sound. He told it to shut up because he was going to kiss Carrie and he was going to do it without a heart attack. Leaning carefully across the seat, he closed his eyes and closed the distance.

But…when his lips met her skin, it wasn't her lips. At least not fully.

His eyes flew open.

He'd caught the corner of her mouth, that tiny spot between her lips and her cheek. She had turned at the last second.

Carrie had turned.

As she studied her hands in her lap, he finally understood. She hadn't given him permission to kiss her. She'd meant that it was fine he had startled her. He was too stunned to apologize. Too stunned to do anything but stare at her as the car went deathly quiet.

"I'm sorry," he said when he found his voice again. "I didn't mean to… I mean, I should have…" What? Asked first? Aimed better?

Never asked her out in the first place?

"No. I'm the one who is sorry, Oliver." Her eyes flickered to him but only for a second. "I'm just not ready yet."

Yet.

With considerable effort, he talked himself into that word. *Yet* had potential. Maybe it wasn't a complete rejection. It was a *not yet*. Only it felt like a rejection, the slap in the face he deserved. Even then, even with the mortification, he had enjoyed kissing that much of her, feeling the softness of her skin. She hadn't pulled back. She'd just turned a few millimeters. Not yet. That was more hope than she'd ever given him because it implied she might be ready someday. He could wait. He could.

He would.

With a tight smile, she grabbed the door handle. "How about I surprise you Saturday, okay? Thanks, Oliver."

Before he could clear his thoughts to respond, she was inside her house. Oliver watched her go, shocked he was still invited to dinner. He would see her again, but this time she was asking *him* out.

Reaching up, he touched his lips.

———◆———

Amber met Carrie in the kitchen. "How was dinner?"

Carrie picked up a muffin. She wasn't hungry, but she needed to eat. To do something. She slathered on a heap of butter.

"Carrie?"

She looked up. "Yeah?"

"How was your date?" Amber asked.

Carrie's mind was a whirlwind. Meeting the man who attacked Greg and Mariah. The mayor who turned Greg down. And then kissing Oliver—sort of. She'd watched the rejection wash over him when she turned. He'd wanted it so badly, and part of her had, too, but...

But what?

"It was..." Carrie looked around her house and out the front window. Oliver's car was long gone, but Greg's house sat across the street. Empty. Dark. Alone.

Amber waved a hand in front of her. "Hello?"

"Sorry." Carrie blinked hard. "It was nice."

"Nice?" Amber scowled. "What's going on? What happened?"

Carrie struggled to breathe normally. Oliver kissed her. That was more than Greg had ever done. And she still rejected him for it.

Setting down the muffin, she turned. "Um...I forgot something outside. I'll be back in a second."

"What? Where are you going?" Amber said, nearly shouting. "It's almost dark and Zach already went to bed."

"I'll be right back."

Carrie raced outside, checked up and down for anyone, and then darted across the street. She didn't dare go in Greg's front door. Someone would see her. So she ran down one more abandoned house, crept around the backyard, and headed back toward Greg's.

In the fading light, she slid up the deck and perched next to the kitchen door. She tried the handle. Thankfully Greg kept his house unlocked like the rest of them to keep patrolmen from breaking down doors during sweeps.

She slipped inside and looked around Greg's kitchen, bathed orange and pink with the last rays of day. It was still perfectly clean. She'd probably spent more time in his new house than he had. Everything looked empty and abandoned, but she knew it wasn't. He didn't have time to pack, which meant his stuff was somewhere inside here.

An overwhelming urge washed over her to see what he'd left behind, to hug a stupid t-shirt, quilt, or anything of his, but she knew that was too intrusive. Besides, she had a hat back home which would do the job. She shouldn't be here, uninvited, intruding, yet she didn't want to leave because she needed to be here.

Desperately.

She sank down on the hardwood floors and wrapped her arms around her knees. Just because Oliver wanted to kiss her didn't mean she had to let him. She'd never seen anyone move so slowly, but she'd only turned at the very last possible moment. Why? One split second decision and the outcome would have been completely different. She could still be kissing Oliver now.

Her throat constricted, feeling like she'd betrayed both men.

She hated herself, hated the situation, hated that Greg was gone, that he didn't love her more than he did, that Mariah was dead, her parents were dead, and everyone was dead.

Everything felt entirely wrong and stupid.

"Greg," she whispered. "Where are you?"

By the time she pulled herself together, it was fully dark in Greg's house. She crept back across the street where Amber waited at the front door, arms folded, looking ready to strangle something.

"I'm trying really hard not to hate you right now," Amber said, "but you promised to be home before dark. What the heck is going on?"

"Are you ready for that talk now?" Carrie said. "Because I could really use it."

thirty-seven

The evening air started to cool, and the small band of rebels gathered around the large campfire while dinner crackled and smoked over the flames. Nobody was pointing guns anymore as Greg explained their "story."

It wasn't hard for Greg to fabricate passionate hatred for the government as he spoke. It filled his soul. He used the same counsel he'd once given to Oliver: *"Truth sells, so use as much as possible."* He spoke of his time in Raleigh, receiving the lashings on his back, his sister dying, and his mom and him coming north. He talked about being recruited and ripped from her arms by David Jamansky and sent off to fight. It only took a few tweaks to allow Isabel into the story. They'd met in training, a woman who'd also been captured and punished. They watched the guards for weeks on end, waiting for a chance to escape. That chance came a short time ago. Since then, they'd been making their way to this area, looking for groups who hated the government as much as they did.

Oh, and Isabel was pregnant.

His story was nothing like the one Isabel wanted, but she sat quietly next to him on the log, taking his hand, rubbing his back, and leaning against him throughout the narrative. A few times she pinched his leg when his story took another unrehearsed turn, but this version rolled off his tongue with little effort. Six years of pent up hatred vented in a single sitting. An easy sell. A few times Isabel looked as mesmerized as everybody else was, surely realizing how much was true.

At first, the two dozen rebels glanced at each other with skepticism. But the longer Greg talked, the more they shook their heads and spouted off rants about President Rigsby, Chief Jamansky, and the whole bitter lot.

"Live free or die," they muttered.

As Greg finished, their leader, a man they called Kearney, stood.

"Well, we can always use more on our side," Kearney said. "So welcome to our sorry lot. In the morning, we'll catch you up on strategy and where we're looking to hit next. For now, do you two have a tent?"

"No," Greg said. "We've been sleepin' under the stars—"

"—or rain," Isabel added, squeezing Greg's hand with a smile. "So we're fine wherever. We're just grateful you'll let us join the cause."

Kearney nodded. "Let's put you in Perry's tent for the night. He's gone to headquarters for a few days. Tomorrow we'll figure out a better place to put you. For now, enjoy your privacy while you have it." He winked.

Isabel's hand slid onto Greg's thigh. "Oh, we will."

Greg ignored the insinuation and instead focused on that one word: *Headquarters.* That sounded more official than he expected. It was disconcerting how easily they'd let Isabel and him into their group. Isabel was right. They'd have no problem getting to the heart of the rebellion. To headquarters.

An hour later, Greg and Isabel laid side by side on the tent floor, no pillows, and one blanket to share. He gave her the blanket even though the air was cooler than comfortable. It was a single-man tent that barely fit the two of them, but it was better than sleeping under the stars. The mosquitoes were out in swarms, plus it smelled like rain.

He brushed the dirt aside and lay on his back, staring up at the dark tent ceiling a few feet above them.

Isabel's leg brushed his. He slid further away. Instead of taking the hint, she rolled toward him and brought her mouth close to his ear. He flinched, wanting distance from her. At least she was still fully clothed. She'd tried to shed a few layers, but he flipped out. Still, she was too close, but it was the only way to communicate without being overheard.

"This group isn't too bad," she whispered. "Better than some I've encountered. And we're in, easy enough."

"Yeah." *Too easy.* The rebellion would never last at this rate. "Did you hide your bag?" he asked in a whisper.

"I kicked it under a bush."

"Me, too. I'll try to sneak away in the morning and bury them."

The only sounds in camp were crickets, frogs, and soft, muddled conversations as people settled into their tents. Isabel rolled onto her back and was quiet for a time.

"If you could have," Greg whispered, barely audible, "would you have stayed in Pete's clan as an illegal?"

"Without citizenship? Are you crazy?"

Yes, but no crazier than Kearney or the rest of this camp. These rebels had fire in their veins. If Greg didn't have a family and Carrie back in Shelton—or virtual handcuffs around him now—he could see himself joining a group like this, living off the land, always on the move. Not just hoping for a better life, but fighting to create it.

He felt Isabel shrug. "If I did, it only would have been for Pete. Nothing else about this life appeals to me. I actually like eating. Why? Would you?"

"In a heartbeat. I'd love to live off the radar again."

She went up on an elbow and leaned far enough into his personal space he felt her hot breath on his cheek. "Even now, after everything you've seen?"

"Especially now, after everything I've seen."

"But you'd lose your green card," she whispered urgently. "Your liberty."

"Actually, I'd be gaining it."

She huffed. "My uncle thinks he can turn you, but he's wrong. So you're a fan of their stupid motto, *Live Free or Die?* If you feel so strongly, why not just run? If you were determined enough, I doubt even I could stop you."

He rolled away from her dark form. "I have my reasons."

"Then you better shut up, because any more of this talk and I'll turn you in myself. I can't have you become a liability on me, Pierce. You're on a mission. We own you now."

His head whipped around. "As if I don't know that."

"Ah," she breathed. "Uncle Charlie really did threaten them. So you'll stab your fellow rebels in the back to keep your loved ones safe?" He heard a smile enter her voice. "And here I thought you were heartless."

Using his arm as a pillow on the scratchy, dirty tent floor, he shifted around until he found a comfortable spot and begged himself to fall asleep.

Greg woke to the sound of a new fire crackling and the smell of breakfast. Bacon. Eggs. Mush. He didn't care what was out there, his stomach grumbled. He'd slept deeper and warmer than expected. Then he realized why. Isabel was curled up beside him, arm draped over his chest.

He threw her arm off him and scooted away until he ran into the damp tent wall.

Still asleep, Isabel snuggled into her blanket.

Greg rubbed the crinks from his neck and stretched out his back. The joy of sleeping on a hard, rocky ground.

Isabel hoped to figure out the general plan of the rebellion today, where and when they would strike next. This group was small, but she hoped they knew enough to help McCormick so she and Greg could move on and do the whole thing over again. And over and over and over until McCormick—or President Rigsby—was satisfied. If there wasn't a dark-haired seductress two feet away, Greg would have laid back down and tried to hibernate away this assignment. Instead, he grabbed his shoes.

Isabel rolled over with a deep yawn. "Sleep well, honey bun?"

"I'm gonna walk around for a bit," he said, lacing his shoes.

She bolted upright. "Wait. Don't go without me, sweetums."

Greg rolled his eyes. She was overdoing the wife bit, but he waited anyway. The sun barely screened through the leaves, dancing on the sides of their blue tent. The morning was cool and damp with dew. Greg planned to head straight to the crackling fire to warm up.

Once Isabel was ready, they emerged from the tent. She grabbed his hand, interlacing fingers with him. He rolled his eyes again but didn't pull free.

The illegals milled about. Some hovered around the fire, some worked on breakfast, and the rest—a small group of leaders—met off to the side, speaking in hushed, concerned whispers. McCormick would want Greg to eavesdrop on that little meeting, but Greg stayed close to the fire, hands outstretched to absorb the heat.

A man handed him a bowl of steaming oatmeal. Greg sat on a log and Isabel snuggled into him with her own bowl. Greg was nearly finished eating when the group of leaders split up and headed back to the fire.

"Sleep well?" Kearney asked, joining them.

"Yeah," Greg said. "Thanks for the tent. We appreciate the hospitality." Greg set his bowl aside. "Just put us to work today. We're real hard workers." At least, Isabel better be.

Kearney nodded. "Good. You can help me dig pits for the new outhouses, Greg."

Although Greg had dug more holes in the last six years than he ever cared to, he nodded. It was something mindless he could do. Something un-devastating.

"How are you at mending jeans, Isabel?" Kearney asked.

"Amazing," Isabel said without batting an eye.

She probably hadn't touched a needle in her life, but this was good. Already they'd been accepted in. If Greg could convince Isabel to lie low for a few days, give them time to settle before they snooped, Greg might be able to—

"Kearney!" somebody shouted, tromping through the brush on a run. "Come quick!"

Kearney jumped up and met the young guy—Travis, if Greg remembered right—outside of the small ring of people. Travis held something up. Greg saw a flash of camouflage and his stomach dropped.

Isabel's fingers dug into his leg. "No," she breathed.

Government-issued bags.

Their government-issued bags.

Kearney ripped open Greg's bag and grabbed a handful of supplies. Radios. Maps. Greg's favorite gun.

Greg's eyes darted around the camp, but Kearney didn't give him time to formulate a plan.

"Grab them!" Kearney shouted.

The entire camp descended on Greg and Isabel.

thirty-eight

Men grabbed Isabel and Greg and dragged them over to Kearney who held the two bags in front of them.

"What. Are. These?" Kearney said, veins popping out of his dirty forehead. On the sides of each camouflaged bag was a single white star, the new seal of the United States.

Three guys held Greg. Isabel was a few feet away in the same predicament. Neither answered, but Greg's mind raced with possible explanations that wouldn't get them both shot.

Kearney dumped the contents onto the dirt. Green cards, radios, pistols, and plenty of other condemning things which Greg didn't see because one of the guys slammed a rifle down on Greg's thigh.

Greg screamed and dropped to the dirt.

Another guy kicked his shoulder. Someone punched his gut. His face. Pain exploded everywhere, a flood of pulsing agony. Greg couldn't breathe. Couldn't think. He could barely hear Isabel's screams above his own, but the hits kept coming. Above the blinding pain, one terrifying thought slipped through: he was going to die. Now. Here.

Then the beating stopped. The men stood back, breathing heavily, leaving Greg to writhe and moan on the dirt. His thigh. His shoulder. Above the chaos and his own moans, he heard Isabel sobbing. Had they beaten her, too?

Greg needed to see. He forced his clenched eyes open, but instead of seeing Isabel, a green citizenship card hung inches from his face, held by Kearney.

"Gregory Curtis Pierce," Kearney read. "Special Operative in the Federal Patrol Unit. I knew something wasn't right." Standing, he flipped the green card, end over end, into the fire. Then he said, "Kill them both."

A man grabbed Greg's pistol. Greg squirmed, trying to scramble to his knees, but two guys held him down. He twisted, kicked, and clawed the ground, desperate to get free until something hard rammed into his temple and he heard the gun's safety click off by his ear.

"Wait!" Greg shouted. "Wait! Let me explain."

"Oh, you've done enough talking, spy," Kearney sneered.

Greg saw Kearney's fist coming but had nowhere to go. It slammed into his jaw. His head snapped back. The world went foggy. Yet through it, he felt metal dig back into his forehead.

Gun.

"Sixty seconds!" Greg yelled. "Just give me—"

A shriek pierced the air. "Greg!"

Squinting through a mass of legs, Greg saw Isabel on her knees, knife at her throat.

"Kearney!" Greg shouted, voice strained with terror. "Give me sixty seconds, then you can shoot us both. Please. Just sixty!"

Kearney crouched next to him. He nodded at the guys holding Greg, and they loosened their grip. "Fine. Sixty seconds. Go."

Greg tried to sit, but pain shot down his thigh. They'd busted his leg and his shoulder felt dislocated. So he spoke from the ground. "You're right. We're government spies. They sent us to find the heart of the resistance."

The man holding the knife to Isabel's neck snorted. "He's not helping your case, is he princess?"

Tears streaked down Isabel's face.

"I know it doesn't look like it," Greg said through gritted teeth, "but I'm actually on the rebellion's side. My story was true. I hate the government more than anybody here, but they forced me into this 'cause they threatened my family. I want nothin' more than to see President Rigsby hang. And to prove it"—he motioned to the pile on the ground— "my commander's tracking our movement right now through those radios. So before you do another thing, you'd better destroy them."

Kearney's gaze flickered to the pile. "How do I know this isn't some ploy and those radios won't blow up the second I touch them?"

Shouts of assent echoed through the camp.

"Let me do it," Greg said. "I'd love nothin' more than to burn the noose they got around my neck."

Kearney considered this a moment. Then he stood and tossed the radios into the fire. "Okay. Your sixty seconds are up."

The pistol rammed into Greg's skull.

"The government's onto you!" Greg yelled. "They know everything. They knew right where your camp was and that there are fifteen camps in this area."

Kearney turned back slowly. "What did you say?"

"They just don't know who's leadin' the pack or where headquarters are," Greg said. "But it doesn't matter. The whole wrath of the U.S. Army is about to descend on this rebellion, so you gotta move out and form a new base somewhere else, and you gotta do it now. Trust nobody. Don't let anybody into your camps, not even people with scars."

Kearney looked around his group. Then he shook his head with a sly smile. "Your numbers are way off, spy. We have twice that many and growing by the day. This area is perfect. We haven't seen a single patrolman since we set up camp. You must know that, so you want us to move to a heavier patrolled area."

"They suspended all local sweeps so you wouldn't run!" Greg yelled in exasperation. "I'm tellin' you, they're onto your game. They're ready to wipe out the whole rebellion. You can't let them!"

For a second time, Kearney's eyes darted from person to person. Greg chanced another peek at Isabel. A guy still held a knife at her neck. She not only looked terrified but sickened by what Greg said. He didn't care. If his life was over, something good better come of it.

Kearney crossed the small circle and crouched in front of Greg again.

"Why are you telling me this?" he hissed. "We're just going to kill you both anyway. Surely you know this."

Live free or die. Greg finally understood. If his death helped some-body else live free, then it was worth it.

The pain in his head, shoulder, and leg pulsed and throbbed, making Kearney's face go in and out of focus, but he set his jaw.

"'Cause you gotta win," Greg said. "The only people I care about live in constant fear and starvation. Your rebellion, this second civil war, is their only chance at a real future. You gotta take Rigsby down."

Angry shouts broke out in the group. Several, including the guy holding Greg, yelled at Kearney not to listen and just shoot them already. Others seemed to believe what Greg said. But Kearney glared at Greg and only Greg.

Then something changed in Kearney's demeanor. His gaze swept beyond the group toward the woods and the sky. Suddenly urgent, he called, "Pack up camp! We're moving out!"

A ripple of surprise rocked through the group.

"We'll keep these two as hostages and make examples of them," Kearney continued. "Let the government know what happens when they send spies. Drew, send word to the other groups and tell them we're on the move. Tell them to head for—"

Greg saw a blur of movement. He heard a grunt, and the man holding Isabel dropped. Isabel scrambled on the ground, grabbed something from the pile of supplies, and shouted one word at Greg.

"Run!"

Before Greg could process, she lobbed something into the air. A second later, an explosion rocked the ground. Smoke, wood chips, and dirt rained down on Greg.

A hand grenade.

It was enough. Chaos erupted.

Greg punched the guy's knees holding the gun to his temple. The guy dropped. Greg swung around and kicked another guy. Something popped in his bad shoulder, causing more excruciating pain, but the guy fell. Greg's path was clear.

Another explosion shook the camp, close enough Greg felt the heat on his back. More screaming and smoke filled the air.

Greg rolled, grabbed his pistol and aimed it at the next guy who grabbed him. The guy's hands flew up, face white as a sheet. He was just a kid, barely older than Zach. That snapped Greg out of what he'd nearly done. He chucked the pistol into the woods and stumbled back. His leg wasn't working, so he dragged it as people ran for cover.

A third explosion, this one near the tents, and Greg searched for Isabel. He couldn't see or hear her through the smoke and mass of people. So he took off into the woods on a lumbered run.

Adrenaline and six weeks of heavy training pushed him through the pain and woods. He darted in and around the thick underbrush, away from the camp. But he couldn't hold the pace. His upper leg was on fire, and his shoulder killed. Finding a thick tree trunk, he doubled over to catch his breath. Then he listened and peered around the tree.

Nobody followed, but he could hear the chaos back in camp.

A few gunshots fired off.

Isabel.

Greg's stomach churned with acid. They'd killed her. She was dead. And all he could think was that should have been him.

Isabel saved his life.

His insides started to shake quickly followed by his hands. Balling them into fists, he assessed the extent of his injuries. His shoulder hung awkwardly in front of him. Dislocated. One eye was swollen shut, his lip was fattened, too, and fresh blood thickened the side of his beard. But his leg worried him most. Hopefully it was just a deep bruise and not a cracked thigh bone. His leg had gotten him this far. It would have to get him the rest of the way.

But first he had to fix his shoulder.

Gathering his courage, he lunged and rammed it against the massive tree trunk. Pain blinded him. He fell back, tripped on his bad leg, and ended up on the ground, clutching his leg one-handed, swallowing back a scream.

Stupid, idiotic move.

The second time he tried to fix his shoulder, he was more prepared for the jolt. He still had to bite back a shout as he threw himself at the tree, but he felt the pop in his shoulder. His arm sat at a more natural angle, but the stabbing pain continued. He tried to rotate it with little success. For all he knew, he'd only made it worse.

Giving up, he spotted the position of the sun and set a course due west, straight for Shelton, Illinois.

As he limped toward home, his conscience began to eat at him. Every step, the same word sounded over and over in his mind:

Isabel. Isabel. Isabel.

He had deserted her. She saved his life creating that diversion, and he ran without a second glance. Just because he'd heard gunshots didn't mean she was dead. He didn't even like her, but she was still his partner. She was the enemy, a true spy, but they'd hold her hostage. Or worse. Make an example of her.

Isabel. Isabel. Isabel.

She was probably dead, he reasoned. Or maybe she had escaped like he had.

But if not…

A few more agonizing limps.

What would they do to her, especially if they found out she was the niece of the commander in charge? They'd torture her. Make an exhibition out of her, the resistance's first hostage. It might even be enough to help the rebellion, to give them the edge to win.

He should let it go. Forget everything—forget her. Isabel was the enemy. They wouldn't let him live if he turned back around. He should go home, see Carrie, and live his mom's last days with her. Be free. He should leave while he still could.

Only…

…he couldn't.

Closing his eyes, Greg wondered which side he was on anymore. Maybe just humanity's.

Then he turned and started back for the camp.

———◆———

Carrie eyed Terrell's rifle as they crouched in a patch of woods west of the Watercrest neighborhood. She really wished he wouldn't bring guns on these "peaceful" delegation missions. They were here to find friends and people to trade with, not start a war.

The second they had approached the outskirts of the subdivision, Carrie could tell things were different. She couldn't even put a finger on why. The area just felt more…alive. Terrell and Richard looked nervous, which in turn made her nervous.

"What next?" Richard said, still crouched low.

"If they post guards," Terrell whispered, "which they'd have to do without Oliver, they've already spotted us. Check for movement on the rooftops."

As one, they scanned the houses. Watercrest was larger than Logan Pond, spanning several streets. There was no way to know anything for sure from their position.

"How are we supposed to snoop around without getting shot?" Terrell said.

"What if we go the obvious route?" Carrie suggested softly.

"Meaning…?"

"Let's start knocking on doors, or just call out to people from the street. Patrolmen wouldn't do that. Neither would government spies."

Terrell rolled his dark eyes. "Because they don't like getting their brains blown out. No one would do something so stupid."

"No one? Are you sure?" Richard questioned. And, without warning, he strode out from behind the hedges, arms waving high in the air. "Ho, there! Hello?" Richard called. "We're looking for fellow illegals like us!"

"Holy heaven almighty," Terrell breathed. "We're all dead."

Probably, but Carrie smiled and joined Richard, walking out into the wide open. Terrell huffed under his breath but followed. The three of them walked down the main road running through the center of the Watercrest neighborhood.

"We're from Logan Pond, your fellow townsmen!" Richard continued to call. "We're looking to make contact with other clans. Hello?"

Carrie checked every house. She couldn't hear anything, she couldn't see much beyond the abandoned-looking homes either, but she swore she felt something move. Her eyes darted around, suddenly feeling like she had a target on her chest. Maybe Terrell was right. Maybe this was a really, really bad idea.

Richard turned onto a side street, winding deeper into the sub as he repeated his message. "My name is Richard O'Brien. I've been a resident of Shelton all of my life, as have my friends, Carrie Ashworth and Terrell Dixon. We're looking to make contact with—"

"Carrie?"

Carrie turned at the sound of a woman's voice.

"Carrie, is that you?" a woman called as she and a few others exited one of the homes.

Squinting, Carrie held up a hand to block the morning sun. The woman had long dark hair and held a small bundle in her arms. Carrie didn't recognize her from this distance, but she waved anyway.

"Hello! It's me, Carrie Ashworth."

"You know her?" Terrell asked under his breath.

"I…" Carrie squinted harder. "I'm not sure."

As the woman approached, Carrie racked her brain to figure out who she was. Terrell and Richard shifted nervously, especially since the dark-haired woman had three men and another woman trailing her, two of whom carried rifles.

Carrie's small group was suddenly outnumbered.

The woman's face stayed shaded, but even then, Carrie saw enough to know she didn't recognize her. It had been years since she'd encountered other people, but so long that she'd forgotten everyone?

A chill ran down her spine. Did this woman really know her, or was this some trick to lure them in?

thirty-nine

Carrie felt stiff with trepidation. The eight of them met in the middle of the street, each sizing up the other group for threats. Their two women looked skinny and worn down while the three men looked shaggy and dangerous. None of them seemed familiar to Carrie, even though she'd met people from Watercrest before. Especially not the younger woman who had called her name.

"It's me, Brooke," the brown-haired woman said. "Brooke Gabriel, from Shelton High? I was in the marching band."

"Yes," Carrie said, finally recognizing the face. Back in high school, Brooke had been a little on the heavy side. Now her clothes hung on her body. But it was still Brooke, and Carrie couldn't have been more relieved.

"You live here?" Carrie asked. "I thought you lived east of the school."

"I did, but these people," Brooke said, looking over her shoulder, "have recently taken in me and my son."

Son. Carrie took in the small bundle in Brooke's arms.

"May I?" Carrie asked, starting to step forward, but Terrell grabbed her arm and kept her back. Understanding his desire to keep some distance, Brooke pushed away the mass of blankets and held up her tiny son to show Carrie. He was sound asleep and smaller than a baby should be, but he had a cute button nose and a few tufts of red hair.

Carrie smiled. "What's his name?"

"Jackson," Brooke said. "He's two months old today."

It was strange that someone Carrie's age had a baby, but then again, she was twenty-three. That was old enough.

"He's beautiful," Carrie said.

Brooke's eyes filled with tears. "Thank you. He looks just like his daddy, but—"

"Why are you here?" one of the men barked, breaking into the conversation. He kept his rifle in the crook of his arm, not pointed at anyone but still at attention, making it clear he wasn't open to a social visit.

Carrie waited for Terrell to take the lead. She'd promised as much. He held his own rifle and had demanded to lead out in this, but it was Richard who stepped forward, hand outstretched.

"We're here on a delegation of sorts," Richard said. "We live in a subdivision northwest of here, in Logan Pond, and we're hoping to make contact with other clans."

The man eyed Richard's outstretched hand. "We were told to steer clear of Logan Pond because it had legals living in it."

Richard dropped his hand but continued to smile through his gray goatee. "Yes. May and CJ Trenton—my in-laws—are yellow card holders, but they have little contact with the government. They've been assisting our small clan of illegals for six years now."

"How do we know you're telling the truth and you're not some green card spies?" the older woman asked.

"I guess you'll have to take our word for it," Richard said easily. "Although I doubt government employees would dress this shabby or look so malnourished."

Carrie smiled at the truth of that statement, but she was the only one. Her smile faded. This wasn't going as she hoped.

"I've known Carrie for years," Brooke said. "She's not a spy."

"Then why didn't she recognize you?" the first man snapped.

Brooke clutched her baby, bottom lip quivering. "Because I don't even recognize myself anymore."

"I'm sorry, Brooke," Carrie said. "I wasn't expecting to see someone from school here, but I recognize you. I'm so happy to see someone I know again." And if Terrell wasn't blocking her, she probably would have given Brooke a hug.

The tall man in the back stepped forward and finally shook Richard's hand. "I'm Gavin," he said. "This is Taylor, Johannes, and Sarina. It sounds like you already know Brooke."

"Nice to meet you," Richard said. "Is Bo Swann still a member of your clan? We go back a ways."

"Never heard of him," Gavin said. "This sub was empty when we got here. We're a Bedouin group."

"Bedouins," Terrell whispered under his breath. "Great."

Carrie frowned as well. How do you trade with people who moved every few weeks? But she was more concerned about the other part he'd said. Empty subdivision.

Gavin noticed their disappointment. "Don't worry," he said darkly. "We'll be moving on soon."

"Do you know where the previous residents went?" Carrie asked.

"A few homes still had things in them," the older woman answered. "So we assume the clan was taken in a raid."

Carrie felt ill. The Watercrest clan once had fifty people.

Terrell leaned close. "They're scavengers," he whispered. "Let's go."

Her eyes widened. Scavengers were worse than Bedouins since they lived off the misfortunes of others. Definitely not people they wanted to trade with. Now that Terrell had said it, she noticed they wore nicer clothes than any in Logan Pond. Except Brooke. Her shirt was stained and stretched thin like it had been worn for years.

"When did you join this group?" Carrie asked her.

"Right after my husband was arrested," Brooke said. "About a month ago."

Carrie gasped. "Your husband was arrested? Oh, Brooke. I'm so sorry."

Nodding, Brooke's eyes watered. "Remember Scott Perry?"

Carrie's stomach twisted further. She knew Scott better than she knew Brooke since they'd hung out in the same social group in high school. Carrie took another peek at the baby and spotted Scott's fair skin and distinctive red hair.

"Of course I remember him," Carrie said. "I'm so sorry, Brooke."

"I don't know if we'll ever see him again," Brooke said, tears wetting the blanket.

"Where was he arrested?" Carrie asked. If it was close, Oliver might be able to look at the records to find out where Scott ended up.

"The other side of Shelton. We planned to find Scott's uncle in West Chicago, but I went into labor early, so we stopped at Scott's old house." Brooke wiped her eyes, but it did nothing to stop the flood of tears. "We were only there a few weeks when a patrolman came through. He had dogs and Scott..." She started to hiccup loud sobs. "Scott, he..."

Sarina put an arm around her. "Her husband ran so they wouldn't find them. Brooke resigned herself and her baby to starvation when we happened across them."

Brooke took a shuddering breath. "They've been so kind to take us in even though I have nothing to offer in return."

Carrie deliberated a moment and then decided to just say it. "I might be able to help, Brooke. I have this friend who is—"

"Carrie!" Terrell snapped.

She reworded her explanation. "My friend might know where they're holding Scott. I could maybe ask him."

"Oh, could you?" Brooke said. "I don't have any way to tell him where I've gone, so even if he was released by some miracle, he has no way to find us. They burned down the house after we left."

Carrie went numb. "What?"

That started another round of tears for Brooke, so Gavin spoke for her. "When I went back to get Brooke's things, they had burned the house to the ground. What a waste!"

Carrie couldn't breathe.

Oliver.

The illegal.

The phone call in the car. The squatter who attacked Oliver. The squatter Oliver arrested.

The squatter who was dead.

Oh, no. Oh, please, please, please no.

"We're taking Brooke and her baby with us," Sarina continued, "so if you're able, tell her husband we're meeting up with the resistance in West Chicago."

Brooke looked up with swollen, red eyes. "It's where Scott and I were heading anyway. He wanted to join the rebellion so badly. Live free or die. He practically chanted it in his sleep."

Carrie couldn't think straight enough to respond. She couldn't even nod. She just kept praying she'd put the wrong pieces together. She'd heard the illegal screaming, yelling nonsense in the background, but for the life of her, she couldn't remember what his voice sounded like. But it couldn't have been Scott. It was just a chilling coincidence.

Then she remembered.

Oliver said he wasn't able to burn the whole house down, mostly just the garage. But the house Gavin saw had been burned to the ground. She took a deep breath. Scott was still alive. It hadn't been him.

The next time she saw Oliver, she would ask him about arrest records and see if he could help track Scott down.

Terrell tugged on Carrie's arm and shot Richard a look that he was ready to leave.

"Well, we won't take up any more of your time," Richard said. "It was nice making your acquaintances. Good luck to all of you."

"Say," Gavin said as they turned to leave, "would your clan be interested in joining the rebellion? If so, there's a group who meets every evening in an old food plant outside of West Chicago. They plan and coordinate the next attacks. I'm sure they can use more people to join the cause."

"We'll keep that in mind," Terrell said, tugging on Carrie's sleeve. She was barely able to wave to Brooke before Terrell dragged her out of there. He looked furious as they double-backed the way they'd come.

They were well out of the neighborhood before Richard broke the tense silence. "Should we try another clan today?" Richard asked.

"Oh, no," Terrell said. "We've done enough damage."

"I didn't think it went too badly," Richard said.

"Me neither," Carrie said. "I'm glad we went."

"Not so bad?" Terrell said, picking up his pace. "They don't live here, they can't trade because not only are they a bunch of vultures, but they're joining a rebellion which is going to make the government even more violent. Oh, and the biggest clan in this area no longer exists! What exactly did we accomplish that has you two all hunky-dory?"

"We made contact," Carrie said. She thought about Greg and a sudden smile warmed her soul. Though it had taken longer than she hoped, they'd finally accomplished Greg's proposal number four. "We made contact with the outside world."

———— ◆ ————

It took Greg a while to figure out which way they'd gone. Kearney and the others had packed up camp faster than he thought possible. He searched around the smoking fire pit, but no sign of Isabel's body—not even that they'd dragged it somewhere. Which meant they had her. Alive, probably. So he searched until he found matted-down grasses and weeds. After that, following their trail was easy.

With every step, his body screamed to give up this suicide mission and head home. With the adrenaline rush gone, his left leg seemed to weigh a hundred pounds, his shoulder screamed with pain, and his other injuries stabbed with every heartbeat. But he kept following the trail until he found them.

Kearney's group had met up with another camp, a larger one. This new camp had fifty or so rebels and they'd commandeered a few small buildings which looked like part of an old weather station. The two groups gathered in a clearing. Greg couldn't see Isabel anywhere, but it was hard to see much of anything from his vantage point through the trees. Then he spotted Kearney's dark hair. With his good leg, Greg knelt on a fallen tree trunk and kept a sharp eye on Kearney.

Kearney was in a heated debate with a few others, probably the leaders. Greg was too far to make out what they shouted, but he guessed Kearney was convincing them to abandon camp. Kearney shifted and pointed into the woods. Right in Greg's direction.

Greg ducked. But after a second, he realized Kearney wasn't pointing at him. He was pointing at a small shed off to Greg's right, a shed guarded by two men.

Isabel.

No longer caring about Kearney or the others, Greg sized up the two guards. They were older than him but close to his size, only they were armed and unwounded.

Greg started moving. With a bum leg, he struggled to keep his footfalls from snapping twigs, so he slowed down and placed every step with care. The low summer brush and tree limbs snagged and scraped his arms, mosquitoes fed on his flesh, but he ignored it all to inch his way toward that shed.

The two guards talked in hushed whispers as they kept watch, looking disturbed by whatever Kearney had said. That was good. They were distracted.

Greg crept up behind the shed. Pressing an ear to the old wood, he heard a woman crying loud sniffles of defeat.

Isabel wasn't dead or unconscious. Also good.

The shed didn't have any windows, and there was only one door in on the opposite side by the guards. The whole shed was made of rotting wood. Greg tried a couple of pieces, but they weren't rotted enough to pry pieces off. Not without taking time and drawing attention.

Stepping close, he pressed his face to the wood and tried to see through the slats.

"Isabel," he whispered.

The sniffling stopped. He heard scrambling inside. "Greg?" she whispered back.

"Yeah. Are you injured?"

"Some. You?" she asked.

"Some." Greg rested his heavy head on the painted shed. "Is the door locked?"

"No." A few more sniffs. "Why are you here?"

Good question, he thought. But he shoved it aside to figure out his options. If the two guards had been on opposite sides of the shed, he could take them down one at a time, but there was little way to do it now without sound or alerting the rest of camp. Not unarmed and alone.

"Think you can take down one of the guards—preferably a silent method?" he asked.

A pause and then, "Yes. Are you sure you want to do this?"

No, but Kearney and the others would be packing up again soon. The longer Greg waited, the harder it would be to free her. Greg listened. Those guards were distracted, talking about how careless Kearney had been to let two spies into his camp. Ironic, considering.

"Can you see me through the cracks?" Greg whispered.

"Just where you're blocking the light," Isabel said back.

"Alrighty. If I take the guard on this side, can you take the other?"

"I think so."

"I'll take both if I have to," Greg whispered, hating this plan more by the second, "but it's gonna be hard without alerting Kearney. You know the sleeper hold?"

She grunted angrily. "Of course."

"Okay. When I knock on the side of the shed, that's your signal to move. The goal is no sound and *no* deaths." He could trust her for the first but not the second. Thanks to training, Greg knew four ways to kill a man without weapons, but hopefully it wouldn't come to that. "Ready?"

When it stayed quiet, he assumed that was a nod and started moving. He inched up to the corner of the shed and peered around.

"I've moved seven times in the last month," one of the guards said. "Here I thought we were going to get settled and now—"

Greg knocked on the side of the shed and then made his move.

The guard turned. "What was—"

That was all he got out. Greg jumped him from behind, arm around his neck, and squeezed his wrist against the carotid artery. The guy struggled, which only sped up the process. Then he dropped, out cold. When Greg turned, Isabel's guy was already on the ground.

Suddenly it was just the two of them crouched over unconscious men. Men who wouldn't be unconscious for long.

Pulse spiking, Greg grabbed her arm and started for the woods.

forty

Isabel was faster than Greg. Her injuries were only surface deep. Noticing he was falling behind, she double-backed and put an arm around his waist to shoulder some of his weight. They darted in and out and sideways through the trees to avoid straight lines that could be tracked.

"Why did you come back for me?" Isabel huffed.

"You'd do the same for me," Greg said through gritted teeth. His bad thigh wasn't going to last much longer.

"No, I wouldn't."

"You just did."

Greg tripped over a fallen stump. Isabel grabbed him before he could fall, but pain still shot through his whole body. He tried to stifle a yell and managed to swallow half of it.

"You were home free," she said, struggling with more of his weight. "You could have run."

He didn't want to admit that he nearly had.

"I'm sorry I told them," he said after another labored minute.

At that, she stopped and looked at him sharply.

"Not sorry for me," he amended. "Not sorry for the rebellion. They need to know what's comin'. But I'm sorry I jeopardized your life—present and future."

Turning, her eyes roamed the thick woods. "I understand why you did. Honestly, it probably saved our lives. It gave me time to distract my guy. But...well...just don't do it again."

Again.

The word knotted his stomach as the full extent of what he'd done hit him. How much would Isabel tell McCormick? What price would Greg pay for what he'd divulged—what price would his loved ones pay? The best he could hope was for McCormick to assign him to another clan. The worst was unthinkable. With luck, Kearney would spread the word to the whole rebellion, but where would that leave Greg and Isabel?

His head pounded. His body begged to be off its feet. But they kept trudging onward.

"Where are we headed?" she asked as Greg urged her to the right.

"Back to the original camp," he said. "The second those radios were destroyed, McCormick should have been alerted. Maybe he's already on his way." Not that Greg wanted to see the commander, but he needed to get off his leg. How could something be so numb and excruciating at the same time?

They were still a ways off when they heard shouting. McCormick's voice.

"Isabel!"

Isabel heaved a sigh of relief. "He found us."

"Just a bit farther," Greg said.

Isabel suddenly dug in her heels. Her fingers clamped on Greg's side to stop him. "Wait."

"What is it?"

She looked up at him, dark eyes urgent. "Don't come with me, Greg. I'll tell McCormick they killed you. You can run—well, not literally, but you can get away from here."

His brows shot up. "What?"

She grabbed his hands. "Go home, Greg. You don't belong here."

"Why would you do that for me?" Yet with only two seconds of time, he'd already allowed himself to hope, to envision his escape.

Her dark eyes shone. "You saved my life. Let me return the favor. You're dead now. So go."

"But…"

"Isabel! Pierce!" McCormick shouted again. "Spread out. They couldn't have gone far."

Greg's mind raced through every possible outcome of being 'dead,' including losing his citizenship, income for the clan, a future for his mom and Carrie, stability—or as much stability as patrolmen ever had. But after all he'd seen, he knew those rebel groups had a chance. But they needed Greg out of the way. Which meant by leaving, Greg was actually helping his own clan. Possibly permanently.

"Okay," he said. "I'm dead."

She nodded. "Just know that once you lose your green card, there's no getting it back. You'll be dead as far as the government's concerned—although I suppose if you got truly desperate, you could fabricate some story about how I thought you were dead, but Kearney just captured you and—"

"ISABEL!"

"I want nothing more than to never be heard of again," Greg said in a rush.

"Then go." She smiled. "Tell your mom hello for me."

"I will," he said, practically bursting with gratitude.

"And tell Carrie I hate her guts," Isabel added.

He laughed. But as he turned to leave, he had one last thought. He leaned close. "Rethink which side you wanna be on—which side Pete would want you on." Her eyes widened, but he went on. "It's not too late. If you wanna truly help these people, find a way to give them back the liberty they were born with, and find a way to do it peacefully. Then convince your uncle to do the same."

She looked stunned but nodded softly. "Good luck, Greg."

"Same to you."

He took off, lumbering through the brush in the opposite direction of the search party. As soon as he was out of sight, he heard Isabel call to her uncle. Curiosity won out. For whatever reason, Greg needed to see. He crept back until he could see Isabel and the others through the trees.

"What happened?" McCormick said. "I saw your bags. What did they do to you? Where's Pierce?"

Isabel turned on the waterworks. "They shot him. They killed Greg right in front of me." She collapsed on her uncle's shoulder and sobbed great sobs. "He's dead, and I thought I was dead, too."

"Alright," McCormick said, patting her back. "It's okay now."

Good enough.

Greg backed away, heart racing faster than his feet could as he set out on a path headed straight west.

Oliver jumped as someone's hands clamped down on his shoulders. Jamansky squeezed hard, pinching the muscle just below Oliver's neck as he leaned down to whisper, "How are you coming on that little project?"

The project involved making three sweep-acquired stashes disappear from the record books. Oliver loathed it. Jamansky and the mayor were working the black market again, but he hadn't figured out how to prove it without getting himself killed.

"Fine," Oliver said.

"Good." Jamansky stood back, releasing his shoulders. "So...how's Carrie?"

Oliver tensed all over again. He managed an indifferent shrug.

Jamansky picked up a random file from Oliver's desk and pretended to flip through it. "How about you give me her address and I'll find out for myself."

Oliver's breath hitched. From across the room, he saw Ashlee's head whip up. He told himself Jamansky was just trying to get under his skin. The guy couldn't seriously be interested in Carrie. He couldn't. He wouldn't.

He better not.

"Excuse me," Oliver said, snatching his file back. "I'm busy."

Jamansky sat on the corner of his desk. "She's a pretty girl. Sweet, too. I like that. So tell me, what was a guy like you doing with a girl like her anyhow?"

"We were just catching up," Oliver said dumbly.

Jamansky's eyes narrowed. "I don't believe you. I think you want Carrie. I think you're making a play for her, which is too bad because I want her, too. She seems like the nice, innocent type. Could be fun." He rubbed his hands together. "Could be a lot of fun. So what's her address? Or is she rich enough to own a phone? I'll just call her instead."

Oliver ground his teeth so hard they could have cracked. But before he could respond, he heard heels clipping across the floor. Suddenly Ashlee was in front of them. Her hand rose and she slapped David Jamansky flat across the cheek. The sound echoed through the office. David's head snapped back.

"You jerk!" Ashlee screamed.

Jamansky held his cheek, frozen with shock. Then his face went red with rage. He grabbed Ashlee's arm. "Who do you think you are?"

She tried to squirm free of his grasp, but his hand tightened on her arm and she yelped in pain.

Frantic, Oliver jumped up. "Let her go!"

"Stay out of this!" Jamansky threw his elbow out, catching Oliver squarely in the jaw. Oliver fell back into his chair with a crash. His head spun, his vision swam, but he jumped up, fists balled.

Jamansky whipped Ashlee around and held her in front of him as a shield. She was crying.

"Go ahead," Jamansky taunted. "Take your best shot, Simmons. She won't even feel a—"

"What is going on?" someone yelled.

Two federal patrolmen ran inside, pulling out their guns. Jamansky immediately dropped Ashlee. She fell to the ground, gasping.

Breathing heavily himself, Jamansky said, "Sorry, officers. We were just messing around. What can we do for you?"

Before they could answer, Ashlee rammed her high heel into Jamansky's toe. He yelped and swore. Then Oliver saw him whirl. His foot swung back.

"Jamansky!" Oliver screamed.

Jamansky's foot stopped inches from Ashlee's ribs. His jaw worked a moment before he gingerly put his foot back down. Throwing a look of pure murder at Ashlee, he stepped over her and went into the front area to greet the two men in black uniforms.

As soon as he was gone, Oliver dropped to a knee. "Are you okay?" he whispered.

"Yes. Thank you," Ashlee said. "Who is Carrie anyway? Her name sounds familiar."

That's because Oliver had slipped Carrie's paperwork in Ashlee's pile of stuff to be signed and documented.

"She's just my friend," he said, taking her hand to help her stand. "Jamansky's just trying to bother me. Don't worry about it. He didn't mean what he said." At least, he better not.

"I hate him."

"Me, too."

"All men are jerks," she whispered, wiping her eyes.

"I know."

Brushing off her pants, she managed a tiny smile. "Thanks, Officer Simmons."

He nodded as his mind sparked with a sudden idea. He'd been thinking about it for a while, but he wasn't sure how to implement it. Now, with Jamansky distracted and Ashlee hating him, Oliver lowered his voice.

"Would you be interested in helping me with a project?" he whispered.

"What kind of project?"

His skin tingled with fear and he checked on Jamansky again. "I need to document some things. Some things that might prove...other things. Things that might get certain people in trouble."

Ashlee's green eyes widened. "You want to take David down?"

Oliver pressed a finger to his lips but nodded. "The mayor, too. I just need proof. I need help with some files, only it might—"

"Looky-looky, Ash babe," Jamansky called from the front room. He waved some papers at her, all smiles again. "Come see what those feds just delivered. This is a huge 'I told you so.' Man, justice is sweet!"

Ashlee turned back to Oliver, eyes lit with fire. "Count me in." Then she walked into the front room and said, "What is it, hon?" as if nothing out of the ordinary had happened between them.

Oliver stared down at the floor, thoughts racing. Ashlee would help. That was a huge hurdle. Now he just had to find enough evidence to prove the level of corruption in this office. But even if he could prove it, who would he report to? Federal patrolmen? Who was to say they weren't just as bad? He decided to worry about that later. Until then, he had a lot of digging to do.

He started for his desk when a sudden scream split the air. Female. Ashlee.

Oliver whipped around, adrenaline spiking for a second time. But Jamansky hadn't attacked Ashlee again. Instead, she clutched the papers the patrolmen in black had delivered.

"No, no, no, no, no!" she cried.

Oliver sprinted for the front room. "What happened?"

Jamansky snatched the papers back and handed them to Oliver. "Remember this guy?"

Oliver scanned the short note quickly:

DEATH NOTICE ENCLOSED FOR <u>Gregory Curtis Pierce</u> :

Inform family that <u> son </u> was killed in action. Please deliver enclosed death notice to: <u>541 Denton Trail, Shelton, Illinois.</u>

Special Patrols Unit

Oliver went numb.

Greg.

"That's the troublemaker you drove to Naperville," Jamansky said with a wide grin. "I knew he'd never survive."

Greg was dead.

It couldn't be true.

Oliver reread the notice. It had to be something else. A mistake. A trick of Greg's. Something.

He felt like someone punched him in the gut. What would Carrie do when she found out? What about Richard, May, and CJ, who already lost Mariah?

He stumbled to the wall and leaned against it. It couldn't be true. He squeezed his eyes shut.

Ashlee was on her knees, hands covering her face. Seeing her there sent a horrible realization through Oliver. If he'd never suggested Greg get his yellow card, this wouldn't have happened. This was Oliver's fault. Carrie would never forgive him for this. *He* would never forgive himself.

Jamansky smacked him. "What's your problem?"

Oliver took two slow breaths. His legs felt shaky and weak, but he straightened. Only when he opened his mouth to apologize, no sound came out.

Greg was dead.

Jamansky glared at him. "Inform his family. If they give you any problems, bring them in. I'll take care of them myself."

forty-one

Carrie stood next to the knee-high corn stalks. With the recent rain, the garden was finally flourishing.

Braden Ziegler walked through May's gate. His eyes stayed on Carrie as he picked up a shovel to start on the goat manure. Anytime she looked back, he was still watching her, as if hoping to get her attention. After giving Amber the cold shoulder, Carrie tried to ignore him.

Rhonda stood with an overflowing basket of peas. "They're not much to look at, but I'll wash them up and distribute anyway."

"Thanks," Carrie said. "I'll have the corn weeded soon."

Rhonda left, leaving Carrie and Braden alone in May's backyard. He shoveled one last load into the corner for composting and then approached her. Carrie kept weeding, pretending not to notice his shadow hanging over her.

"Hey, Carrie," Braden said. "Can I talk to you?"

She really didn't want to be dragged into the drama, but she sat back on her heels and wiped her forehead. "Sure. What's up?"

"Can we talk somewhere private?" he asked, looking around. "Maybe behind the pond? Not now, but after you're done working?"

"I don't know, Braden." If Amber spotted them alone—regardless of the reason—she'd flip out.

"Please. This is important."

Sighing, she nodded. "Okay. I can go now if you want."

"No!" Once again, he scanned the yard for any observers. "I'll meet you behind the pond when you're done. I'll be waiting for you."

She'd never seen Braden act so strange, but she agreed, hoping an explanation was coming.

By the time she finished, Braden was already behind the pond in a spot deep in the trees, hidden from the homes. He sat on a fallen log but stood the second he spotted Carrie.

"Thanks for coming," he said. "Here. Have a seat."

Reluctantly, she took the log he vacated. He started pacing in front of her, hands clasped behind him, eyes down on the dirt and weeds.

"I want to ask you some things," he said, "but I need to know that what we say won't get back to Amber. Is that okay?"

"Braden," Carrie said, "you have to know that I'm completely loyal to my sister. I can't hide things from her." *Especially* not now.

"I know, but I don't want to have to edit my thoughts. Please?"

Carrie was torn but said, "Okay. If I have any problems keeping something from her, we can discuss it later."

"Fair enough." He faced her and started right in. "What do you think of patrolmen? Like what they do and how they live? People around here hate them so much, but after Oliver—and now Greg—I just..." He ran a hand through his sandy-blond hair. "I'd like to know what you think. You're the most level-headed person I know on this subject."

Her shoulders lifted. "I guess they're just fulfilling their job. Some of them abuse their power"—she shuddered thinking of David Jamansky—"but I hope those are few and far between. Then again, who knows? Oliver is...well, he's different."

"Yes, and without him our life would be miserable, right? And he's done more for us than we could have done for ourselves, right? So why do people hate him so much?"

She could think of several reasons, but she suddenly pieced together where he was headed. Her gut tied itself in knots. "Do you want to become a patrolman?"

His gaze swept over the pond. "Yes. Quite seriously."

"But how? You're illegal."

"The government is desperate for help right now. I think they'd take volunteers if I offered."

Yes! her mind screamed. *To fight the rebels. To arrest people like us!* Somehow she managed to respond calmly. "May I ask why?"

He threw his hands in the air. "Because I don't want to live like this forever. I'm an adult now. I need to plan for my future. I want to have a home—my *own* home—where I don't have to worry about my family's safety every single second of the day. Is that too much to ask?"

"No," Carrie said, heart breaking for the next generation—her generation.

"I keep reasoning that being a patrolman wouldn't be so bad if I could help people like us. Maybe I could focus on the real bad guys, the ones killing and stealing and hurting others."

"Only Amber doesn't want you to," Carrie said, putting the final piece into place.

He picked up a stick and peeled off some bark. "Amber hates patrolmen, *especially* Oliver. The things she says about him... I just don't get it."

"I think some of Amber's resentment is because Oliver is showing interest in me." Carrie felt heat creep up her neck. "Amber thinks I have a hard time speaking up for myself, so she pushes Oliver away because she thinks I don't know how to let him down easy." And maybe Carrie didn't.

After the date, Amber had given her one advice: *"Dump Oliver. Now."* Not wholly unexpected, but not all that helpful either. *"If Greg didn't exist, would you have let Oliver kiss you?"*

When Carrie couldn't respond, Amber took that as confirmation.

"But I think it's more than that," Braden went on. "Amber truly hates patrolmen—any government workers, actually. Everyone does. And yet, I can't see any other way out of this."

"Yes, but what you're suggesting..." A chill ran down her arms. "You need to talk to Oliver."

His head hung. "I know. I want to. I can't stand Amber hating me anymore, but I'm scared of her reaction when she finds out I'm serious. What if I go to training and don't come back like Greg? But I also can't handle living like this forever."

The mention of Greg upped her desperation. "That's why we're reaching out to other clans. To find other options."

"Yeah. And how's that going?"

"Not good, but it's still something. With time,"—*a lot of time*, she added silently—"we might get enough income to buy a house or two."

"A house or two? For thirty people to split?" He gave her an incredulous look. "That's the best we can hope for?"

"You really need to talk to Oliver," she said because she trusted Oliver to steer Braden clear of this madness. "He's coming over for dinner Saturday. You can talk to him then."

"Okay. I hope I can wait that long. Every time I see Amber, it kills me. I know it might sound stupid, Carrie, but I love her. I think we could have a happy life together, maybe, but when I picture her living here, starving like we are, scared like we are, or worse, pregnant and dead like Jenna, I just…" His countenance fell. "Amber deserves better. We all do."

"Yes. But at what cost?"

"That's what I'm trying to figure out."

Carrie couldn't help but think that a guy like him with a stable head on his shoulders would be good for her head-in-the-clouds sister. "How about I send Oliver to your house first on Saturday. Then Amber won't know—"

Carrie stopped, hearing some shouting from around the pond. Braden heard it also and turned. She couldn't see anything from their secluded spot, but someone was calling her name.

"Sounds like Amber is looking for me," she said, standing and brushing off. "I better go."

Braden caught her arm. "Wait. You're not going to tell her, are you?"

"No." She smiled. "Let me know how it goes with Oliver."

Carrie quickly made her way back around the pond. Braden lagged behind, but when Amber's shouting turned frantic, both of them broke into a sprint. Something was wrong.

Amber spotted Carrie and met her by the muddy shoreline, out of breath. "Carrie, where have you been? I've been looking everywhere for—" Her dark eyes went past Carrie and narrowed suddenly. "What's he doing here? You guys were together?"

Braden stopped dead in his tracks.

"Doesn't matter," Carrie said. "What's wrong?"

Amber glared at Braden.

"Amber," Carrie said, grabbing her arm. "What happened?"

Amber finally remembered herself, and her face tightened with that same look of urgency. "It's Greg."

Carrie's heart screamed with terror. *No!* She clutched her stomach. "What about him?"

"He's back." The tiniest smile lit Amber's features. "Greg is back."

Carrie stopped breathing. "What?"

"He's back, but he's hurt."

"Wait. What? How bad?" Carrie struggled to keep up, but already Amber's gaze had wandered back to Braden who also stood anxious for news of Greg. Her dark eyes filled. "Why were you two alone behind the—"

Carrie grabbed her shoulders. "Amber! What's wrong with Greg?"

"I don't know. I tried to find you everywhere, and now I know why I couldn't. Sorry to have..." A few tears fell down her olive skin. "...interrupted."

Carrie couldn't deal with this right now. "Where is Greg?"

"May's," Amber said, wiping her cheeks angrily. "Everyone is going there right now."

"Can I come, too?" Braden asked.

Without answering, Amber's chin lifted and she started up the hill. Carrie didn't answer either. Greg was back.

She broke into a sprint and flew up the hill past both of them.

forty-two

May's house was crowded with people thronging Greg. Carrie tried to press in to see him, but she couldn't see. Couldn't see! But she heard him trying to keep up with the questions being hurled at him.

"When are you going back?"

"Is training finished early?"

"How did you get hurt?

At that last one, she jumped to see over the heads. Tall Terrell Dixon finally shifted, and she caught her first glimpse. Greg looked scraggly with his brown beard and shaggy hair. His clothes were filthy and rumpled, and his coloring wasn't quite right. But that wasn't what caused her stomach to drop. One side of his face was scraped and bruised, and he was cradling his left arm close to his chest. She wanted to fling herself at him, but he was too far, too many people, and like everyone else, she had a million questions. He already couldn't keep up.

Then she heard him say something that caused the entire room to go silent.

"Where's Mom and Richard?" Greg asked.

People looked around, wondering who would answer. Greg searched the room, too, and spotted Carrie by the door. His face brightened and he smiled that half-quirked smile. Her smile.

Limping, he pushed his way through the group and stopped in front of Carrie. His eyes roamed over her face at the same time she searched every inch of him. He leaned heavily on one foot, and beyond the bruises, one eye was swollen. He didn't wear a uniform and was in his old UNC t-shirt. He'd bulked up through the arms, shoulders, and neck, casting a thousand more questions in her mind. She could hardly believe he stood in front of her. Alive.

"You're here," he said, sounding almost surprised.

Her eyes filled with hot tears of gratitude. "You're back."

"Back for good."

"For good?" she whispered, hardly daring to hope.

He smiled again. "Yeah."

May clapped her hands. "Did you hear that, CJ? Gregory is home for good!"

A cheer went up in the room, but Carrie barely noticed. Greg had locked eyes with her. Those green eyes, so steady and warm. That face so perfect and haunted. That smile only for her.

Greg was back.

His arms opened, and Carrie fell into him, throwing her arms up around his—

"Ow!" He jerked back. "Ow, sorry," he said, cradling his arm. "A little tender."

Carrie backed up. "What happened? How did you get hurt? Is something broken?" He'd obviously been beaten, but the thought was so horrid, so sickening she couldn't believe it.

"Long story. I should probably wait to tell my mom and Richard at the same time." He craned his neck to search the room again. "Where are they? They weren't at their house."

His mom.

Carrie's insides twisted into a huge ball of dread. He never got the note. No one told him.

He didn't know.

Greg turned back to her, smile fading. "Why isn't anybody answering?"

May covered her face and started crying. CJ looked down at the floor. No one else seemed willing to break the news, leaving it up to Carrie. But her throat constricted and even simple breaths seemed suddenly impossible.

She swallowed twice. "I don't know where Richard is, but your mom...she..." Her eyes filled and her nose began to run. "She..."

Greg's battered face turned white. "No. Please no."

"Didn't you get the note?" Carrie whispered. "Oliver tried to get you word. Didn't they tell you?"

Greg backed up, shaking his head over and over. He backed up until he ran into the wall. Carrie felt every heartbeat in her chest, breaking all over again for the loss of Mariah. For Greg.

When his eyes lifted to her again, it took him a moment to speak, and then he only spoke one word. "When?"

Before she could answer, Richard burst through the back door. "Greg's back!" Richard said excitedly. "Where is he?"

But Greg hadn't looked away from Carrie. His face twisted with agony. "When?"

As Richard pushed into the living room, Terrell grabbed his arm and whispered something to him. Richard's head whipped up, staring at Greg in dismay. Still, Greg's gaze stayed fixed on Carrie, waiting, desperate.

Carrie pressed her fingers to her trembling lips and forced the words. "The night you left."

Greg stopped moving. Stopped blinking. Yet even in his stillness, she watched the transformation within him: from shock, to disbelief, to pure rage.

"We think she had some internal bleeding from her fall in town," Carrie said quickly. "I'm so sorry, Greg. So, so sorry."

"From her fall," Greg repeated, nostrils flaring.

Hot tears flowed down Carrie's cheeks.

Suddenly every muscle from his neck to his fists clenched with anger. "I'll kill him. I swear I will kill him."

David Jamansky.

A dark chill ran through the crowded room.

Richard jumped forward. "Alright people, let's give Greg some space. We'll catch up with him later. Maybe we can have a clan dinner tonight. Let's go," he said, urging them for the door. "We'll catch up later."

Following Richard's cue, Carrie helped to herd everyone out May's front door. The last thing she wanted was to leave. She was desperate to know what happened to Greg, but he needed time to come to grips with losing his mom. Still, she hung by the door, waiting for some sign from him.

May, CJ, and Richard gathered around him as he leaned against the wall. His fists were still clenched. The muscles in his neck were still taut. And he hadn't looked up from the floor.

A few more tears slid down Carrie's cheeks as she quietly slipped outside.

Greg couldn't sleep. His emotions swung wildly from overwhelming grief to boiling rage. He kept reliving that day in the township office, wondering how he could have done things differently. Wondering how much pain his mom had been in when she died. Wondering why he hadn't gone back with Oliver to drive her home, to make sure she was okay. But most of all, wondering how to get revenge.

He could have been there when she died.

He *should* have been there when she died.

And if it wasn't for David Jamansky, he would have been.

His training kicked in, and as the dark night hours passed, he dreamed up a dozen ways to get rid of the local patrol chief. He tried to push the thoughts from his mind, knowing they were wrong, evil, and dangerous, but at the same time, thinking it only fair and just. Jamansky killed his mom—indirectly maybe, but still. Justice said he deserved to die. An eye for an eye.

The darkness gnawed at Greg from the inside out.

Tossing and turning in the dark room, his nightmares were back with a vengeance. And anytime he was awake, his injuries kept him miserable. His thigh ached something fierce, the cuts and bruises on his face itched, but his shoulder killed the worst. It still felt dislocated even though he'd tried to pop it into place multiple times.

Greg was grateful Richard sent everybody home when he had, but he hadn't realized Carrie left with the others until she was gone. Maybe it was for the best. He didn't want her to see him like this. He needed to get his feet under him again, figuratively and literally.

Even then, he was relieved she still lived in the clan.

When he told Richard and his grandparents he wasn't up for a clan dinner, he expected his grandma to protest. She hadn't. Instead, the four of them walked to the small neighborhood cemetery so Greg could see for himself. His grandma cried the entire time, but the three men stood in silence around his mom's small grave, giving Greg a chance to get used to the idea that his mom wasn't coming back.

"She said to tell you she was sorry," Richard had said.

Of course his mom would apologize for dying. Just thinking about it made his fury rage all over again. But Richard also said she'd been anxious to see Kendra. Lying on his dark bedroom floor, Greg tried to picture that happy reunion, mother and daughter together and free. He'd never given religion a second thought until people started dying on him. Now he clung to the possibility of a happy, painless afterlife.

Up and down, forward and back, in and out of disturbing dreams he relived it all, tripping over the same details. Kendra's death. His mom's death. Training. Isabel. Jamansky. Carrie. Raleigh. Jeff and Jenna.

His whole life felt like one giant mistake.

He got up several times to walk the empty floors of his dark house. His grandma invited him to sleep at their place so he wouldn't have to be alone. Even Richard offered his place, but Greg needed time to sort through things before he did something dangerously stupid. David Jamansky didn't deserve to be a man of position. As of two days ago, Greg outranked him. Jamansky was just a snake, a pesky, puffed-up nuisance Greg could dispose of with—

Stop! he yelled at himself. His mom would box his ears for such thoughts. He could even hear the lecture.

"I raised you better than this," she would say, shaking a finger in his face. *"What's done is done. I'm happy now, so it's your turn. You've been given a second chance at life, so fight for happiness. Fight and win."*

Greg wandered to his window. He stared out into the black night at the two-story house across the street. In the three minutes he'd seen Carrie, he should have asked if she was married—or at least asked Richard. But strangely, Greg no longer cared. He was back and Carrie still lived in Logan Pond. That was good enough for him.

Walking back from the cemetery, Richard told Greg about Carrie's newest plan. Even now, even with the flood of grief, it made him smile. Her idea bypassed the mayor and corrupt government entirely to create a trading system for illegals. It was brilliant. They didn't have any clans on board yet, but Greg couldn't wait to jump in. Assuming Carrie wanted him to. Assuming she wasn't married.

Why hadn't he asked Richard?

After a minute, he squinted out the window. A dark shape moved on the Ashworth's front porch. Carrie. The sky in the east was barely starting to lighten. Carrie was a morning person, but even this was early.

It looked like she was tying her shoes on her cement steps. Then she stood, looked around, and walked down her sidewalk. Greg grinned, thinking she was headed for his house, but when she reached the street, she turned.

He didn't know where she was going or why she was leaving before dawn, but he grabbed his shoes and sprinted downstairs.

forty-three

Greg nearly missed Carrie, but then he spotted her dark shape heading down the street and into the woods beyond. He probably shouldn't have followed her like a creep, but curiosity won out. She never checked over her shoulder to see if somebody followed her, which meant she had no business being in the dark woods alone. She wore her blue blouse, so she was planning to meet somebody special. That only confused him more.

When he was about to call her name, he heard her humming softly, a sad, lonely melody. The sound of her voice and the way her hand trailed over the long grasses enchanted him, so he kept following. It wasn't until the first rays of day turned her hair gold, that he realized where she was headed:

The Ferris Clan.

Why was she going there so early on today of all days? Richard said they planned to contact Ferris next, but why did that take priority over everything else this morning, especially Greg? She'd left his grandparents' house last night with everybody else. Surely this morning she'd want to talk to him, to see him. Wouldn't she?

He stopped.

Maybe this was her way of avoiding him. Maybe things had progressed with Oliver in the last six weeks, and she'd finally made her choice—which explained why she was wandering alone. If she had her green card, Mrs. Oliver Simmons, she wouldn't worry about being arrested.

His jaw tightened. He'd come back too late.

Too late for everything.

Something inside him snapped. He refused to lose another person to some government scumbag. Not that Oliver was a scumbag, but in that moment, he felt like one for stealing Carrie. Not that he'd stolen her either since Greg encouraged it, but none of that mattered.

Greg made his move.

Silently, he sped through the long grasses, practically dragging his bad leg.

When he was within ten feet, he called, "What's the weather?"

Carrie screamed and whirled around. "Greg!" Her hand went over her heart. "What are you doing here?"

He grinned. He couldn't help it. He'd always loved sneaking up on her, a bad habit he didn't plan to break.

"I was gonna ask you the same thing," he said. "What are you doin' sneaking off so early all by your lonesome?"

She cocked her head, throwing her thick, honey-colored waves over her shoulder. She studied his face—or more accurately, his lack of beard. He'd shaved the whole blasted thing off last night. Best thing he'd done so far.

Besides following her.

At the same time she studied him, he drank in the sight of her. He'd always loved her in her mom's blue blouse. It brought out her eyes. And with the first rays of day, her hair practically glowed. It was lighter than when he'd left, and her skin had tanned and sprouted a few more freckles. Summer had been good to her. Real good. The morning sun framed her whole being in light. He wanted to snatch her up and never let her go.

"Sorry," she said. "I couldn't sleep. I just needed to get out."

Get out or avoid him? That was the question and the only thing keeping him from stepping forward and engulfing her.

"Where you headed?" he asked, even though he'd already guessed.

"The Ferris Clan."

"Without me?" He smiled a little. "This little trail hasn't had the best of luck for the two of us, but maybe the third time's a charm?"

Her cheeks colored in memory as he'd hoped they would. The first time, he'd proposed. She declined. The second time, they'd been looking for Zach. He snatched her hand and then told her off ten minutes later. He refused to strike out a third time.

"I just…" she started. "It seemed like Terrell and Richard were busy today, but I thought maybe I should—I don't know—try anyway. But, but…"

She continued to stumble over her words which would have been adorable if she wasn't avoiding his direct gaze, looking everywhere but at him. His heart sank. He wasn't invited.

But he had to be sure.

"Mind if I join you?" he asked.

She broke into her beautiful, wide smile. "I'd love the company, but are you sure you're up for it?" She eyed his leg with more concern than it deserved. "It's a long walk."

"What, this old thing?" He patted his thigh. "Old football injury."

She laughed, a melodic sound that melted his insides. Seeing her brought him warmth he hadn't felt in weeks. He just needed her ten feet closer.

Stepping through the weeds, he closed the distance. Then he reached up and tucked a gold lock of hair behind her ear, giving into the temptation of her skin. His fingers trailed her cheek, her jaw and chin, savoring her softness.

"I missed you, Carrie girl," he whispered.

Her lashes lowered at his touch, heightening her loveliness. "I missed you, too."

"Can we try that hug again?"

With his good arm, he pulled her against him. She barely wrapped her arms around him, giving him the kind of careful hug a teen boy would give his grandma. Determined to man up and not let her see how bad his shoulder killed, he urged her arms up around his neck where she'd tried the night before. Then he wound his arms around her small waist, pulling her close. She gave in. Her cheek pressed against his shaved neck, making him grateful he'd cleaned up.

He inhaled the floral scent of her thick, wavy hair, the softness of her cheek, the feel of her delicate body, and the last six weeks dissolved into nothing.

"Don't let go of me," he whispered into her sun-warmed hair. "Ever again."

"Ditto."

They stayed that way for a long time. In the end, Carrie let go first. Greg supposed it was only fair. Eventually they'd have to do things like eat and sleep. Still, his arms felt empty without her. He meant to grab her hand as it fell away, but she folded her arms as she started off toward Ferris. He limped behind.

"I hardly slept thinking about your mom. I'm so sorry, Greg. None of us realized how bad she was until…" Carrie hugged herself. "She went quickly if that helps."

Some, but not enough.

"I'm glad you were there. She loves you." He flinched, realizing his mistake a second too late. "I mean, she *loved* you."

Carrie glanced at him. "She loves you, too. She doesn't want you to feel bad. She wants you to be happy."

He could have kissed her for using the present tense, but even then, the whole thing conjured up too much anger he didn't know how to process, so he changed the subject.

"Richard told me about your plans to trade with other clans. It's amazing. Brilliant, actually. I wish I'd thought of it."

"You did," she said. "I just tweaked your idea a little."

"No. You tweaked it a lot, and that's why it'll work." He clutched his bad arm to his chest while studying her hand tucked out of reach. "So…why now? Couldn't reaching out to another clan wait?" At least until he wasn't dying to see her, hold her, or even talk? It was a slap in the face that she'd taken off for several hours on today of all days.

"I'm hoping to find some medical help," she said. "Ferris is our best chance."

The bitterness crept back in. "It's a little late. Six weeks too late."

"Too late for your mom," she said gently. "Too late for Jenna. But not too late for you."

Surprised, he stopped. "That's why you left? To help *me?*"

"Yes. Don't be mad," she said in a rush. "Those just don't seem like simple football injuries. I'm worried you've broken something, maybe two somethings. Do you know what's wrong with your arm and leg?"

It was his shoulder and thigh, but he shook his head. "They're not broken. Just tender. Another day or so and I'll be back to normal."

She rolled her eyes. "I knew you'd say that, which is why I'm going no matter what. Nobody thinks my mom's friend was any good at medical stuff, but Gayle's the only one I know who might be able to help you. Even if she can't, she might know someone who can."

Carrie left to find him help. That alleviated most of his anxiety about her. Most, but not all. Her hands were still folded away out of reach. Was she that clueless or was it intentional?

"Alrighty," he said. "Lead the way."

"You're not going to fight me on this?" she asked skeptically.

He didn't need medical help, but a chance to be alone with her—without the clan or his grandma bombarding him—was worth it.

"Nope."

She still didn't look convinced, but she started off again. "Can you tell me about it? Training and everything?"

So he did.

He told her more than he planned to, probably more than he should have. The whole time, he waited for an outward signal from her that he hadn't lost her, that he could reconnect with her somehow. She kept her arms folded as if she was freezing even though the summer morning was plenty warm. It was too blatant to be a coincidence. Those blasted marriage papers. Were her and Oliver more than paperwork now? The longer he talked, the more he fretted that he'd missed his chance with Carrie long before he ever left.

"Will Isabel be okay?" Carrie asked as he finished.

"Yeah. Wish I could say the same for the rebels. I hope they're not destroyed already—or that I didn't single-handedly undermine the rebellion."

She shot him a sideways glance. "From the sounds of it, you saved it. I doubt they'll trust anyone again. They'll spread the word."

He sighed. "As long as McCormick hasn't already exacted revenge. That retaliation could get ugly."

"So..." Carrie said hesitantly as they entered a large abandoned cornfield, "she's pretty?"

"Who?"

Her cheeks went bright red. "I meant, are you really here to stay?"

Slowing, Greg looked at her. Carrie wanted to know if Isabel was pretty. A slow smile spread on his face. She didn't seem like the type to care about that sort of thing. Maybe he should have toned down his story—the bar, the tent, calling Isabel a dark-haired seductress—but he figured Carrie had nothing to worry about. Now he was thrilled to see that much reaction in her.

"Yeah. They think I'm dead," he said, answering her second question. "Being dead means we can stretch grandpa's money a bit longer 'cause I won't be payin' taxes. Neither will my mom, I guess." An unexpected wave of grief hit him, but he shoved it aside. He held his good arm out wide. "I look pretty good for a dead guy, don't I?"

The color in her cheeks grew, a trait he'd missed dearly. He grinned. Married or not, Carrie Ashworth still found him attractive. Plus, she cared enough to be jealous. He hadn't totally lost her. She just needed time to come out of her introverted shell.

He could wait.

Sort of.

Pulling her to a stop, he said, "Carrie, are you okay that I gave up my citizenship? I know it coulda helped things in the future." Possibly even with the two of them. "It just caused so many other issues that I figured—"

"You did the right thing," she cut in. "You're free now, Greg, and I'm thrilled. I guess you're as pathetic as the rest of us illegals now, huh?"

"Illegals?"

She smiled. "Don't worry. It's not as bad as it sounds."

Greg stared at her. She didn't know about her citizenship. Six weeks and Oliver hadn't told her a darn thing about those papers.

Oliver!

Although…maybe that meant she and Oliver had a falling out.

"How are things with Oliver?" Greg blurted.

Her eyes flickered up. "Fine." It was a knee-jerk response, one that came too quickly. But before he could press, she pointed past him. "Oh, look. We're halfway." Then she took off for the old stone wall that ran between their clan and Ferris, practically running to escape his question.

Grunting, Greg followed. The rock wall was chest high and easy to climb when he had working legs and shoulders. Now it looked like a mountain.

Carrie hoisted herself up on top and offered him a hand up like he'd once offered her. Manly pride insisted he refuse her help, but a chance to grab that hand was worth surrendering.

Taking her hand, he swung up. Only she didn't have the arm strength. His hand slipped from hers and he landed hard, chest on stone. Pain flared everywhere, radiating from his shoulder to his fingers. He yelped. He couldn't help it. Then he scrambled for a foothold. His left toe found a rock jutting out and, without thinking, he pushed up. It felt like somebody smashed his thigh with a baseball bat. That time he full-on yelled. It was all he could do to squirm the rest of the way up.

Once on top of the stone wall, he held his thigh, teeth gritted, waiting for the pain to subside. He rocked back and forth. Man card was definitely surrendered.

Carrie crouched next to him. "Sorry, sorry, sorry! My hand slipped. What can I do?"

"I'm fine. Just need…oooh," he said, sucking in air. "Just need a second."

Man up. Man up. Man up.

Then he realized he'd dropped her hand and he wanted to punch his injuries all over again.

Finally, the pain subsided to a dull throbbing. At least enough he felt he could breathe again. Carrie was glancing down the other side of the wall.

"How will you get down?" she asked.

"Not sure. Maybe you could catch me."

He hadn't meant it, but she pursed her lips, calculating. That relaxed him enough to smile. He was twice her size, yet the poor woman was figuring out how to catch him.

"I'll be fine," he said. "I just might need another hand."

She jumped down first, turned, and offered him that same hand which he was only too happy to take. As he started to drop, her other hand slid around his waist and she used her shoulder to carry his weight, bringing her even closer. Bonus. He slowly eased himself down, stone by stone, using his good foot until he was at her side.

Grinning, he realized he'd done it. And he'd gotten off the wall, too.

"Are you okay?" she asked, a little breathless.

"I am now," he said, squeezing her soft, delicate hand in his.

It took a second for her to understand, and then she yanked free like he'd electrocuted her. Turning, she started off at a fast, hurried pace.

Stunned, confused, and dejected, he limped behind her.

"So," he said after a minute, "I guess Oliver finally made his move, huh? You two a thing now?"

Without denying or confirming, she pushed through some waist-high weeds and sped across the large field. Greg struggled to keep up. And not just physically. Bitterness spread through his veins like wildfire. She didn't even know about the papers and she and Oliver were still an item?

So why did she still look at Greg like she did?

Why act like she still cared?

His bad leg felt heavier with every step. He fell further behind until he gave up completely and just stopped in the middle of the open field.

"Carrie," he called, "just talk to me. What happened while I was gone?"

She stopped but stayed faced away from him. She stared down at her hands, nervously picking at a spot on her blouse. With effort, he crossed through the thick weeds until he was in front of her. She still didn't look up, so he lifted her chin and waited for her to meet his gaze.

"I told you when I came back I'd be ready to pursue a relationship," Greg said. "Why are you pushin' me away?"

"No. You said you'd *try*." Her blue eyes flashed with pain. "Try, Greg."

That's what he thought he was doing, but maybe he wasn't trying hard enough.

Those beautiful blue eyes looked up at him, so bright against her blouse. But in that moment, she had a more appealing feature. Her lips looked so soft and inviting, and he wanted nothing more than to kiss her.

So he did.

Hands cradling her neck, he leaned down to her. His lips barely brushed hers before she flinched back.

"What are you doing?" she asked.

"What's it look like I'm doin'?" he said with a sly grin.

He tucked another loose strand of hair behind her ear and then his thumb strayed to run along her bottom lip. Her lips were softer than should be humanly possible. The color matched the lovely blush in her cheeks.

"I don't think this is a good idea, Greg," she whispered. Yet her eyes closed against his touch.

"Me neither," he said, feeling wonderfully heady.

He pulled her closer, savoring her warmth. Carrie was everything he wanted but didn't deserve. She was light and happiness and all that was right in the world. Leaning down, he kissed her forehead. Kissed the summer freckles on her nose. Then he lowered his head to explore those soft, pink—

Suddenly, she twisted out of his grasp. "I can't do this."

Carrie started off again at a frantic pace. She was six feet away before his sluggish brain caught up.

"Why not?" he called.

"You don't want this, Greg. Not really."

"I beg to differ!"

His feet finally moved, but she took two steps for every one of his. He fell further behind but dumbly kept following.

"No. You're just confusing passion with compassion," she said. "Your mom just died, and she wanted the two of us to be together, so you're trying to make her happy by trying to love me, which is sweet, but I can't do it. I can't pretend it's enough or guilt you into being with me because other people want this. So I think we should leave things how they've been, okay?"

The whole thing rolled off her tongue in seconds, only every word flew over his head.

"What the heck are you talkin' about?" he called in exasperation. "Carrie, will you please tell me what's goin' on?"

Stopping abruptly, she turned. "I kissed Oliver."

That brought him up short. "What?"

"I kissed Oliver."

forty-four

Like a punch to Greg's gut, Carrie's words sunk in. Greg couldn't believe it. Oliver beat him to it. He kissed her first.

Carrie and Oliver were together.

Greg felt his world implode. The longer he thought about it, the sicker he felt, because he realized not just what she said, but how she'd said it.

"Oh. *You* kissed Oliver," he said. Which shouldn't have surprised him either because Oliver didn't have any gumption of his own. Then again, neither did Carrie. She'd never initiated anything with Greg. Knowing she'd made the first move with Oliver stung.

She stared down at her hands. "Technically, he kissed me, and it wasn't even a full kiss, but…" She sighed. "I'm sorry, Greg."

"No, it's fine," he lied. "I told you to give him a chance and you did." She really, really did.

He started off, limping through the abandoned cornfield past her. He didn't know the way to Ferris, but that seemed inconsequential now. She followed, the sound of their feet swishing through the brush. No amount of words could fill the void between them. This trail to Ferris really was cursed.

"I'm sorry, Greg," she said again. "We had dinner and it just kind of happened."

Kisses didn't just happen. They were planned. Premeditated.

He wanted to lash out but couldn't. Oliver was the better choice. Greg knew that. Yet all he could think was, first he lost his mom. Now Carrie. But ever the glutton for punishment, he couldn't seem to shut up.

"Dinner, huh? I bet he's a good cook." For all Greg knew, the guy was a sous chef. *Jerk.*

"Oliver didn't cook," she said softly. "He took me to a restaurant."

Greg whirled around so fast she nearly stumbled back. "He took you into public?"

She bit her lip. "Yes. A small deli far from here. We only saw a few people. I felt safe with Oliver. I always do."

"Safe?" And yet in six weeks' time, Oliver never had the decency to mention why she felt safe. Greg felt like strangling something—namely a tall, awkward patrolman. "You need to ask him about those papers, Carrie."

She gave him a puzzled look. "Why?"

"You just do."

Then he took off as fast as his bad leg would allow. He should have been paying attention to the direction they were going so he could make his way back home, but he couldn't rid the image of Carrie in public. Carrie and Oliver linked at the mouth.

"Was he a good kisser?" Greg refrained from adding, *Better than me?*

"Please don't do this," she whispered.

"Sorry. Just tryin' to catch up. We're still best friends, right?" His jaw tightened. "Or did I lose that, too?"

She stopped and stared at him, looking seconds shy of crying. That was his cue to shut up and grow up—probably apologize, too—but the questions came faster and faster.

"So what are your plans?" he asked. "You gonna leave the clan or stick around for a bit longer? When's the big day?"

She threw her hands in the air. "It was one date and one kiss that wasn't really even a kiss. I just thought you deserved to know. I don't have any plans beyond this moment. I'm taking things one day at a time because any time I get my feet under me, life knocks me down and I have to figure things out all over again."

"Tell me about it," he muttered.

For the second time, her words registered three seconds too late. He felt another stab.

"Oh…" he said slowly. "You weren't expecting me to come back." Every muscle in his body tightened with complete and utter betrayal. "Sorry to have made things awkward for the two of you."

For the first time, her eyes flashed with red-hot anger. "I wanted you to come back, Greg. I've wanted nothing more since you left. You should have been here with your mom. You should have been here with me! But what was I supposed to do? You told me to give Oliver a chance, so I did, and now you're mad at me. But if I hadn't, you would still be mad at me." Her voice broke. "Just what was I supposed to do?"

His anger dissipated. "Exactly what you did. It's fine. I'm happy for you." It just sucked big time on his part.

His mom would tell him to keep fighting for her, but between losing his mom, the mess with the rebels, his leg, shoulder, Jamansky, and everything else, Greg had no fight left in him.

"At least tell me we're still friends," he said lamely.

"Always," she whispered. "Always, always, always."

Friend.

The word turned to acid in his gut.

"Wait," she said, slowing down. "I think we're close. We enter the neighborhood over there."

Greg followed her gaze and spotted rooftops. A twinge of nervousness cut through everything else. With all the civil unrest in the area, he decided it was time to pay attention to their task at hand. He could worry about Carrie and Oliver some other time.

He lowered his voice. "I'm not a huge fan of tromping into some clan without a way to defend ourselves. What were you thinking, comin' by yourself unarmed? Had I known, I woulda grabbed the rifle."

She scowled at that. "This isn't West Chicago, Greg." Turning back, she surveyed the scene. "I hope."

———— ◆ ————

Ten minutes later, Carrie still crouched with Greg behind an old shed on the far corner of the Ferris neighborhood, watching for any signs of life. She should have been trying to remember names and homes, but her thoughts were a muddled, disjointed mess, vacillating between what Greg had been through and what he'd just done to her. She begged her pounding head to sort it out later.

But that kiss...

Even as brief as it had been, goosebumps ran down her arms. Had she not turned to mush the second he touched her, she would have stopped him like she had stopped Oliver. For preservation of her fragile heart alone, she should have. But all she kept thinking as he leaned down was, *Impossible. He can't want this.*

Once his head cleared and he properly grieved for his mom, he'd realize Oliver had taken his place and he was no longer obligated to Carrie. But right now, her skin was in a constant state of chills, remembering the brush of his lips against hers.

Why did he do that to me?

Blinking back to her surroundings, she focused on the Ferris neighborhood. Greg crouched several feet away, keeping a safe distance like he'd done since she told him about Oliver. The way he moved and hid seemed government trained, almost stealth. He'd followed her all that time without a sound. Even now, he looked like he'd be more comfortable with a gun, making her wonder how much someone could change in six weeks.

Having him in Ferris would simplify getting him help. Gayle could look at him and determine if he'd broken any bones right here— assuming they made it to Gayle before sundown.

"Looks harmless to me," she whispered, trying to urge him on. "Gayle's house is on the farthest street. Let's just go."

"Our neighborhood looks dead this early in the morning, too," Greg said. "I wanna watch a bit longer, and if all stays quiet, we'll head over."

As she waited, she wondered how painful it would be to see her mom's old friend. Watching Greg go through the pain of losing his mom brought Carrie's grief for her parents back to the surface. Another minute, and she said, "You know, Richard's style is to walk down the middle of the street and call out to see if anyone's around."

Greg's dark brows shot up. "And that works?"

"Pretty well, actually," she said with a smile.

"Well, it's not my style," he said, turning back. "Still too traumatized by that last clan."

Her smile faded. She studied his injuries. His brown hair hung down over his bruised forehead, longer than she'd ever seen, and he kept his arm close to his chest. At least his gash and other scratches seemed to be healing. His whole body was thicker, more muscular than when he'd left, making her wonder how many men it had taken to hold him down in that camp. She shuddered. This week wasn't the only beating he'd endured.

Her eyes traced the lines of his muscle along his back and shoulders, down his arms and up again to his jaw line. Absentmindedly, she wondered how long after she left the Trenton's house he had shaved. Probably minutes. She didn't mind, though. She liked seeing the angles of his face, feeling of the soft skin of his neck. His lips.

How was she supposed to get over him now?

With a sigh, she sank onto the grass and leaned against the shed, not caring what spiders might be lurking. The morning sun pierced straight to her brain, and she closed her eyes to ward off the headache she'd woken with after tossing with worry all night.

"How much longer?" she said. "Zach and Amber don't know I left or where I went. Did you tell anyone you left?"

"Nope."

Great. The whole neighborhood would be out searching for them. What rumors would circulate then? After punishing Zach for the same thing, she decided to speed things up.

Standing, she brushed off her jeans. "These are peaceful people, Greg. Let's go."

He stayed crouched, watching, scanning.

"Gayle's husband is their clan leader," Carrie tried. "When my parents died, Gayle and Frank came all the way over to pay their condolences. They'll remember me, I promise. So…I'm going, okay?"

She started forward, heading out around the side of the shed. Greg followed reluctantly. She only made it a few steps when her eye caught hold of something two yards down.

"Look at that," she said.

Back beyond the original property where the leftover grass grew the thickest, she spotted something among the weeds. She squinted, making her head pound harder, but she definitely saw huge, yellow flowers.

"What is it?" Greg asked.

"A garden," she said with a smile. Then she took off, darting across the yards.

"Carrie, wait!"

She ran until she reached the spot. Crouching down, she fingered the huge leaves. Squash plants. The bright yellow flowers popping out were so eye-catching that no clan could think they had hidden them well.

She stood and turned, taking in the rest of the area. Beyond the squash, tomato plants rose above the other weeds. Maybe these clansmen hoped patrolmen didn't know plants, but to her it was obvious this was a vegetable garden. A weedy, disorganized one, but still.

When Greg reached her, she pointed to the nearest squash plant. His head snapped around. "Somebody lives here?"

"Yes, but…" She circled the area. "These aren't planted in rows. It's like someone took a handful of seeds and tossed them into the air." Which was fine if they were trying to hide their food, but they'd done a bad job of that, too.

Then she spotted some pea vines and a strange wave of dizziness washed over her. They were filled with pea pods. Bulging, dry, and yellowed. Unused.

"Oh, no," she whispered.

"How long ago was this garden abandoned?" Greg asked, putting together what she had.

"They planted summer crops but never harvested their spring ones, so sometime in May? But…they could have abandoned it last summer. Without anyone to harvest the crops, some seeds sprouted this year on their own. What kind of people abandon perfectly good food?"

"Dead ones," Greg said soberly.

The thought got Carrie moving. She walked smack into the middle of the backyard.

"Hello?" she called loudly. "Hello! Is anyone here? I'm Carrie Ashworth from the Logan Pond Clan."

Greg crept up to the nearest window and peeked inside. "There's stuff in there. A small table. A few books." He pounded on the window. "Hello?"

They both waited, tensed for a response. When none came, Greg stood back. "How long ago did y'all have contact with Ferris?"

"Gayle helped with Zach's ankle three years ago. Maybe six months after that." The hair on her arms prickled. "Is it possible this clan consolidated like we did and moved to a different part of the sub?"

"Yeah, but why abandon perfectly good food?" He glanced nervously around. "Where's Gayle's house?"

"End of the next street."

Unable to wait for Greg's bad leg, she broke into a run, passing home after abandoned home. Gayle couldn't be gone. Carrie's mom was gone. Mariah was gone. Every other clan was gone. Not this one, too. She had to reach Gayle's because right now it felt like their clan was the last one left.

Turning a corner, she skidded to a halt, nearly tripping on the paved road.

A house sat blackened and charred in front of her. Mostly the garage, but parts of the rest of the house had been burned as well.

Exactly as Oliver had described.

Only Carrie recognized this house beyond Oliver's description. She hadn't seen it—or at least noticed it—in six years. But those tall white pillars. The long, circular driveway. She'd come here once in high school for a study group. Because Scott Porter invited her. His house was so fancy inside, and she'd been mortified because she dropped a fruit smoothie on their white carpet. Scott just laughed it off.

Scott.

Oliver.

Her knees went weak.

Greg caught up to her. "What is it? What's wrong? Oh," he said, spotting the blackened home. "Is that Gayle's house?"

She shook her head. "Oliver."

"Oliver?" Greg looked around in confusion. "Where?"

Suddenly she remembered the call in the car and the crazy man screaming in the background. That had been Scott. Scott was the crazed illegal which meant...

Scott Porter was dead.

The world spun around her. She stumbled, and Greg caught her by the waist.

"Sit," she said. "I have to sit down."

Greg helped her to the nearest curb and crouched in front of her, waiting for an explanation.

Her head fell into her hands. "Oliver did this. He told me. He had dogs and his boss made him..." The whole story was a giant blur of emotion, but Scott's voice, so hysterical on the phone, echoed loudest. Oliver's partner had said he was trying to kill himself, so they shot him. Because Oliver hadn't made it back in time.

Because of her.

"I killed Scott," she said, choking on the words.

Greg's eyes widened. "Who's Scott?"

With throat swelling and raw, Carrie explained everything. The real cause of Oliver's injury that day of the drive. The phone call in the car. Brooke's baby—Scott's baby. Jamansky's order to burn the house.

"I heard Scott," she said. "I heard him, and he's dead, and Brooke doesn't know, and I told her I'd help, but I can't because he's dead." Her breaths grew painful. "I did this."

"This Scott guy," Greg said, "was in the same clan as your mom's friend?"

"No. That's why I'm confused. I didn't even remember that Scott used to live here until I saw those pillars. I don't know why, but he and Brooke weren't in the Ferris Clan when we had contact with it."

Greg stood. "Then let's go. We need to figure out what happened to your mom's friend."

"They won't be there!" A sob of terror rose in her chest, begging for escape. "No one is here. Oliver did this!"

He'd arrested them, all of them. Him or one of his coworkers—what did it matter? She wanted to take the blame for Scott's death, but if Oliver hadn't arrested him, Scott couldn't have died in the station and Brooke wouldn't be alone now. And what about Gayle and the Ferris Clan? No matter what she thought of Oliver the person, Oliver the patrolman was still her enemy.

"You stay here," Greg said. "I'm gonna check out the last street."

"No!" Carrie said, getting to her feet. "I'm coming."

They started slowly and then, without discussion, broke into a run.

"This is it," she said, huffing at the end of the last street. Out of breath and out of answers, she ran to the front door and pounded on it.

"Frank? Gayle? Emma? Maggie?" She pounded so hard her fist hurt. "It's Carrie Ashworth. Please be here. *Please.*"

Greg tried the handle. Locked. He searched for something and grabbed a large rock. Carrie would have stopped him, but she was feeling the first effects of the shock numbing her. What the rock didn't break of the window, Greg kicked in. He climbed in and disappeared inside. A moment later he unlocked the front door for her.

One step inside and Carrie knew the house had been deserted for years, even longer than Scott had been gone. The air was stagnant, oppressive, and musty. Maybe that was good. Maybe Gayle and her family left of their own accord. Maybe Oliver hadn't arrested them— killed them.

"They had kids?" Greg asked.

"Two. Emma was in Zach's kindergarten class, and Maggie was..." She stopped as her eyes spotted broken shards of dishes scattered across the kitchen floor. A chair was overturned, wood brutally splintered.

"No," she breathed.

Greg searched the main room and headed up the dusty stairs. Carrie followed, each step taking longer than the previous.

At the doorway of the first bedroom, she dropped to her knees. A few girl clothes were scattered on the floor. A Barbie without a head. Everything had been left behind. Their family hadn't packed up and moved out. They'd been arrested.

By Oliver.

Or David Jamansky—it didn't matter who.

The dizziness assaulted her again. Her hands found the wall and held on. One raid gone wrong and this was her. Zach. Amber. They'd become wards of the state. Gone forever.

"Should I search the other homes?" Greg asked.

She shook her head. "No. They're all gone."

Scott. Gayle. Mariah. Her parents. Every single one.

For several minutes, the two stared at the disturbing scene. When Carrie found the strength, she stood.

"We should go," she said numbly. "It doesn't feel right to be here, like we're intruding on their last moments together as a family."

Greg followed her downstairs and outside. But on the porch, Carrie couldn't seem to go another step. She felt trapped by the looming, empty homes.

"Do you think they're okay?" she asked. "Do Emma and Maggie know their parents were just trying to protect them by living illegally, or have they already been brainwashed? Do they hate their parents for what's happened to them, or are they all dead?" Her eyes burned. "Dead like Scott?"

Greg put an arm around her. "Come on. Let's go home."

forty-five

Oliver had never been a praying man before, but he prayed the entire drive to Logan Pond. The death notice stayed on the seat next to him in an unmarked envelope. He had no idea how to break the news to Greg's family or Carrie. It seemed cruel and unfair, especially coming from him since Greg's recruitment was partially his fault. That's why he'd put it off, hoping for different news. But when different news hadn't come, he knew he couldn't wait any longer.

He owed Carrie that much.

Oliver wasn't sure which house to try first, but he decided to obey his boss for once and headed right for the Trenton's. Knocking on the front door, he stood back, mind racing with how to say it. Some days he hated his job. Others, he loathed it.

CJ Trenton answered the door, looking far happier than he had the last time Oliver saw him. "Officer Simmons, how nice to see you. Carrie isn't here right now."

"Actually, I'm here for another reason." Oliver stood straight in his green uniform. "Mr. Trenton, by chance have you had any contact from Greg in the last few weeks? Any at all?"

"Yes," CJ said. "He returned last night. Why?"

"He's back?"

CJ beamed. "Yes. We've only heard half of his story. It sounds like a wild one. But he says he's back for good now. Isn't that wonderful?"

Relief washed over Oliver. *You have no idea.* "That is great news. Is he here? I have a note for him that I should probably deliver in person."

"No. He slept at his own house last night, but he was gone this morning when his grandma went to invite him to breakfast. However, Carrie's missing as well, so..." CJ trailed off, seeming to remember who he was talking to. "Can I give him a message for you?"

Oliver blinked. He told himself to nod. Greg was back and disappeared with Carrie. Of course. He should be happy for her—for them—but he was lost in conflicting emotions, smart enough to know what this meant for him and selfish enough to be devastated by it.

CJ waited for him to answer, but Oliver couldn't even remember the question. "Or..." CJ said, "you're welcome to wait here for Greg and Carrie to return."

Wait around to see that reunion? No thank you.

Oliver handed Mr. Trenton the envelope. "Actually, will you give this to him? It's confidential so I'd appreciate it if no one else opened it."

"Sure. Is there a message you want me to pass along with it?"

"No. Well, yes. Do you have a pencil?"

CJ smiled. "Haven't had one of those for years."

"Right. Sorry. Um..." Oliver scratched his receding hairline. Greg had faked his death. Not a bad idea—hopefully. "Just tell him that this is official, so he doesn't have to worry anymore." Not that Greg was worried. He was too occupied with Carrie. Oliver thought about adding a quick, *And thanks for the heart attack in town. A little heads-up would have been nice.*

CJ studied the envelope. "Alright. Anything else?"

"There's no sweep this week," Oliver said, passing along the message he usually reserved for Carrie. CJ could tell the clan just as easily. Maybe Oliver would give it to CJ from now on.

With a lurch of dread, Oliver remembered Carrie's dinner invitation for this Saturday. Was he still invited? Is that when she'd break the news to him that it was over? He could back out, but Saturday might be the best time to give her those papers. It's time she knew what he'd done once and for all, regardless of who she ended up with. Because her citizenship wasn't official until he got one final signature:

Hers.

"Great. Anything else?" CJ asked, noting his reticence to leave.

"No, that's it," Oliver said.

His prayer leaving the neighborhood was different than the one going in.

———————◆———————

Carrie felt trapped in a wall of silence on their long walk back.

"It's not Oliver's fault," Greg said after some time. "You know that, right?"

She knew that.

In theory.

Greg picked up a small stick and whipped it back and forth over the tall grasses. "The greater good has to outweigh the current bad. It's the only way to find some sanity in this insane world."

She knew that, too. By following his boss's orders, Oliver kept his job which, in turn, kept her clan safe.

The greater good.

But why did her clan matter more than Gayle's? Why did her life matter more than Scott's? It was unbearable to think that her freedom came at the expense of someone else's.

"That coulda been me burning down that house," Greg said, voice growing with frustration. "Arresting illegals—if not worse. We're all tryin' to do our best to protect those we love, and sometimes that protection comes at the cost of others, but what else are we supposed to do?" He swung his whip over the tall grass hard enough that seeds went flying.

"I know. I know. I just…" *What?* She couldn't find the words.

He sighed a long, tired sigh. "I know."

Greg's lopsided pace slowed as he struggled home, reminding her that, on top of everything else, he still didn't have medical help.

"Would you ever want to join the rebellion?" she asked, even though the thought petrified her. But Greg had the personality, determination, and training now to be one of the front leaders against Rigsby. "Brooke's group invited us to join them."

"No," he said, still swinging his stick.

Surprised, she glanced sideways. "Why not?"

"Would *you* want to join them?"

"No, but I'm not…" A fighter. A leader. Greg.

"You're not one of them, and I don't wanna be either. Not anymore. Besides." Another swing. "I have too much pullin' me here to ever leave again."

A curious response.

Carrie always figured that once his mom passed, he'd skip town as fast as he'd come. Greg hated Illinois. He didn't even like most of their clan. He couldn't be talking about her. He wanted to stay for his grandparents, and his projects, and...and...

Her migraine pulsed.

Desperate for distraction, she broke away from the trail to explore a small patch of trees. Greg was just confused, she told herself. Broken, lonely, and confused.

"What's up?" he asked, joining her.

When she kept searching without answering, he leaned against a large tree and rubbed the muscles in his upper leg. It took a bit of searching before she found what she was looking for: a large, dead branch. She broke off the side twigs and handed it to him.

"Here. A walking stick."

"Am I that slow?" he asked with a quirked smile. But the way he said it implied more than walking abilities.

Yes! she wanted to shout. She was with Oliver now. Not really, but all Greg needed to know was that he was free to move on. The sooner he stopped looking at her like that, talking to her like that, the sooner she could move on, too.

Without meaning to, her gaze flickered to his lips. Not in desire—or at least, not entirely—but in memory. There had been no hesitation when he leaned down to kiss her.

Why?

Worry less. Love more, Mariah whispered. Which was useless advice because Carrie already loved Greg too much.

One of his dark, expressive, battered brows cocked, noticing where her gaze had stopped. Nothing pleased him more than knowing he was the center of her thoughts. But that was just his ego. He was beautiful and wonderful to look at, and he loved being the center of *all* females' thoughts.

Didn't he?

He hadn't entertained Isabel's attentions.

Or that blonde's in town.

His green eyes danced with pleasure. With a flush of mortification, she realized she was *still* studying his lips. The shape of them. The surprising gentleness of them. Shaking out of it, she forced herself to start off again. He'd catch on soon. He had to because it was killing her.

Silence smothered them as they headed back. He used the new walking stick to help with the limping, and his eyes no longer danced with amusement.

"I'm sorry," she said.

She didn't say what for, but he nodded. "I know."

When they reached the stone wall, they both stopped. Her body felt twice as heavy as it had before and she was healthy. She couldn't imagine how Greg felt. If she'd planned ahead, they could have gone the long way around. As it was, her hands went on her hips, calculating.

"Want help up?" he asked.

The absurd comment made her laugh in spite of everything. "No. Give me a second, and I'll help you up."

With effort, she climbed the chest-high stone wall. Her head pounded and her vision swam a moment before she regained her balance. Then she turned and offered Greg a hand. She wouldn't drop him this time.

He stared at her hand with a long, sad expression. "No. I got it."

Using his stick and sheer muscle, he climbed one-footed, one-armed, until he hoisted himself on top. Then he sat on the wall, clutching his thigh and breathing heavily.

She scanned the trail ahead and so did he. Both of them seemed to think the same depressing thing. They still had a long ways.

"You shouldn't have come," she said.

"Wow," he said with sudden bitterness. "You keep throwin' the punches, don't you?"

"That's not what I meant. I'm glad you were with me in Ferris. I'm just worried about your leg."

"My body's fine, Carrie." The rest of his thought was implied: his heart wasn't.

His constancy with that subject made her temples throb. Coupled with standing atop the wall, the world swayed. When he was done grieving for his mom, he'd see clearly—see Carrie clearly. He'd remember how uninterested he had always been.

"You ready?" she asked.

He looked up at her. "Not really. Mind if we sit for a bit?"

Yes. Zach, Amber, and everyone else would be worried about them, but she couldn't desert Greg in his condition. "Okay. We can rest as long as you need."

"I don't need to rest. I'm just not ready to face the world yet. That and"—he flashed a sad smile—"I'm not ready to give you up either. Sit for a second so we can talk."

Talk?

The word terrified her.

"But the people back home—"

"Can wait. What time is it anyway? Seven in the morning, maybe eight? C'mon." He patted the rocks next to him. "Keep me company before the entire clan descends on me wantin' answers. You said I'm still your best friend. I promise not to bite."

She sat by Greg, though not too close, with her legs dangling over the side. Sitting on the round stones wasn't comfortable, but Greg didn't seem to mind. He just rubbed the scar on his calloused palm as if in deep thought—the scar he said would forever remind him of her.

"You gonna be okay?" he finally asked. "About Scott and every-thing?"

She shrugged. "How long before that's us and our stuff is strewn about? What happens when Jamansky asks Oliver to burn *our* homes?" Question after question pounded against her, but she saved the most terrifying for last. "What would I do if I lost Amber and Zach?"

"That won't happen. Oliver made sure you're safe."

"Travel papers can't prevent something like this, Greg."

"They aren't travel papers."

He said it so softly, she nearly missed it. She turned. "What do you mean?"

His hand clenched over the scar. "I mean, they aren't travel papers, Carrie."

"Then what are they?"

Sighing, he glanced over his shoulder behind them. Instead of thinking about today, her thoughts skipped back to their first walk to Ferris. Greg had thrown out that marriage proposal like it was another of his business plans—which it had been. Just a way to get her legal. He'd hated her back then, so she turned him down flat. He'd never proposed since. And she suddenly realized he never would. He'd lost his citizenship.

Her stomach lurched in sudden understanding.

Papers.

Oliver.

"No," she said, shaking her head adamantly. "Oliver wouldn't. Not without asking me."

Greg rubbed the scar on his palm, slow and steady.

"A marriage license?" she whispered. "No, no, no." She couldn't be married. Oliver wouldn't. "Did you see it?"

"Didn't have to. Oliver told me they weren't travel papers and then swore me to secrecy, only he broke his end of our bargain, so I shoulda told you." His expression softened. "I'm sorry. You deserved to know."

She was married. Had been for weeks, possibly months.

And Greg knew.

Her eyes widened. "That's why you begged me to give him a chance. You thought I'd actually be happy about being married without my permission? That...that I'd choose Oliver because of it?"

"No. I figured you'd be furious." He shook his head. "I tried to warn him."

More and more things fell into place. Her drive with Oliver. The restaurant. Things Greg said in CJ's garage.

"So..." she said, muscles tightening, "Oliver knew about your draft papers, and you knew about his marriage license, but neither of you bothered to tell me, hoping to keep me in the dark like...like I'm some kid or something?"

Greg's hands lifted. "Hey, in my defense, I figured havin' me disappear might help you figure out what you wanted. And in Oliver's defense, he's scared of you, scared of this reaction. He doesn't want you to think you owe him anything. It's just a paper, Carrie, a way to protect you."

Exactly what Greg told her months ago.

But what neither man understood was that, to her, a marriage was so much more. Only she never expected Oliver to go behind her back like this. Greg, the impulsive, headstrong one, maybe. But Oliver? And Greg hadn't told her either even though he knew how opposed she was to this.

Her pulse hammered.

She was married. To Oliver.

What else were they hiding from her? Lying about? The bitterness burned through her like wildfire.

"You know what?" She scooted to the edge of the wall and jumped down. "I'm done."

"Done?"

She glared up at him. "Done with relationships. Done with the games. I think I'm done with both of you, actually. See you back home."

Carrie started off.

"Wait." Greg scrambled to the ledge and, using the walking stick, hopped down. She heard him grunt in pain, but he quickly hobbled after her. "Think about how *I* felt finding out about those papers, Carrie. Where does that leave me if you're married?"

She whirled. "Then why didn't you talk Oliver out of it?"

"'Cause it was already a done deal. Believe me, I was furious, but then I pictured you never being arrested, taken, or killed. What's the greatest gift Oliver could give you?"

"The truth!" she cried in frustration.

He pointed back to Ferris. "You sure?"

Her chin dropped, but the betrayal refused to release her. "What am I supposed to do now? I don't even want my stupid citizenship! I'll tell Oliver to revoke the marriage or divorce me or…" She cringed. Divorce. She'd known she was married for all of two minutes and already she wanted out?

"Look, Carrie, I know you're mad, but give it time before you do somethin' that can't be undone."

"Like marrying a person without asking them?" she snapped.

"Yeah. Like that." Sighing, he rubbed his bad shoulder. "Oliver's given you your liberty. Amber and Zach, too. Only green cardies don't have monthly check-ins, taxes, or recruiting officers dragging you away." His gaze swept over her face, her hair, her lips. "Was I really supposed to stand in the way of that?"

"So why tell me *now*?" she whispered, heat building behind her eyes. "Why kiss me and confuse me all over again if you'd already resigned to let me go?"

His face twisted in pain. "'Cause I don't wanna lose you, Carrie girl. Call me selfish."

Carrie girl.

She felt herself sliding again, falling even though she knew better. She started to turn, desperate to think about anything else, but Greg grabbed her hand.

"Carrie, please. You keep pushin' me away, but I swear you still feel somethin' for me. Am I just reading you wrong? Am I off my rocker to think you and I still gotta chance even with all this madness?"

His face, so battered and bruised, filled with pleading and she had to look away. Greg didn't mean this, not deep down. He was just grieving for his mom, recovering from West Chicago, and scrambling for someone to grasp onto, a way to give his mom her dying wish.

"Honestly," she said, pulling free of his warm, strong hand, "I don't know what to think anymore."

She watched the dejection wash over him, but he nodded slowly.

"You know," he said after a moment, "when you came into my mom's room, I was in the middle of explaining everything about Oliver's marriage license and my draft papers. I listed every reason I should walk away from you, but my mom told me to not give up. She told me to—"

"—fight for happiness," she said softly, remembering. "I thought she was talking about your training."

He smiled weakly. "Nope. She told me to fight for you—fight and win—which I'm willing to do, but only if you want me to." Reaching up, he stroked her cheek, sending a flame of heat through her. "I love you, Carrie girl. The time I spent away only solidified that. But I swear I'll understand if you still choose Oliver."

She jerked back. "What did you say?"

"I'll support whoever you choose: me or him—or neither of us jerks. I just need to hear you say it."

"No. Not that. Never mind." Her cheeks flushed and she dropped her chin to hide behind her thick hair. Those three little words had slipped out without him even noticing. She'd almost missed them, too.

I love you.

Closing her eyes, she begged her feet to take her away from here. She couldn't do this anymore. But she stayed rooted in her spot, her body stilled by those words.

Were they true?

He looked confused for a moment, and then suddenly broke into a grin. "Oh, that? Is it so surprising that I'm in love with you? I thought that'd been obvious for a while."

He tilted her chin up and gazed intently into her eyes. "When I asked you to not let go of me, I meant it in more ways than one. I love you, Carrie. You're all that's good in this world, and I don't deserve to be part of your life, but I want to be. Selfishly. Don't give up on me." His voice caught and he cleared it gruffly to finish. "I don't wanna lose you, too."

Lose you, too.

And just like that, she remembered why she had to walk away.

"That's just it." She grabbed his hands and lowered them from her face so she could think clearly. "You don't have to love me to keep me. I'll always be your friend. Your mom is gone, and I understand emotions are running high, but I can't handle you doing something for the wrong reasons because—"

He kissed her again.

No warning whatsoever, he just leaned down and planted another one on her, slamming her with a million sensations. All good.

Everything buzzed and swirled around her. His lips were warm and confident. And quite insistent. Her hand rested on his muscled chest, determined to push him away. But somehow she found herself clinging to his shirt to keep him from leaving.

He kissed her like she'd dreamt about. He kissed her like he should have a long time ago. She was overwhelmed by the feel of him, the taste of him. His fingers wound through her warm, golden waves sending bursts of chills through her.

Only when he pulled back did she remember to breathe.

Somewhat breathless himself, he leaned his forehead against hers. "Why is it so hard to believe that I love you?"

"Because," she said, heart shattering into a thousand pieces. "I'm your Oliver."

forty-six

"My what?" Greg said in confusion.

"I'm your Oliver. The person you're trying to love because your mom wants it, your grandma wants it, and…" Carrie's blue eyes filled. "And I want it. Everyone wants you to love me, so you're trying to make it work like I tried with Oliver. Only deep down, you don't want it—want me—like I don't want Oliver."

"You're my Oliver," Greg repeated, trying to wrap his mind around it. And then in a flash, he understood. Everything she'd said. Why she kept pushing him away.

"Wait, wait, wait," he said. "Hold on a sec. That's what you think?"

She blushed and tried to escape, wrenching his bad shoulder, but he locked his good arm around her, refusing to let her run again.

"Carrie, I'm not you," he said firmly. "I'm not exactly what you'd call a people pleaser. I do what I want, when I want, unless absolutely forced. Even then, I usually end up doin' my own thing anyway. My mom wanted you and me to work out 'cause she knew how I felt about you even before I did. She just didn't want me to give up on somethin' 'cause it seemed impossible. But this—us—is somethin' *I* want. I want it bad."

Carrie stared down at his t-shirt. "What about your grandma? She wanted us to be together before we even met."

"Since when have I ever listened to my grandma?" he said in exasperation.

She opened her mouth to respond but then clamped it shut again.

With a slow smile, he wiped the moisture from her lower lashes. "Why have you never asked who *my* perfect woman is?" She blanched, but he continued anyway. " about 5'4", gorgeous hair, blue eyes to drive a man wild, horribly self-conscious yet unbelievably selfless, adorable freckles and a rose-colored view of the world that inspires me to—"

"You don't have to do this, Greg."

He kissed her again.

Probably shouldn't have, but self control wasn't really his thing. This kiss was the kind that shot hot electricity all the way down to his toes. He could have kissed her forever, but he forced himself to stop long enough to ask, "Does that seem like a guy tryin' to convince himself of anything?"

Her eyes struggled to open. "No."

"Look, I know I was horrible to you when I first moved in, and obviously I ruin everything in my life, but my mom wanted us together because *I* wanted us together. She wanted me to be with somebody who inspired me to be a better person, but she also knew I needed a swift kick in the head 'cause I'm stupid, remember? Real, real, real..."

The words caught in his throat as he remembered his mom's rebuke. Of the thousand times she'd told him to get his head on straight.

What would he do without those lectures now?

He tried to clear his throat, but it filled with cotton as he thought about how much his stupidity had cost him over the years—cost those he loved. Even now, Carrie struggled to believe he loved her because he'd pushed her away so many times.

Would it ever stop?

How was he supposed to do anything right ever again without his mom keeping him on track?

His eyes burned and he breathed deeply to clear his thoughts. He wasn't going to do this. He wasn't going to break down. Not here, and *definitely* not now.

"From the beginning, my mom knew I'd fall for you," he tried again. "And now..."

And now she'd never know he was back, safe, alive, and doing what he should have long ago. She wouldn't be around to see him and Carrie end up together—or worse, tell him to keep fighting when Carrie rejected him. His mom was gone and it killed on so many levels, he didn't know how to process it.

He pinched his eyes shut, but they filled anyway, hot moisture that had no business intruding on this moment.

"And now…" he said, voice growing ragged.

Carrie grabbed his good arm and pulled it around her. She wrapped herself against his chest like a cocoon.

"I miss her, too," she whispered.

Greg broke down. The worst moment for his emotions to hijack him, but they spilled over. Carrie held him close and squeezed him harder than his broken body could handle.

When the worst of it passed, he stroked her warm hair, feeling bad he got it wet.

"Sorry," he whispered.

She tipped her head back and looked up at him with those deep blue eyes. "I love you, Greg. I'm sorry I'm so dense, but with everything with Oliver, the paperwork, your mom, and now Ferris, it's just…it's a lot. And now I can't seem to…to…"

Commit.

Believe him.

He put a finger to her soft lips. "It's alright. You don't have to decide anything right now. I'm back, and we've got all the time in the world to figure us out. I just don't want you to doubt where I stand. But I swear I won't pressure you into anything—or at least, I'll try not to," he added with a wink. Because for once in his life, he'd be patient and do things right. He'd win Carrie back.

But first, he had to let her sort through her fake marriage.

"I promise to give you time," he said. "After everything I've put you through, I owe you that much."

Her eyes lit up, quickly followed by the rest of her, making her glow in the morning sun. "Thank you. That means a lot to me." Then she turned and looked over her shoulder. "We should probably get back."

Nodding, he clutched his walking stick and started off beside her.

Time.

Carrie needed time.

"Just to be clear," he said, "what exactly is allowed while you're sortin' all this out? Can I do, say, this?" He snagged her hand and threaded his fingers through hers. "Or is that too pushy?"

She smiled. "No. It's fine."

"Good. How about another kiss, just for good luck?"

With a laugh, she shook her head.

"Fair enough," he relented.

They walked the rest of the way home, hands clasped, discussing Ferris and what it meant going forward if their clan couldn't find anybody to trade with. He kept stealing glances at her, trying to capture this image of her forever in his mind. He should have paid better attention to what she said, but he kept thinking of those stolen kisses, the feel of her, and where the future might take them.

When they neared his backyard, her hand slipped from his.

"Was it something I said?" he asked, only half-teasing.

"No." She tucked a golden lock of hair behind her ear. "I'm just not ready for the whole world to see us together. Do you mind?"

"No." Mostly.

Her cheeks still looked flushed. While he wanted to believe it was his unbelievable kissing abilities, he knew she'd taken losing her friend and her mom's friend hard.

"You gonna be okay?" he asked, stroking her warm cheek. "You look worried. You're kinda wincing, too."

"Sorry. I woke with a headache, and all of this hasn't helped," she said, rubbing her forehead. "I just don't know what to tell Brooke. Not that I'll ever see her again, but still..."

He slipped an arm around her small waist, appreciating the curves of her back. Then he pressed his lips to her forehead. "It will be okay. You'll see. Oh, wait," he said, leaning back a little. "Is that kind of kiss still allowed?"

"No," she said, and yet she leaned into him. Her eyes closed and her hand rested on his chest. So he pulled her tight against him and kissed her forehead again, kicking himself for cutting off the other kind of kissing. Already he craved those moist lips, but he forced himself to behave.

Mostly.

As she started to pull away, he tightened his grip. "Don't go," he whispered.

"I have to. Amber and Zach are probably wondering where I am."

Slipping from his grasp, she started up around the side of his house. He followed, too addicted to her to do otherwise. When she reached the street and saw him still following her, she shook her head with a rueful smile.

"Go spend time with your grandparents, Greg, before May kills me for stealing you all morning." She waved. "See you tonight at the adult meeting."

His mind said, *I gotta wait that long to see you?* while his mouth said, "Y'all still do those?"

"Yes. I'm sure everyone is anxious to hear what happened to you."

He dreaded reliving the story again, but hopefully if he told them all at once, that would be the end of it.

"Alrighty," he relented. "See you tonight. By the way, you still owe me a walk around the pond. Maybe after the meeting?"

She didn't say yes, but neither did she say no. She just smiled her radiant smile again, which was close enough.

"I'll save you a spot at the meeting," he called. Then he winked at her, not caring who might see.

As she crossed her wild front yard, he wondered what she'd do if he jogged up on her porch and kissed her in front of the world. Probably smack him.

Still tempting.

His grandma was only mad that he'd disappeared until she found out who he had disappeared with. Then all was forgiven. Before he could escape to catch up on projects with Richard, his grandpa handed him an envelope.

"Oliver delivered this while you were gone," his grandpa said.

Tensing, Greg broke the seal and slipped out a half sheet of paper.

TO THE FAMILY OF: _Gregory Curtis Pierce_ :

We regret to inform you that your _son_ *was killed in the performance of* _his_ *duty and service to* _his_ *beloved United States.*

Remains buried locally.

Condolences,
Commander McCormick, Special Patrols Unit

Shuddering, Greg realized he'd barely beat this letter home. What would have happened if he hadn't pressed hard to arrive last night? Probably heart attacks for both grandparents and who knew what for Carrie.

"Good news?" his grandpa asked.

"Yeah." Greg handed it over.

His grandpa paled as he read it. "No wonder Oliver looked so distraught. Oh, goodness. Poor Oliver."

Greg didn't feel too sorry for the patrolman, not after seeing Carrie's reaction to her fake marriage.

As the adults began arriving at his grandparents' house that evening, Greg noticed everybody seemed to be in good spirits. He'd avoided most questions as he worked with Richard, saying he'd explain things at the meeting. Maybe Carrie hadn't told them about Ferris either.

When Carrie walked in, she looked worse than before with a sad, blank stare, but that dissolved the moment she spotted Greg standing against his wall. Her eyes brightened with a smile she tried to hide. He pointed to the couch where he'd asked his grandma to save a seat. If it hadn't meant somebody else had to stand for the meeting, Greg would have squeezed next to Carrie on the couch, maybe even held her hand if she'd let him, but he stayed leaned against his wall, arms folded.

The second Carrie sat, his grandma chatted away a mile a minute. From the way Carrie blushed and ducked her chin, Greg could guess the topic well enough. For once he didn't mind his grandma snooping into his love life. He loved watching Carrie squirm up answers.

"I think we're ready to start," his grandpa said, a cue for Greg to wipe the grin off his face. "Richard, can you open the windows in the kitchen to get some air flowing through here?" Then his grandpa turned to Carrie on the couch. "Any updates from Oliver?"

"No," Carrie said. "Oliver didn't stop by today, so I assume there's no raid this week."

Raid? Greg echoed. Carrie was the only person he knew who still called it a *sweep,* its official term. Or she had been until this morning.

"Actually," CJ said, "Oliver dropped something off for Greg this morning. He said there's no raid this week, but I wasn't sure if he'd mentioned anything else of interest to you, maybe during your dinner out on Monday?"

"Oliver came this morning?" Carrie's eyes flickered to Greg. "Amber didn't say anything about him stopping by. I must have missed him."

"Doesn't sound like you missed him too badly," Sasha said, fanning herself idly. "Have a nice walk?"

Carrie's face went beet red as snickers erupted around the room. Greg's grandma patted Carrie's hand in congratulations, and Greg had to study his feet to keep from grinning again. With the world falling apart, he really should quit smiling. His emotions felt bipolar, swinging from one side of the pendulum to the next. A relationship—that wasn't even that solid—shouldn't have this much effect on him after everything else. Then again, he was alive, home, free, and had a chance with Carrie. Nothing else seemed to matter anymore.

"Well," his grandpa said, "if there's nothing else, I think most of you are anxious to hear from Greg. If it's alright, Greg, I'd like you to fill everyone in on where you've been and what it might mean for us. Don't water it down, either."

Sobering quickly, Greg made his way to the front. The room was hot and muggy, reminding him of summers in North Carolina. People fanned themselves while he recounted his experience training, the government's plans for infiltration, the state of the rebellion, and how he was able to return—including the letter Oliver delivered today. Then he decided they needed to hear about Ferris as well.

He looked at Carrie. "Wanna take the reins? You know more about the Ferris situation than I do."

She shook her head.

That left Greg to explain the empty clan, Carrie's dead friend, Scott, the burned out home, and Oliver's hand in it. Carrie kept her gaze on the floor as he spoke, and everybody else went silent.

"I'm thinkin' we need to build up our defenses here," Greg said. "Maybe start posting guards again, even with Oliver. Carrie and I still hope there are other clans in Shelton. Maybe we should go down the list of potentials."

"But Ferris was our last chance at a decent-sized clan," Terrell said. "Even if there are others still out there, who knows if they'll be hostile or lead us into more trouble. The last thing we need is some crazed rebels like that Scott guy bringing the wrath of the government down on our heads."

"The wrath of the government is coming either way," Carrie said softly.

There were a few surprised glances at that, but Greg nodded.

"And I think we need allies," Greg said. "Just in case. In my mind, the benefits still outweigh the risks."

"I agree," Richard added. "If it wasn't for Greg and Oliver, we would be in the dark about this civil war. Perhaps our neighbors are as unaware. I feel it's our responsibility to warn them about what might be coming."

"And possible spies tryin' to infiltrate," Greg added with a nod. "Everybody agree that reaching out is still in our best interest?"

Sasha raised her hand. "Before we decide that, Greg, can we go back to the Ferris Clan? You said they left things behind: clothes, food, and that kind of stuff. Shouldn't we go through their homes and find what we can?"

"No!" Carrie blurted.

Startled, Greg turned. So did the rest of the room.

"Why not?" Sasha said. "Times are desperate. If they left stuff behind, maybe we could—"

"They didn't just walk away," Carrie said bitterly. "They were arrested. Taken against their will."

"Right. So they're not coming back," Sasha said.

Carrie's jaw tightened but she looked away, so Greg spoke up.

"From the little we saw," he said, "most was broken or trashed. I'm sure the patrolmen already took all the good stuff."

"Still..." Sasha glanced around the room. "If we look hard enough, we could probably find tools, clothes, and who knows what else. How thorough are patrolmen anyway?"

A quiet rumble started as people considered that. Greg watched Carrie, waiting for her to speak up. She'd seen the homes, the items, the damage. But she stared down at the floor, hands clasped in her lap.

"What do you think, Carrie?" Greg urged from ten feet away.

People quieted down to hear.

Carrie pushed herself up to stand. Her sad eyes roamed the room as if counting the cost of each person. When her gaze went back to Greg, she said, "Actually, I might head home. Do you mind?"

"What?" Greg said, startled. "Now?"

His grandma tugged on Carrie's yellow work shirt. "We need you, dear. You were there. We want to hear what you think."

Carrie rubbed her arms, looking cold in the hot room. Now that she was standing, she looked white as a sheet, making Greg worry that this was affecting her physically and not just emotionally.

"I know times are desperate, Sasha," Carrie finally said. "But those people were our friends and neighbors. If we go into their homes and take what doesn't belong to us, then we're no better than the patrolmen who raid ours. Which is fine. It is. But I would hope to never hear another word about '*low-life patrolmen*' again."

Greg stared at her in shock. So did the rest of the room. Quiet Carrie just put bossy Sasha in her place. Quite pointedly, too.

Sasha didn't even bat an eye. "What about the boys? Jenna hardly had clothes for Little Jeffrey and Jonah in the summer, let alone winter. The kids in the clan go barefoot to save their shoes that will be too small by winter anyway. It's madness, Carrie. Do you..." Sasha's voice broke. "Do you realize who I used to be? What I used to wear? Now look at me." She held out her arms as if people hadn't memorized the stains in her Banff National Park shirt.

"I know," Carrie said, "but what if that was us? How would we feel to have our neighbors come in and steal the last of our things? Are we scavengers now, too?" Her shoulders lifted. "Maybe we would understand, and maybe the Ferris Clan would, too, but I'm not that desperate. Not yet. I still hope they'll return to their homes someday—maybe someday soon if this rebellion takes hold. I'd hate for them to come back to nothing." With that, she turned and met Greg's stunned gaze. "Sorry to leave early. You already know my vote."

Again he was struck by how drawn she looked. "Can I walk you home?" he asked. "No offense, but you don't look too hot."

"Ouch," Dylan called. "That's no way to treat your lady."

Carrie didn't seem to hear Dylan. "No, I'm fine," she said to Greg. "Stay and finish."

Before Greg could argue, Braden jumped up and started climbing over people. "I'll walk you home, Carrie. I need to head that way anyway."

"I'm fine," Carrie protested. "Really."

"Ah, Carrie," Terrell called, "give Braden a glimpse of Amber."

She nodded and took in the room a last time. "I know I should stay, but I'll understand whatever decision you make." She turned to Sasha. "I really will."

forty-seven

As Carrie and Braden walked the few houses home, Carrie felt the evening chill her bones. It was going to be a cold summer night.

"I just wanted to let you know that I changed my mind," Braden said.

She looked up. "Really?"

"At least for now. After hearing Greg's story..." Braden shoved his hands in his pockets. "I need to see what happens with this rebellion. I don't want to get caught on the wrong side."

"That's wise."

Her head pounded with each step. Today was the first time Oliver had dropped by and not even tried to see her. That hurt. It's like he knew Greg was back and he'd already given up. Maybe it was for the best. Then again, maybe not. She sighed. At least Greg was giving her time to sort through everything. When Oliver came Saturday, she'd ask him about the papers and set things straight.

Carrie didn't notice Braden had followed her all the way to her front door until she opened it. If she hadn't felt so foggy, she would have remembered why he walked her home—the real reason behind his chivalry.

"Oh, come on in," Carrie said. "Let me find Amber."

She dragged herself upstairs and knocked on Amber's bedroom door.

Amber opened it. "Yeah?"

"Braden is downstairs," Carrie said. "He wants to—"

The door started to slam, but Carrie's foot shot out to block it. "Just give him a chance to explain."

"Why should I?" Amber said, plenty loud for Braden to hear. "You two are all cozy now. Maybe *you* should give him a chance."

"You're right. Maybe I will," Carrie said, too tired to fight her. "Goodnight, Amber."

"Wait! You can't have Braden. He's mine." Amber grabbed her arm, eyes narrowing on Carrie's face. "Are you okay?"

Carrie rubbed her head, tempted to go to bed before the sun set. She really hoped she wasn't coming down with something. She didn't have time to be sick. "Just be nice to him. He's a good guy."

When she went downstairs for a cup of water a few minutes later, Amber and Braden sat on the front steps. Braden had his arm around her, and Amber's soft laughter drifted inside.

Well, that was easy, Carrie thought. Easier than with Greg. Then again, Braden was less complicated. Carrie felt like she would never understand Greg.

Zach sat at the kitchen table, two slingshots in front of him.

"Ready for bed?" Carrie asked.

Zach gave her a strange look. "No. Can I stop by Greg's house after the meeting? I wanna show him what I've done."

"No. It's going to be dark soon." Though not soon enough.

"But I have to give him back his slingshot. You haven't let me see him all day," Zach whined.

"Greg has a lot on his mind right now with his mom, trying to find other clans, and…" She leaned against the counter. "And everything."

Zach froze. "Greg's trying to find other clans?"

"We all are. Maybe we should try a different direction, like Centennial?" She drank the cool water, struggling to remember the map they'd sketched. "Too far. Orchard Vines?"

Zach suddenly shot to his feet. "No, you can't!"

Startled, she turned. "What's wrong?"

"You can't go looking for other clans. It will ruin everything!"

"Why? What are you talking about?"

His eyes went big, deer-in-the-headlights size. "Nothing. Never mind." He dropped back on his chair and pretended to study his slingshots. He was obviously hiding something, but it took her a moment to realize what.

His disappearance.

She sat next to him. "Zach, what do you know?"

His jaw tightened.

"Please, Zach. What did you see?"

"There are others," he said softly. "Other people in other clans."

Carrie's heart skipped. "How do you know?"

"Because I met them."

———••———

Zach knocked softly on the Trenton's door, but no one answered. He could hear the adults talking inside, making him want to turn tail and book it home. But Carrie threatened him that if he didn't tell everyone what he and Tucker had been doing, he'd be grounded for the rest of his life. For real this time. So he cracked open the door and sneaked in.

May's house was stuffed with adults. Greg was in the middle of talking when he spotted Zach. He straightened. "What's up, Zach? Is somethin' wrong with Carrie?"

Zach played with his hands. He was the only kid there, and everyone stared at him like he had something nasty on his face. Carrie was mad enough. Tucker would kill him for breaking their pact—plus everyone else in this room. Tucker's dad sat on the side, watching him. Zach and Tucker were going to pay for this big time.

"No. Carrie sent me because…" Heat crept up Zach's neck. "I know something and she thought it was important for your meeting."

"Come on up where we can all see you," Greg said, waving him forward.

Hating his life and everyone in it, Zach shuffled up front. Then he stared down at the floor as he started. "Everyone here thinks there aren't any clans left, but there are. 'Cause I've seen them."

Greg's eyes widened and Zach could see him figuring it out like Carrie had.

If only they knew how many times he'd actually sneaked out.

He scratched his head, looked at Tucker's dad again, and then it all blurted out. How he and Tucker went exploring one day and came across a couple of kids. Those kids invited them to their secret meeting they had once a week, only teenagers allowed.

"It's supposed to be top secret," Zach said, "and they'll never let me back in for telling all of you, but…" Wincing, he finished. "They all come from different clans."

"How many clans?" Greg asked eagerly.

"Four or five. I can't remember."

"Do you know the clan names or where they're located?" Terrell asked.

Zach finally had enough brains to shut up. They'd kill him if he said, Delaney especially. She'd never talk to him again. It wasn't worth it. He'd rather die.

Greg took him by the shoulders and bent down to look him in the eye. "Zach. This is real important. We need your help to make contact. Please, buddy."

"I don't remember the names," he lied, "but I could maybe ask them sometime."

Fat chance of that.

"Or, you and I will ask them together." Greg smiled. "'Cause I'm comin' with you."

forty-eight

Carrie fell onto her ugly couch to wait for Zach. She hadn't realized she'd dozed off until he burst through the front door.

"Greg said I can go with them," Zach announced. "He said he was proud of me for being honest."

Forced honesty, but she didn't point that out. "Good. You're still in a lot of trouble." She couldn't think what kind, so she waved him away. "We'll talk tomorrow. Go to bed. It's late."

Amber came in soon after on cloud nine. Braden had explained everything, and Amber was elated that he'd moved past that "obsession." She even did a little twirl.

"We kissed and made up and everything," Amber crowed.

"Good," Carrie said. "We'll talk tomorrow. Go to bed. It's late."

But instead of leaving, Amber sat next to her on the couch. "You haven't told me about your walk with Greg. Everything okay? You seem sad."

Carrie gave a weak thumbs up. "Things are good with Greg. Everything else, not so much. Bad day. Plus, I think I might be getting sick." She threw an arm over her hot forehead, tempted to sleep right there on the couch.

"Sick?" Pulling a face, Amber backed away from her. "You're not going to throw up are you?"

"No. Just a headache."

"Oh. Good. Want help upstairs?"

"No. I got it."

Carrie dragged herself off the couch and up to her room where she rolled out her blankets and pillow and collapsed in relief.

The first time she woke up freezing. The next time she was sweating and throwing off her blankets. Feeling her way to the dark bathroom, she grabbed a drink from the water bucket to relieve her dry throat. If only she had ibuprofen for her throbbing head. Once she changed into pajamas, she crawled back under her blankets, but she couldn't sleep anymore.

The first rays of morning lit her window and she decided to watch the sunrise from her porch, craving the crisp morning air. She sat up slowly, feeling every achy joint, and wrapped her blanket around her as she headed downstairs.

It was surprisingly cold for July but also peaceful and serene. She watched the sky in the east turn from dark navy to pink. The sunrise gave her hope. Nights could be ominously black, but day always came. While times could be tough, the human will to survive was strong. Greg had proven that. Of course, that same survival instinct made people do things they wouldn't normally do.

Like stealing from friends? she wondered. She meant what she told Sasha. Zach's shoes were falling apart and Terrell hadn't found replacements yet. Plus, they always needed—

"You okay?"

Carrie jumped. Blinking hard, she focused on a person on the sidewalk in front of her. Greg. Though for once, he hadn't tried to sneak up on her. It was strange. She'd watched him come out of his house and cross the street toward her, but it hadn't registered until he spoke that he was right there.

He crouched down and peered at her. "Okay. You're really startin' to scare me. I know I'm an amazing kisser, but this kinda reaction is a little much, don't you think?"

She would have rolled her eyes if they didn't burn so badly.

"What's up?" he said, feeling her forehead. "Wow. You're burnin' up. Is this why you ditched me by the pond?"

"Oh, no," she said with a groan. Their walk. She'd been looking forward to it. "I forgot. I'm sorry. I feel asleep early."

He winked. "No worries. I knew you weren't up for a midnight stroll—not that I didn't wait out there just in case. Why didn't you tell me you were sick?"

"It's nothing. I just didn't sleep very well again." She rubbed a pulsing, tender spot behind her ear. "How was the rest of the meeting?"

He sat next to her on the cement step and slipped his hand into hers. It was so warm and strong and heavenly she didn't pull free like she should have. "Dylan suggested we inventory the supplies in Ferris," he said. "Then we can use them on a need-only basis."

"Oh. Good." That was better than taking things outright.

Her head fell on his shoulder. She hadn't meant to, but her head was unbearably heavy and his shoulder was so close. The second she did, he slipped an arm around her blanketed waist and pulled her closer.

"You comin' on to me, Miss Ashworth?" he whispered into her hair.

She should have been embarrassed, but his shoulder was too warm and comfy.

Shoulder.

"Oh, no," she said, trying to sit up again. "I forgot. Your bad shoulder."

"Whoa, there. You got the good one," he said, pressing her head back down against him. "The other one's gettin' better anyway. Don't be goin' anywhere."

She didn't believe him, but she didn't fight him either. Resting against him, she closed her eyes against the piercing morning sun. Sunshine shouldn't hurt so much.

He kissed her forehead. "Man, you really are hot. Oh, and you're burning up, too."

That time she did roll her eyes. There was nothing appealing about her right now. She wasn't sure if she could handle this side of Greg. The side that said what he thought, what he felt, and teased mercilessly with no regard for her reserved, easily-embarrassed nature.

"Mind if we take Zach with us today?" he asked. "He can point us in the direction where those kids came from."

She was still furious Zach had been sneaking out, but punishment could come later. "Okay. How soon do you want to leave?"

"The sooner the better. I was gonna head to Terrell's after I talked to you. Then we'll meet Richard at the front of the sub."

Another long walk sounded like torture to her, but she hoped once she got moving, the haze in her head would clear. As hard as it was, she shifted away from Greg's warmth and stood. "Okay. I'll go wake him up. We'll be ready in a minute."

Greg looked up at her. "Heya...maybe you should stay home for this one."

"Why?" she said, stung. Just because she broke down in Ferris didn't mean she was weak. She wasn't.

"No offense, but you look like death. I don't know how far we're gonna have to walk."

"Says the guy with the bad leg," she pointed out. "If you can walk, so can I. Besides, I want to see other clans for myself. It might ease my mind." Plus she didn't trust Greg to ask for the kind of medical attention he needed. She dropped the blanket from her shoulders and immediately regretted it. Goosebumps ran down the length of her arms. "Maybe we should get Terrell first."

Greg scrutinized her with a strange expression.

"What?" she said more sharply than intended, but the cold was already seeping through her clothes.

"Somethin' tells me you don't want Terrell seein' you like this. I mean, I'm a big fan of your pajamas, but..."

Her gaze dropped to her dad's old t-shirt and ratty sweats hanging on her body, both thread-bare. She'd come straight from bed, not thinking she'd see someone.

Cheeks flushing, she leaned against her porch railing. "Oh, man. I'm really out of it."

"Yes, you are," Greg said with a laugh. "I'll probably have to drag Terrell's lazy hide outta bed, so don't rush. We'll be back in a bit."

As expected, Terrell had been sound asleep, and so had Jada. Greg finally convinced their nine-year-old twins to quit chasing each other long enough to wake up their parents. Terrell straggled downstairs, rubbing his afro with a scowl. He grumbled the entire way to Carrie's, but Greg ignored him, anxious to be doing something productive again.

Greg knocked the clan signal on Carrie's door.

"Carrie didn't take Ferris too well yesterday," Terrell said. "I don't really take her for the emotional type—at least not like other women around here."

"Definitely not like other women," Greg said, knocking again.

"Are you sure she's awake?" Terrell asked.

"She was."

Greg knocked again and then peeked inside. Immediately, he wished he'd done the two actions in reverse. Carrie had changed into her blue blouse and her hair was pulled back in a pony-tail, but she was curled up and sound asleep on her old couch.

Zach whisked open the door. "Carrie, they're here!"

She didn't budge.

Greg crept into the living room and felt her forehead again. Hot and flushed. There was no way she was up to a long day of walking. She'd probably kill him for going without her, but he backed up.

"Let's go," Greg whispered. But before he closed the front door, he said, "Hey, Zach, where's my slingshot?"

Zach whipped it out of his back pocket. "Here. Why? Are we gonna need it?"

"Possibly."

"Tell me you're not going to protect us with that little thing," Terrell said darkly.

"Nope. Zach is," Greg said.

Terrell's mouth dropped and Zach looked seconds shy of fainting.

Greg smiled. "Richard's meeting us out front of his house. He has both rifles. Let's go."

forty-nine

When Carrie woke, she wasn't thinking about Greg, Zach, or anything besides herself. She had chills like never before, and no matter how hard she tried, she couldn't stop shaking. The aches were bone-deep. Her head, her neck, her legs. Even her skin hurt. And all of it seemed to originate from one spot. Like someone was stabbing the back of her skull with a dull knife.

She was back in her bedroom even though she couldn't remember getting there, and it was dark outside again even though it didn't seem like a whole day had passed. Rolling over, she pulled the blanket over her head to sleep.

The dreams she had.

Vivid nightmares of Zach and Amber being ripped away by David Jamansky. One time she woke panting so wildly it felt like her heart would burst from her ribcage. In that dream, her house had burned with her siblings inside. Worse, Oliver had done it.

Shivers racked her body. If she'd had any energy, she would have put on another pair of socks. Maybe her winter coat. As it was, she didn't want to move more than she had to.

Squinting in the dark, she noticed Amber's blanket already on top of her own. Carrie half-remembered Amber asking if she needed anything, but she couldn't remember answering. Now all she wanted was sleep, sleep, and more sleep. She tried, but each time she woke up, she felt worse. The migraine. The aches. Her neck. Time stood still. Even the crazy dreams stopped.

It had been years since she felt this ill, definitely before the Collapse, and she wished for some medicine to knock her out. She couldn't remember anyone in the clan being this sick either, at least not since that first year, as if there was a limited germ pool they'd used up and there was nothing left to pass around. Living like a recluse had a few benefits.

So why now? she wondered.

Then she remembered. Kissing Greg.

Mortification rolled through her. He'd exposed her to something from training.

As embarrassing as that would have been, her headache started before their walk to Ferris, before a single kiss. And she'd barely seen Greg the night he returned. He wasn't sick anyway. No, this had to be from somewhere else. She'd met Brooke's group, but Terrell had kept her back. Richard was the only one who had shaken hands. Which meant she'd contracted this on her date with Oliver back on Monday. Her first real exposure to society.

Groaning, she laid a frozen hand on her burning cheeks to help both body parts. The relief was only temporary, and she flipped her hand over to swap temperatures again. While her internal thermostat craved the fetal position, her neck and back ached too badly from lying so long. She uncurled slowly.

"Ow," she moaned.

Opening her mouth brought a dryness of its own.

"Amber?" she called in a whisper that barely crossed her parched lips. Somehow it was day again. Amber shouldn't be asleep. Hopefully she was home. Carrie sucked in a little more air and tried again. "Amber?"

"What do you need?" a voice said.

Carrie tensed. Not only was that *not* Amber's voice, but it came from inside her bedroom, down by her feet. She knew that voice anywhere. Deep. Southern. She lifted her head and saw Greg sitting at the foot of her mattress.

"Why are you here?" she asked. More importantly, how long had he been there? She hadn't heard him come in. The sun cast afternoon shadows on her wall, even though she distinctly remembered it being night not that long ago.

"You doin' any better?" he said, crawling over beside her mattress.

Mattress?

Carrie looked underneath her. She no longer lay on the hard carpet, which didn't make sense. She'd lost her mattress in the raid back in March. "Where did this come from?"

"The better question is why you didn't have one in the first place," Greg said with a scowl, "but I'll lecture you about that later. How do you feel?"

"Lousy."

She threw an arm over her head, partly for relief to her feverish forehead, partly to block the painful light streaming in from her window, but mostly to hide. If she had looked bad on the porch, she could only imagine how horrible she looked now. Her hair was plastered to her head from sweating.

"I'm not surprised," he said. "Why didn't you tell me how sick you were?"

"Oh!" It finally dawned on her why Greg was in her room. "Are you ready to go?" That seemed like weeks ago, but she tried to sit up.

He pushed her back down. "Don't you dare. We already went. There was nothin' to see and Zach couldn't remember which direction the kids came from—at least not enough to be helpful. The kids meet again in a few days, so we'll just have to wait. Now…where are you sickest?"

"Mostly my head." She closed her burning eyes. A second later she felt something cool and wonderful on her cheek. Greg's hand pressed against her skin. "You're so cold," she said. Like he'd dunked his hand in a bucket of ice. It felt divine.

"No. My temperature is normal. Yours is not."

She jumped as his hand slid onto the side of her neck. Checking her temperature or not, the gesture felt too intimate. Whatever her temperature had been before, it spiked now.

A worry line pinched between his perfect, dark brows. "I'll grab a cool washcloth. What else do you need? Somethin' to eat? I've got noodles downstairs. Or how about water?"

Noodles?

Carrie pulled the blanket around her shoulders wishing she'd changed back into her pajamas. She was still in her jeans and blue blouse, dressed to go with Greg and Terrell. Now the clothes felt rough on her skin. Not enough to leave the warmth of her blankets and change. Fevers always baffled her. One part burned while the other froze. She was fairly certain if she had five more blankets, her toes would still feel like ice blocks. But that would have to wait until Greg left and she could get Amber.

"Carrie?" he pressed. "What do you need?"

"I'm fine."

That only deepened his scowl. "You're not fine, so just tell me what—Carrie!" he said, interrupting himself. "You're shivering!"

He grabbed another blanket from somewhere and piled it on top of the others. With a huff, he knelt beside her again. "Now, will you please tell me what you need?"

He was mad at her which didn't seem fair considering her weakened condition.

"I just need to sleep it off," she said. At least she hoped she could. She'd always received antibiotics as a kid. She just hoped Greg didn't catch it.

Her burning eyes flew open. "Greg! You have to get out of here!" Her desperation came out weak and pathetic. "You'll get sick. You have to go!"

"Not gonna happen. I woulda already caught it. Now, what do you need?"

True. Greg would have already caught it. Sadly though, she couldn't bring herself to regret those kisses. But still…

She squinted up at him. "I need Amber actually. Where is she?"

"Amber and Zach are at Tucker's. They're gonna stay there until you're better."

Amber was at Tucker's, not at Maddie's or Lindsey's—with their 'dreamy' older brother? Great. More Braden drama. For now at least her siblings wouldn't catch this. Then again, that left her all alone. Or worse…with Greg. She didn't want him seeing her like this. Not now. Not ever.

But then he left.

He walked out of her room—or rather limped. Her own muscles begged for another position, but it seemed like too much work. She couldn't even turn her head. So she settled onto the soft mattress and reentered the wonderful world of unconsciousness. She woke to a cold washrag being placed on her forehead. Her body let out an involuntary sigh. She vowed right then never to take good health for granted again.

"Serves me right for going back into civilization," she said.

"What do you mean?"

"Dinner with Oliver."

Greg stroked her cheek with his wonderful icy fingers. "Actually, I think I gave this to you."

She peeked an eye open. "Are you sick?"

"No, but…" A corner of his mouth tugged up. "I'm pretty sure we exchanged a few germs."

She was too tired to blush. "No. I had a headache before Ferris. I think I got this on my date."

His countenance did a one-eighty. He growled under his breath. "Another reason you shouldn't have kissed that guy."

That barely-there kiss from Oliver couldn't have done much more than make her and Oliver uncomfortable. Besides, she saw Oliver all the time, and he'd never gotten her sick before. This had to be from shaking hands with his coworkers, touching doors, booths, or who knew what else.

Greg sighed deeply. "Now for the last time, you stubborn woman, will you please swallow some pride and just tell me what you need?"

Considering she was tempted to suck the water out of the wash rag, she decided to ask. "I could…use a drink."

"Dehydrated. Great." He grabbed a cup of water already waiting on the floor next to her. With effort, she propped herself up. The first gulp made her wince. After that, she had the dilemma of pain or thirst. She chose thirst knowing the pain would only be momentary. She finished the glass with a quiet "ouch."

As she lay back down, Greg stared at her, face suddenly devoid of emotion. "Is it just your head, or do your lungs hurt, too? Does it…" He paused. "Does it hurt to breathe?"

He almost looked scared. Traumatized, maybe. And no wonder. Kendra and his mom both died of breathing, coughing issues.

Carrie took a slow, deep breath. It hurt everywhere, but not in the way he meant. "No. It's just the flu or something. I just need to sleep it off."

"Sleep? People used to die of influenza all the time. No. You need to get to a hospital."

She moved the washcloth off her eyes. Unfortunately, he wasn't teasing. "I'd rather be sick than arrested, Greg."

"You won't be arrested, remember?"

Right. Stupid papers.

"You need medicine," he said, "and I've gotta plan."

Of course he did. He always did.

"If anyone needs a doctor," she said tiredly, "it's you."

He ignored that. "It's all figured out. If you're not better by morning, you're goin' to the hospital in Aurora. I don't care what you say."

She pressed the washcloth to her eyes, too tired to fight such a ridiculous idea. She hated Aurora. Six years ago, her family nearly starved there in a tiny government apartment they shared with nine other people. Her parents and siblings fled before the fences and blue cards had been mandated. Carrie refused to go back.

He stood. "Alrighty. I'll let you sleep again."

Only instead of leaving, he moved to a folding chair—her kitchen chair—which, for some reason, sat in the corner of her bedroom. He sat, elbows on his knees, and watched her, clueless about how awkward it was to sleep with someone staring at you.

Go away, she begged silently.

He just sat there, absentmindedly twirling something in his hands. When she realized what it was, she wanted to slink under her covers.

His NY Yankees hat.

Thankfully, it wasn't under her pillow anymore. She could only imagine how he'd exploit that. But still…

"Please go, Greg," she whispered.

"Not a chance."

"I don't want you to catch this."

"I'm not leavin', Carrie."

"But—"

"Carrie," he said, "just sleep, alrighty? Let me know if you need anything."

Embarrassed, exhausted, crusty-haired, and all around unsociable, she tucked her face inside her dark cave. Her skull pulsed and stabbed, making sleep difficult, but she faded in and out, sometimes jerking awake and sometimes being roused by the pain. Her mom used to get migraines, but Carrie never appreciated them until now. The light in the room inched across the far wall. Even that much light was painful, so she stayed hidden beneath her dark blankets. Mostly. Each time she woke, she had to check. Greg still sat in her corner, twirling his hat.

More miserable than she could ever remember being, her thoughts wandered to her mom, suddenly missing her. Isn't that what moms did? Take care of sick kids? At least Greg had sent Amber and Zach away.

The last thing she wanted was for anyone else to catch this. Gratefully she hadn't been around anyone besides Greg and…

"May," she croaked.

He straightened. "You awake again?"

"Greg," she said, frantic, "I sat by your grandma at the meeting. She held my hand the whole time. What if she gets this?"

His face darkened. "Grandma started with a headache and chills last night."

Carrie fell back on her pillow. May was sick. If it really was strep or flu, then a few days—maybe a week—and Carrie would feel back to normal. But May was old. She'd have a harder time recovering. It could turn into pneumonia or something worse.

"Anyone else?" she whispered.

Greg tossed his hat on the floor. "Braden woke with a pounding headache, and Terrell started a few hours ago."

"But…how did they all get it so fast? I only started feeling lousy yesterday."

"Yesterday?" He looked at her. "Carrie, you've been in bed for a day and a half. Who knows how long you were sick before then."

"What?"

With a slow nod, his eyes seemed to lose focus. "Everybody keeps sayin' this *infection* just needs to run its course, but there's no way to know for sure. Who knows what it could turn into."

That's why Amber was at Tucker's. Carrie had talked to Braden behind the pond—and then walking home—and she'd been with Terrell the whole Watercrest day. Who else had she been around? She closed her eyes, feeling nauseated on top of everything else.

"For some reason, Amber and Zach haven't shown any symptoms," Greg went on. "Neither have I, even though we've all been exposed to you—some more than others," he added with a smirk. "We've got all of you quarantined to be safe, but even then, we could have a serious epidemic on our hands."

Her migraine pulsed. May could get medical help if desperate—and now Carrie could, too, thanks to those stupid papers. But what about Braden and Terrell? Then again, CJ didn't have any extra money. He might not even have enough to treat his wife, let alone others.

"Please go, Greg," Carrie said desperately. "Please?"

For a second he looked hurt, but then he nodded. He stood and stretched in a way that made her wonder how long he'd been there. But instead of leaving, he knelt by her mattress again.

He pressed his palm to the side of her neck and then moved the washcloth away to feel her forehead, but her thoughts were far from her own temperature. She studied those worry lines around his bruised face. When his eyes met hers, they didn't blink or twitch. They just stared through her like a lost, scared soul. He looked worse than she felt, and she couldn't help but think how awful the last six weeks had been on him. His mom's death and everything was still too raw. He couldn't handle one more thing.

She slipped her hand out of her blankets and found his. Squeezing his hand tightly, she said, "I'm fine. Really. We'll all be fine."

"You've got twelve hours to prove it. If not, you and Grandma are goin' to the hospital. I'll take you myself if I have to."

"You? With what citizenship? You're dead, remember?"

His jaw tightened.

Something clicked in her head. *I gotta plan*, he had said. Isabel told him if he ever changed his mind, he could fabricate a story about his disappearance and he'd be reinstated. Special Op. Green card.

Greg the spy.

He said that card gave him special perks—perks that even Oliver didn't have.

"No!" she yelled. The outburst stabbed her brain, making his face go in and out of focus, but she continued anyway. "You can't give yourself up for something stupid like this. If we get desperate, we'll find Oliver."

He stroked her cold fingers without looking at her. "Dylan's been camped in town since last night. No sign of Oliver."

"Are you nuts? Dylan doesn't have his citizenship—and neither do you. Neither of you should be *anywhere* public!"

Greg just kept stroking her hand.

What was he thinking, taking such huge risks for a simple illness? He'd just barge into some government hospital, ask for a phone to contact his former commander who would cart Greg off before he could even check Carrie and May in.

His wounds hadn't even healed yet. He was crazy. Insane!

Though it hurt to do so, Carrie fixed him with a steady gaze. "Twelve hours isn't long enough to get over this, so don't do anything rash. If your grandma gets worse, we'll find Oliver. Just swear to me you won't do anything stupid." Her throat started to close off. "They can't have you back."

"I haven't decided anything yet," he said softly.

It was a blatant lie. She could see it in the set of his clean-shaven jaw. He would turn himself in, get his green spy card and whatever money his Commander owed him, and then spend the rest of his life—however long that was—in their control. All for what?

The flu?

"You can't do this to me," she said, voice cracking. "You almost left once without telling me. You can't do this again. Promise me, Greg. Promise."

His shoulders lowered. "I won't do anything without tellin' you first, but I won't promise anything beyond that. If you're not better by morning, you're goin' and that's final."

"We'll see," she whispered.

She lay back. If the light from the window would quit stabbing her temples, she could sleep deeply enough to recover and show him she would be fine. Terrell and Braden would be fine, too. But what if May kept declining? What if they couldn't find Oliver?

Carrie's stubborn side dug in. Greg wasn't the only one who could come up with crazy plans. He and Carrie had switched roles. She was the legal one now, which meant she'd take May to the hospital herself. She'd scrounge up the last of CJ's money and…walk to Aurora? She didn't know how she'd make the long trip, but she'd find a way.

If only she could stop shaking.

Hunkering down, she pulled the blankets tight and clenched every muscle to stop shivering. It didn't help. Greg tucked her hand back under and pressed down on her arm.

"Tell me what to do," he said. "Can I rub your arms to warm them up? Cuddle close? Build you a fire? What?"

"Stay dead. Stop overreacting." *Stop scaring me to death.*

"The greater good," he whispered.

She glared at him. "Right. Which means no destroying neighborhoods or killing my friends. Whatever happens tomorrow, one month, five years, or five decades from now, you find a different way, Greg. You stay free." The burning in her eyes won out and tears pooled, blurring his bruised, haunted face. "Promise me."

With a long sigh, he finally nodded. "Fine. I promise."

Breathing easier, Carrie sunk into her pillow, finally ready to sleep.

After a minute, she felt Greg shift away from her. Her eyes fluttered open.

"I'm gonna let you sleep now," he said. Then he leaned down and kissed her. A long, lingering, hot kiss that made the room spin. Even as he broke off, the room continued to twirl around her. But before she could scold him for exposing himself to more germs—or breaking his agreement to give her space—he stood.

"I'll be downstairs. Holler if you need me." Then he slipped out of her room.

It wasn't until he left that she realized his kiss had the chilling sentiment of someone saying goodbye. And she knew his promise meant nothing.

fifty

Amber swept out the nasty-smelling chicken coop, plotting ways to make Zach pay for this. It wasn't her fault Carrie found out about his escapades. But she kept sweeping because she promised Greg things would get taken care of while Carrie was sick.

Richard slipped out the Trenton's back door, heading for the well. Amber dropped the broom and started over to him.

"Not too close," Richard called, waving her back.

Amber folded her arms. "How's May?"

"Worse. So is Carrie."

That wasn't good. At least Greg was there. He would know what to do. "Have you checked on Braden again?" Amber said.

Richard grabbed the water bucket. "Last I heard, he just had a slight fever. Nothing to worry about yet."

"Yet?" Amber echoed.

"Tell you what," Richard said with a smile, "after I get May water, I was going to make the rounds and check on everyone anyway, including your sister and Braden. If you'd like—"

"I'll go!" Amber said, jumping forward.

Richard chuckled. "I was going to offer to give them a message for you."

"Oh, please can I come? I promise to stay far away from everyone."

"Alright," Richard said. "Give me a few minutes and we'll go."

Amber washed her hands and finger-combed her hair even though she wouldn't be allowed to see Braden. She'd never seen her clan so paranoid about germs. Once Richard finished, Amber followed him a safe distance down the street.

"Is this really that serious, Richard? I thought Carrie and the others just have colds or something."

"Hard to tell," Richard said. "It's spreading rapidly, so we thought we'd better be safe, especially without access to doctors or medicines."

Amber thought about the number of graves in the cemetery. Most of those started as simple illnesses, too.

A wave of panic swept through her. Braden promised he wouldn't let anything happen to her—wouldn't let her die—but he never promised the same for himself.

Or anyone else.

While Richard grilled Mrs. Ziegler, Amber stayed on Braden's front lawn, fretting and watching the upper window. After a few seconds, Braden appeared. He looked tired but gave her a tiny wave, flashing his red bracelet. She wanted to smile but couldn't quite as she waved back.

———— ✦ ————

Greg ended up on Carrie's front porch, too wound up to nap like he should have. After several nights of fitful sleep and a full day in Carrie's unbearably-hot room, he was on edge. His leg and shoulder were definitely on the mend but still ached, so he closed his eyes and let the summer breeze cool his damp skin.

He left the front door cracked open so he could hear if Carrie called him. Not that she would. Really, he was just waiting for her to fall back asleep so he could sneak back into her room.

He spotted Richard and Amber coming down the road. Richard waved and stopped on Carrie's sidewalk fifteen feet away, what they had determined was a safe distance.

"How's Carrie?" Richard asked.

Greg frowned. "Still declining, but she finally woke up for a few minutes. She's burning up and squints a lot. The light really bothers her eyes." More than it should for a fever. He sighed. "How about Grandma?"

"About the same," Richard said. "Has Carrie said anything about being dizzy?"

"No, but she hasn't been upright that I've seen."

"Your grandma can hardly walk. She says the room keeps spinning. CJ hasn't left her side, so he'll probably start with it next."

So would Richard with the amount of time he was spending at his in-laws. Greg still wasn't convinced he hadn't given this to everyone. Who knew what he'd been exposed to in his time away. Except he hadn't been sick during training. Not even once.

"Braden didn't seem too bad," Amber said behind Richard.

He'll get there, Greg thought.

"Well," Richard said, "your grandma agreed to go to the hospital if she's not feeling better. She put up a fuss about money, but I reminded her that you and your mom aren't paying taxes anymore."

Greg nodded. Now for the problem of getting them there. Ten miles, one way. "Don't suppose Dylan's back?"

"He came back to report, but no sign of Oliver or his car. Dylan's back in town again."

If Oliver didn't show up soon, Greg would have to move to plan B, regardless of what he'd promised Carrie. But that still didn't solve the transportation issue. Unless Isabel had a car she might lend him.

"Carrie refuses to go," Greg said. "She wants to *sleep* it off, but if she's not better by morning, I'm makin' her go with Grandma. Any suggestions how to get them there?"

Richard jerked back. "Carrie? She's an illegal. She can't go."

When Greg said nothing, Richard shook his head. "What grand scheme are you planning now?"

Greg folded his arms. "Carrie has papers."

"What?" Richard and Amber cried at the same time.

"How?" Amber added.

"Doesn't matter," Greg said. "Oliver got them for her a few months back. She just found out."

Richard let out a long breath. "If that's the case, we really need to find Oliver. Don't do anything until we've talked again, Greg. Amber and I are making the rounds to make sure no one else has contracted it. Then I'll head back to your grandmother's and stay the rest of the evening. We'll talk in the morning."

Morning seemed like forever away, but Greg nodded. "Okay. Thanks for keepin' an eye on them for me." He rubbed his weary eyes. "Hey, Amber, before you head around, can you find me a couple nails? Ron should have some. Just leave them on the front porch, and I'll grab them."

"Sure," Amber said. "Catch you in a bit, Richard."

Richard watched her go but didn't leave. When she was out of earshot, he turned back. "Greg..." he said in a slow, fatherly tone, "I know you're worried, but Carrie will be fine. Sometimes these things just need to run their course."

Like Kendra? Greg wanted to snap. *Like everybody else?*

He wasn't risking it.

"Carrie is strong, young, and healthy." Pausing, Richard waited until Greg looked at him. "You won't lose her, too."

Too. A horrible word.

Greg stared down at the cement.

"I don't know what craziness you're planning," Richard continued, "but whatever Carrie has, whatever this is, it's not the same as—"

"Check on the others," Greg interrupted. "Let me know if anything changes."

Sighing, Richard nodded.

Greg watched him go, feeling more sleep deprived by the minute. He kept snapping at people, but his nerves were strung too tight. There was something off about this illness, about the way Carrie squinted and shook like crazy that told him this was more than the simple flu.

Heading back inside, he crept upstairs and found Carrie where he left her: curled up under her mass of blankets in a room that could melt metal with its trapped heat. She was out cold, but the heels of her hands were pressed against her eye sockets to block the light.

He went to Zach's room and grabbed the last blanket. Amber dropped off the nails a few minutes later. Then Greg found a rock and nailed up the blanket to block Carrie's window. It wasn't quite big enough and a small sliver of sunlight still streamed in, but hopefully it would help.

She hadn't even budged with the hammering.

Greg checked out the window, hoping Dylan would show up with Oliver, and then checked Carrie's forehead hoping her fever would break. Maybe then he could crack a window. But her forehead stayed red hot and the rest of her stayed ice cold, making him wonder how long she could maintain a fever that high.

He ran a finger along her parted lips. They were no longer moist and soft. The dehydration was worsening.

That got him moving.

"Carrie?" He nudged her. She needed to drink. Food would be even better. "Carrie?" he said more loudly.

She peeked around her hand, but only for a moment. Her eyes closed again and her breathing deepened.

"C'mon, Carrie girl. You gotta drink somethin'. Up and at it."

She moaned but gave in. Helping her up, he got a few sips of water in her before she started to reach for her pillow.

"Wait. How about some food?" he said. "Noodles? Soup? What sounds good?"

She grimaced. "My head hurts."

"I know, but you should eat anyway. Or maybe more water?"

But she was already curling up under her blankets. With a sigh, he let her go. Maybe sleep was for the best.

Sitting next to her, he brushed some damp hair off her forehead. Her eyes fluttered open, squinty and still pained, yet she gave him a weak smile.

"Thanks, Dad," she said.

His hand froze.

She pressed the heels of her hands back into her eyes, and her breathing returned to a soft hush-hush in the silent room. Greg's pulse drummed in his ears.

Her father had been dead for five years.

Tired, hot, and admittedly ornery, he laid down on the carpet next to her mattress—the mattress he'd stolen from Tucker's brother. His eyes drooped under the strain of the day, the week, the year. Giving in, he closed them. But sleep still escaped him.

You won't lose her, too.

An ironic statement because you couldn't lose something you never had. With her lashes on her cheeks, her light hair spilled across the pillow, he pictured lying beside Carrie every night for the rest of his life.

She was going to be just fine.

He would make sure of it.

McCormick said Greg's green card came with special privileges, a way to get around government red tape. Wiggle room. If Oliver didn't show soon, Greg was going to need a lot of wiggle room. He just hoped it was enough. If needed, he'd go into town and borrow the phone there. One call. That was all it would take.

He didn't realize he'd dozed off until he heard an engine outside. Even then, it took his sluggish brain a moment to realize who it was.

Oliver!

Finally.

Greg rubbed his eyes, wondering how long he'd slept. The small sliver of light shining in Carrie's window had a golden, early evening hue. He ran downstairs and whisked the door open before Oliver could knock.

The patrolman couldn't have been more shocked to see Greg of all people standing in Carrie's doorway. Oliver wasn't dressed in uniform but looked more casual in jeans and a button-down shirt. He held a handful of wildflowers. Flowers that seemed to droop at the sight of Greg, blurry-eyed and disheveled.

Greg stepped onto the porch and shut the door, forcing Oliver back as well. "Finally. Where have you been?"

"Nice to see you, too," Oliver said. "Nice to know you're not dead. I don't suppose you could have warned me *before* I received your death notice and had a heart attack? I assume there's a logical explanation why the government thinks you're dead?"

"Yeah. Long story," he said, finger-combing his messy hair. It felt like years since Greg had last seen Oliver. Too much to explain now. "Thanks for helpin' my mom, by the way. Richard said you're the only reason she made it home alive, so I'm eternally indebted to you. However"—his muscles tightened—"I have a beef to pick with you. A few beefs actually."

"Don't you always." Oliver eyed the closed door. "Look, I'm sorry to have interrupted…whatever, but I need to see Carrie. She invited me to dinner, so I'll talk to you another—"

"Dinner?" Greg cut in. "Dylan didn't find you?"

"No. I've been in Joliet all day for some training. Why? Was he looking for me?"

Greg's temper flared. Oliver was here for a date.

Date number two.

"Follow me," Greg said, starting down the sidewalk.

Oliver huffed. "I'm not in the mood for this, Greg. I really need to talk to Carrie." And yet he followed Greg to his car.

When they were far enough away Carrie couldn't overhear, Greg whirled on him. "What were you thinkin' taking Carrie into public?"

Oliver's brows shot up, but only for a moment. Then his jaw set tight. "I understand your concern, but I didn't know my boss was going to show up. But I assure you Carrie was safe the whole time. She handled Jamansky perfectly."

Greg's blood pressure shot through the roof. "She met Jamansky? The slime ball who murdered my mom!"

Oliver took a step back as if to ward off a possible punch to the face. "Nothing happened."

"Like her getting sick?"

Oliver blanched. He glanced back at the house. "Carrie's sick?"

"Yeah. Real sick. My grandma, Braden, and Terrell, too. If this continues to spread, we could have an epidemic on our hands, only unlike you people," he spat, "we're helpless to deal with it."

"Carrie's sick," Oliver repeated. He stared down at the ground as if trying to pinpoint the exact moment she'd caught something. Greg could have, and he wanted to deck the guy for it.

"Look," Oliver said apologetically, "I realize you're mad at me—which you have every right to be—but let me help her."

"No. *I* will take care of this. *You* will stay away from her from now on."

Oliver went rigid. "That's not your choice to make."

"You're right," Greg said. "But it's hers, and she's made it."

Mostly.

Greg knew he was pushing it, but the lack of sleep and trauma of everything made civility impossible.

"She said that?" Oliver said, sounding hurt. "That I should stay away from her?"

When Greg couldn't respond truthfully, the tall patrolman glared at him. "I didn't think so. Need I remind you that you're dead, Greg. You're in no position to help her financially or legally, but I am. I can take her to a doctor. Let me see her."

Deep down, Greg knew Oliver was right. This was the reason he'd sent Dylan into town, but Greg couldn't give it up—give her up. Not again.

Arms folded, he blocked the sidewalk. "You're not goin' in there. The house is quarantined."

"Quarantined? What does she have?"

"She says it's the flu, but it's different. She's actin' weird. Even if it is just the flu, it could easily turn into..." Greg trailed off when Oliver's face went white. "What?"

"What are her symptoms?" Oliver asked suddenly.

"Crazy high fever, migraine, aches, chills, and she's slept two days straight. My grandma is dizzy, too. Why?"

"Is her neck stiff?" Oliver asked.

"I don't know. Why?"

"Is her neck stiff?" Oliver said, practically shouting. "Does she have pain behind her ears?"

"I don't know! She might have mentioned something about her neck."

Oliver backed up, shaking his head for a moment. Then his head snapped up with a sudden look of determination. "I have to see her."

He started around Greg, but Greg grabbed his arm. "Nobody's allowed in there."

Oliver yanked free and shoved a finger in his face. "Don't touch me again! I'm going in there, and you will not stop me. You have no idea what's going on."

Oliver pushed past and ran through the front door, taking the stairs two at a time. With his bum leg, Greg struggled to follow while his mind spun with those words. *You have no idea what's going on.* By the time he caught up, Oliver was kneeling next to Carrie's mattress.

"Carrie?" Oliver whispered. "Carrie?"

No response.

"Carrie?" he said a little louder, shaking her gently.

"She's only woken up a few times," Greg said, "and it's getting harder to wake her up."

Oliver grabbed her hand. "Carrie, I'm really sorry, but can you try to wake up?"

Her lashes flitted open. She squinted hard and finally noticed someone crouched in front of her. "Oliver?" she croaked.

"Sorry to wake you," Oliver said. "I just need to—"

"Dinner," she moaned. "I'm so sorry."

"Don't worry about that. I just need to ask you something. Greg said your head hurts. Can you tell me where?"

She closed her eyes. "Everywhere."

"I know, but does it hurt one place more than another?"

Though it took a moment, her hand slipped out of her blankets and patted a spot behind her ear. Oliver's eyes flew to Greg in a panic. That panic transformed into sheer terror for Greg, and he didn't even know why. Was that not a normal place for a migraine?

Oliver turned back to her. "Is...is your neck stiff?"

"Yeah." Her words were slow and slurred. "Sorry about...dinner."

He managed to smile down at her. "Don't be. Go back to sleep, okay?"

Oliver stood and walked past Greg, down the stairs and all the way out to his car. Greg limped behind, feeling himself go numb with dread.

"What is it?" Greg asked. "What does she have?"

Oliver paced in front of his car, hands running over his thinning hair. "No, no, no."

"Oliver! What is it?"

"I think, I think she has G-979."

"Which is...?"

"I hadn't heard of it until a week ago. They said"—Oliver swallowed—"it's similar to meningitis, but more...severe. The brain swells. Symptoms include a high fever, neck stiffness, and a horrible headache originating behind the ears."

Meningitis. From the little Greg knew, meningitis wasn't great, but it was treatable. At least, he hoped.

"So what do we do?" Greg asked.

Oliver stopped and stared at him, looking suddenly ten years older. "I don't know. I heard rumors. I mean, I heard things during training that this...this isn't..."

"Isn't what?"

Oliver started pacing again, faster, nearing the hyperventilation stage. "I think the government created this. I think it's their newest weapon. They tweaked the disease, messing with it to make it purposely deadly. They never said as much, at least not officially, but..." He shook his head. "But why else warn us about it? Why give us so many shots? People were talking, Greg, and, and..."

"A weapon?" Greg's stomach dropped to the cement. "As in biological warfare?"

Pale and terrified, Oliver nodded. "President Rigsby's way to win the war."

fifty-one

Greg thought about the shots he'd received during training. He'd assumed they were immunizations, and maybe some were, but they also gave him boosters before he left with Isabel. And now he wasn't sick even though he'd been exposed to Carrie more than anybody.

Neither was Oliver.

He felt like somebody kicked him in the gut. He put a hand on Oliver's car to steady himself.

Swelling of the brain. What did that even mean?

"No," Greg said. "No, you're wrong."

Oliver didn't respond. He didn't even hear as he paced in front of Greg.

Something Isabel had said sparked in Greg's mind—or maybe it had been McCormick. About them delivering a weapon to the rebels, even if they couldn't get information. Isabel and Greg had been more than spies. They were hosts of some virus, some plague of President Rigsby's creation. And it made sense. Rigsby couldn't find all the illegals, so he'd wipe them out through simple strategy. Introduce a new strain of disease and let it spread among people with no access to medical help. Immunize those you want to save. Let the rest die. No guns would be fired. No civil war. They'd be peaceful, seemingly natural deaths.

Genocide.

How could you do this to Carrie? Greg wanted to scream, but he didn't because he could have exposed her—and the others—just as easily. And maybe he had. His grandma went downhill so fast, she probably caught it from Greg, not Carrie.

How many others had he infected? What happened when it spread through the clan? West Chicago? The whole rebellion?

"It wasn't supposed to be in this area yet. It wasn't supposed to be," Oliver said, still rambling. "It's deadly—purposely deadly. They said we had time, but-but-but obviously…"

Greg looked up. "Tell me there's a cure."

Oliver's eyes darted back and forth over the driveway. "I don't know. We received immunizations, but I don't know if there's anything they can do once you have the actual disease."

Greg grabbed him by the shoulders. "Tell me there's a cure!"

"I don't know. I don't know!"

"What in the world is going on?" Richard said, running up to the two men. Amber was right behind him.

Greg released Oliver and fell back against the patrol car, unable to speak. As Oliver filled Richard and Amber in, a single word kept chanting in Greg's mind: *Genocide. Genocide. Genocide.* By the time Oliver finished, Richard looked like Greg felt, and Amber burst into tears.

"How long do they have?" Richard asked.

If that didn't sound like a death sentence…

"I don't know," Oliver said softly.

Greg pinched his eyes shut. This couldn't be happening. Not now. Not after everything.

Richard eyed his stepson. "They need doctors, Greg. Real doctors. Oliver, can you take them to the medical unit in Aurora?"

Greg whirled. "Can they even treat it when it's this advanced? Carrie started symptoms two and a half days ago."

"That long ago?" Oliver whispered.

Amber whirled and started for the house. "I have to see her," she said. Richard grabbed her, but Amber fought against him. "I want to see my sister!"

"Not yet," Richard said. "We can't have you getting this, too. Just wait a minute and let Oliver and Greg figure this out."

Greg stared at Oliver, feeling more despondent by the second. Brain swelling. Even if they could treat it, Carrie and the others could already have permanent damage. A thousand questions swirled in his mind with a thousand possible outcomes. None good.

"Take her," Greg said to Oliver. "Carrie already knows about her papers, so go."

Oliver's jaw dropped. "Carrie knows?"

"Yes. Go! You gotta take my grandma, too. She's sick and Braden's sick and..." Greg's hands ran over his hair, ready to pull it out. How many would they lose? How many people would he watch die while he went on living a healthy life alone?

"But, but, but," Oliver stammered, "her papers haven't been processed yet. They still need Carrie's signature. She has to sign them before I can—"

"Give me the blasted papers!" Greg roared. "I'll sign them myself!"

"Greg," Richard said. "Let's not do anything rash."

Greg whirled. "Like killing millions of Americans? This is genocide, Richard. He's gonna win. He can't win!"

"Who?" Richard asked.

Greg pinched the bridge of his nose, struggling to find some semblance of control. "President Rigsby will not take another person from me. Give me the papers, and I will forge Carrie's name."

Though it took a second, Oliver nodded. He opened his car door and bent over the glove box a moment before handing Greg a set of folded documents.

"Let me find a pen," Oliver said.

As Oliver searched his car again, Greg unfolded the papers. He read the title and froze. "What's this?"

Oliver was still digging through his car.

Greg scanned the words. The papers weren't a marriage license or even citizenship papers. They looked like business papers. Real estate papers. He pulled them close in the fading sunlight and scanned the heading once, then twice to be sure.

Greg's head whipped up. "You bought Carrie's house?"

"He what?" Richard cried.

"Let me see." Amber practically climbed over Greg to get to the papers.

Greg finally had enough sense to swat her back. "What are you doin'? I've been exposed, Amber. You wanna die, too?"

Amber held out her arms. "I've been around Carrie, too. It's only a matter of time."

Greg cursed under his breath. She was right. Still, he backed away from her and stormed over to the patrol car.

"This isn't a marriage license," he said, holding it up as if Oliver hadn't seen it himself.

Oliver's brows shot up high. "Why would it be a marriage license?"

Greg reread the tiny print. He'd never read a deed to a home before, but that's the only explanation for what he saw. He'd assumed Oliver went the same path Greg wanted to in getting Carrie legal, but Carrie wasn't married. She was a homeowner. Like his grandparents.

A yellow card holder.

"Holy heaven almighty," Greg breathed. "You bought Carrie's house. How?" It's not like patrolmen made oodles of money. They got a living stipend for food and clothing.

Oliver's face went red. "I've been saving for a while."

"How long?" Greg asked.

Oliver shrugged, which Greg took to mean years.

"I started the paperwork after that raid a few months ago," Oliver said, "but it takes a while for the government to clear homes. I got the final papers last week."

"Why didn't you tell her?" Greg asked. *Why didn't you tell me!* he thought desperately. She was free.

She'd been free this whole time.

"I don't know if she wants this," Oliver said. "Look at what your citizenship did to you, Greg. This could backfire."

All Greg could think was another home for the clan, another yard for a garden, chickens, goats, or whatever they wanted. All without ties to Oliver. Carrie was free in more ways than one. And she wasn't the only one.

Greg's gaze lifted to Amber.

"Does this mean what I think it does?" Amber whispered. When Greg nodded, her hands flew to her mouth. "Oh, my gosh. Oh, my gosh! I love you, Oliver!"

"This is amazing," Richard added, looking at the paperwork.

"No!" Oliver insisted. "You people don't understand. This deed is nothing without Carrie's signature, and processing, and cards, and so much other stuff we don't have time for. Everything takes time, and it's the weekend, and I can't do it without—"

"I'll forge her name," Greg said, snatching the pen from Oliver. He'd never seen Carrie's signature. Heck, he'd never even seen her handwriting before, but he could fake a few girly loops. "Where do I sign?"

Oliver pointed out the spots, but before Greg could, Amber yanked the pen from him.

"Let me. This is my house now." Amber pushed the papers against Oliver's car and signed every spot he pointed to. "Now what else do we have to do to get my sister legal?"

"I have to get this processed," Oliver said, "and then somehow get her a yellow card—which is a whole new set of paperwork and signatures and—"

"But you were gonna show these papers on the drive," Greg said. "Why not in the hospital?"

"Because the hospital's different!" Oliver said in exasperation. "They track patients through their cards—their actual cards. They use scanners to disperse medicines and payments and everything. Your grandma already has her card, but I can't fake Carrie's or tell them that her paperwork is being 'processed.' We have to do this the right way."

"Which means...?" Richard prompted.

Oliver ticked off the list on his fingers. "I need Carrie's picture, several signatures, and so much paperwork that I just...we just can't..." His shoulders sagged. "That's not even the worst part. I'm out of money. This house drained my resources. If I pay Carrie's taxes to get her the green light, I won't have enough for the hospital."

"CJ has money," Richard said.

But it wouldn't be enough. Greg knew it wouldn't be enough to treat Carrie and his Grandma—plus more people as this kept escalating. He just shook his head. "Forget the money. You just get Carrie through those hospital doors and we'll figure out the rest."

"But it's the weekend," Oliver said. "The offices are closed until Monday. I don't know how to make this work in time."

Time.

Something they didn't have.

Greg had been trained all about citizenship scanners. If Carrie's card didn't turn the light green, officers were required to take her into immediate custody, no questions asked, no exceptions. She'd never get through the hospital doors, let alone treatment.

"Please," Greg begged. "You gotta help her. There's gotta be a way."

"Please, Oliver," Amber added, tearing up again.

Oliver thought for a moment, and then his head rose. "What about Ashlee?"

"Yes! Ashlee will help," Greg said. "Bribe her if you have to."

"Okay. That might help with processing," Oliver said, "but I still need Carrie's signature at least a dozen more times, plus her picture. Do you really think she's up for a trip into town?"

"I'll go with you," Amber said suddenly.

All of them turned.

"Why not? This is my house, too," Amber said. "I can sign Carrie's name as many times as Oliver needs. I can help him with anything else, too."

Greg considered it before looking at the others. "Well?"

"No way," Richard said adamantly. "It's too dangerous."

"But isn't Amber protected by that deed, too?" Greg asked.

"That's right. I am," Amber said.

Oliver nodded slowly. "Having you there would help. Are you okay with being gone a day or longer?"

Greg tensed. "Carrie doesn't have that long." Not with her brain swelling. "You gotta make this work tonight."

"Tonight?" Oliver choked.

"Yes."

"No problem," Amber said, taking Oliver's arm. "We can do this, right?"

Oliver didn't seem to share her optimism.

"I have my yellow card now, too," Richard said. "If it will help, I can accompany you to the hospital when it's time. And if there's something else I can do before then, let me know."

"It's probably best for you to stay with May for now," Oliver said. "But it will help having you at the hospital." Scanning their small group, he finally squared his shoulders. "Alright. I still need a picture of Carrie for her ID card."

Greg studied Amber's dark features at the same time the others did. Unfortunately, the Ashworth sisters looked nothing alike, and this wasn't something they could fake.

"Do you have a camera with you?" Greg asked.

Oliver frowned. "A lousy one on my phone."

"It's gonna have to be good enough." Greg turned to Richard. "Have Grandma ready to leave the second they get back. Amber, run around and tell everybody they're on house arrest until further notice. Oliver, grab your phone. Let's go see if we can wake Carrie up."

Amber tugged on Greg's arm before he could leave. "What about Braden? You can't forget Braden and Terrell. They're only a couple days behind Carrie, and if anyone else gets this..."

"We have to see if this works first," Greg said. "Then we'll work on the next step."

Her dark eyes filled. "Which is...?"

Another burst of rage shot through Greg as he thought about Rigsby and his plan to kill millions of his own people. Worse, McCormick and Isabel had known about it, too.

It was unforgivable.

"If there's a cure," Greg said, "we're gonna have to steal it. A lot of it."

Oliver gasped. Richard did, too. But Amber threw her arms around Greg. "Thank you. Tell Carrie that I love her."

"I will." Greg looked her in the eye. "I'm countin' on you to help Oliver to be bold and bossy. Don't let him take *no* for an answer. Ashlee's gotta get this processed tonight. Make sure it happens."

"I will," Amber said.

"Good." Greg motioned to Oliver. "Let's go."

fifty-two

"Knock louder," Amber hissed from the dark bushes.

Oliver grunted under his breath. Amber was bossier than Greg, if possible. A few hours together and he was ready to handcuff her to the car. He raised his hand to knock again but stopped to glance around the dark neighborhood. House after white house of government housing sat with porch lights on like this one. His own house was a few streets over. It was nearly midnight. If Jamansky was staying at Ashlee's tonight, Oliver could kiss this whole plan goodbye.

"Come on!" Amber said impatiently.

Oliver's muscles tensed as he went through everything that could go wrong, but he knocked louder than before. Seconds later, he heard soft footsteps inside Ashlee's home. The footsteps stopped on the other side of the door.

Oliver stood directly in front of the peephole. "Ashlee," he whispered as loud as he dared—at least he hoped it was Ashlee. "It's me, Officer Simmons."

The door cracked open and Ashlee peeked out with puffy, sleep-weary eyes. "Oliver? What are you doing here?"

"Is David here?" Oliver whispered.

"Yeah, he's asleep." She tightened her pink bathrobe. "Do you want me to get him?"

"No!" If Jamansky caught wind of this—especially who Oliver was doing this for—they'd all be dead. Amber grunted from the bushes, and Oliver took a deep breath. "No. I'm here for you. Is there any way you can help me? As in, right now?"

She gave him an incredulous look. "Do you have any idea what time it is?"

"Yes, I'm sorry. But I have a life or death situation."

Her eyes widened and she scanned him head to toe. "Are you hurt?"

"No. I, I..."

Why hadn't he practiced?

Moths buzzed around the porch light as he struggled with how to ask. From the bushes, Amber rolled her hands, urging him to use the excuse she'd created, some contrived story about the Shelton township office catching on fire.

Oliver lowered his voice and asked straight out. "Can you come with me to Shelton right now to process some paperwork? It will only take a few minutes. Well, an hour. Maybe two."

Ashlee eyed him. "Have you been drinking, Officer Simmons?"

"No." He knew this was a bad idea.

"Ohhh," she said slowly. "Is this about that project?"

"No." If only it was something so easy. Feeling his options dwindling, he said, "I just really need your help, but we can't discuss it here. I'll explain in the car. No one can know about this, *especially* David."

She glanced over her shoulder as if she was actually considering his insane request. But if she waited much longer and David Jamansky woke up, Oliver would have a whole new set of problems.

"We can wait until you're able to sneak away," Oliver said. "Actually, we can't wait very long because it's an emergency, but if you need a few minutes to—"

"We?" Ashlee whipped around and searched the darkness.

On cue, Carrie's dark-haired sixteen-year-old sister stepped out from behind the bushes. "Hi," Amber said with a wave.

Ashlee jumped back with a cry of alarm. She clapped both hands over her mouth and closed her eyes until she regained control. Then she glared at Oliver. "Officer Simmons, what kind of mess are you in?"

More than he could handle.

"I swear I'll explain," he said. "Please. We need to hurry."

"I can't believe I'm doing this." Barefooted, Ashlee stepped onto the cement porch, pink robe and all, and quietly shut her door. "Alright. Let's go."

Oliver gaped at her. "Really? You'll help me?"

"Yes. Don't ask me why."

"What about David?" he said. "What if he wakes up and sees that you're—"

"Oliver!" Amber hissed from the grass.

"What?" he said. It was a valid question.

"David is a deep sleeper," Ashlee said. "Plus, he can go to hell. Where's your car?"

———— ◆ ————

"How long are you staying?" Tucker asked.

Zach settled on Tucker's floor, trying to find a comfortable spot. Tomorrow Tucker would take a turn on the floor. Zach twisted onto his back again. "I don't know. Until Carrie gets better."

"You mean, *if* Carrie gets better," Tucker said under his breath.

"What?"

"Never mind. I'm glad you and Greg didn't find anyone at the barn," Tucker said. "Those guys will kill us if they know you squealed on them."

"Yeah." Tucker had been quick to forgive Zach, but Delaney wouldn't be.

The boys settled back. Normally Zach would have been thrilled at the chance of an extended sleepover, but he felt fidgety and he didn't know why. The quarter-sized moon cast long, creepy shadows across Tucker's floor.

"Do you think Carrie will die?" Tucker whispered.

Zach sat upright. "No! Don't ever say that again!"

"Chris said her brain is swelling, and she's going to die. My dad said that we should be praying hard for her. He said we should pray for the all of us so we don't die, too."

"He did?" Panic seized Zach's chest. He couldn't remember much of his childhood, but his parents' deaths felt like yesterday. People kept telling him they would be okay. They wouldn't let him see them because they swore they'd get better soon. Then they were gone. And now Greg wasn't letting Zach see Carrie. Maybe Greg was lying, too. Maybe Carrie was going to die and Greg was keeping Zach hidden away at Tucker's.

What would Zach do if Carrie died? Live with Amber?

He grabbed his shoes. "Don't tell anybody."

"Where are you going?" Tucker said, sitting up.

"I...forgot something at home. I'll be back in a minute."

"But it's dark."

Zach didn't answer. He was already sliding open Tucker's window.

———————— • ————————

Greg lay on Carrie's moonlit floor, mind swirling even several hours later. The disease. The rebellion about to be stomped out. His own arrogance assuming Oliver drafted a marriage license.

The guy bought her house.

Getting her picture had taken both men. They propped her up against the wall and begged her to keep her eyes open for more than two seconds. She didn't have enough sense to ask why they were torturing her. Thankfully she still wore her mom's blue blouse, helping the picture look a little more official.

Still, she looked like death.

Once Oliver took off, Greg had lain next to her mattress. He could barely see her shadowed form in the darkness, but he continued to hold her ice-cold hand. She no longer shivered. In fact, she was too still except her breathing which had become quite rapid in the last hour. He listened to every shallow breath, driving himself mad with worry.

His felt like life was on repeat. Different women. Different illnesses. Same blasted outcome.

A sound downstairs brought his head off the carpet. He heard Carrie's back door slide open. Oliver wasn't supposed to be back until morning, so hopefully this was good news.

Greg stood and stretched, and then he peeked out Carrie's dark window. The moonlit driveway was empty.

No car.

Another movement downstairs. Somebody sneaking around. Had he been asleep, he would have missed it, but as it was, his heart kicked into full throttle.

Somebody was breaking into Carrie's house. A patrolman doing a silent raid? Vagrant wanderer needing a warm place to sleep? Homeless psychopath looking for a beautiful woman to cart off?

The adrenaline combined with a surge of rage.

Greg felt his way to the hallway and crept down the pitch-black stairs. Footsteps padded softly through Carrie's kitchen on a direct path toward him. Greg pressed his back to the staircase wall and waited, wishing he had a club, bat, or something besides two clenched fists.

A dark shape started up the stairs.

Greg raised his fist to strike but suddenly stopped. The intruder was small. Too small. It almost looked like...

"Zach!" Greg barked, grabbing the kid's shoulder. "What are you doin' here?"

Zach jumped a foot and let out a blood-curdling scream, piercing the silent night. He bolted out of Greg's grasp.

"Carrie!" Zach yelled. *"Carrie!"*

Greg chased him up the stairs and caught hold of his ankle. Zach went down, screaming her name even louder. Greg clamped a hand over his mouth, ready to give Zach a verbal lashing, but it was too late.

"Zach?" she called out groggily.

Carrie's voice broke Greg's concentration. Zach kicked free and scurried up the last steps. Greg followed clumsily. From Carrie's doorway, he saw Zach throw himself over his sister's body, breaking into hysterics.

"Zach?" she repeated more coherently. "What's wrong?"

The young teen couldn't control himself enough to answer. He just sobbed into her blankets.

Greg's instinct was to drop-kick him all the way back to Tucker's. Another person exposed. But listening to the agony rip through the kid's body, reasoning returned to Greg. Amber was right. They'd already been exposed. Plus, with Zach living in this house, technically he could get his yellow card now, too.

Not that they had money to treat him.

With a deep sigh, Greg traipsed back downstairs and searched for a candle. By the time he returned, Carrie was stroking Zach's thick hair.

"What happened, Zach?" she asked, near to tears herself.

When Zach still couldn't answer, her sunken, tired, and squinting eyes moved to Greg for an explanation. Greg shrugged. Certainly a little startle—or even a big one—couldn't have provoked this much emotion.

"Carrie," Zach finally said, taking huge gulps of air in between sobs, "you can't...you can't die."

"What?" she said.

"They said your brain...and Greg wouldn't let me see you, and...and..." That got Zach going again.

Carrie tried to glare at Greg. But she had no clue she was on a downward spiral induced by a government plague, and Greg couldn't bear to tell her.

He left the candle in the hallway to ease the strain on her eyes and crossed the room to sit by Zach.

Carrie rubbed Zach's back but kept her pained, blinking glare on Greg. She waited for him to apologize and say he'd overreacted, to tell Zach she'd be fine. Greg refused, especially seeing how bad she looked.

"I'm just sick, Zach," she whispered.

Zach wiped his nose on his sleeve. "But they said Mom was just sick, and then she and Dad, they..." He started sniffing again. "People said 'Go away,' and I never...I never got to see them, and now Greg said I couldn't come, and...and..." He buried his face in her blankets.

The picture in front of Greg flipped. Carrie wasn't Zach's sister. She was his mom—or at least, as close as he had to one.

Greg's chest constricted, feeling Zach's pain afresh.

"Sorry," Greg whispered. "I didn't realize."

Carrie nodded tiredly.

Though Greg dreaded her reaction, it was time she understood the gravity of the situation. "Zach, Oliver is takin' Carrie to the hospital in the morning."

"What!" Carrie said at the same time Zach said, "Really?"

"It's done, Carrie," Greg said firmly. "No more fightin' on this. It's time to get you some meds." If they even had medicine for this.

She closed her eyes and huffed every word. "I'm. Just. Fine."

So fine it took a minute for her to open her eyes again.

Zach lifted his head. "Carrie, you have to go. Chris told Tucker that you'll die without medicine." His Adam's apple bobbed, sending more tears down his freckled cheeks. "You can't die, too."

She gave a small sigh and stroked his hair again. "Fine. If it will make you feel better, Zach, I'll go."

Greg felt every muscle relax. At least the kid had been good for something.

Turning, Zach looked up at Greg. "Can I sleep here tonight? I promise to be real quiet. I won't wake Carrie up. I swear."

Greg had no fight left in him. "Sure."

As Zach rested his head on her legs, Carrie met Greg's eyes. "Thank you," she mouthed.

Greg nodded.

Her pained grimace remained after her eyes closed, making Greg wonder how it felt to have your brain swell. She continued to stroke Zach's thick mop of hair, so Greg knew she hadn't drifted off yet. It only took Zach a few minutes—seconds practically—before his breathing deepened into sleep. Lucky guy. Greg felt like he'd never sleep again.

"My eyes," Carrie whispered, nearly inaudible.

"I know," Greg said. "Just rest them. Here. I'll blow out the candle."

But as he started to stand, she said, "They won't focus."

He froze.

She peeked one eye open at a time, blinked several times, and then shook her head.

She was losing her vision? Greg felt ill. What other long-term effects would she have if they couldn't get her help soon? You didn't mess with the brain without it messing up other things. How long before her vital organs shut down? And what if Oliver couldn't get her citizenship finalized?

If this had affected a healthy twenty-three-year old this much, what would it do to his grandma and the others?

"Did…" Carrie took a slow breath. "Did Oliver take my picture?"

"Yeah," Greg said. "We needed it for your yellow card."

"Green card?"

She still thought she was the wife of a patrolman. Since she was awake anyway, Greg decided to work on that pained line between her eyes.

Sitting close to her head, he started massaging between her brows. "You up for a little story?" he whispered.

He felt the tiniest nod, so he told her everything. The papers. Being a homeowner. Even the little he knew about G-979 and Rigsby's strategy.

"So you have to go," he said. "No negotiation."

After a long pause—so long he wondered if she'd drifted back to sleep—she said, "A cure?"

A knot formed in his gut. Her eyes peeked open and found him above her in the darkness. "There better be," was all he could manage.

Shifting, she rubbed the side of her head.

"Let me do that," Greg said. "There?"

He tried to rub the spot she had, but she grabbed his hand and pressed it flat against her skull behind her ear. Hard. Surprised, he followed her lead, hoping the extra pressure would alleviate the pain and not cause worse damage.

"Not married," she said after another minute.

He smiled. "Nope, so feel free to propose to me anytime, Miss Ashworth. Anytime at all. It's killin' me that everybody else is goin' to the hospital, and I'll be stuck here." Although marrying Carrie wouldn't work either since he was 'dead' now.

"Trade you places," she whispered.

His smile faded. "In a heartbeat."

He traced her brow down her cheek to her jaw. Fire and fever followed. Leaning over, he kissed her dry, cracked lips. "Don't leave me, Carrie girl, alrighty?"

"Ditto."

He frowned, remembering his promise. As a special operative, he could probably get her into the hospital without paperwork—or money. One call, one lie, and Greg would have it all back.

Why fight for the greater good if you lost your last reason to live?

Carrie peeked an eye open.

The guilt ate at him. How could he join Rigsby's side knowing what the President was capable of? Knowing McCormick was in on it? Knowing that Kearney and his clan—plus all of the rebels—could be dead already?

With a sigh, Greg said, "Don't worry. I'm not goin' anywhere."

That seemed to relax her, and her breathing started to slow like Zach's. Greg quickly reached over and grabbed the glass of water.

"Wait," he whispered. "Before you fall back asleep, you need to drink somethin'."

She groaned.

"I know, but you have to. C'mon," he said. "I'll help you up."

Greg nudged Zach awake, and the two of them eased her into a sitting position. Greg held her around her waist, letting her rest against his arm.

"Ow," she moaned, grabbing her head. "Ow."

"We'll be fast," Greg said, lifting the water. "You just need a little—"

A sudden scream burst from Carrie's lips. She wrenched back.

Greg caught her before her head smacked against the wall. Eyes wild, she grabbed her stomach as a choking sound bubbled in her throat. It only took a second to realize what was happening.

"Zach," Greg said, "grab a bucket!"

Zach stared in horror as Carrie suddenly vomited over the blankets.

"Zach!" Greg screamed.

Zach jumped up and flew out of the room. Greg grabbed Carrie's hair out of the way as she vomited again. Hardly anything came out—she'd hardly eaten—but she kept heaving over and over until it was nothing but air. Eight times. Nine. Greg held her tight around the waist to keep her steady, praying with every ounce of his soul that it would stop. That it wouldn't turn to blood.

When the retching changed to coughs and gasps for air, Greg knew he had a small window. She needed to be horizontal again to relieve the pressure in her brain, but her pillow had been soiled. Mostly acidic water, so he flipped it over.

"Lie back," he said. "Easy."

Tears streamed down Carrie's face as she lay on her pillow, cradling the back of her head.

"It's okay." Greg huddled close, stroking her face. "It's okay. You're okay. It's okay."

Her tears flowed harder, ripping at his heart. She looked terrified. He felt it. His hands shook like mad as he stroked her skin—skin that was no longer hot but cold and clammy. Zach stood by the flickering candle, bucket in hand, a picture of sheer terror in the hallway.

"Here, Zach," Greg said. "Put the bucket by me, and then get me a wet rag."

Zach was only too happy to leave again.

Carrie still clutched the back of her skull. She was rocking slightly on the pillow, watery eyes squeezed shut. She was breathing fast, crying, and nearing the sobbing stage, which wasn't good. Greg knew from sad experience that crying caused more vomiting, and he was desperate to calm her down.

With face inches from hers, he stroked her hair, her cheek, her forehead. "It's okay. It's okay. It's okay," he whispered, hoping she couldn't feel his trembling hands. "It's okay. It's okay. It's okay." He said it twenty more times before her breathing finally slowed.

"Sorry," she whispered.

His insides still shook like mad, but he forced a smile. "No more drinks for you, Miss Ashworth."

It was the wrong thing to say.

New tears leaked down the bridge of her nose. He wiped them as his own eyes filled.

"It's okay. You're gonna be okay," he said.

She nodded and squeezed her eyes shut, still clutching the back of her head.

Greg took a slow, shuddering breath and looked around. Her top blanket got it the worst, so he rolled it up and tossed it into the corner. When Zach brought the wet rag, Greg cleaned up the rest, including some on his own shirt. There wasn't much, less than there should be, but his hands trembled like crazy as he worked.

What would he do if he couldn't even get water in her?

He tossed the rag onto the soiled blanket and sat next to her again. Zach draped himself over her legs, burying his face in her blankets as he cried a high-pitched squeal in the dark candlelight. As Zach cried, more silent tears slipped down the bridge of Carrie's nose.

Greg curled himself around her head, half on the mattress, half off. She pressed his hand to the back of her skull. He didn't know if it would make it worse. He didn't know if he should make her drink water anyway. He knew nothing other than in that moment, as the two Ashworths cried soft, frightened tears, his heart felt like it was being shredded. And he had the overwhelming urge to slit President Rigsby's throat.

"Amber," Carrie whispered. "Zach. You have to take care of them for—"

"They need *you*," Greg said before she could finish. "You're gonna take great care of them when you recover," he said, because anything else was unacceptable. He probably should have eased her worries that they wouldn't be left alone and neglected, but right now she needed every reason in the world to keep fighting. "Just hold on a bit longer, alrighty? Just a bit longer. Please."

She nodded.

He knew when she drifted off to sleep because her breathing settled into a slow, steady rhythm. But the muscles in her face never relaxed and her hand never left his, keeping pressure behind her ear. He should have tried to sleep, but he stayed curled around her in the dark as he started to count each and every breath, braced for it to be her last.

fifty-three

Oliver grabbed Carrie's yellow card, fresh from the laminating press. "Thank you, Ashlee," he said.

Ashlee shut down the computer, leaving a single lamp and the dim emergency fluorescents overhead as their last light sources.

"Your friend should be all set now," Ashlee said, "but let's double-check to be safe." Standing, she tightened her bathrobe. "Here. Let me see the card."

Oliver followed her to the verifying machine. Carrie's new citizenship card lit up green. His insides swelled with relief. Another hurdle cleared.

"I owe you," Oliver said. More than he could ever repay.

"Don't worry about it," Ashlee said, waving him off. Then she admired the odd picture of Carrie in the corner. "You still haven't told me who this Carrie girl is—or why David is so interested in her."

He understood her skepticism. Poor Carrie looked like a druggy he'd pulled off the streets. Ashlee had pestered him with questions all night, and so far he'd kept his answers vague. He'd said that Carrie was a former illegal who inherited some money, so he'd helped her purchase a house. Only now she was sick but she hadn't had a chance to get her citizenship yet. But still, at the root of her question, Ashlee wanted to know why he had been acquainted with an illegal in the first place—or why he cared now.

Oliver glanced behind him at Carrie's little sister crashed and snoring softly on his desk. "Carrie's my friend," he said. "Just a friend."

"Well," Ashlee said with a sad smile, "I hope this *friend* loves you as much as you love her."

Not a chance.

Oliver took the card from her and slipped it in his pocket. Then he gathered up the last of the scraps and tossed them in the garbage, hoping the Monday morning crew wouldn't notice anything amiss. His eyelids burned with exhaustion. Crossing the room, he nudged Amber awake.

"Time to go," he said.

As they pulled out of the dark parking lot, Oliver glanced over at Ashlee. "What if David's awake when you get back?"

She shrugged. "I'll just tell him I went for a walk."

"In the middle of the night?"

"He was so drunk when he came to bed, I'm not worried. But you…" Ashlee looked over at him in the dark car. "What happens when he finds out you skipped out on another patrol? He hates you enough already."

"No idea," Oliver said honestly. He'd have to come up with some excuse about being sick in bed—so sick he hadn't even called in the absence.

He sped up for Sugar Grove and Ashlee's home. Amber was curled up in the back seat, already back in Dreamland.

"Why does David hate you so much?" Ashlee said. "You're such a sweet guy." But before he could think up an answer, her eyes went wide. "Oh my gosh, it was you! You ratted him and Nielsen out. You're the reason they went to prison." She broke into a giggle. "And you're going to do it again. I love it!"

Right now, Oliver could only think about Carrie.

He sped up.

"What do you know about this new illness?" he asked.

"Just that it's nasty. By the way, that federal task force who immunized us wasn't the nicest. I still have a bruise." She rubbed her arm with a pout. "Supposedly there's a shipment of immunizations coming in for local citizens. Do you know that they trained me, and now I'll be giving the shots? I swear I'll be nicer than they were."

A shipment? "How soon will it come in?" he asked.

"Late next week."

Too late for Carrie's clan—and who knew how many others.

Figured.

When he pulled into the government housing, Ashlee grabbed his arm. "Just drop me off here," she said.

"But it's three houses away," Oliver said.

"I'll just walk. I don't want David to hear your car."

"Can I walk you the rest of the way then?" Oliver asked. It was still pitch black out with only a little moon to light the sidewalk.

"No, I'm fine. You take care of your *friend*." Ashlee winked at him.

"I'll find some way to repay you," he said quickly.

Her hand rested on his. "Thank me by taking David down, okay?" Then she stretched up and, before he knew what hit him, kissed his cheek. A gentle, lingering kiss. When she sat back, her eyes were large and soft in the darkness. "You're a good man, Officer Simmons. Thank you for trusting me tonight."

Then she whisked open the door and was gone.

Oliver's cheek tingled. He wanted to rub it—needed to rub her touch from his skin. Instead, his eyes flickered to the rearview mirror, hoping Amber was still asleep. She wasn't. She was staring at him, mouth wide open. Thankfully the darkness hid his face since he could feel it burning with embarrassment.

"Well," Amber said, "that was interesting."

Not really. Ashlee Lyon was the biggest flirt Oliver knew. She thought nothing of gestures like that—of kisses like that. However the temperature in the car doubled and he felt he needed to explain so this didn't get back to Carrie.

"It's nothing," he said. "You don't know Ashlee like I do."

"Apparently not," Amber said, breaking into a wide grin. "You know, I like her. She's different, but I like her."

That grin, that blessing of sorts for him to pursue Ashlee, tore the last piece of his heart because it said what he'd feared: he'd already lost Carrie.

He flipped his car around and headed out the patrol neighborhood. Once he hit the main road, he pressed the accelerator to the floor.

His mind was a garbled mess of worry and dread. What if Jamansky had been awake when Ashlee got home? What if he forced her to talk? The guy was already obsessed with Carrie, and Ashlee wasn't a locked-vault kind of girl. All it would take was one click of the computer, and Carrie's card could be rendered invalid. A thousand and one things could go wrong in the next hour, all of which left Carrie dead, Oliver arrested—possibly dead, too—and her clan on the same path of destruction.

Yet Amber kept grinning in the back seat.

As the sun hit Carrie's window, Greg watched the road like a hawk, waiting for Oliver's car to appear. Every minute felt like a year.

Carrie had woken once more in a delirious state that scared the daylights out of him. She kept asking him to slow down. He hadn't been moving and neither had she—plus it was as dark as a cave in her room—but she kept begging him to slow down, hysterical.

Greg and Zach tried everything: rubbing her forehead, stroking her arms, speaking softly. Nothing reached her. Finally, she slipped into a deep sleep and hadn't budged since. Now with the first light of day, her skin was as gray as the sky, the muscles in her face sagged unnaturally, and her breathing came out in soft puffs. The longer Greg waited, the harder his heart pounded.

Oliver should have returned by now.

Several agonizing minutes later, Greg spotted a patrol car pulling down Denton Trail.

Finally!

Oliver parked at Greg's grandparents first. Richard and Greg's grandpa came out, each on one side of Greg's grandma who was wrapped in a blanket. Oliver jumped out to help. Every step seemed to hurt her, and she was stooped lower than normal, but at least she was upright. That was good.

The five of them drove to Carrie's. Oliver was back in uniform and Amber rode in the front seat. Greg's mind spun with worry. Just because they were back didn't mean it had worked.

As soon as Oliver parked on Carrie's driveway, Amber opened the front door and spotted Greg in the upper window. Grinning, she flashed him two thumbs up.

Greg released his breath. He felt every muscle loosen. First step accomplished.

Carrie was going.

Crossing the room, he shook Zach. "It's time, Zach."

Zach rubbed his eyes and then jumped up, instantly awake. He moved aside so Greg could kneel next to Carrie.

"Carrie?" Greg said, brushing some hair from her forehead.

She didn't move.

"Mornin', beautiful," he tried louder, rubbing her hand. "C'mon. Time to take a little ride."

He felt her cheek and neck. Both were cool. Too cool. So he bent down and kissed her lips, desperate for a response. They were dry, cracked, and cold, a frightening combination, but that's not why Zach pulled a face.

"Ew," Zach said. "I'm right here."

"So am I," another voice growled.

Oliver stood in Carrie's doorway.

Greg ignored both of them. Carrie hadn't even twitched. He'd seen that waxy, gray skin too many times on too many people. Panicked, he felt the side of her neck for a pulse. Faint, but there. Though there was no logical reason, he felt like if he could just see a flicker of those blue eyes before she left, everything would be okay.

"Carrie," Greg said, loudly. "It's time. C'mon. You can do it."

"When was she last awake?" Oliver asked.

"A few hours ago, but she was delirious," Greg said.

"It was freaky," Zach added.

Amber pushed past Oliver and knelt next to Greg. "Carrie," she said, shaking her shoulder. "Wake up!"

Nothing.

Sliding his arm under her neck, Greg pulled Carrie tight against his chest. "C'mon, Carrie girl," he whispered in her ear. "Just let me see those baby blues." He stroked her cheek as his chest seized up. "One glimpse and then you can go." Then he could let her go. "Please." His voice started to give. He might never see her again. "Please," he begged.

Her eyes remained closed, but she gave the tiniest moan.

Close enough.

Hugging her tight against him, he slipped his other hand under her knees and lifted.

Oliver was instantly at his side. "Let me carry her, Greg. You have a bad leg."

"No. Get her blankets," Greg ordered as he stood. His thigh throbbed and the muscles in his shoulder pulled, but he leaned back to help Carrie's head fall against his chest instead of flopping back. Then he carefully hobbled down the stairs and outside to Oliver's police cruiser.

As soon as Richard spotted them, he jumped out and opened the passenger door. Greg set Carrie gently inside Oliver's front seat and then took the blankets from Oliver and piled them in around her even though the morning was already hot.

"Is she okay?" his grandma asked from the back seat. "Carrie? Carrie dear?"

"Carrie's not doin' so hot right now, Grandma," Greg said. Her whole body had slumped, chin on chest, like a newborn without any muscle strength. Greg leaned her seat back to help straighten her out. Then he looked up. "How about you? You hangin' in there?"

His grandma didn't answer. She stared at Carrie. Her wrinkled skin looked whiter than a sheet. So did his grandpa's.

Greg swallowed back another wave of emotion. "Oliver's gonna get y'all help now. Hang in there, alrighty?"

When they nodded, Greg shut the door and faced Oliver and Richard. "Grandpa's startin' now, isn't he?"

Richard still hadn't torn his eyes away from Carrie. "He started chills in the middle of the night. Wow. I didn't think Carrie would look so..."

"Yeah," Oliver whispered.

Greg's eyes narrowed on both of them. "I'm trustin' the two of you to make this work. Y'all have to do whatever it takes to save them. You understand? *Whatever* it takes."

They nodded soberly, both still watching Carrie's hunched form. Distracted. Disturbed.

Greg shook his head angrily. There's no way they would do what he would. He sidestepped, bringing their gazes back to him. "That means one of you," he said pointedly, "is gonna have to steal some medicine."

"Steal?" Oliver choked.

But Richard nodded. "I'll do it."

"Good," Greg said. "Tell the doctor that Carrie's eyes are bad, so maybe there's pressure on the optic nerve. And she was delirious last night, and the spot behind her right ear is the worst, so make sure they check—"

"We've got this, Greg," Oliver interrupted. "We have to go." Running around his car, he got in.

Richard put a hand on Greg's arm. "We'll get you word as soon as possible."

Word. As if that was comforting.

Greg stared at Carrie's lifeless body, wondering if he'd ever see her again, wondering if he'd ever see *any* of them again or if they'd end up as three fresh mounds in some hospital cemetery.

"You gotta save her," Greg said, voice suddenly husky. "You gotta save all of them. I can't be there, so you gotta do it."

"We'll get you word soon," Richard said again. Then he opened the door and squeezed into the backseat behind Carrie's reclined seat.

Greg backed up as the engine revved to life, feeling the world implode. Amber and Zach held each other on the front porch, both crying. Sasha Green and others stood in their yards, watching Oliver back out of Carrie's driveway. But none of them could feel like Greg did. That car held every last person on earth that he loved—the very last of his family. How was he supposed to let them go? To trust their fate to the hands of others? Again.

Time rewound.

Greg felt like he was standing on the outskirts of Shelton, watching Oliver drive away. His was mom injured in the township office, left in the hands of Ashlee, Jamansky, and Oliver Simmons.

He never saw his mom again.

His feet started running before he knew what he was doing. Picking up speed, he sprinted across Carrie's front yard and ran right in the middle of the road. Right in front of Oliver's car.

Oliver slammed on the brakes. Greg jumped back to keep from being hit.

"What are you doing?" Oliver yelled through the glass.

"Pop the trunk," Greg ordered.

"What? Why?" But before Greg could answer, Oliver rolled down his window. "Oh, no. No way! You're not coming with us, Greg. You're dead, remember?"

"Pop the trunk."

"Greg…"

Greg pounded the car hood. "Pop it before I bust the lock!"

Oliver did but jumped out of the car and stormed around in time to meet Greg by the trunk. "I just spent ten hours making sure every person going to the hospital was fully legal. You're not going to ruin it with some stupid selfish stunt! We're already treading on thin ice. So many things that can still go wrong, I can't even begin to—"

"I'll stay dead," Greg interrupted. "I'll even stay in the trunk the whole time if you want. I just...I can't be left behind again."

Oliver's eyes narrowed to tiny slits. "The whole time?"

"Most the time," Greg said honestly. "But nobody will see me. I won't cause a single issue. You have my word."

Huffing, Oliver glanced over his shoulder at Richard. Richard shrugged as if he didn't know what to do with Greg either.

Greg pointed. "Listen. That's my family in there. Every last one of them."

"Not all of them," Oliver said darkly.

Maybe not yet.

Greg folded his arms. "I'll walk to Aurora if I have to. I'm goin' to that hospital one way or another, so you might as well make it easy on me."

Swearing under his breath, Oliver slid some boxes in his trunk to the side. "It's going to be cramped and hot."

"It's fine." But before Greg climbed in, he remembered Amber and Zach crying on the porch. "You're in charge, Amber!" Greg called. "Stay here. You're still quarantined. No mixing with anybody else. That's an order."

"You want us to stay here alone? All night?" Amber squeaked.

"How old was Carrie when your parents died?" Greg said.

Amber wiped her eyes. "Seventeen."

Close enough. "You've got this," Greg said. "If either of you get sick, lie down and drink lots of fluid. One of us will be back soon to check on you."

With that, Greg lifted his bad leg in first and then climbed inside. The trunk was smaller than it looked, but scrunching in, knees to chin, he somehow fit.

"There's an emergency latch in there somewhere," Oliver said, peering in. "If you have any issues, pound on the lid and I'll pull over— but don't have issues because we don't have time." His eyes narrowed. "I'm trusting you, Greg. Don't. Be. Stupid."

People said that to him an awful lot.

Greg nodded. "Got it. Let's go."

fifty-four

Oliver flipped on his flashing lights. Even with a seatbelt, Carrie slumped to the side with every turn, but he didn't slow down. He hit the highway pushing 80mph.

"Can you turn up the heat?" CJ asked from the backseat.

Heat? Oliver was already a sweaty mess and it was barely morning. But he did. May and CJ huddled under their blanket, looking carsick on top of everything else.

Glancing in the rearview mirror, Oliver's barrage of questions came barreling out. "You all have your cards, right? Can you take care of them, Richard, so I can take Carrie? What if they don't know how to fix Carrie? What if it's too late? What do I say if they look too closely at her card or try to verify when it was processed?"

Richard gripped Carrie's seat, looking a little green himself. "You'll know what to do."

Horribly placed confidence. Oliver had been up all night running ragged, and now he worried what signature he'd missed, what hoop they'd forgotten to jump through.

"What about the money?" he fretted. "I withdrew every dollar I own, but it's not enough. I know it's not enough."

"I brought all of CJ's money," Richard said. "It will have to be enough."

"But it's not!"

"I don't need treatment," CJ said. "I'm not that sick."

"Me neither," May croaked. "We'll stay in the car. You just get my Carrie what she needs."

"No one is staying in the car," Richard said with a pointed look at Oliver in the mirror. "We'll figure out finances later."

"You don't understand," Oliver said, unable to stop freaking out. "Hospitals require payment first now. We won't even get through the front door if the staff doesn't think we can cover the expense."

A muffled voice shouted something from the trunk. Oliver grunted angrily, wondering for the thousandth time why he'd let Greg tag along. His nerves were frazzled enough without a headstrong, reckless nut job hiding in his trunk.

Richard turned and spoke through the seats. "What was that, Greg? I couldn't understand."

"Be a patrolman!" Greg shouted, followed by a few choice words Oliver heard well enough.

Oliver bristled. "What's that supposed to mean? I *am* a patrolman."

"I think he means that you can be forceful in your delivery," Richard said. "Most people are frightened of patrolmen. Perhaps you can be a little…bossy?"

"Yes! Yes!" came another shout. Followed by something that sounded like, "Threaten them!"

Oliver's eyes popped open. "Threaten them? How?"

"Guns! Guns! Guns!" Greg shouted.

Oliver gripped the steering wheel. "Will you shut him up?"

"Greg," Richard said loudly, "Oliver will know what to do when the time comes."

Richard wasn't helping either. Oliver had no idea what to do.

No one did.

When they reached the hospital, Oliver drove right for the ER. Dozens of people lined the sidewalks outside the entrance, hunched over and looking ill. But the people who had Oliver's heart jumping were the ones holding assault rifles. He'd never seen the hospital so heavily guarded.

Oliver screeched up to the curb and jumped out.

"Hey! You can't park there," one of the guards called.

"I'll move the car," Richard said. "Just get Carrie inside."

Oliver opened Carrie's door, careful to catch her shoulder before she slumped out. Then he slipped a hand under her legs and lifted.

Two security guards met him at the car, waving their guns around as they spoke.

"No one is allowed to park here," the first guard demanded.

"Sorry. My friend is really sick," Oliver said, straining to keep hold of Carrie. "She needs a doctor right now."

The security officers tightened their grips on their rifles, blocking the door. "Cards first."

Each of them wore green uniforms like Oliver, but both had more gold arm bands. They outranked him, and he was desperate.

"Please," Oliver begged. He couldn't hold Carrie and grab the cards from his pocket. Richard had already pulled away to find a parking spot. "I'm an officer in Kane County, and she's dying. Please let me get her inside and then I'll show you our cards."

"No entry without ID," the first guard said. "No exceptions."

A nurse came barreling out of the hospital wheeling a gurney. "Here, officer. Put her on this."

Oliver laid Carrie down. The sight of her frail body on a stretcher about put him over the edge. Her limbs flopped in whatever position he'd laid her in, and he was too frazzled to tell if she was still breathing. She looked dead.

In a daze, he pulled out his and Carrie's cards and handed them over. The guard swiped them through his devices and Oliver held his breath. The lights flashed green on his card first and then—miraculously—on Carrie's.

Thank you, Ashlee.

The guard held Carrie's card next to her face. Both showed her drawn, gray skin and her mom's blue blouse askew on her body. Plus the picture quality was sub-par. Ashlee forged the date, making it look like Carrie's card was issued months ago, but Oliver could see the wheels churning in the guard's brain. The picture was obviously less than twelve hours old.

Be like Greg.

"We don't have time for this!" Oliver shouted. "Let us through!"

Nodding, the guard dropped Carrie and Oliver's cards into clear pockets hanging from lanyards. Then he hung the lanyards over their necks, pictures facing outward. With the nurse's help, Oliver pushed Carrie's gurney through the glass doors.

The waiting room was packed. People crowded every inch, old and young, in wheelchairs, regular chairs, window ledges, and sprawled on the tile floor simply for a place to sit.

"Take a number there," the nurse said, helping Oliver steer Carrie through the bodies. "They'll call you when you're ready."

"But she's dying," Oliver protested, eyeing the crowds.

Her eyes softened. "So is everyone else. I'm sorry, officer, but you'll have to take a number."

Oliver left Carrie near a far wall to grab a paper ticket from the reel.

"Ninety-eight!" a receptionist called.

Oliver glanced down at his number. *One hundred and sixty-two?* The room spun. He was too exhausted to do the math, but he knew it was too long. Too long! They hadn't come all this way to have her still die.

Around the room, people held their heads or shivered in blankets, pale with cold. Babies were crying, adults were moaning, and others tried to console loved ones. It was one giant sound of misery that Oliver felt as much as he heard. Most looked like yellow card holders—people the President shouldn't be trying to kill. Oliver couldn't believe how fast it had spread. Where did it end?

A few minutes later, Richard walked inside supporting a hunched-over May around the waist. CJ struggled behind them, wrapping a lanyard around his neck.

"Heaven almighty," Richard breathed as he looked around. Spotting Oliver off to the side, they lumbered over. "What number are you?"

"One hundred and sixty-two," Oliver said, feeling hollow inside.

Richard's eyes snapped to Carrie's still form. "You have to do something."

"I know, I know." But everyone was in the same predicament.

Oliver and Richard helped May and CJ to the wall where they could lean. That was the best they could offer. May immediately sunk to the hard tile floor, head against the wall, blanket around her. CJ did the same. Oliver wondered if they'd ever get back up.

Richard studied Carrie. "Is she...?"

"Still breathing," Oliver said. "I think." Then he double-checked her blue blouse. It moved up and down with tiny breaths.

The white-haired nurse who brought Oliver the gurney walked past.

"I'll be right back," Oliver said to Richard. Then he stormed across the waiting area, each step growing angrier until he snagged the nurse by the arm. "I can't wait for them to call our number. My friend is dying."

"I'm sorry, officer," the nurse said, "but—"

Oliver rocked forward. "Do you really want to bring down the wrath of the entire Illinois State Government on this hospital? That is the daughter of a high-ranking official. Her father ordered me to bring her here because he's off fighting rebels. But if her father finds out she died because of some stupid number, he'll…he'll…" The lies ran out, but the nurse still paled.

"Yes, sir," she said. "Sorry, sir. I didn't realize. Just give me a moment."

The nurse disappeared down a hallway.

Richard was nodding when Oliver headed back. "I believe even Greg would have been impressed with that performance," Richard whispered. "Nicely done."

For all Oliver knew, he'd put Carrie in greater danger by claiming she was government material. Daughters of officials had green cards, not yellow. But seconds later, the nurse was back waving Oliver forward.

"Right this way, officer," she said.

Richard clapped Oliver on the shoulder. "Good luck."

Oliver eyed May and CJ huddled together on the floor. "Same to you. Here. Take this," Oliver said, handing Richard his ticket. "I'll try to find you soon."

Then Oliver pushed Carrie's gurney down the long hallway.

———— ◆ ————

Greg drove himself mad as he waited. He tried to catch up on sleep, but Oliver's dark trunk steamed with trapped summer heat, making him sweaty and miserable. He could barely breathe let alone nap, and his brilliant plan no longer seemed so brilliant.

So close and yet a million miles away.

What good did it do to rot, trapped in temperatures nearing the surface of the sun while Carrie and his family suffered inside? With luck, they'd be in there for days receiving treatment. Oliver couldn't expect Greg to stay in this trunk that long, could he?

Patience, he told himself.

By now, Carrie should be on medicines. She should be hooked to IVs and machines and all sorts of life-saving needles. He shuddered. He'd never been a fan of needles, but that had been cemented in Raleigh where he'd watched his sister die. Once the money ran out, they cut off Kendra's medicine. She hadn't lasted an hour.

And now Oliver didn't have enough money.

How would a quiet guy like Oliver demand the same thing didn't happen to Carrie?

The thought put Greg over the edge.

Feeling around the dark trunk, he found the release lever, careful to keep hold of the lid so it didn't fly open in the middle of the crowded parking lot. The hot air whooshed out and he took a few breaths, feeling his thoughts clarify with the cooler air.

For a time, he just peeked out. Whenever a car passed, he shut the trunk again. After an hour of this—or what felt like an hour and was probably only three minutes—he climbed out and hunkered behind the back tire. He tried the driver's handle, but Richard had locked the doors and taken the keys with him.

Crouched low, Greg surveyed the hospital. It was several stories tall with loads of security officers guarding the entrances. There was no way he could slip in unnoticed.

At least not the conventional way.

He started creeping toward the hospital. Whenever a car approached, he stopped at the nearest parked car and pretended to search for his keys. All the while he scanned every inch of that hospital for another way in. Doors. Windows. Roof. He crossed two full parking lots before he found it.

A food service truck pulled into a fenced area. The gate around it was shut, but Greg didn't let that deter him. The fence connected to the hospital in two spots, one in the wide open, and the other within a patch of huge shrubs. Greg worked his way over to those shrubs. They were thicker than they appeared, but he ducked inside them anyway. They scratched, pulled, and stung his arms by the time he inched up to the fence.

Peering through the slats, he saw three men and a woman unloading food supplies from that truck. Two guards with rifles kept watch while they worked. In Greg's mind, assault rifles were major overkill for a hospital—although this was food. His empty stomach growled. He couldn't even remember his last meal. The guards were distracted as they complained about over-extended work hours. Neither checked the shrubs.

As the four unloaders took another armful inside, Greg scaled the fence and dropped to a crouch behind another tall shrub. Then he worked through his options: lie to the workers—say he stepped outside for a smoke and forgot his green card—or take down all six of them, including the armed guards. He'd been trained to do as much. Swift upper punch to the smaller guard's jaw, then use the gun to take down the others. With his aim, he could incapacitate them without major injury. However, he refused to use violence. So he scanned the area for another option.

The longer it went, the more appealing the McCormick fallback became.

A sudden boom sounded as the hospital metal doors slammed shut. The two guards pulled down the truck's hatch. All the others had disappeared inside the hospital. Then the guards climbed in the truck, pushed a button to open the gate, and drove off.

Greg stayed behind his shrub, cursing himself. Once the truck disappeared, he tried the large metal doors, but they didn't have outside handles. It was just a giant, gray barricade he wanted to kick in frustration.

All of his "specialized" training, and he couldn't even break into a stupid hospital. Maybe they should have spent less time teaching him survival skills and how to shoot kids, and more time teaching them—

His thoughts skidded to a halt.

Survival skills.

Whirling around, he eyed the huge dumpsters in the far corner of the fenced area. He ducked low and slid behind the first dumpster. He lifted the lid. Everything inside was bagged, making it impossible to decipher the contents. He and his mom escaped Raleigh's Municipality in a dumpster similar to this one. They spent a full night sleeping under piles of rotting garbage. The smell had clung to them for weeks.

Knowing where he was headed but not all too thrilled about it, he searched for a better option. But the last few days had worn him down, and his ideas were mush.

Sighing, he used his good leg, caught a foothold on a ridge of the dumpster, and heaved himself inside. He dug through the reeking filth, tearing bags open as he went to find anything with one specific trait:

Flammable.

Because while Greg might not know how to break into a guarded hospital without violence, he'd spent the last six years starting fires in the most dire of circumstances. And right now, his circumstances felt pretty dire.

fifty-five

The medical staff opened up other sections of the hospital to accommodate the bulging ER.

Oliver waited with Carrie's gurney in a small corner of *Obstetrics*. Three minutes. Five. At fifteen minutes, he fretted that they had forgotten them. He had a staff meeting in a half an hour, and he was at least twenty minutes away. If he missed it, Jamansky would call his house. If Oliver didn't answer, Jamansky would go looking. But Oliver didn't dare leave Carrie in this abandoned part of the hospital. So he paced and fretted. A lot.

Finally he saw a doctor coming down the hallway with two nurses wheeling machines behind them.

"I apologize for keeping you waiting, officer," the doctor said. She picked up Carrie's yellow card, scanned it into her handheld computer, and then added, "We didn't realize we had a VIP here because this patient doesn't have a green card."

"Her father wanted to protect her identity," Oliver said. A lame excuse. Even *he* didn't know what he meant by it, but the doctor nodded as if it made perfect sense.

Grabbing her stethoscope, the doctor listened to Carrie's heart, lungs, and neck while the nurses hooked Carrie up to several beeping machines.

"Who is her father?" the doctor asked. She lifted Carrie's eyelids and shined a light to check her pupils.

"Blood pressure at 88/59," one nurse reported.

"I'm not allowed to say," Oliver answered, feeling his own blood pressure surge. He would pay for these lies later.

"No. Of course not. My apologies," the doctor said. "How much money did her father send to cover her expenses?"

Sweat trickled down Oliver's forehead. He'd forgotten. In all the guard mess downstairs, he never grabbed CJ's extra money from Richard.

"I think...I think fifty." The doctor's eyes darted up to him, and Oliver added, "But he's sending more. I'll have the rest tonight." Not that he knew where to get more money. If his uncle had a dollar to his name, he could try there, but the old drunk already lived off Oliver's paychecks. There weren't even banks to rob anymore.

"Oxygen at 87%," one of the nurses said. She attached a clear tube under Carrie's nose.

The doctor checked Carrie's wrist for a pulse and then moved around to slip off Carrie's socks. She felt her ankles as well. "How long has she been unresponsive?"

Oliver couldn't answer as he stared at Carrie's bare feet. They were blue. Not gray. Blue. It was 90 degrees outside, but her feet were blue. The reality of losing her fully hit him.

It was too late.

They were too late.

"Do you know what her have symptoms been?" the doctor asked as if this was just another typical day at the office.

No time, no money, no sleep, and Oliver snapped.

"Look at her! She's dying. She obviously has G-979, so do something!"

The doctor looked up. "She has what?"

"Don't play stupid. You know what this is. You have to fix her. You have to fix all of them. People are dying!"

The doctor seemed to age ten years right before his eyes. "I'm afraid this woman has a progressed case. It might be too late and we can't afford to waste our—"

"No!" he roared. "It's not too late. You will help her and you will help her now!"

With a weary nod, the doctor turned back to the nurse. "5 milligrams every hour. Let me know if it's having any effect."

———◆———

The numbers in the ER ticked by painfully slow. A few chairs finally opened up, so Richard was able to move May and CJ. Then he leaned against the wall next to them, taking in the gobs of people. A few had abrasions or other emergency-type injuries, but most looked like May and CJ. Closed eyes. Pinched foreheads. One poor man kept vomiting in his own hat. Several parents hovered frantically over their children. How many realized their brains were swelling? How many knew the government was behind this 'plague?'

The longer it went, the heavier Richard's body became. He hadn't told anyone that he'd woken with his own stabbing headache.

He distracted himself by watching others. A few chairs down, a mother was trying to console her crying baby. The child, no more than six months old, was hoarse with tears, barely able to catch a breath through its raspy wails. The mother rocked him faster, desperate for their number to be called.

"What is going on?" someone shouted.

Wincing, Richard turned. A man had come up behind him. The man looked mid-forties and had his arm around a woman who wore a heavy winter coat even though it was July.

"There's nowhere to sit," the man yelled. "My wife can't stand up!"

Richard flinched as the man's booming voice sliced through his headache. "Do you have a number yet?" Richard pointed to the number reel. "I can stay with your wife while you get one."

Huffing, the man handed her off to Richard. The woman leaned against Richard without even looking at him. Her face stayed pinched.

"Your head?" Richard asked.

She nodded.

Mine, too.

It took a few minutes for the man to work his way back through the crowd. By then, his face was red with fury. "Two-hundred-and-three? This is madness!"

Richard nodded. At least CJ and May were holding up. May's chin was on her chest, and she was snoring softly, but that was better than some in the crowd who looked to be on death's door.

The man grew quiet. "Is it just me, or does everyone here seem to have the same illness? Is this an outbreak or something?"

"I believe the official term is genocide," Richard said, rubbing behind his ear.

The man whipped around. "Genocide? What do you mean?"

Richard didn't clarify because he noticed the mother out of the corner of his eye again. She had stopped rocking, and her baby had stopped crying. Both should have been a good sign, except the way the mother stared straight ahead and the way the baby slumped on her shoulder.

"Dead," Richard whispered.

These people had their citizenship. What would happen to the millions without?

The man tugged on Richard's sleeve. "Are you implying the government did this to us?"

"That is precisely what I am implying."

"But, but, but...we pay our taxes," the man stuttered. "My wife and I have been dutiful citizens all this time. Why would they do this to us? We're the good guys!"

"One-hundred-sixty-two!" someone called from the front.

"That's my number," Richard said, straightening. But before he left, he leaned close. "Spread the word. People need to know what's happening—what our president is capable of." Then he left the couple and shook CJ's shoulder.

"That's our number, CJ. Are you ready?"

With effort, CJ used the chair handles to push himself up on shaky feet, but May didn't move. Without CJ's support, her head slouched lower on her chest.

Richard crouched and patted her knee. "May, can you wake up?"

"One-hundred-sixty-two!" the man called again.

"Here!" Richard said, waving a hand. "Just a moment. May, are you ready?"

She sniffed awake, looked around in momentary confusion, and then nodded. Richard and CJ each took an arm to help her up.

"Wait!" she cried, eyes closing to stave off the dizziness.

"One-hundred-sixty-three!" the man up front called.

"No!" Richard shouted. "Stop!"

He had no choice but to hand dizzy May to CJ. Then he pushed through the crowd to the row of desks. A young father and his children were moving to the open seats. Richard cut in front of them.

"My apologies," Richard said, "but we're here. One-hundred-sixty-two. Look, here is my number," he said, pulling it out. "My in-laws are old and struggling to make it up here, but we're here. Please."

The man behind the desk didn't seem happy to be kept waiting, but he waved the father and his children back. Then he held a hand out to Richard. "Cards."

"Let me grab them." Richard ran back to help CJ and May move through the crowd. He handed all three of their cards to the man. The hospital worker swiped them and checked each card against their faces.

"Is Curtis John Trenton the patient?" he asked.

"Curtis John and May Trenton," Richard said. "Both of them have taken ill." He didn't mention himself because there already wasn't enough money.

The man gave all three of them lanyards with their citizenship cards inside. "How much money do you have available for treatment?"

"I'm not really sure," Richard said, suddenly remembering that he hadn't given Oliver any money. "Let me see. I have around three hundred and—"

The man snatched the bills clean from Richard's hand. He counted the money twice and put it in his drawer. Then he wrote Richard out a receipt.

Panicked, Richard eyed that drawer. It held the entire financial security of his clan. "How much treatment will that cover? We were hoping to not have to use all of their money."

"Do I look like a doctor? The medical staff will decide what treatment to give based on the money written on this receipt. If there's any leftover money, it will be returned to you upon checkout, but *only* if you have this receipt, so don't lose it."

"Okay," Richard said, feeling even more exhausted. "Just out of curiosity, is it normally this busy?"

All anger seemed to dissolve from the man's face. "I've never seen it like this in twenty years."

Probably why he was so short-tempered.

"Well," Richard said, "thank you for your help and good luck." Because if this epidemic kept sweeping through the population, the man would need it.

They all would.

———— ◆ ————

Once the fire was strong enough it wouldn't blow out, Greg stepped back into the shrubs and waited for somebody to notice. The dumpster was made of metal, and there would be plenty of water in the kitchen on the other side of that gray metal door, making his plan harmless. Except...the fire kept growing, catching more and more things ablaze within the dumpster, and not a soul in the hospital came out.

When the orange flames rose above the top of the dumpster, Greg started to panic. He could feel the heat from 15 feet away and he feared for the wood fence and nearby shrubs. Yet the gray metal door stayed sealed. If somebody didn't notice soon, the fire would be beyond control.

Don't do anything stupid. Don't do anything stupid. No matter how many times people told him, he couldn't—

A tiny boom sounded, and the fire leapt another five feet. Greg knew he had overdone the flammable materials.

Other people in the parking lot noticed, and cries of alarm went up. A few people peeked out from upper hospital windows to see the cause of the black rising smoke, but no hospital staff.

Wanting to shoot himself and his stupid plans, Greg ran to the metal door and pounded on it.

"Open up!" he yelled. "You've gotta fire out here!"

He kept pounding until the metal door flung open. Seeing the fire in the dumpster, a woman cried out in shock. A man swore loudly.

"What did you throw away?" the man shouted.

"Nothing!" the woman said.

Ditching all previous plans, Greg stepped into full view. He was going on instinct now, and instinct told him they only had a few minutes before the fire reached the trees and the hospital itself.

"You got buckets in there?" Greg asked. "A hose? Anything? We gotta get this under control."

The workers ran back inside and the metal door slammed shut. The fire dipped below the top of the dumpster, making it look like it might go out on its own. If that was the case, his plan was still idiotic because the door was—

Another explosion sounded. Greg jumped back as the fire leaped up, snagging the first branches of a nearby tree. Black, thick smoke billowed. He shielded his face, but the first of the smoke hit his lungs and he started to cough.

Even more desperate, he pounded on the door again. "C'mon! We don't have time!"

The door flew open. Several people rushed out, each with buckets and huge pots. They threw water on the flames. It did nothing to squelch them.

"Where are more buckets?" Greg asked the nearest man.

"On the left," the man said, waving Greg inside. "Hurry."

Greg sprinted inside and ignored every desire to make a run for it. He'd started the fire. He'd finish it. Through the chaos of people running into the kitchen, he found a large pitcher and darted after the others.

Stupid, stupid, stupid! Greg continued to yell at himself.

As he ran to the nearest massive sink, the inefficiency of their work struck him, and he shouted at them to switch to a water bucket line. People listened. Up and down they passed buckets, tripling their efficiency. The flames disappeared below the top of the dumpster. Several more buckets, and it was nothing but smoke, but they kept working. By then, scores of people had gathered in the parking lot on the other side of the fence to watch. More huddled around windows overhead.

As the smoke filtered, the other half of Greg's brain kicked back into gear. Things seemed in control outside, and every person dumping water wore their citizenship cards in lanyards around their necks. Any second, somebody would notice that Greg didn't have one.

Pretending to search for more buckets inside, Greg left the line and slipped into a corner of the kitchen near the giant ovens. He coughed and swallowed hard to clear the irritation in his lungs while watching the people streaming in from the hall. When there was a break in people, he quietly made his exit.

The hospital hallway was just as chaotic with people rushing back and forth. A man wearing scrubs saw Greg and ran toward him.

"Which way to the fire?" the man asked.

Greg covered his mouth with both hands to keep his chest—and lack of ID—hidden. "That way," he said in between coughs. "Out the kitchen. Careful of the smoke."

Greg turned the corner and sped-walked down another hallway past the cafeteria, coughing enough to justify both hands at his mouth. But that wouldn't hide his lanyard-less-ness forever. He needed a lanyard.

He hobbled toward an elevator as if he'd done this every day of his life, hoping the confidence made him look less suspicious. Once the doors closed, he didn't push any buttons to give himself a moment to figure out his next move. His skin and clothes were smeared black. That would distract people, and his lungs still felt on fire with smoke, making a few coughs legit.

But still.

According to the buttons, there were six floors. He had no clue where to find Carrie and his grandparents. None of the buttons were labeled with departments, and he hadn't seen a hospital map. How was he supposed to find anybody this way? Oliver and the others went to the ER, but would they still be there, or would the staff quarantine this cursed disease to a special section of the hospital?

Should he be searching the morgue instead?

Greg whirled and punched the wall of the elevator. Not hard—just enough to expend some pent-up frustration—but the elevator dinged and started moving upward. He straightened in time for the doors to open on the second floor.

Two nurses were waiting to ride up, so Greg covered his mouth to cough and shot out of the elevator as if he'd wanted to be on the second floor the whole time. The last thing he needed was to be stuck in a small confined space with hospital staff.

The longer he wound through hallways, the faster he went. Radiology, Cardiology, and too many other -ologies. He'd always prided himself on a good sense of direction, yet a few minutes inside and he didn't know north from south. Thankfully, the only people who spoke to him asked him which direction the fire was, but every time he passed a guard with a gun, his pulse leapt.

In the next hallway, he saw a cart of unattended linens. The guy who had been pushing it stood near a window watching the smoke, telling a janitor how awful it was that "the rebels were targeting hospitals now."

Without slowing, Greg grabbed a stack of sheets from a shelf and kept walking. He hugged the sheets to his chest. Not a perfect way to hide his lack of ID, but better than keeping both hands at his mouth.

That's when he heard the sirens. Fire trucks.

He was distracted enough by the sound that he nearly ran over a large ornery-looking woman.

"What are you doing?" she said, stumbling back. "You're not supposed to be in this area. Where is your ID?"

"Sorry." Greg bent in half and mimicked his mom's raspy cough. "Where do I go for..." Another cough. "...smoke inhalation? Somebody said ER?"

Her eyes narrowed on his dark smudges, and she pointed him back the way he'd come. "Go down to the first floor. Turn left and take your second right. There's an information desk there. They can direct you to the ER. Unless you need me to escort you? Are you well, sir?" she asked as Greg continued to hack away, doubled-over.

Nodding, he waved her off.

When he reached the information desk, he changed tactics. The ER was sure to be packed with people and security guards. Clutching his pile of bed sheets, he asked, "Can you page somebody for me?"

"Who would you like to page?" the receptionist asked, barely looking up.

"Officer Simmons. Tell him he's needed in"—Greg looked down the hallway—"the outpatient lab, stat."

fifty-six

"Took you long enough," somebody said. "Where have you been?"

With effort, Greg straightened. A tall, balding patrolman strode toward him, looking haggard and spent.

Oliver.

Greg could have kissed him.

"You knew I was gonna break in?" Greg said.

Oliver rolled his eyes. "I knew it the second you climbed into my trunk. How did you get past security?"

"I had to get a little creative."

Eyes narrowing, Oliver took in the dark smudges covering Greg. He shook his head. "That was you?"

"Maybe." Greg looked around. "Where are the others?"

"This way."

Oliver ducked past a nurses' station and headed for the stairwell. They took the stairs two at a time, Greg still clutching his pile of linens.

"How's Carrie?" Greg asked, voice echoing in the empty stairwell.

"She's been on an IV for over an hour," Oliver said. "The only improvement I see is her feet aren't blue anymore. I have no idea where your grandparents and Richard ended up. Sorry, but it's been crazy."

Oliver gripped the hand railing, huffing with the assent. "How are you going to hide the fact that you don't have a citizenship card—or do you plan to hold those sheets forever?"

"Seen any dead guys?" Greg asked. "I need to swipe somebody's lanyard."

Oliver glared over his shoulder. "If you're arrested, I'm not bailing you out."

"Don't worry. I have a get-out-of-jail-free card."

"Which is…?"

Greg didn't say. He just kept climbing. His bad leg ached, and the rest of him didn't feel so hot either. Not enough food or sleep to fuel the body. "Did the doctors give you any indication if the treatment will work?"

"Not exactly. They almost didn't treat her, so I had to get creative, too. By the way, they kind of think Carrie is the daughter of a high-ranking official."

"Nice," Greg said.

"No, it's dangerous, but I didn't have a choice. I'm glad you're here, though. I have to leave."

"Leave? Why?"

"I'd like to salvage my job," Oliver said.

Before Greg could ask what he meant, Oliver reached a door. "Alright," he said softly. "Stay close."

They exited the stairwell on the third floor and headed for a sign which read *Obstetrics*. Greg hung close to Oliver, hoping nobody would question a soot-covered guy with a patrolman. When Oliver reached a set of double doors, he pressed a button on the wall.

"Yes?" somebody said through a speaker.

"Officer Simmons back for room 322."

As the doors swung open, Greg frowned at the speaker. He wasn't getting back in here without Oliver.

Neither man spoke as they passed room after room. It was a quiet corner of the hospital, and Greg only saw three nurses. When they reached room 322, he held his breath, anxious.

Carrie.

She was alone in the darkened room. Machines beeped and hummed around her. She had an oxygen tube taped beneath her nose and an IV strapped to her hand.

An unexpected wave of emotion hit Greg. The IV. The dark room. The smell of disinfectant. The fear of death. In a pale hospital gown, Carrie looked so similar to how Greg's sister had looked the last minutes of her life—so peaceful—and his chest constricted. He didn't want Carrie to look peaceful. He wanted her pained grimace back, her hands covering her eyes. He wanted some sign that she was still aware, still feeling, still…here.

Sitting next to her, he took her free hand. It wasn't as cold as before, and while her coloring was still pallid, her cheeks had more form, more bulk. The IV liquids were helping even if the medicines weren't. He told himself she was getting better. She was.

She had to.

"Hey, beautiful," he whispered, squeezing her hand. "You doin' any better?"

He didn't expect a response, but Oliver shifted uncomfortably behind him.

"If the doctor or nurses ever come back like they promised," Oliver said, "you're going to need some kind of ID. I'll go peek around." But before he left, he stabbed a finger at Greg. "Don't wake her up."

As Oliver left, Greg scooted his chair closer to Carrie. He brushed some hair from her forehead, adjusted her blankets even though they didn't need adjusting, and read the screens on the machines until his eyes blurred. Then he figured he needed a backup plan.

He searched the room for a hiding spot in case somebody came in who wouldn't appreciate his illegal status. No closets, dark corners, or curtains, but there was a tiny bathroom. Unfortunately, it was next to the door where the staff would enter. He wouldn't reach it in time unless he hid there now. He refused to leave Carrie's side.

As he waited, his eyelids grew heavy. He kept telling himself that she looked better. That it was working. But the despair was as consuming as the exhaustion.

The door cracked open, and his heart kicked into full throttle, but it was just Oliver ducking back in.

"Here," Oliver said, handing Greg a lanyard. "It's not perfect but better than nothing."

Greg inspected the green card tucked inside the plastic sleeve. A middle-aged Asian lady smiled up at him. Good enough. Greg wrapped it around his neck so the lady's picture faced his chest.

"Is she gonna miss this?" he asked.

"She was covered with a sheet a few rooms down. Hopefully the staff won't notice her card is gone. Now," Oliver said, "I really have to go. I'll be back when I can. If I find Richard, I'll tell him where you are. Oh, and they're expecting Carrie's *father* to send more money tonight, only I'm broke, so I'm not sure what to tell you on that."

"That'll make things interesting," Greg said. "Anything else?"

"Probably, but I don't know what." Oliver rubbed his eyes. "Man, I dread going back. Jamansky is going to be furious. He's paged me four times in the last twenty minutes. I missed his mandatory meeting, and I completely skipped my patrols last night. He was already making my life miserable. How will he punish me now?"

Probably in a way that would punish Greg's clan as well.

"You know," Greg said, "if there's ever a day you gotta quit your job, the clan will support your decision."

Oliver eyed him skeptically.

"Or I'll support you," Greg amended. "Carrie will, too."

"Yeah, because getting fired right now is such a great idea." Oliver motioned at Carrie in the government hospital bed with her yellow card around her neck.

"Hey, I'm here, aren't I?" Greg said. "We can get creative."

"Even if I wanted to, I'm not allowed to quit. Patrolmen who quit conveniently disappear."

"All the more reason to bug out," Greg said. "There's somethin' vastly refreshing about livin' off the radar. We've got plenty of empty houses in Logan Pond, and I heard a rumor that one was recently purchased, too, which gives us twice the garden space and twice the space to hide."

Oliver shook his head, but the tiniest smile played at the corners of his mouth. "You're crazy."

Crazy, sleep deprived, and hungry. Both of them were.

Sighing, Oliver studied Carrie's sleeping form. "I'll do my best to come back tonight. I'll also try to stop by the neighborhood to check in."

"Thanks," Greg said. "Tell everybody I'm workin' on gettin' a cure."

"How?"

"Not sure yet, but I'll figure somethin' out."

Another shake of the head as Oliver moved to the door. Before he left, he turned back with a long, sad look. "Take care of her." The way he said it implied more than just the immediate future.

Sobered by that, Greg nodded. "Keep safe and don't let Jamansky push you around."

"Yeah." Pointing at Greg one last time, he said, "Don't wake her up."

"Look who finally showed up," Jamansky sneered, pinching that same nerve in Oliver's shoulder he loved to aggravate.

Half asleep, Oliver jerked out of his grasp. "Sorry, sir. My pager battery died and I didn't realize it until I got here."

"I don't care if you have car problems," Jamansky said. "You report to *me*, not Ashlee. You call *me* if you have issues. Am I clear?"

Oliver had no idea what he was talking about, but he nodded. Car problems was a better excuse than being sick—the excuse he'd planned to give. Patrolmen weren't allowed to get sick, at least not in Jamansky's precinct. Oliver would thank Ashlee for bailing him out later.

Jamansky glared at him. "I'm writing you up on formal charges, Simmons. Any more of this and you'll lose that car."

"Yes, sir," Oliver said while thinking, *Drop dead.*

As Jamansky left, Oliver grabbed his mug and sipped what was left of his luke-warm coffee. A movement on the other side of the office caught his eye. Ashlee was waving him over. Oliver dragged himself over to her counter.

"Officer Simmons," Ashlee said, sounding formal, "can you help me with this file?"

"Sure?" It came out as a question because she'd spread a blank travel permit in front of him.

As he looked at it, she leaned close and whispered, "Everything okay with your friend? Did it work?"

"So far," he said. "She's there now."

"Wonderful. I tried to hold David off as long as I could." She smiled. "Sorry about the car excuse. It's all I could think of. I told him you called in the middle of the night, and then later found a mechanic who was able to fix your car already, so you're all set. Is that okay?"

It was as lame as the lies he'd fed the hospital staff, but for whatever reason, karma seemed to be on his side. "That's great. Did he suspect anything about you being gone last night?"

She shook her blonde head.

That was a relief. "Thanks for all your help, Ashlee."

"No prob," she said with another warm smile. "Let me know if you need anything else."

"Actually…" The second the word was out, Oliver changed his mind. "Never mind."

She turned. "What?"

"Nothing. Sorry." She'd already done too much—she already *knew* too much.

Ashlee cocked her head to the side and looked up at him beneath her thick, black lashes. "Just ask me, Oliver. It's okay."

He took another sip of coffee and avoided her steady gaze. "Can I borrow some money? Carrie's medical expenses are a lot, and I, I…I'm out of money." He felt like a desperate fool, but he kept going. "I swear I'll pay you back with my next paychecks. I'll even pay interest—a lot of interest—if you can help."

She studied him with an unreadable expression.

"Never mind. Sorry," he said. "It was inappropriate to ask."

"You really love her. Don't you?"

He sighed a long sigh. "I shouldn't."

"Why not?"

"It's not a relationship that can work."

"I know all about those," Ashlee said with a sad smile. "But she's legal now. You're free to love her."

"It's not that. Carrie, she…" He took another sip. "She loves someone else." He couldn't say who because Ashlee not only knew Greg—and kind of had a thing for him—but she also thought Greg was dead.

Instead of nodding as if his answer was completely obvious—who wouldn't love someone else?—she actually looked surprised. "After all you've done for her?"

"Yes. I mean, no. It's…complicated."

"Ah. I know about that, too. But don't give up on her. You deserve happiness." Standing a little straighter, she said, "How much money do you need?"

He stared at her. After hearing how pathetic he was, begging money for a woman who didn't love him back, she still wanted to help? Apparently so. She grabbed her purse from her desk. Glancing over her shoulder to make sure they were still alone, she pulled out a fat wad of bills.

"Will this cover it?"

His eyes widened. She hadn't even counted the money. She just held the wad out to him. When he couldn't move, couldn't budge, she grabbed his hand and placed the money inside.

"You'll pay me back," she said. "I'm not worried."

The money felt heavy, and Oliver was at a loss for words.

She closed his hand over the money. "You shouldn't be so surprised when people do something nice for you. This world needs more people like you. Which reminds me." She scanned the room again and lowered her voice. "I might have found something to help you on that other project, the one with David and the mayor. Come here."

———◆———

David Jamansky's insides shook like flood waters ready to burst a dam. He tapped his pen on his desk faster as he watched Ashlee and Oliver Simmons through the small security screen. The audio wasn't great, but he heard enough. The lies. The money. The betrayals.

He'd kill them both.

"David doesn't know that I know," Ashlee was saying. "But I heard him and the mayor talking, and I think this might be what you need."

Oliver flipped through the papers. When he replied, his whiny voice was too soft to hear. Not that it mattered. Jamansky knew exactly what those papers were. He snapped his pen in half, splaying dark ink all over, but he restrained himself from going out there because he suspected there was more to their little budding relationship.

He just needed proof.

Ashlee took the papers and slid them beneath a stack of empty travel permits, hiding them. Out of sight but easy to find. Then she followed Officer Simmons to the door, smiling a wide smile Jamansky recognized easily. The whore.

The two traitors ended up below the camera mounted on the wall, out of sight but closer to the microphone. David was finally able to hear both sides of the conversation.

"How long will you be at the hospital this time?" Ashlee asked.

"Not sure," Oliver said.

David leaned toward the screen even though he couldn't see either of them.

"Well, good luck," Ashlee said. "I'll tell David you're having more car problems." And then Ashlee stepped back into view. "Tell her I hope she feels better."

David didn't know who 'she' was—as far as he knew, Oliver Simmons didn't have family left—but he'd find out, and then he'd make them *all* pay.

"I will," Oliver said. "Thanks again. I'll find a way to repay you. For last night and this, too."

Last night?

Oliver Simmons left the station. Still, Jamansky waited, inked fist clenched. A plan was forming in his mind, but he had to verify something first. Ashlee disappeared into the bathroom a few minutes later. She'd be primping that fake blonde hair for a while.

Jamansky strode out of his office and into the front room. He pulled out the sheets Ashlee hid beneath the empty travel permits and cursed loudly. For all her supposed love and devotion, Ashlee ratted him out.

He fed the papers into the shredder and turned back to straighten the stack, debating how soon to confront her: now, and watch her squirm up another lie, or later, when the trap had been fully set?

Something caught his eye. Another sheet was half-pulled out of the bottom of the pile. It was filled with tiny writing. Legal jargon. Something else Ashlee had hidden.

Jamansky held it close and read the small print. It looked like a deed to a home in Shelton, which was a strange thing for Ashlee to hide from him. But then he read the date, the address, the owner's name, the buyer's name, and the notary's signature at the bottom.

"Well, well, well," he said slowly.

Two of the names made him want to hurl Ashlee's computer against the wall, but the top name, the owner of this home in the Logan Pond subdivision, had Jamansky smiling for the first time. Carrie Lynne Ashworth.

"Found you," he whispered.

When Ashlee came out of the bathroom, David Jamansky was leaning against her desk, waving the deed in the air.

Ashlee glanced at the stack of empty travel permits. Her hands flew to her mouth. Terror flashing, she took a step back, but Jamansky ran across the office and grabbed her before she could escape. She screamed. He shoved her against the wall.

"You will tell me exactly what you know," he seethed, "and you will tell me right now."

"I-I don't know what you're talking about," she said.

He slapped her across the cheek like she'd once slapped him, only harder, hard enough his hand stung with hot pain. Crying out, she doubled over. But just as fast, she straightened, chin held high. Her cheek was red from his handprint, but her eyes spit fire.

"We're through," she said.

"Oh, no, we're not, Ash babe. We're just getting started."

He knew she was going to run, he could see it in her traitorous eyes, so he grabbed her and threw her back against the wall.

"I'll make this easy on you," he said, pinning her so tight she gasped with pain. "You and I are going to visit Mayor Phillips and let him know what you think you've found. But first, you're going to tell me everything you know about Oliver and Carrie Ashworth or I will snap your neck."

fifty-seven

Greg watched the nurse adjust Carrie's IV. For some reason it had stopped flowing right, and the nurse didn't want to start a new IV since it had taken them so long to get this one into Carrie's weak veins.

"Come on," she said, adjusting the needle.

As the nurse jiggled it in and around Carrie's pale skin, Greg nearly passed out. His forehead went cold, his hands felt clammy, but he forced himself to keep watching. Unfortunately, the nurse added the medicines to the mass of clear bags and tubing—things Greg wouldn't have access to in the clan. Still, he needed to learn all he could about this medicine.

"There," the nurse said. "Yes. There we go."

Greg sat back and wiped his hands on his jeans. The IV was flowing again. She adjusted a few more things and scribbled notes in Carrie's chart. She had been ridiculously punctual, coming in every hour at exactly ten minutes after the hour. But she never asked who Greg was or why he was there instead of Oliver. In fact, she barely spoke to him, but he got braver with every visit, asking more questions—like if they offered pills for people who had horrible veins like his grandma. He had no idea if his grandma had bad veins and only hoped she was already on her own IV, but he needed something transportable, something administer-able by a clueless, needle-fearing guy like him. But the nurse gave vague answer, and whenever he asked if Carrie's meds were working, she told him the doctor would be in soon. Only the doctor never came and Greg was slowly going mad.

Five hours.

A cruel form of torture for a man who struggled to sit and do nothing on a good day.

"When will the doctor be in?" Greg asked again. "Miss Ashworth's father is anxious for a report."

At that, the nurse gave him a nervous glance. "I'm not sure, but I'll go check."

With the room silent again, Greg watched each blip of Carrie's pulse, each drip of the medicine, each rise and fall of her chest, analyzing whether a single thing was improving. In his limited knowledge, nothing changed except the seconds on the clock. Time became his enemy. She should be getting better by now. She had shifted a few times in bed, and maybe that was an improvement, but when he called her name or rubbed her hand, he got nothing.

The door creaked open. It wasn't the doctor. It was a man, an older gentleman with wrinkled clothes, tired eyes, and long, graying hair going every which way. Greg's stepdad looked like he'd been hit by a bus.

"Greg?" Richard whispered.

"Yeah," Greg called. "Come on in."

Richard entered the small birthing room. "I wasn't sure if I had the right spot. Wow. A room to yourself? I'm jealous. They have us packed in downstairs."

"Special privileges for the upper class," Greg said. "How's Grandma?"

"It doesn't seem like the medicines are helping—at least not yet. What about here?"

"Same," Greg said. The despair rose up on him again. He brushed some hair from Carrie's forehead.

"She looks better," Richard said. "At least better than she did before. Where did you get that?" Richard asked, pointing to Greg's tag.

Greg flipped his lanyard over to show him the Asian lady. "Looks just like me, doesn't she? Poor lady—may she rest in peace. Were they able to get an IV into Grandma?"

"They didn't even try." Richard rubbed the back of his head. "Apparently they're running out of equipment, so she and your grandpa get shots every two hours. They finally gave your grandma a bed, but your grandpa is in a chair."

"And you?" Greg leaned down to eye him. "No offense, but you're not lookin' so hot. You've started, too, haven't you?"

Richard waved that off. "I'll be fine, but I was hoping Carrie had progressed more than this by now. They're kicking us out in the morning, and at this rate, your grandma—"

"Morning?" Greg cut in. "Why?"

"Money. Always money. Which reminds me. I promised I'd give Oliver money to help with Carrie's costs, but we already don't have enough, and I doubt your grandparents will be better by morning, so I'm not sure what to do."

"Great." Although if his grandparents were on shots instead of an IV, that answered his other question. He could steal shots—in theory. He could administer shots. In theory.

He just had to find them.

"Well," Richard said, "I don't dare leave May and CJ for too long, but I wanted to check in here. We're in room 259 if you need us. Enjoy your solitude—and your chair. I'll check back later."

"Richard?" Greg asked as he turned to go. "What if this doesn't work?" The meds. The money. Carrie's supposed father. Since climbing into Oliver's car trunk, Greg hadn't allowed himself to consider that this was all for naught, that he could still lose her—lose them. But at some point, he might have to accept the writing on the wall.

Things were on a downward spiral.

Richard studied him with a long, tired look before answering softly. "I suppose we'll cross that bridge when we get there."

When.

Greg felt numb.

As Richard left, Greg couldn't wait any longer. Instead of going back to his chair, he limped over to Carrie's bed and sat next to her legs on the hospital blankets.

"Carrie?" He rubbed her arm. "Hey, beautiful. Time to wake up."

Oliver would shoot him, but Greg didn't care.

"Carrie?" he said a little louder. "Please try to wake up for me. Please."

Her legs shifted. That was it. But he scrambled back to watch, to see. When nothing else happened, he grabbed her hand.

"C'mon. Time to wake up." Time to ease his fears. Time to move on with life, reaching out to other clans, her garden, Greg, and everything else that needed her. "Please. Ashworths are fighters, remember? I know you can do it."

Her fingers twitched in his hand, and while her eyelids didn't open, he saw them moving. He wanted to jump, shout, and strike up the band, but he just rubbed her cool skin.

"Just a little more," he urged.

With a grimace, her eyes finally cracked open. She squinted and blinked a dozen times against the light even though the room was dim with late afternoon sun. She could still see light. That brought a smile to his lips.

He leaned over her body to enter her line of vision. "Hey, beautiful."

She blinked a few more times before her squinty eyes found his face. A tired smile lifted the corners of her mouth.

"Hey," she breathed.

One word—a simple word at that—but he grinned like a kid at Disneyworld.

Her eyes roamed the semi-lit room. They were only open a crack, but he could see more life in those baby blues, more coherency than before. He wanted to kiss her senseless, but he refrained himself to ask, "How's the head? Any better?"

Without answering, she stroked the IV strapped to the back of her hand and then reached up to touch the tube attached beneath her nose. Confused, she looked at Greg.

"How long have I been here?" she asked.

But before he could answer, her hand lifted to her left ear. She covered it, patted it a few times, before her eyes flew back to him. "What's wrong with my ear?"

His stomach dropped. "Is it both or just the one?"

She patted the other ear and then went back to the first. "I can't...it's not right." She rubbed and patted her ear like somebody trying to get water from it.

"Both or just the one?" he asked more loudly, feeling sick.

"Just this one." Her gaze, terrified and vulnerable, lifted to his. "Is it...permanent?"

How did he respond? The doctor told Oliver her brain had been under 'duress' long enough she might have permanent damage, but they wouldn't know how much until she woke up and they could reassess. Greg wasn't ready to assess anything. He took her hand and pulled it gently from her ear.

"It'll be okay," he promised. Hearing loss, vision problems, or anything else seemed inconsequential now. Carrie was alive. The medicine was working.

Though it took a moment, she nodded. "How is your grandma?"

Settling next to her on the bed, he caught her up on everything, making a conscious effort to speak louder. The whole time he stroked her hand, her arm, her cheek, probably driving her insane with all the stroking, but he needed to feel her warm and alive.

"I've still gotta find a way to steal some meds," he finished. Especially now that he knew they worked.

Her head cocked on her pillow. "Wait. How are *you* here?"

"You think you could keep me away?" he said with a sly grin.

Carrie spotted the lanyard around his neck, and her eyes went wide, wider than they had in days. "No, no, no!" Her eyes pooled with tears. "They can't have you. You promised me, Greg. You promised."

"Hold on. Look." He flipped his ID over so she could see the lady's stolen green card. "I kept my promise. I'm as dead as ever."

Relieved, Carrie laid back and closed her eyes.

"Are your eyes any better?" he asked, noting how much she still squinted. Maybe she would always be sensitive to light. If so, he'd find her sunglasses. Somehow.

"I think so," she said.

She fell silent and rubbed her bad ear again. He didn't press her to speak even though he wanted to hear her voice, to know her thoughts. But she looked spent. And overwhelmed. And sad, too.

When she looked at him again, her hand slipped across her blanket and wrapped around his. Then she slid her fingers into his.

"I'm glad you're here," she whispered.

That little gesture meant more to him than she'd ever know. He stared at their hands entwined, and a burst of emotion rose inside of him. He leaned down and kissed her softly.

"I'm glad you're here, too," he said. "I mean, not glad you're in the hospital—well actually, I'm thrilled you made it and are gettin' the help you need. But I mean that I'm glad you're *here* here."

As in, not dead.

She seemed to understand and even managed a tiny smile. "Me, too."

Then, totally and without warning, the tears started again. Only this time they overflowed and leaked down the sides of her cheeks.

"Hey, whoa," he said, wiping them back. "Everything's gonna be okay, you'll see. Don't be sad, Carrie girl. Not now."

"Oliver bought my house," she whispered.

He smiled. "Amazing, isn't it? You're a free woman in more ways than one."

"Why me?" She sniffed. "Why did he buy it when he knows that I love you?"

"Ah. So you *do* love me?" Greg winked at her even as his heart swelled another notch. "So tell me, was it my good looks? My unbelievable charm?"

She gave him a tired look.

"Sorry." He tried to sober up—a difficult task, considering. "You know Oliver. You know the kind of man he is. He cares for you and just wants you to be safe. It was a gift to you. A gift to all of us, actually."

"Then why couldn't he buy the house for someone who would appreciate it and not slap him with a rejection afterward?" Her voice trembled. "I told him that I love you, Greg. I told him. He knows, but he still bought it. Why?"

"Because I wanted to," a quiet voice said from behind them.

Greg turned to see Oliver in the doorway. Standing, Greg moved off of Carrie's bed, wondering how long he'd been there.

"Hey, Carrie," Oliver said with a tiny smile. "You're awake. That's...that's good. Really good."

More tears slid down her cheeks. She didn't bother wiping them back—probably too much effort. Greg didn't either, not with Oliver there, hearing what he'd heard. The last Oliver and Carrie had talked—really talked—had been on their date, the one where Oliver kissed her.

Carrie didn't look embarrassed. She didn't even blush. She just looked heartbroken by the rejection she had known—even from the beginning—would be inevitable.

"How'd it go?" Greg asked Oliver as a diversion.

Oliver's eyes finally shifted away from Carrie. Remembering himself, he crossed the room and handed Greg a folded wad of cash. "Here. This should be enough."

Brows lifting, Greg flipped through the bills. There were hundreds of dollars. Plenty to cover Carrie's expenses—plus his family's.

"How?" Greg asked in amazement.

Oliver shrugged. "Oh, and I stopped by the neighborhood. Braden and Terrell are worse but are resting. However, Mrs. Watson started. Sorry."

"Rhonda, too?" Greg said. He blew out his breath. "Are they still quarantined?"

"Yes."

"Then how is it still spreading?" It was a question more for himself, but Carrie sniffed back more tears behind him.

"Amber and Zach are fine," Oliver said quickly. "They're fine, Carrie. I talked to both of them, and neither have any symptoms. None."

A strange phenomenon which made Greg think President Rigsby's cronies had somehow engineered the disease to skip the teen generation, the ones who could be molded, influenced, and brainwashed.

Oliver and Carrie were still looking at each other.

Greg didn't know everything that had happened between the two of them in the six weeks he was gone, but he suddenly felt like the third wheel. So he moved to the door.

"Hey," he said, "I'm gonna poke around for a bit. I'll be back."

Neither glanced his way as he slipped out of the room.

fifty-eight

Carrie and Oliver stared at each other for a full minute before she found the courage to speak.

"I'm sorry, Oliver." Her emotions were overflowing, her throat was raw, dry, and swollen, but she kept going. "I'm so sorry that—"

"Please don't," Oliver said softly, so soft she almost missed it with her bad ear. "You did nothing wrong."

No. I just broke your heart.

"Are you…" Oliver paused. "Are you okay?"

"Fine," she said, throwing out an automatic response. In reality, she was far from fine. Her ear. Her head that killed. Still. Her stomach that rolled with nausea. Her eyes that only focused if she blinked a dozen times, but if she looked away, even for a second, she had to refocus all over again. Then there were those in the clan on the same path, Greg limping around with a fake badge, and Oliver. She was on the verge of losing it mentally, physically, and emotionally.

Well, she'd already lost it emotionally.

Wiping her cheeks, she took a few calming breaths. It would be okay. Her symptoms would improve. Her sick friends would be okay. May. Braden. All of them. They would be okay somehow. And Oliver would be…

Oliver was…

Crushed.

"Thank you for my house," she said, lips trembling. Another house for the clan. Another garden. More safety, less hiding. Citizenship for her and her siblings. It was too much. She struggled to keep her head above water.

He played with a gold button on his uniform. "Sorry it took so long. I wanted to buy it for you years ago. Sorry I bought it without asking you. I tried to tell you. I tried so many times, Carrie, but I just..." He sighed. "I'm sorry."

Of course Oliver would apologize for such a gift.

"What can I do?" she whispered.

"Get better."

He blurred beyond recognition. "Why are you so good to us? So good to me?"

Oliver shook his head fiercely. "Not good. I got you sick. I've endangered your whole clan. I've been so scared—so, so scared—that I've killed you all. I'm still scared, but I'm glad you're getting better. And I'll do whatever I can to help the others, too. Is there..." He thrust his hands in his pockets. "Is there anything I can do for you right now? Do you need anything?"

The question was so backward and guilt-inducing, but she forced herself to smile.

"Can you keep me company? Maybe catch me up on what I've missed?"

His face, so long and concerned, so tortured and lonely, finally relaxed into a smile. "I'd like that."

————◆————

Greg watched the flurry of doctors, nurses, and sick people moving through the hallways. *Obstetrics* was no longer a quiet place, and standing around with a fake badge made him feel like he had a target on his chest. He folded his arms while watching the direction the nurses moved. Whenever one passed with a pile of meds, Greg stole a foot that direction. They had to be getting the medicine from somewhere.

Carrie's nurse turned a corner and spotted him. "What are you doing out here, sir? You're not supposed to be in this hallway. Is there a problem? I haven't been able to find the doctor yet."

"No. There's no problem," he said, not mentioning that Carrie had woken. Carrie and Oliver didn't want to be disturbed. "I'm just lookin' for a place to score some food."

"The cafeteria is on the main floor."

"Great. Thanks," he said, heading toward the front of *Obstetrics* while knowing he'd never risk passing that many hospital staff for some food. He was famished. Not suicidal.

Once Carrie's nurse disappeared, he sneaked back to the hallway he'd been watching. He was pretty sure they were getting medicine from one of four rooms at the end of the hall.

When the next nurse passed, Greg bent down to tie his shoe. The nurse pulled out his badge and swiped it through a security panel on the wall. The door opened. The nurse was inside a minute before he reappeared with a small pile of meds. Greg was still tying his shoe.

When the man left, Greg stood and studied that security panel. The nurse had used his citizenship card to open it. Desperate, Greg tried his own stolen green card. He was shocked when the door swung open.

"Huh," he whispered. More green cardie privileges.

He quickly shut the door behind him and looked around. Shelves of medicine lined the room. Bottles, boxes, needles. Clueless, he started searching the stacks for a box that matched the label on Carrie's medicine. Everything was written in medical, chemical jargon. He hadn't the foggiest what he was looking for.

He was on the second row when he froze. He heard women laughing in the hallway, right outside of the door.

Greg dropped to a crouch.

If they opened the door, they wouldn't see him. But if they came inside, he was dead. There was nowhere to hide. The room was too small.

Keep going, he begged the women.

No such luck.

The door opened and two women in scrubs walked in, continuing their conversation about a combative patient. He saw their shoes and bent lower behind a small stack of boxes. They walked right past, too distracted to notice him glued to the floor.

Still crouched low, he started to move, to slip back toward the door. Only the door shut after they entered, which would pose a problem. They'd hear him—

"Ah!" One of the women cried. "Who are you?"

Flinching, Greg looked over his shoulder. The other nurse, a younger one, turned and saw what her older friend had seen. She jumped back as well.

"Who are you?" The older nurse demanded again. She had graying hair and put an arm in front of her younger partner, as if that could protect her. "Why are you in here?"

Greg looked around for a valid reason, but too many days without sleep and too many close calls left him fresh out of lies. He stood slowly and held his hands up to show he wasn't armed.

"I just need some medicine," he said.

They seemed to understand in an instant. He wasn't lost. He was stealing.

The younger nurse picked up the nearest box and held it high in a semi-threatening position. The gray-haired lady took four brave steps forward and flipped Greg's lanyard over.

She saw the Asian lady and gasped. Then her jaw tightened. "I'm getting security," she said. She moved as if to pass Greg, but he sidestepped, blocking her.

"Listen," he said quickly, "my friends are sick. Real sick. Only they can't come to the hospital. They're gonna die if I can't find them help and they don't deserve to die. I just need a little medicine, and then I'll go. I can even pay for it," he added, reaching into his pocket.

"Don't move!" the younger one yelled, raising her box again.

Greg was twice her size, yet she still looked around him as if calculating what he'd do to her if she made a run for it.

Or screamed.

"Look," he pled, lifting his hands higher in a show of peace, "I know what this disease is. I know it's G-979 and it's designed to wipe out people like us who can't get help. I know Rigsby wants us all dead." His muscles clenched. "I just can't let that happen."

The older nurse's brows shot up. "How do you know about that? Who are you?"

Greg wondered if it was time to pull the McCormick card. *I'm a special op, so move out of my way. Sure. Go ahead and verify. My busy commander loves to be interrupted.* The lie would probably work. They might not even try to call McCormick to verify. But if they did…he'd just assured Carrie that he kept his promise.

His hands fell in surrender. "I'm nobody. Just a guy with friends who are dying. A guy with nothin' left to lose."

"Are you part of the rebellion?" the gray-haired woman whispered.

Technically no. He planned to stay in the shadows for the rest of his life. But if President Rigsby kept taking down those he loved, Greg couldn't—he wouldn't—stand idly by any longer.

Though he would probably regret the answer once security arrived, he nodded slowly. "Yeah. I am."

The two nurses eyed each other, speaking some unspoken language. Based on the fear in their eyes, he guessed they were deciding who had to run for security and who had to detain him. He wouldn't fight them, but he couldn't let himself be taken. So he took a step back. Neither noticed. He stole another step toward the door.

"No," the younger one hissed at her partner. "We can't."

"It's the right thing to do," the older nurse said. Then she turned and smiled at Greg.

Smiled.

He stopped.

"Here," she said, moving to a side shelf. "Your friends will need this." Going up on tiptoes, she grabbed a box down and held it toward him. "This will treat eight people. Is that enough?"

Greg's gaze flickered from her to the box and then back again. Her younger counterpart didn't look thrilled, but neither did she run for help.

"Is it?" the older nurse asked again, less sure of herself.

He shook his head to clear it, realizing what she was offering. Eight people. "Uh, I think so. Then again, it's spreadin' fast. Six of our group have already contracted it."

"Then here's another, just in case."

As she handed him two small boxes, disbelief spread through Greg. Treatment for sixteen people.

"Why?" he asked.

The older nurse's eyes grew moist, but it was the younger one who answered. "Live free or die," she whispered.

Understanding spread through him at the same time a smile did. These women might work for the government—for President Rigsby. They might have green cards in their lanyards, but... His smile grew. The rebellion wasn't just for illegals anymore.

"Live free or die," he echoed.

"Here," the younger one said. "Let me get you a badge that isn't so suspicious."

fifty-nine

A doctor was examining Carrie by the time Greg returned. Greg wasn't handcuffed or beaten, but he'd been gone so long Carrie was sure he'd been caught. Then she realized her doctor or nurse could check his citizenship just as easily. Carrie tried to ward Greg off with a look as he entered. He needed to wait in the hall, but he just flashed her that crooked, cocky smile of his.

Why did he think he was invincible?

He dropped a small sack behind the door and strode across the room to Oliver in the corner. The two men whispered quietly, catching each other up on things she couldn't quite hear.

"Miss Ashworth?" the doctor said, leaning into her view.

"Sorry." Carrie faced front.

The doctor shined a light in her eyes. She tried not to shrink back or close her eyes against the blinding light, but it was unbearable, like staring at the noonday sun.

"Is the room still spinning?" the doctor asked.

"Not now," Carrie said. "I'm just light-headed."

"Hopefully that will improve with time. Sorry, I know the lights bother you. I'm almost done."

The doctor finally finished and wrote some notes in her chart. Carrie sat back against her inclined bed and clutched her hospital gown, needing something to ground her. She hadn't asked where her mom's blue blouse went or who changed her into the thin cotton gown—hopefully not one of the men in the corner who continued speaking in hushed tones.

Her strength was returning, but not as fast as she needed. She needed to get out of this place. She needed to make sure everyone else wasn't following her fate—or worse.

"Seventy percent?" Greg suddenly said, loud enough they all turned.

Oliver nodded.

Greg turned and stared at Carrie, horrified.

The emotions hit her again and she had to look away. Her hand went to her left ear even though no amount of tugging made the sound improve. Seventy percent hearing loss in one ear was better than a hundred percent in both—or so she told herself. It just made her feel lopsided, like she was missing something or turned sideways.

"Is it permanent?" Greg asked.

"Appears to be," the doctor said. "Miss Ashworth's heart and lungs are strong, her vital organs are functioning normally, however she's experiencing residual effects in her hearing, vision, and vestibular-related functions. We'll run some tests to give us a better idea of the damage."

Tests sounded expensive to Carrie—too expensive for their situation—but both Greg and Oliver nodded.

"When will her father be visiting?" the doctor asked.

Father? Carrie shot Greg a look. He barely locked eyes with her before answering.

"Not sure," he said evenly, "but he sent more money, around four hundred."

Carrie shook her head—a bad idea considering her *vestibular-related* issues. Oliver definitely hadn't caught her up on everything, but she was wise enough to stay quiet.

"That should be enough to start the tests," the doctor said. "We'll begin within the hour. If her father wishes to speak to me directly, I can be reached at extension 1205."

As the doctor and nurse left, Carrie fell back against her pillow, wondering how many lies it had taken to get her here. Or how much money it was going to take to get her out.

Greg came to her side and squeezed her hand. "You okay? Your coloring is a little better." He spoke louder than necessary, and she tried not to let it irritate her.

"Yes," she said. "Where were you?"

"Well, I have a little gift for you. A gift for both of you, actually." Grinning, he grabbed the bag he'd dropped by her door. He pulled out two white boxes and handed one to her and Oliver. "There's enough medicine in there to treat sixteen people. If we need more, I was told that I can come back anytime."

"Sixteen people?" Carrie stroked the box. They were going to be okay. She couldn't believe it.

"You didn't set any fires to get these, did you?" Oliver asked, opening his box to peek in.

Greg chuckled. "Nope. Not this time."

Carrie's head lifted. "This time?"

Oliver really had told her nothing.

Greg shot her another quirked smile. "You've missed out on some fun times. But no. I just made a couple new friends. They gave me a new hall pass, too."

He lifted his lanyard to show off a new ID badge. Though it hurt to do so, Carrie squinted to make it out. His new badge was green like the other, but more square-ish with the word HOUSEKEEPING written across the top. Somehow, his small picture was in the corner.

"How did you get that?" she asked. Then again, how did Greg do anything he did?

He sat next to her on the bed and lopped an arm up behind her, almost around her shoulders but not quite. As he kicked his feet up on her blankets, he was the picture of complete ease. A smile crept up on her. Greg was back—her Greg was back.

"Apparently," he said, "there are a couple nurses who are fans of the rebellion. If people back home stayed quarantined, sixteen should be plenty. It makes me wonder if we should take my grandparents home now. They're not gettin' much treatment here anyway, plus they're just burnin' through money we don't have."

"Do you know how to give shots?" Oliver said, pulling out a syringe.

Greg grimaced. "Not really. I'm not a huge fan of needles, so I might have to convince somebody else to do the stabbing, but the nurses explained it three times and swore it wasn't hard."

Nodding, Oliver said, "Then maybe it's a good idea to salvage some money. If Richard and your grandparents are up for it, I can drive them home now if you want."

Home.

That was all Carrie needed to hear.

"I'm coming, too," she announced. She sat up too quickly and the room spun violently. Gripping the blankets, she squeezed her eyes closed until she felt steady again. By then, Greg was pushing her back against the bed.

"Hold on," Greg said. "You're stayin' until you're better."

"I *am* better," she said.

He eyed her. "You're a little better, but still worse off than anybody else. No. You need to stay and get those tests."

Tests. That solidified her decision.

"We don't have money for tests," she insisted, "and the doctor already said the damage was permanent. Amber and Zach are home alone, and I don't want to be here anymore, so I'm leaving."

Greg's expression softened. He stroked her arm, sending fire and warmth through her. "Zach and Amber are fine, and you won't be here alone. I'll stay with you. We'll just stay long enough to see—"

"Don't fight me," she whispered. "Please don't fight me on this."

"Carrie…"

Her throat started to burn and she felt her strength wane. But Greg was one of the most stubborn people she knew, so she turned to Oliver instead. "Will you please take me home?"

"Carrie," Oliver said, "I think Greg's right. I think you should stay while…" His mouth kept moving, but the rest of his quiet plea faded into hearing-loss oblivion.

Hot tears of frustration filled her eyes, but she refused to cry. Gritting her teeth, she swung her feet over the other side of the bed. "Fine. I'll walk home."

She waited for the dizziness to pass and then planted her bare feet on the cold floor. At the same time, she started peeling off the white tape on her hand to remove her uncomfortable IV.

"Wait," Greg said, trying to snag her arm.

Scooting farther away, she ripped off the first row of tape.

"Carrie, wait," he said, grabbing her shoulder instead.

That didn't stop her. The next row of tape took her arm hair with it, but she was almost free.

Greg sprinted around the bed and grabbed her hands before she could yank the IV out. "You crazy woman, will you just listen?"

Poor choice of words. Listening took too much work. She shook him off.

Greg bent down and looked her directly in the eye. "Look, I know you wanna go home, and I know you're worried, but for cryin' out loud, you don't know what it took to get you here!"

She stopped.

His green eyes pled with hers, and she could see the weariness in them, the mused hair, the wrinkled, soot-stained clothes. In those eyes she saw the absolute, complete, and utter desperation Greg had experienced—Greg *and* Oliver had both experienced.

She would have died.

Without those two men—and who knew what else—she would have been grave number nine in their clan's cemetery. A chill ran through her that she felt to the depth of her weary soul. Her gaze dropped to the yellow citizenship card around her neck.

"You're right," she said. "I don't."

She felt him exhale.

But before he could get too comfy, her gaze lifted to his. "But I also can't forget the future. Money means taxes, and taxes mean houses and gardens and safety for thirty-four people." She found his warm hands and squeezed them tightly. "You left the clan to save it. Let me go home to do the same."

Greg looked at Oliver. Looked back at her. He grunted, shook his head, even growled a little, but finally dropped his chin.

"Fine," he said. "But *only* if we do this the right way. The nurse unhooks your IV and gives us the green light before we do a single thing, alrighty?"

"Alrighty," she echoed with a smile.

Straightening, he ran a hand over his brown mop of hair. "You know you're gettin' bossy in your old age." He tried to give her a stern look, but she could tell he was fighting off a smile.

"I learned from the best," she said.

That won her a laugh.

"Well," Greg said, turning to Oliver, "you go find Richard and I'll track down Carrie's nurse to see what it takes to get us the heck outta here."

———◆———

"How did we all fit before?" Carrie asked, shielding her eyes from the bright sun. With paperwork signed and money paid, they were finally free.

Almost.

They stood in the hospital parking lot around Oliver's patrol car—or Greg and Oliver stood while Carrie, Richard, May, and CJ leaned against Oliver's hot car, needing something to keep them upright. With each hour, Carrie felt a little stronger, but walking still took work. At the top of the hospital stairwell, a huge wave of dizziness hit her, making her feel like she was going to tumble down all three flights. Greg kept tight hold of one hand while she gripped the handrail, hand over hand. By the time they made it down, she felt like she'd walked a tightrope in a tornado. If they didn't solve the car situation soon, she'd sink down to the hot asphalt for relief.

May and CJ claimed they were feeling better, but both still looked pale and drawn and needed help walking. But Richard concerned Carrie most. He'd hardly said a word and wore a pained expression she felt. Anytime they stopped, he found a wall or car to lean against. Richard got the first shot when they made it home. *If* they made it home.

Oliver unlocked the car doors and trapped summer heat rushed out.

"You three sickies take the back again," Greg said.

Richard, May, and CJ didn't argue. Richard slumped against the window as soon as he slid in. That left two seats up front for three adults. Carrie's head pounded from the bright daylight.

Greg opened the front door for Carrie and then turned to Oliver. "Pop the trunk."

"Wait," Carrie said, "can't we just squish? I'm not letting you ride in the trunk again."

Greg smirked. "I'm all for squishing, but you'd have to ride on my lap. You okay with that?"

Oliver shot Greg a dark look. "Or…you can ride in the trunk."

"Whatever we do," CJ said, "we should do quickly. That larger security officer is watching us."

"Get in," Carrie said to Greg. Then she added, "Which is your bad leg?"

"Neither." Sitting, Greg took her hand and pulled her after him. She sat on one of his knees and leaned as far forward as she could, resting her heavy head against the dashboard.

He mumbled something she couldn't hear.

"What?" she asked.

He shifted to speak in her good ear. "Sit back. C'mon. Get comfortable. It's a long ride."

Wrapping an arm around her waist, Greg pulled her legs across his lap and leaned her sideways into his chest. She pressed her cheek against his forehead, and somehow, all squished, he got the door shut. She felt herself blush at their close proximity—especially when she noticed Oliver watching them—but Greg just smiled.

"I could get used to this," he said. "Alrighty. We're ready."

As they drove home, the exhaustion set in. And yet overshadowing Carrie's exhaustion was a feeling of peace. And gratitude. And love, relief, and many others. Richard and Greg's grandparents slept in the back, and Carrie couldn't help but drift in and out. She woke when they reached the neighborhood.

Oliver stopped at the Trenton's house first.

"Sorry," Greg said, shifting beneath her, "but I should probably help them inside."

"I'll help, too," Oliver said, jumping out.

Carrie would have offered as well, but in her state, she'd only make them more unsteady. Back stiff, she climbed out of the front seat to let Greg out. The quick rise made her head spin, but he just gave her a quick peck on the cheek.

"I'll be right back," he whispered. "Don't go anywhere."

As if she could.

She lay back on the seat, eyes closed to wait for the dizziness to pass. When Oliver and Greg came out a few minutes later, she started to scoot up to make room, but Greg just grinned and climbed in the back seat. He was smiling an awful lot which, in turn, made her smile.

By the time the three of them reached her house, Amber and Zach were on the porch, waving wildly. They looked perfectly healthy—how, Carrie didn't know, but she was thrilled to see her two goofy siblings again. Sasha Green stood on her front lawn with the little boys, and Jada Dixon was further down, stretched up high to see. The whole neighborhood had come out to see their return.

Carrie got out and gave a little wave. She wanted them to know that the medicine was working and help was on the way.

"Carrie!"

Turning carefully, she saw Amber barreling down the sidewalk. She would have knocked Carrie over if Oliver's car wasn't behind her. Amber squished her in a huge hug. Zach joined in, too, creating a giant tangle of arms.

"You're okay, you're okay, you're okay!" Amber squealed.

"Alrighty," Greg said, prying them off. "Go easy on her. She's still wobbly."

They backed off, and Greg took their spot, wrapping an arm around Carrie's waist to help her up the sidewalk.

They only made it halfway to the house when Carrie suddenly stopped. Her feet refused to go another step. She looked up at her two-story brick home. Then she scanned her jungled front yard.

"What's wrong?" Greg asked.

Her house.

Her yard.

"This is mine," she whispered.

"Yes, it is," he said with another smile.

She looked at every spot, every crack in the ground, every overgrown bush and tree that had sprouted in the last six years. She could weed. She could plant vegetables. She could fix leaky roofs and broken doors. She could even hang pictures and do anything she wanted because this was *hers*. The house she'd lived in her whole life. The yard she'd played in as a kid. Tossing baseballs, skipping rocks, singing Christmas carols, and every other wonderfully ordinary moment with her family. It had all been lived here.

The memories. Her parents. Her pond.

"This is mine," she said again as her eyes filled with gratitude. And not just hers. It was the clan's, too. Twice the food. Twice the space. Twice the safety. Plus citizenship for her siblings.

"What's wrong?" Oliver said, running up to join them.

Carrie was too overwhelmed to answer, so Greg did. "I think she's tryin' to figure out where to put her new garden. Possibly a swimming pool."

Laughing, Carrie broke away from Greg and threw her arms around Oliver.

"Thank you," she whispered. "Thank you, thank you, thank you."

For a moment, Oliver froze, arms suspended in mid-air. But then he relaxed and patted her back. "You're welcome."

After a minute, he released her and stepped away, looking a little awkward. "I should get to work. I'll be back to check in on things later."

Greg helped Carrie the rest of the way up the cement stairs and to the porch. At the doorway, he stopped and pulled her close. He tipped her chin up and leaned down for a long kiss. It was the kind of kiss that would have made her head spin regardless of her vestibular-related issues.

When he pulled back, she wound her arms around him and lay on his chest to steady herself.

"Thank you," she said. "Thank you for everything."

He kissed her forehead and then pulled her tight against him again. "Does this mean I gotta move that tomato plant of yours?"

She smiled. "No. I just might have to plant a hundred more."

"A hundred? Why so few?"

Laughing, she cocked her head back to look up at him. She intended to say something witty and hilarious—not that she knew how, but she wanted to make some joke about her garden spilling across the street into his yard. But then everything hit her all over again. What she had. What Greg had done for her. Her family. Her friends. Her home and her wonderfully perfect life.

Her eyes pooled with tears.

"Thank you," she whispered again.

Greg squeezed her close. "Welcome home, neighbor."

epilogue

Oliver dialed the office as soon as he was on the road, dreading the next round of reprimands. Jamansky had paged him six times in the last hour, but Oliver had ignored every one. How many more excuses could he create before his boss fired him?

"More car problems?" Jamansky said by way of hello.

"I'm sorry, chief," Oliver said into the phone. "I thought the mechanic fixed the problem, but apparently—"

"How was the hospital?" Jamansky interrupted.

Oliver nearly drove off the road. He hit the curb and swerved back onto the street. "What?"

"Did you have a nice visit? Tell me, is it hard to drive a broken-down car all the way to the medical unit in Aurora?"

Oliver's pulse leapt. Jamansky knew. How did he know? How *much* did he know?

"You will be here in five minutes," Jamansky said, low and deadly. "Not a second more. Am I clear?"

"Yes sir. I'm already in Shelton."

"Oh, I know."

By the time Oliver screeched into the station, it had only been two minutes, but he was sweating up a storm. He resisted the urge to run inside and instead walked calmly up the front steps.

Jamansky stood against Ashlee's desk, arms folded, eyes cold and turbulent. Officers Portman and Bushing were there, too, and for some reason, so was Mayor Phillips. Ashlee was nowhere in sight.

"I'm sorry, sir," Oliver said, breathless in spite of his desire to look calm. "I should have told you, but I was visiting…my aunt. She's very ill with this new illness and I-I-I'm not sure she's going to make it."

"Ah, so Carrie's your aunt now?" Jamansky said. "She seems a little young, don't you think?"

Carrie.

Oliver couldn't breathe.

He looked around. Ashlee was gone.

Ashlee told.

Jamansky pushed away from the desk and circled him like a vulture. "How about you try your story again, this time without the lies—although at this point, it's not going to help your case. But I am curious if you're capable of any truth whatsoever."

"Carrie was dying," Oliver said weakly. "I had to help."

"Ah. How noble of you." Jamansky stopped in front of him. "Why you?"

Oliver closed his eyes, sick. Carrie was legal now. She had her yellow card, making her safe from Jamansky's clutches.

She was safe.

She was.

Jamansky leaned close and whispered, "Ever wonder why I didn't have you arrested with Chief Dario?"

Oliver couldn't have answered if he wanted to. His heart pounded out of his chest. He checked the doors, calculating how fast he had to be to get out of there alive. Reading his mind, Jamansky motioned to Portman and Bushing. Oliver's former partners jumped into action and grabbed his arms, rooting him in spot.

"I knew you were hiding something," Jamansky continued. "Something bigger than Chief Dario. Bigger than even your lovely Carrie Lynne Ashworth. You're just a bit too awkward, too quiet, and too…accommodating. You wanted to work alone all those years, and I played right into your hand, didn't I? You're a lot more brilliant than I thought, Simmons. You've been up to something all these years, and it's been eating at me. But today"—Jamansky smiled a dark, chilling smile—"I finally figured it out."

Crossing the room, Jamansky snatched a single paper from Ashlee's desk. He waved it high in the air.

No. No. NO!

Oliver didn't have to read the words to know what it was. He felt like he'd been sucker-punched.

"This claims you bought Carrie's house months ago," Jamansky said, pretending to read it. "But Ashlee assures me that the final paperwork wasn't pushed through until recently. In fact, it cleared just last night during the early morning hours. Isn't that something?"

"Ashlee," Oliver whispered. What had she done?

Jamansky's expression darkened. "Oh, don't worry. I've already dealt with her. That wench will pay dearly for her hand in this."

Oliver's head snapped up. He tried to rock forward, but Portman and Bushing's grips tightened on his arms.

"What did you do to her?" Oliver shouted.

Ignoring his questions, Jamansky scanned the deed. "You know the best part of all this? Not that I found out about your girlfriend—although that is a huge, huge bonus," he added with a chuckle. "But Carrie's new house just so happens to be in the same neighborhood where that raid fell through last March. The same raid where we found twenty squatters who had slipped through your patrols all these years. That's also the same raid where our acquired stuff went missing. That's a pretty big coincidence, don't you think, Mayor Phillips?"

"Yes, it is," the mayor said, eyes tiny slits of fury.

Oliver gulped. "That stuff wasn't yours," he squeaked.

Jamansky threw back his head and laughed. "After everything I've accused you of, everything I now know, that's the best you've got? Are you still going to claim you and Carrie are just friends?"

"Leave her alone!" Oliver yelled.

Jamansky waved the deed again. "No. I don't think I will."

Carrie's address.

Her house.

The clan.

Oliver's knees went weak. Portman and Bushing had a hard time keeping him upright.

Jamansky stepped forward. "Oh, this is payback time," he whispered in Oliver's face. "I spent two months in a smelly, rotten prison because of you, wondering how to get revenge. I just found it—or should I say, I just found *her*. Guess I don't need you to give me Carrie's address anymore, huh? In fact, I think I'll pay her a visit right now. The hospital said she was just released, so she should be home by now. Isn't that where you just were? Driving your sweet, pretty little Carrie home? Tell me, is she still wearing a cute little hospital gown? The one with the—"

Oliver lunged. Portman and Bushing weren't expecting it, and he broke free. In one giant leap, he was on Jamansky, fists swinging.

The first blow caught Jamansky squarely in the jaw. Jamansky's head snapped back, but Oliver kept going, fists wild with rage. Chest. Head. Stomach. He hit every part of Jamansky he could reach before the others pulled him off.

Then Jamansky leaped up with a scream of rage.

His fist cocked back and rammed Oliver's gut. Air whooshing out, Oliver dropped. Another blow to the head, and the world rang. Jamansky's foot connected next, sending Oliver flailing across the room. Oliver tried to scramble free, but Jamansky kicked again, connecting with his ribs. Oliver gasped in agony. Everything went in and out, black and white.

With his foot, Jamansky rolled him onto his back. That same foot went on the center of his ribs, squishing out the last of Oliver's air.

Breathing heavily himself, Jamansky stood over him, wiping the blood from his swollen lip. "You're under arrest for harboring illegals, using government-earned funds to support the rebellion, lying to your boss, running around with my old girlfriend, sleeping with my *future* girlfriend, treason against your country, and so many other things you'll never see the light of day again." Swinging back, he gave Oliver's ribs a final bone-breaking kick.

Oliver couldn't breathe. His whole body burned. His fingers dug into the blue carpet, desperate to escape. To warn the clan. But Portman and Bushing yanked him up.

"You can't...you can't do this!" Oliver said in between gasps. "I earned every...dollar of Carrie's house!"

"Just be glad I'm not having you killed. Take him away!"

With everything he had, Oliver dug in his heels. "Live free or die!" he bellowed. "There are things far worse than death!"

Jamansky turned slowly, murder blazing in his eyes. "Oh, believe me, I know. Which is why you don't have a bullet in your head. Get him out of here. No, wait. I want him to see this."

Jamansky walked up to the map of Shelton mounted on the wall. His finger traced the streets. "342 Woodland Drive. 342 Woodland Drive.

Ah, there she is." He tapped the house by Logan Pond. "Where are my keys?"

"NO!" Oliver screamed, flailing with his last ounce of strength.

Carrie, still weak and recovering.

Greg, supposedly dead.

May, CJ, Richard.

The whole illegal clan.

Jamansky would see them. He would know. Oliver had condemned every last one of them.

The last glimpse Oliver saw before he was carted off was of David Jamansky whistling to himself as he strode out to his car.

the end

more

Meet the citizens, explore Logan Pond, and find more at
www.rebeccabelliston.com

(scan QR codes)

| Website | Meet the Citizens | Explore Logan Pond |

Books in the Series

| Life | Liberty | The Pursuit |

Thank you for reading *Liberty*. Please consider telling your friends or
posting a short review. Word of mouth is an author's best friend and
much appreciated!

acknowledgements

Thank you to my loyal readers. You inspire me to keep writing.

Thank you to Google for letting me research at home. In my pajamas.

Thank you to my husband, my dad, Sarah, Tricia, Sharon, Gerri,
Amanda, Jen, and Cindy who read and proofread and read a little more.
This book is better and stronger for your input,
and my life is better and stronger for your friendship.

More than anything, thank you to the many unsung heroes of the past
who sacrificed to give me the liberties I enjoy today.
I'm grateful to write this story under the "fiction" umbrella.

I am truly blessed!

discussion questions

1. The title of this novel is *Liberty*. How does that fit with the story?
2. This story alternates between different characters and points of view. Did one story speak to you more than another? Do you identify with one character more than another?
3. How does guilt affect the actions of characters in the novel? How does love? How does fear?
4. What is the central theme in this story? How do other themes support the main theme?
5. What are Carrie's strengths and weaknesses? How did they help or hinder her throughout the novel? What about Greg's?
6. Greg convinces himself to stay away from Carrie for 'her own safety.' Do you think his actions were justified?
7. Do you think Carrie should have gone out with Oliver?
8. Do you agree with Mariah's advice to *Worry less and love more?* What about to *Fight for happiness?*
9. In this novel, Oliver and Greg are asked to do things that go against their moral judgment, but they do it anyway to save someone they love. Do you agree with their actions? Would you have done differently?
10. Do you think the clan should join the rebellion?
11. The rebels started quoting John Stark, a Revolutionary War general. *Live free or die. There are things far worse than death?* How do you feel about this sentiment?
12. Did this book end the way you expected?
13. Did this book affect your view on your own liberties? How would you answer the question: *What price would you pay for the liberty of those you love?*

Coming 2016

the PURSUIT

CITIZENS of LOGAN POND
BOOK 3

Let the chase begin…

———◆———

Rebecca Lund Belliston is the bestselling author of the
Citizens of Logan Pond trilogy and the LDS romantic suspense novels,
Sadie and *Augustina*. She is also the bestselling composer of religious
and classical-style music that has been performed around the world.
When she's not writing fiction or music or chasing her five kids,
she likes to cuddle up with a good book.
She lives with her husband and five children in Michigan.

Rebecca loves to connect with readers.
Visit her online at rebeccabelliston.com.

———◆———

LINKS:

Facebook: @rebeccalundbelliston
Twitter: @rlbelliston
Pinterest: @rlbelliston
Instagram: @rebeccabelliston

CPSIA information can be obtained
at www.ICGtesting.com
Printed in the USA
LVOW01s1610300317
529063LV00014B/1300/P